COLLEGIUM SORCERORUM:

Thaddeus of Beewicke

* * *

by

Louis Sauvain

Printed USA
Second Edition
Protinus

This is a work of fiction. All characters and events portrayed in this book are either products of the author's imagination or are used fictitiously.

Maps, Illustrations and Cover by Sean Bodley

Lingua Imperatoria translations by Laura Barnard, PhD.

ISBN: 0615503292
ISBN-13: 9780615503295

Library Congress Control Number: 2011912896
CreateSpace Independent Publishing Platform
North Charleston, South Carolina

The COLLEGIUM SORCERORUM *Trilogy*

by Louis Sauvain

Volume I *Thaddeus of Beewicke*

Volume II *Thaddeus and the Master*

Volume III *Thaddeus and the Daemon*

Acknowledgement

* * *

To:
BarBara Fricke and Janet Cummins –
tireless Editors without peer

Dedication

* * *

In memory of Joe W who often said,

"Great literature is hard to do,
but most everybody likes a good yarn."

Contents

* * *

Prologue			xiii
Chapter	1	Domo	1
Chapter	2	Cincinni, Papiliones et Amici	39
Chapter	3	Tertius	77
Chapter	4	Fur, Fides, Vesica, Vesanus et Canis	119
Chapter	5	Pilae et Puellae	157
Chapter	6	Sub Diem Media Aetate	207
Chapter	7	Somnia et Nasus Caeruleus	243
Chapter	8	Anus Arborea	287
Chapter	9	Conventus et Castra	327
Chapter	10	Discere Leger et Iudicare Liberi	365
Chapter	11	Ad Collegium	405
Epilogue			447
Appendix		Dramatis Personnae	481
Glossary		Lingua Imperatoria	521

List of Illustrations

* * *

Frontispiece "The Westlands"	x, xi
"Beewicke"	2
"Ormerod's Vineyard"	40
"Journey"	78
"The Great Spansion"	158
"Garrungroot"	288
"Convent of the Silent Sisters"	328
"City on the Plains"	346
"Mountaingaard"	406
"Orbis Magnus"	435
"The College of Sorcerers"	445

THE GREAT GLACIER
THE WEST
THE FROZEN SHALLOWS
ICE PORTS
THE ICE
N
GAGDELLE RIVER
NORDEN ROAD
NORDEN ROAD
THE NORZIL PLAINS
LAKE NILIN
NORTER RIVER
NORDENGELL
LUDIA
NORTHFAST
MIDINA ROAD
PONTES PORT
TRAILIC ROAD
TETHYS SEA
THE HORN COAST
THE INNER SEA
TECEN MOUNTAINS
PARI ROAD
PARI ROAD
TRESHIVINN
SUT ROAD
COBBLY EKNOB
LEGEND
RIVER
ROAD
CITY/ TOWN
MOUNTAINS
HILLS
FOREST
WETLANDS
WESTWALLIA
TUR
TURIAN RIVER
THE WALLIAN MARSHES
ADALANTINE OCEAN

LANDS
The Great Ice Wall
Collegium Sorcerorum
Northirst Peaks
Irez
The Northern Road
Arx Montium (Mountaingaard)
Lands
The Great Flatstone River
The Barren Flats
Bulcoran Forest
The Southern Caves
Gagden River
Bannock
The Great Striunn Forest
Mei Wood
Lake Cirum
The Golden Range
Lake Marn
The Great North Road
Mercea
Lake Gernem
Bakem Road
Mekern
Merneca
Rirgev Forest
Fremor Road
The Great Bramill Forest
River's Wood
Moorstown
Ardennia Pass
Bramillean Wetlands
City on the Plain
Beewicke
Moorsland
Lake Thean
Fountaindale
Cricklewood
Frantillia
Wood
Scralia Pass
Frantille Road
Frantil Road
The Great Frantillean Grass Lands
The Great Flatstone River
Bonedellum Swamps
Frocian Woods
Frantilla
Vexare
Blackcove
Port Stellatus
Port Ostia
Frantillan Sea

Prologue

* * *

Laughing, the young couple ran hand in hand up the gentle slope of the forest path. When they reached the small clearing, they fell into each other's arms at the foot of the ancient sarsen and embraced. The Old Moon, *Luna Senex,* full this All Hallows' Eve, had been laughing with them but now grew silent, observant, expectant. Around them, gnarled trees stood tall and waited. The youth and maiden shed their festive clothes and gazed lovingly at each other.

"Wife," the man said.

"Husband," said his bride.

They embraced again, each kiss more joyful and fervent than the one before.

Later they lay asleep in each other's arms, blissful and spent in the shadow of the old standing stone that towered above them, pulsing with a faint blue light. They were unaware of the ring of eyes regarding them from the surrounding tree line, quizzically, protectively.

Chapter 1

DOMO

* * *

The weathered, white-haired man reappeared from behind the sentinel elm and adjusted his garments. Tall and bony, his ragged frame suggested an austere life lived among the elements. Retrieving his staff from where it leaned against the trunk, he briefly surveyed the lingering drought of early summer, patted the tree, and smiled.

"There, now we are both refreshed."

Regaining the dusty road, Silvestrus shuffled over to his cart and affectionately rubbed the ears of his steadfast mule. "Asullus, my old friend, our goal lies but a short way over that hill, I trow—the village of Beewicke. There you will get water, food, and a well-deserved rest. And I, well, we shall see. So please bear us there with as much haste as you can manage, however, not to forget a degree of decorum."

When the old man climbed up onto the cart seat, the mule snorted and began his usual plodding pace, apparently resigned to further toil.

As they neared the stone bridge that spanned the Old Mill Stream, a splashing sound drew the traveler's attention. The man pulled back on the reins and climbed down to investigate.

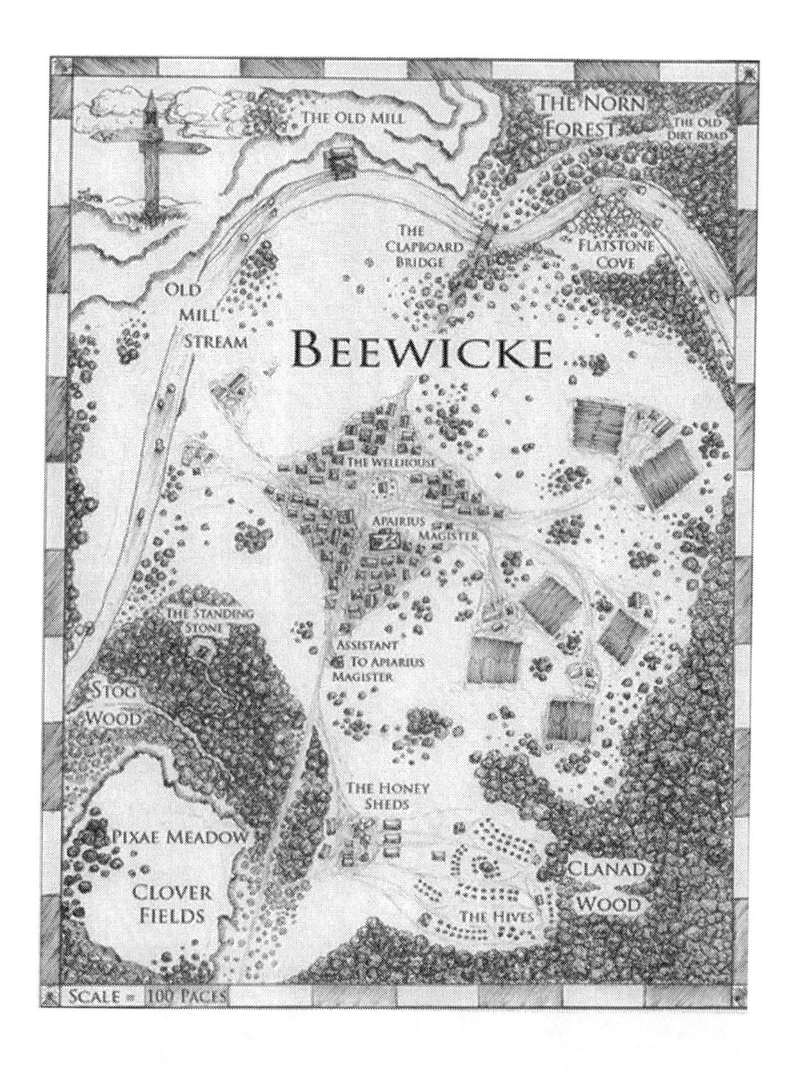
The Old Mill
The Norn Forest
The Old Dirt Road
The Clapboard Bridge
Flatstone Cove
Old Mill Stream
Beewicke
The Wellhouse
Apairius Magister
The Standing Stone
Assistant to Apiarius Magister
Stog Wood
The Honey Sheds
Pixae Meadow
Clanad Wood
Clover Fields
The Hives
Scale = 100 Paces

"Wait here," he said. "I shall not be long."

The stream gurgled as it flowed over its rocky bed, here and there forming small pools of backwater. The splashing sound came again, followed by the lilt of a whistled tune. The man made his way down the embankment and peered through the semidarkness formed by a copse of overhanging willow trees to catch sight of those across the stream. Holding a fishing pole, a young boy sat on a great red rock on the bank, a bag on one side and a large, nondescript hound on the other. Silvestrus smiled. He knew with certainty the boy was one of those he sought. He pushed through the branches.

The old brown dog jerked his head, barked twice, then settled down, seemingly as annoyed at having been disturbed as he was at having been surprised.

"Ho, there, lad. How is the fishing?"

Warned by the dog, the startled boy had jumped to his feet as if confronted by an apparition. He stared hard, his eyes flicking warily.

Apparently deciding the old man presented no immediate threat, he replied in a friendly tone, "Fine, sir, I have two now." He indicated the bag. "And hopes for a third. Fair size, too, for trout."

Silvestrus moved closer to the stream's edge and surveyed the young boy. He would be about fourteen, and was sandy haired and freckled. The old man thought the boy's eyes were green—green as river water—and both earnest and curious. Good. The boy had an open manner as well. Excellent.

"That sounds like success to me. Do you always have such luck with fish?"

"Why, yes, sir, ever since I can remember. My father has often marked me on this."

"Do you mind if I watch you, then? I would truly like to observe one with such a gift. Perhaps it might improve my own luck."

"If you wish it, sir."

The old man made his way over to a large rock just opposite his quarry and settled down. "Allow me to introduce myself. My name is Silvestrus, and I will share a secret with you. I am traveling toward Beewicke on a matter of some importance. But not of such import that I cannot take the time to learn something useful. What of you, then, young *Magister Piscatorum*? What are your secrets?" The old man's glance sharpened.

"Secrets, sir? Of fishing? I mean, it's not just one thing. It's the weather and the season and the bait and...I can't exactly say. I..." His voice trailed off as he caught the old one's gaze. "Well, it's not that hard, really. You just have to pay attention and be patient."

"I see. And your name, lad? If I may have it, that is."

"What? Oh. Thaddeus, sir. Cedric's son. I'm sorry—I didn't mean..." Recovering quickly, he nodded toward the dog. "And this is Argus. He's my watchdog. My parents got him to look after me just after I was born."

"Very pleased to meet you, Thaddeus." The stranger turned and nodded to the hound. "Enough eyes for your job, then, Argus?" The dog made no response.

Silvestrus turned his attention back to the boy "What is it your father does, Thaddeus?"

"He's the assistant to *Apiarius Magister*, sir," the boy replied with pride. "The Keeper of Bees in Beewicke."

"Are the hives good in Beewicke, then?"

"Oh yes, sir. Beewicke is well-known for its bees and the quality of its honey. Have you never heard of it, sir? Our honey is very famous."

"Perhaps I have, now that I think on it. And do you enjoy the honey, young Thaddeus?"

"Uh, well, no, sir. I've become rather tired of it, really. We have it a lot. But everyone says it's very special, sir. My father says that the clover fields where the bees gather are blessed by the *Pixae*, and that's what makes our honey so good."

"Ah, yes, the *Pixae*. That would account for it, I suppose. So tell me, Thaddeus, Cedric's son, do you believe the *Pixae* exist? Do you Believe they are...real?"

"Well, they must be, sir. I mean, if my father says they are. I've never seen one, myself, however. But everyone agrees our honey is the best. So it must be true."

"Of course. No doubt, no doubt. Now perhaps you can do me a service, and in return, perhaps I can do one for you."

The boy looked more interested. "Why yes, sir. If I can."

"Fine. I am seeking directions to this Beewicke of yours. Is it far?"

"Oh no, sir. You are practically there already. Just keep to the road and pass over the bridge. It's but a few moments further."

"Thank you, Thaddeus. Are you fished out here—or is there another spot you favor?"

"Oh, I believe I'm quite done, sir. I was getting dinner for my family. Besides, I don't think there are any more left as good as these." He indicated the two large bulges in his bag, one of them still quivering.

"Ah. Well, it is always good to feel certain of the future. Now for my part of the bargain. You might wish to cast your line one more time. I suggest that eddy pool across the way, underneath the large willow there. Sometimes it is good to have an additional fish or two. You never know when you might be having an extra mouth for dinner. Fare thee well, lad."

"Yes, sir. I will, sir. And thank you."

Silvestrus rose to his feet with a wink for the dog, climbed carefully back up the embankment and, strode to his cart.

"Well, Asullus, I think the lad is not the only one to land his catch today. Let us make our way to this Beewicke and meet its good folk."

The old man clambered back onto the cart seat, checked the westering sun, and gave a short whistle as he flicked the reins. The mule shook his head and began to trudge toward the bridge.

From the river behind them came a splash and a whoop of delighted surprise.

* * *

Silvestrus sat sipping a mug of honey-laced herbal tea in the sparse but cheery interior of Cedric and Hycynthya's home. He gazed around the hut. Two pallets were laid out in one corner, a third in another. An open fire pit lay at one end. Terra-cotta pots stood on the rough-hewn table, and a large kettle hung from a hook in the fireplace. Three clay lamps added only minimally to the room's meager light. The dirt floor of the hut was covered with clean rushes. One earthenware jar, larger than the rest, occupied a place of honor in the middle of the planked table. Silvestrus knew it contained the local specialty.

Suddenly the doorway darkened as Thaddeus skidded through the opening, animated and breathless. A moment more and the old hound rounded in, wheezing with the effort. He gave two obligatory warning barks for the visitor and shuffled over to the corner, circled twice, settled down, and fell asleep.

"Father! Mother! Look what I caught! I've never seen a fish so big, and the others as well. And, I almost forgot—there's a traveler in the village! A Master Silvestrus. He's old and tall and—"

"Thaddeus," his father said, "we have a guest. Remember your manners!"

"I'm sorry, Father. I—" Catching sight of the old man, he turned toward him. "Sir, I am sorry. I meant no disrespect."

"It is of no moment, my boy. I was able to reach your village due to your good directions and decided to seek out your parents to advise them of your excellent assistance. And to ask a boon of them as well. A service, actually, that concerns you."

Silvestrus judged Thaddeus to be slightly taller than average—already the same height as Cedric—and not yet done with growing. He had a lithe frame that promised strength one day. His father, on the other hand, ran to the stout. A stolid man, Cedric was dressed in the same type of tunic and jerkin as the boy, but his hair and short beard were already showing signs of pepper-salt. His face was open and honest, like his son's. The boy's mother, Hycynthya, seemed a quiet, caring sort. Her hair was pulled back in an iron-gray bun held with twine. She was full figured and dressed in the simple homespun smock that seemed to be favored by the ladies of Beewicke. Over it, she wore a patched and frayed apron. Cedric appeared to dote on her.

Thaddeus moved closer. "I'm sorry, sir, you said this service concerns me?"

"So I did. As your village has no inn, your parents have graciously invited me to stay the night, along with my companion."

Thaddeus's eyebrows rose.

"I refer, of course, to my mule, Asullus. We have been together for many years, and for that, I name him companion. But we will discuss this matter of service later."

After an interval of pleasant conversation, they were interrupted by Thaddeus's mother, who bade them come to table.

Thaddeus's father cleared his throat. "Master Silvestrus, could I call upon you, please, to speak the benediction?"

"Of course. I would be honored, Goodman Cedric."

The old man spoke briefly in a soft voice. Though he was sure they could hear him well enough, he suspected the words were unfamiliar to them. Shortly thereafter, they began their meal.

The three freshly caught fish, nestling in a bed of boiled onions, had been fire cooked and garnished with herbs from the family garden. Accompanying the modest but succulent fare was a round of coarse, dark bread, a modest wedge of white cheese and, of course, a measure of honey from the gray crock. They washed it all down with thick, sweet purberry wine. As the last of the juices was sopped up from the wooden trenchers, Silvestrus brought forth four large green apples from somewhere in his robes.

"Apples? In *Iunio?* That is a wonder indeed, Master Silvestrus," Thaddeus's mother said, a note of awe in her voice. "How came you by them?"

"A simple matter of a preservation technique, my dear lady, I was taught by my own master when I was but a learner." He then produced from the same source a blue-bladed dagger with a worn leather handle and proceeded to core each in turn, sharing them out to the delight of all.

"Many thanks for an excellent dinner, Mistress Hycynthya, but, getting back to the service I mentioned earlier, Master Cedric, might I borrow your son for a time? I have heard you have hereabouts a sarsen, one of the Old Guardians, what you would call a 'standing stone.' If it is not too far from here, perhaps young Thaddeus could take me to it? I realize it is late, but I understand sometimes these relics are best viewed by moonlight such as we have tonight. I have some torches in my cart we can use to light our way."

Cedric glanced at his wife before replying. "Of course, Master Silvestrus, the lad will be glad to direct you. We know the stone you speak of—know it quite well, as it turns out." He paused and smiled briefly at his wife. "You might say Thaddeus and the stone are connected in a way. Let me know if you need anything further."

"Thank you, but the lad and I will be fine. Please do not wait up for us. We may be a while. Come, my boy, you can help me with the torches."

With a small bow to Cedric and his wife, Silvestrus gathered his cloak around him and stepped across the threshold into the night. Thaddeus followed to find the old man rummaging through the supplies in his cart.

The traveler glanced at the boy. "You are quiet, lad. Is there something that troubles you?"

"I'm not sure, sir. I guess I don't understand what any of this means and what business you could possibly have with the stone or the likes of me."

Silvestrus found the torches and passed them to the boy.

"Here, light these, and we will be off. Well, now, your father told me something earlier that was quite interesting. It turns out that your parents, um, visited the very stone we are going to see some fifteen years ago on a night very much like this one. In my travels, I have found that some of those stones have a certain *Potestatem,* or power. Under the right circumstances, strange and unusual things can occur around them. I think this stone might be one of those."

Thaddeus handed a lighted torch to Silvestrus and kept one for himself. "Really, sir? Strange things? What would they have to do with me?"

"Well, now, it is said by the Wise that such power can often influence people and events for those who believe in that sort of thing. Sometimes, if conditions are right, a portion of this power may leech out of those stones into surrounding objects or even people. Your parents were there at an auspicious time under special circumstances. That is why this may involve you. It is possible that this stone has influenced you in some way. That is why I have come to Beewicke. I search for ones such as yourself. I want to know more about them."

"But, sir, I know nothing of any of this. I mean, wouldn't I know if there was anything special about me?"

"Perhaps so, perhaps not. How much does anyone really know about themselves—especially at the ripe old age of fourteen, eh?"

Thaddeus ducked his head and turned away.

"Now, lad, take no offense. I assure you none was intended. I only meant to say that we have an unusual mystery here that may involve you. And such mysteries interest me mightily." Silvestrus shifted the torch to his other hand. "All right, lay on, boy, the night is not getting any younger."

* * *

Thaddeus headed south, past the fields spotted with beehives, toward the end of the greensward. Soon he found the opening in the forest wall that marked the beginning of a trail.

"So, after you look at the stone, you will be leaving in the morning, sir?"

"Well, now, as to that. If I am able to puzzle out some of this mystery tonight, and if it does involve you, I am of a mind to ask your parents about their plans for your apprenticeship. I may be able to offer an interesting alternative. Perhaps you could accompany me to your benefit. For example, I could teach you about such mysteries as these and how to go about solving them. It would also give me an opportunity to learn more about whatever effect this stone may have had on you."

The boy turned and stared at the old man with his mouth agape. "I'm to become your apprentice? Here, sir?"

"Well, not here. At my school. It is a place where other young fellows like yourself come to learn."

Thaddeus resumed his pace, peppering the traveler with questions. "You have a school? What's it like? Is it far from here? In Bostle? Or as far as Fountaindale?"

"My goodness, what a lot of questions. No, it is neither at Bostle nor Fountaindale. It is a bit further away than that, actually, and—" He stopped and peered into the gloom ahead. "Well now, this would be the place, would it not?"

They had come up the path through the trees from the meadow and now entered a small clearing. Toward the back of a grassy knoll stood an old stone of giant's height and so black it seemed to absorb every drop of moonlight shining down upon it. Even the light from the torches seemed diminished.

Perhaps because of a trick of light and shadow, the old megalith appeared to Thaddeus to be outlined in a faint bluish haze. He blinked, but the effect remained. He was, of course, familiar with this part of the woods and its surroundings, despite repeated parental admonitions to avoid the place. But he'd never seen it as it appeared this night. It seemed to pulse. How odd.

Without hesitation, Silvestrus walked up to the stone and placed his left hand on it, murmuring several words in the same strange language he'd used for the blessing of the meal. Suddenly the ring on the old man's forefinger began to glow a brilliant blue, the same shade as the haze that now surrounded the stone—but more intense.

The scene before Thaddeus was somehow familiar, though he would swear on any *Librum Sacrum* that he had never seen anything like it before.

After a moment, Silvestrus withdrew his hand, and the glow from his ring abruptly vanished, as did the haze surrounding the stone.

"All right, lad, I believe I have found what I came for. It is getting late. We had better return to your home before your parents begin to worry."

The old man and the young boy turned and made their way back to the rough-hewn wood hut. Despite his host's protestations, Silvestrus declined one of the pallets in favor of sleeping on his own bedroll near the banked fire pit. He was soon snoring vigorously.

Thaddeus, though, found sleep elusive. His thoughts raced from one experience to another, keeping him from shutting off his mind for some time. Strange dreams chased him doggedly throughout the night, leaving only empty cobwebs by the graying of dawn. After a time, he became aware of a muted conversation between the old traveler and his parents. He eavesdropped unashamedly.

"...so you see, Master Silvestrus, his mother and I are getting on. And, it is time—past time, really—for Thaddeus to begin his apprenticeship with *Apiarius Magister*. We made the arrangement many years ago, and it is expected. There is no finer work for the lad—your own craft excepted, I'm sure—and it will give him a certain position in the village as well as a means to keep body and soul together. He'll be finding his own lass soon enough and wanting a family in due time.

Of course, they will stay here with us—won't be too crowded—and when the time comes, why, they can see us out and have the place to themselves and their children. That is the way things have always been done in these parts. Hycynthya and I have given it much thought, and that is what we see for him."

Thaddeus was well acquainted with this plan, having heard it regularly for most of the years of his youth—though more frequently recently. It had not particularly troubled him before. But now, with the arrival of the stranger, it seemed somehow confining, restricting. Something had changed, but he could not say exactly what.

"Of course, good Cedric, that is clearly a well-thought-out plan with the boy's best interests at heart." Silvestrus paused and, from the slurping sounds, was sipping his morning tea. "I say, this honey really is quite excellent. However, from what you have said, and my own observations, there is a bit of a mystery about the boy. And it is a mystery that I am not likely to solve here, as I am sure you can understand. Though I have known you for only a short time, it is obvious that you and your wife have loved and cared well for young Thaddeus and want only the best for him. At the *Collegium*, he will be well trained and prepared for a profession of hard work, honest thought, and unstinting reward. And he will be at a place where such questions as I have already alluded to can be delved into, and their answers uncovered. I will also give you my own guarantee of his safety, as well as his eventual success in the learning of a useful craft."

Thaddeus's heart leapt. The old man meant it—he meant to take him along! To take him away. His stomach clenched. He had never been away from home before, away from his mother, his father, from Argus. Away from his friends, the village, from all he knew. He drew his cloak more tightly about him.

Silvestrus cleared his throat. "However, I know his absence could lead to hardship, so please allow me to leave with you a small amount to reimburse you for the expense of finding a replacement apprentice. And to compensate you for a helper's position to manage the lad's chores."

To his astonishment, Thaddeus heard the clink of a hefty sackful of coins. But how could this be? The man was only a traveler, a stranger, not much more than a vagabond, really. Thaddeus opened his eye a crack. The old man and his parents were deeply involved in their conversation.

He studied Silvestrus's white hair and beard, dusty robes falling to his knees, all gathered about with a wide tooled-leather belt. His sandals were laced up in the imperial fashion. And his eyes—even from this distance, Thaddeus could see the old man had one green eye and one brown. The boy's gaze slid to the old man's ring. It was glowing blue again, though not as brightly as it had the night before at the stone.

His father gasped. "*Sacra Mater!* Master Silvestrus, we cannot take this! It's—"

"No more than you deserve to give up your only son at this vital time. I assure you, good sir, I proffer it as a gesture of good faith and to ease your loss. Take it, please. I—ah, I see the boy is awake. No doubt he is also concerned about his future."

Thaddeus sat up and rubbed the remainder of sleep from his eyes.

"Son," his father said, "Master Silvestrus feels you would make him a good apprentice at his school and wishes to take you with him when he leaves. I am inclined to allow this. What do you say, lad?"

Thaddeus's heart hammered. "I would like that, Father. But to be away, especially now with the collecting season coming on..."

"Don't you think on it, my boy. We will make out, as we always have."

And with that, the first exhilaration of freedom thrummed through Thaddeus's veins. Then, unbidden, doubt crept into his awareness. Could he merely be trading one master for another? He looked up to find the old man regarding him closely.

"Young Thaddeus, if you are to accompany me, it is needful that we depart this day—this morning, in fact. I will go see to Asullus. Why not gather the things you will need for our journey and say your good-byes? When you are ready, join me outside. But do not tarry. We have a long way to go, and the day is getting on. Goodman Cedric, Goodwife Hycynthya, I thank you for the bounty and hospitality you have shared with a stranger." With a nod, the old man rose from his chair and went out to make his preparations.

An awkward silence followed. Finally, Thaddeus's father spoke.

"Well, lad, it seems you will be leaving us now to start a new life. I never dreamed it would happen so. But the Gods sow as they will, and men reap as they may. Now remember all the things your mother and I have taught you. Be wary of strangers, and keep the family name proud. Come back to us when you can, perhaps during the summer. I..." His voice trailed off. "You know that we both love you," he whispered, overcome.

"Oh, my boy!" his mother cried and rushed to Thaddeus, crushing him to her ample bosom.

Thaddeus, throat constricting and eyes watering, was having difficulty saying, or seeing, anything.

"Good-bye, Mother. Good-bye, Father. I-I love you, too. I will make you proud of me. I will be home as soon as I may."

"Yes. Well, come, Hycynthya. The boy has to get ready. You heard Master Silvestrus. He wants an early starting."

Thaddeus's mother nodded briskly, wiping her eyes on her apron.

Thaddeus glanced around the small house, the only home he'd ever known. He didn't really have that much to take—his knife, his walking stick, carved for him two summers ago by his father from the limb of an old forest oak, his fishing gear, a small bundle of clothes. That was all. He rolled them into a pack.

Cedric met him at the door. "Here, lad, you'll be wanting to take these." He pressed three coins into his son's hand.

Thaddeus glanced down and gasped. "Father, I can't take these! This gold is for *Apiarius Magister!*"

"Never you mind, my boy. He won't be missing it any." His father squeezed his son's fist shut around the coins.

Thaddeus was stunned. He'd never had any gold of his own before and had only seen it once, perhaps twice, in his entire life.

His mother came to him, holding a carefully wrapped package. "Here, my Taddy, I've fixed a small food poke for you, for your journey. You are likely to be hungry. But be sure to share it with your master, giving him the larger portion, as needs be."

"Yes, Mother, I will."

She embraced him fiercely and dabbed at her eyes again, then went to join her husband, who was waiting outdoors.

Thaddeus took a last lingering look around his home, then walked outside, shutting the door behind him.

Shading his eyes from the glare of the late spring sun, he found Master Silvestrus hoisting several bundles into the cart as the mule waited patiently. He walked to the cart and peered curiously at its contents. Wedged protectively in one corner was a large, slightly sticky stone crock with a lead seal.

Thaddeus turned and knelt by his old dog, who had followed him outside. He scruffed the hound's neck, then hugged him close. "Good-bye, Argus. You've been the best watchdog ever. Now you have to take care of Mother and Father." For his trouble, he received a face wash before the old dog lay down and fell asleep.

Thaddeus's parents stood off to one side, his father's arm protectively around his mother's waist, as if bracing them both for what was to come.

Silvestrus nodded. "Well, Thaddeus, are you ready?"

"Yes, Master Silvestrus, I believe I am."

"Good lad. Belief is the key, you see. It all starts with Belief."

"Begging your pardon, sir? Belief? I don't understand."

"Later, Thaddeus. There will be time." He turned to the boy's parents. "Now, Cedric, Hycynthya, try not to worry. I know it will be hard, especially at first. I assure you, I will let no harm befall the boy. Thank you again for your hospitality and kindnesses. Fare thee well." With that, Silvestrus shook hands all around, then climbed onto the cart seat and turned to Thaddeus.

"Come, lad, let us be off."

"What? Oh, sorry, sir." Thaddeus leaped up to sit beside the old man on the narrow bench. "'Bye, Mother, Father. I will see you soon as I may."

"*Prodi!*" his master commanded, and the mule, with a flick of his tail and toss of his head, set off down the path to the coarse dirt road that led to the clapboard bridge over the Old Mill Stream. Thaddeus looked back over his shoulder and waved until he could no longer make out the figures of his parents.

The trio made their way through the small collection of wood and stone huts and up over the bridge. They turned east, past the weathered, long-deserted mill, and on out of the village, heading toward the Little Flatstone River.

After a time, Thaddeus turned toward his new master. "Please, sir, where is it we are going?"

"We will head east, then north, to the *Collegium*. Along the way, we will be joined by others, I think. But our route will be first to Figberry, then Meadsville, Bostle, and, finally, Fountaindale."

"All the way to Fountaindale, Master? That's at the end of the world!"

"Well, perhaps not quite so far as that, but far enough to begin with. We'll pick up some supplies and other needful things there, strike out to Moorstown, and then—north."

"It seems a long way, Master," Thaddeus said, thinking perhaps he had made his decision to leave home and see the world a little too hastily. A part of him already regretted his choice.

"Yes, it is a long way. A very long way, actually." Silvestrus flicked the reins and nodded toward the mule. "Now, Asullus, here, is not nearly so dull as he looks. He knows the way quite well. As I am indeed an old man and had a long night last eve, I find I require some rest. So, if you will be so kind as to take the reins, I will make a bed in back and try to get some sleep. Thank you, lad." He turned to the mule and spoke to it in that same strange language he'd used in the benediction and at the Old Stone. The mule turned his head and spoke a word in answer.

Thaddeus, who had just taken the reins, sat frozen, his mouth open. The animal had spoken! Or had it? Perhaps he had misheard.

"Master Silvestrus! The mule—he…he just talked!"

"Did he now? Are you quite certain?"

"Why, yes. I mean, I believe so. I mean…"

"Well, lad, if that is what you Believe, then it is likely so. Quite an interesting idea, don't you agree?"

"Excuse me, Master, but what idea?"

"Why, Belief, of course. Yes, quite interesting." With that, the old man clambered into the back of the cart and settled down in the midst of the bundles. He closed his eyes and within moments was snoring peacefully, despite the jouncing cart.

For a long time, Thaddeus stared at the mule's backside as it plodded along, trying to absorb the situation. Finally, there was nothing left for it but to ask.

"Excuse me, mule, I mean Asullus, but did you speak just now? I mean, can you really speak?"

The mule looked back over his shoulder and regarded Thaddeus for a long moment. "Aye," he replied and turned back to the road.

Thaddeus nearly fell off his seat. "You do talk! How—how can that be? How is it possible? I mean, you shouldn't be able to, should you? I mean…" Words again failed him.

The mule looked back at him once more. "Look ye, boy, I canno' watch the road an' talk at ye o'er me shoulder all at the same time. I might run into a tree or put me foot in a pothole. If ye wishes conversation, then get off yer buttocks, come down here, an' walk beside me. I do no' fancy a sprained fetlock on yer account."

The boy scrambled down and strode forward until he was even with the mule's head.

"How do you, um, that is to say, well..."

"Ye boys do always ask the same questions. Ye'd think once in a while...Look ye, just ye listen an' donno' interrupt. I was born towards the end o' the *Anno Cometae Magni*—the year of the Great Comet—on a small farm in the Red Forest, near the village of Cobbly Knob. No' so much o' a village it was, come to that. Smaller than Beewicke, anyways. An old witchin' woman there, Lady Lillith, she's the one as taught me to speak. So after that, I always could, don' ye know, though she ha' told me often enough to be extra careful who it is I speak to.

"Then, oh, say ten years ago, Silvestrus, he shows up. 'Just travelin' through,' he says. An' he says he knows the Lady Lillith, tells me the two o' them go way back, he did. They talks a while, an' he comes o'er an' says hullo an' asks me how'd I like to come work fer him? So I says, 'What's in it for me?' He says, 'Lots o' travel, lots o' interestin' people, an' lots o' oats.' I says OK an' came away wi' him, an' here I be, pullin' a cart down this dusty road fer an old scarecrow an' some gawking hayseed. Anyway, 'fore I left, Lady Lillith, she warns me, 'Ye be cautious, Asullus,' she says. 'That Silvestrus is a sorcerer, he is. Ye takes him in the wrong direction, an' ye're likely to end up yer days as a persimmon. But he's a good man, he is, an' will treat you right—mostly.' An' that's how it is."

If Thaddeus was surprised before, now he was stunned. "A sorcerer? Are you certain? I mean, with magicks and all? I thought…I mean, he seems so…"

"Aye, a sorcerous one. An' one o' the most powerful as well. He's next in line fer *Princeps Academiae* at the *Collegium* if ye asks me. The College o' Sorcerers—that's where we're goin', boy—be our final destination. Mayhap he told ye that already. 'Tis a nice enough place an' all. Most o' the time I'm in me stall there or lollygaggin' around the yard, grazing the meadows or blouzing the ladies. But ev'ry once in a while, he'll come out to the tack room an' loads the old cart an' tells me, 'Well, Asullus, we've got to go get us some more likely lads. Are ye ready to go?' An' I says, 'Hell no,' but I go anyway. I think this is, maybe, the seventh or eighth trip out fer me. Ye're the first one from round here, though. The old man's got some others to pick up on our way back, too, he says."

"We're picking up others? Other boys?"

"Aye. Aye."

"Where are they? How does he know? Where does he find…?"

"That I donno' know, boy. He just comes to the stable an' tells me, 'We're off!', an' off we are. The work's no' so hard, an' ye boys are no' so bad a lot as things go, though that one boy a few years back, a real pain in the ass he was, e'en if I does say so meself. Silvestrus dinno' always use a mule, though, ye know. He tells me he used to use one o' those man-horses, but that un dinno' like to be ridden much, an' they kept arguin' aboot whether to go here or there, so he quit. So here I am. I donno' argue so much, but I do eats summat. The old man, now, he never complains. He's good company, really, though he's always going on aboot how stubborn I be. But like I always says, people as live in glass houses should no' call the kettle black. I think we're supposed to find the next boy in Bostle, but I forgets the name. Ye lads are all pretty much the same—stupid, scared, an' pee in your beds at first. But ye all grows up pretty good. Most o' ye, anyways."

They traveled on in this manner, and Thaddeus learned much about the great outside world in general, and the sorcerer's world in particular—from a mule's point of view, of course.

Keeping Shell Creek on their left, the small procession made its way down to the New Stone Bridge, which spanned the Little Flatstone River. Once across, Asullus turned southeast, and the party headed into the Central Hills, usually a drier stretch of country but greening up now. They followed the *Via Prima* that led to Figberry. Thaddeus had been to Figberry only once before. He'd gone with his father to take a wagonload of Beewicke's Best sent by *Apiarius Magister*, but he'd never been as far as Fountaindale. Excitement began to replace sadness and doubt. He was going to see the world!

"...so I says to her, I says, 'Well, sure, that stallion there might be a little higher off o' the ground, but if ye be talkin' aboot lanks an' shanks an' such, mind ye, then ye need look no further, missy. I got all the—'" Asullus's voice stopped abruptly, and he stilled. His ears pricked as he cast his gaze back and forth among the nearby bushes and the low-lying hills. "Hold on, boy, there's summat not right here."

"What? What is it, Asullus?"

"Get ye behind me, boy! Master! In the bushes!"

Thaddeus, however, instinctively sprang to the cart for his quarterstaff. The next instant, sharp, burning pains blossomed simultaneously in his left shoulder and right side as a great force knocked him off the side of the cart, onto the ground. He lost his breath, and an instant later was sobbing in agony. Blinking back tears, he looked down to see two gray-feathered arrows protruding from his body. Mother! Father! Of a sudden, Asullus tossed his head in a peculiar manner and was free of his harness. He sprang off to the right, braying with all his might. The mule's charge bowled over a roughly dressed man with a bow. Then the mule reared up on his hindquarters and came down hard with his front hooves where the man's legs met. The man howled in pain and vomited. Asullus turned and galloped off out of Thaddeus's line of sight.

A brilliant flash of light accompanied by a great roaring sound blazed and thundered in the glade. Behind him, a voice deep and terrible intoned, "*Illos Destrue!*" From Thaddeus's left, a giant of a man, all in brown, shambled into his line of vision and passed in front of him, heading toward two roughly dressed men armed with bows who had just emerged from the brush. Though initially surprised, they immediately began shooting at the larger figure.

Thaddeus stared at the big brown man—he wasn't like any man he'd ever seen. The strange figure was tall, well muscled, his brown color mottled. His long arms dangled below his knees, each hand ending in razor-taloned fingers. He did not seem to be clothed. The head was squat and hairless, and he gave a guttural roar as he advanced on the hapless brigands.

The one on the left turned to run, but the creature reached out a long arm and snagged his foot, sending him sprawling. The other man fired more arrows at him. The man-thing backhanded the archer, who flew head over heels to land in a heap. The humanoid ambled over to the first thief, grabbed him around the neck, and dragged the struggling ambusher behind him. As he advanced on the thief's fallen comrade, the man desperately scrabbled back from the huge figure. The creature, however, pinned him to the ground with one clawed foot and squatted down. Casually inspecting the struggling man he held by the neck, he calmly tore off the other man's arm and began to eat.

Blinding pain now claimed Thaddeus, and he lost consciousness to the accompaniment of the armless man's terrible screams.

Through a fog, someone called Thaddeus's name, then once more. Slowly, he opened his eyes. Silvestrus stood over him, a look of concern on his face. Thaddeus was no longer on the ground, but in the back of the cart. His arm and side hurt, but less so than before.

His arm had been tied with a cloth that bulged and smelled odd. His side had been bandaged as well. He found he did not wish to move. He was drowsy and, if not for the aching pain from his wounds, would have been content to stay exactly as he was.

"Thaddeus, lad, how fare you?"

"I'm all right, Master. There is only a little pain. What was it that happened?"

"Ah, well, it was brigands. Highwaymen—common thieves is my guess. At least that's what one of them admitted to before he died from his…wounds. As I understand it, they had but recently taken to banditry, and we were to be their first catch of the day. He implied they were not expecting much of a fight from a boy, an old man, and a mule pulling a cart, a cart possibly loaded with treasure. As for you, you took two arrows—left shoulder and right side—but the poultice and salve should help. As soon as you have rested a bit, we will be on our way to Figberry. I had planned to push on through to Meadsville by nightfall, but now I think it best we dawdle a bit, all things considered. I am going to have a look around. More of those fellows might be lurking about. Most likely not, but it is always best to be careful. No use having some unaccounted-for ragtag sneak up on you and want to open your neck while you are sleeping. Try to get some rest, lad. Asullus will stay with you."

"Thank you, Master. But, really, I'm fine and have no wish to be a burden. I'm ready to leave whenever you wish."

"Rest, Thaddeus. Be not troubled."

The sorcerer turned, spoke briefly to the mule, and entered the wood. Thaddeus's gaze followed the old man until he was lost among the trees. When he looked back, he could find no sign of the large brown man. Had it all been a dream?

"Well, laddie, how be ye farin'?" the mule asked. "I saw those thorns they put in ye. Nasty business, but they'll no longer be troublin' decent folk in these parts—or any other parts, now that I thinks on it."

"I saw what you did, Asullus. You were very brave charging that man with the bow."

"Ah, think nothin' o' it, laddie. He got me peeved, was all. Imagine! Three people—well, two people an' a mule, that is—out on honest business, an' one o' 'em a lad not yet shavin'. An' they goes an' wants to put slivers into us all. Pfah! What kind o' men would do such things? Well, they've paid fer their mistake, an' that's the certain o' it. Paid in a large way, I'm thinkin'."

"Asullus, may I ask you something?"

"Ask away, laddie."

"You know, earlier today, I thought I saw…a sort of man. He was big and brown and ugly. And he fought those bandits, but then I thought I saw him…"

"Ah, aye, I knows who you mean. But don' ye think on it, lad. Master Silvestrus says ye need yer rest, no' summat to stir ye all up."

"But, Asullus, please, I really do want to know. Who, or what, was it, and why did it do what it…did?"

"Hmm. Well, I see ye'll no' be lettin' me go till I spills it, will ye? All right, but donno' be tellin' the old man where ye heard this. This is just 'tween ye, me, an' the feed bag, aye? So, I told ye Master Silvestrus is a sorcerer. Well, this do give him certain advantages in a scrap, don' ye know. This creature ye saw—an' make no mistake, 'twas no man, laddie—was a *Daemon Minor,* an' a mean un into the bargain. I always knows when he's around, smells bad an' makes me nose burn. Canno' pronounce his real name, though, so I just calls him Charles. Well, Charles's just like me, been working for Silvestrus for a time. They have some sort of arrangement, I twig. I think it's he deals wi' the unpleasant folk, an', as a compense, gets to stay fer lunch, if ye take me meanin'. Not a pretty sight. Mostly, I donno' watch, but I ha' seen it a few times. I'll say this fer him, though, he's thorough. Also, ye know, the word gets around after a while. These days, anyone who's ever heard of Master Silvestrus likely knows about Charles, too. Smart folk—meanin' those still livin'—knows as to avoid pesterin' the old man unless they wants to end up as buffet. I think that's what surprised us today—these fellows was new at their work. Probably had no' gotten the word yet. Well, now they never will. Hope it was no' situation like these men was starvin' an' could no' find work an' only took to robbin' 'cause they was desperate to feed their wee ones. I hate it as that happens."

Silvestrus's abrupt return startled the pair. "You will find, Thaddeus, that Asullus here is, beneath his leathery hide and in spite of his black heart, rather a sentimentalist. It gets in the way, sometimes, as he and

I have had occasion to discuss from time to time. But there it is—stubborn."

The mule snorted loudly.

"But I thought I told you to rest. Asullus, come over here and let me look you over. A mule with an arrow wound somewhere would only slow us down." The sorcerer placed a gentle hand over the boy's eyes. "*Dormi.*"

Thaddeus knew nothing more.

When he next awakened, he felt much better and found, after testing himself gingerly, that he could sit up, then get up. Judging by the sun, it was late afternoon. With some effort, he picked his way out of the back of the cart and slid down to stand, wobbly legged, on the ground. Silvestrus was sitting on a fallen tree trunk a short distance from the cart, engrossed in conversation with Asullus. Neither had noticed him yet. He peered at the bushes where the bandits had hidden. A wide swath of trampled grasses was covered by a dark stain. Thaddeus shivered as he realized what he was seeing. Just then, Silvestrus looked up and saw him. The sorcerer rose and walked back to the cart.

"Ah, up at last. Good lad. How do you feel?"

"Well enough, Master. It hardly hurts at all."

"Excellent. Well, there's not much more to be done here, so I suggest we pack up and head on to Figberry. We'll stay with an acquaintance of mine there, a successful merchant with a large house. Exactly what we require. Come, Asullus, time to be off."

Thaddeus rode in the back of the cart—one more bundle amidst all the other baggage—while

Silvestrus sat on the cart seat, occasionally conversing with Asullus and enjoying a pipe he had produced from somewhere in his robes. They passed southeast through the last of the Central Hills and began climbing the sloping terrain to Figberry. They turned from the grassland trail onto a country road, then followed it around the town to the north. The road eventually led by a large villa, beyond which were spread several hectares of neatly rowed vineyard. As the sun sank in the west, they pulled into a long, curving drive that wound its way to the villa's portico and there came to a stop. Tall lattices outlining the entranceway were bending under the weight of a tumulus of blossoming flowers.

Silvestrus clambered down from the cart just as a man in his middle years emerged from the building waving a greeting.

"Master Silvestrus! Hail and welcome! How long has it been? How are you? What on earth brings you to these parts? Can you stay with us for the Solstice? Where—"

"Peace, Ormerod. We were traveling from the west and were assaulted earlier today by bandits. One of our number is injured. I stopped here to beg succor."

"Oh my goodness! Bandits, did you say? You know, I myself have had some of the same sort of trouble with no few of my wagon shipments recently. I have sent several urgent missives to the Shire Reeve in Fountaindale requesting aid but have had no response—though I notice his tax agents appear always to be well escorted. But here I am blathering on, and you have an injury."

"Not I, good Ormerod, my apprentice. He is in the back of the cart. If one of the servants could, perhaps, aid us in getting him down and to rest…"

"Of course. Of course. Annis! Gethin! To me! They'll have him down jack-short and to bed. Ah, here they are. Boys, take the lad in the cart up to the green room—with care, mind you. He's been injured. My, um, niece, who happens to be visiting, has some skill in the healing arts and will look in on the lad. But please come, please come. My, what a long time since our last visit. You know, it's been so dry this spring, not a drop from the clouds, and I am worried about my press. You see…" The vintner escorted the older man into the villa, talking and gesticulating as he detailed the misfortunes of the current growing season.

The two servants helped Thaddeus down from the cart and supported him into the columned courtyard, through the atrium, up a marble flight of stairs, down a richly carpeted hall, and into a large, airy room filled with the deep reds of a waning sunset. They placed Thaddeus atop a large pallet set on a raised platform, which they called a "bed," despite his protestation that he could move under his own power. The elder of the two tsk-tsked over his clothes and said something about "a bath," then both left the room.

Thaddeus had never seen a room so large and splendid—vases and amphorae filled with bright blue flowers were everywhere—nor any furnishings so ornate. Some things puzzled him, however, like a large copper cauldron in one corner, and a box about chair height with a lid in the opposite corner.

Within moments, an old woman came in with a tray holding a gray, moisture-beaded metal pitcher and a cup that she set on a table by the bed. As the old servant straightened, a younger woman entered with another tray, but this one, Thaddeus could tell from the aroma, held food.

"You're to eat and drink your fill, Young Master," the first woman said, setting the tray on the table. "The Lady will be in shortly to see to your other needs." A slight frown of disapproval crossed her face but was gone in a trice.

The two women filed out quietly, and Thaddeus was left to his own devices. He wanted to explore the tray and see what lay beneath the bleached linen, but hesitated. He wasn't used to being waited on and was unsure how to proceed.

A slight cough made him look up. A willowy young woman stood in the doorway. He had never seen anyone so beautiful. She was slim and pale with dark hair in ringlets that tumbled down over her shoulder to her waist. She had what appeared to be paint on her face—red lips and cheeks, blue eyelids, and black lashes. And she was dressed in a gown of sky blue, the style and composition of which Thaddeus could not fathom. From her slender neck hung a bright blue gem suspended from a finely wrought golden chain. The gem, the size of a bird's egg, matched her earrings. She approached Thaddeus with a grace that made his heart ache.

"Hello, boy. I am Ethne. You are the old sorcerer's apprentice, are you not? I see the servants have brought you your food. I advise you to eat and drink sparingly. You have taken a great hurt today, as I understand it, and temperance is best for now."

Thaddeus could only stare stupidly.

"Do you speak?" she asked pointedly.

"I, um, yes, ma'am. I mean, miss. I...uh, you're beautiful!" Immediately, Thaddeus's visage matched that of the setting sun.

The girl, who Thaddeus judged—when he could think again—to be only a few years older than himself, laughed a bright, silvery laugh. Her teeth were white but uneven. No matter. It was a wondrous smile. Thaddeus's heart melted all over again.

"Why, thank you, um...?"

"Oh. Thaddeus, miss. From Beewicke." Now why had he said that—his flyspeck of a village—to this Imperial Princess?

She smiled. "Ah, that's where we have our honey from. It is very good. Do you enjoy it, Thaddeus?"

"Well, not exactly, miss. You see, that is to say—"

"You may call me Ethne. Everyone does."

Everyone? Other boys? He would kill them all. Or Charles could, and he would watch. Either way...

He swallowed. "That's a pretty name."

"Thank you again, Thaddeus. I am...niece...to Master Ormerod. He has sent me to tend to your wounds. I have some knowledge of the healing arts from my days in Fountaindale."

Fountaindale? That was at the end of the world! She must remain here and never go back to such a distant place!

"Now, Thaddeus, please put aside your clothes. They will be cleaned and returned to you—or, perhaps, replaced. Yes. I will examine your hurts now. Just lie back on the bed. This will not take long. And Thaddeus, your teeth are one of your good points, but they surely need scrubbing, and I do not need to see them always." She smiled as he snapped his mouth shut and reddened further.

Thaddeus did as he was instructed, wondering just what it was she was about to subject him to, then decided she could do whatever she wished—remove his liver, for example. As she drew near him, he caught her scent and was again transported. She then reached out her delicate hands and gently probed his body from head to foot. She missed nothing, and by the end of the examination, Thaddeus felt himself near the point of spontaneous combustion.

Ethne indicated a modest robe draped over the back of one of the chairs and signaled that he should put it on. He did so, then waited patiently.

"How strange. Those wounds seem but star points, nearly healed. Not what I had expected from the old sorcerer's report. Otherwise, you seem healthy as a young bull. Here, sit up now, and let me see you eat. Begin with some of this broth." She stood back and removed the cloth from the food tray. Thaddeus did as he was told, but his eyes never left her.

Ethne took a seat nearby and observed his efforts patiently. Thaddeus noticed she was thin, thinner than he had first thought, and really quite pale. Every so often, she removed a small linen from her belt, turned her head, and coughed delicately into it. Once, after a particularly deep spell of coughing, she wiped away a drop of red spittle from the corner of her mouth. He became alarmed for her.

"Are you not well, Ethne?" he asked.

"It is the consuming sickness, I fear. I had it when I first met Master Ormerod. It was one of the reasons he brought me here. I think he felt the sun and breezes from the Central Hills would be felicitous for my condition."

"When you first met him? I thought he was your uncle."

"Ah, Thaddeus, he is not my blood relation. Rather, we first met in Fountaindale, perhaps a year ago. He was there on business—a wine delivery, I believe. We spent some time together, and he offered to bring me here. He seems to care for me, treats me well, and provides for all my needs. It is customary for a girl such as I to refer to her benefactor as 'uncle.'"

Thaddeus nodded as if he understood what she meant. It didn't matter. Finishing the last mouthful, he belched appreciatively, then smiled shyly.

"Hmm. Thaddeus, you are from what we would call the back country. More importantly, you are now the apprentice of a wise and powerful man. You would not wish, through mis-action on your part, to embarrass him, would you? I thought not. Customs and manners differ widely, it is true, but you will be traveling in higher circles now and must needs act in accordance. I am not required for a time. Let me teach you something of how to go about the business of creating a good impression when you are in society and bringing a credit to your master. First, those objects on your tray next to your plate are called utensils. They are used to get the food to your mouth without dribbling it down your tunic and soiling your fingers. Now…"

The instruction went on for some time, with stops and starts for questions, demonstrations, and practice. Thaddeus's eagerness to please the young woman smothered the perplexity he might have felt under any other tutelage. The lessons progressed from table, to matters of hygiene, to raiment and its use, and, finally, to social intercourse. By repose, his head was spinning. But he was an apt pupil and eager to excel.

At last, she turned to him. "You have done well, Thaddeus. If you practice what I have taught you, you run little risk of being turned out or receiving a cuff for your troubles. But I require rest now, and you need it as well. I will be by to see to you in the morning."

He watched her leave, heartbroken, but buoyed by her promise. He was certain the night would be interminable. It was not, but it was filled, at first, with pleasant thoughts that, inexplicably, became rousing and troublesome before sheer exhaustion took him.

Chapter 2
CINCINNI, PAPILIONES, et AMICI

* * *

Thaddeus awakened gradually. His wounds seemed much better, though he felt a trifle guilty about lying abed so late in the morning when surely many chores needed to be done…somewhere. Sunlight falling on the fields outside the window gave him the time of day. He stretched and inhaled the fragrance of dozens of flowers the color of butter placed in various vases about his room. He ran his hand over the snowy linens and plump headrest—a "pillow" Ethne had called it—filled with goose feathers. He felt himself an equal in luxury to the high king of the Parthi—a reference his mother made from time to time. His thoughts returned to Ethne, so beautiful, so wonderful! If only he was a sorcerer, he would wish her here in an instant.

A knock came at the door, which then creaked open. And there she was, the object of his deepest heart. Today she was dressed floor to crown in yellow. Coherent thought fled away.

ORMEROD'S VINEYARD

"Thaddeus, I am returned as I promised. Do you fare well this day?"

"Yes, miss—I mean, Ethne. I feel quite well. I hope you do also."

"Yes, all things considered. Now I have come to continue your instruction. Have you finished your morning functions?"

"My functions?"

"Thaddeus, have you used your chamber pot? You will recall we spoke of this last night."

"Oh, yes, that. Uh, no. Not yet."

"Then will you please do so? I will wait outside the door for a few moments."

Thaddeus jumped up from the bed and hurried to the box-shaped chair in the corner. After he finished, he used the cloths lying close by to cleanse himself and closed the lid. He put his robe back on and stood uncertainly in the middle of the room, waiting.

The door opened, and Ethne entered followed by the two women servants from the previous evening. One carried a tray of food, while the other had several folded towels and a variety of stoppered bottles in a wicker basket.

The younger servant placed the tray on the bedside table and took up the two from the evening before. The older servant went to the chamber pot, pulled it away from the wall, and removed the bowl. She covered it with a towel and put a new one in its place. After opening one of the bottles, she sprinkled a portion of its contents on and around the chair. Leaving the remaining bottles by the commode, she gestured to her companion and, with a curt bow to Ethne, left the room.

Thaddeus eyed the covered tray eagerly. He looked to Ethne, however, for a cue on how to proceed. He didn't want to put a clumsy foot forward with her now.

"Wait, Thaddeus. You will eat soon enough, but ablutions come first."

He was not sure of her meaning, but began to get an idea as Annis and Gethin trudged in with steaming buckets of water, which they poured into the large copper kettle. Several trips were required before it was full.

Ethne retrieved two of the deep-blue stoppered bottles and poured their contents into the hot tub. She looked at him critically. "Now, Thaddeus, it is time for you to bathe."

Thaddeus had certainly heard the term before, but it had always referred to a weekly command from his mother to go down to the river, plunge in, and roll over at least twice. Although it was usually pleasant, it was occasionally difficult to endure, especially *Ianuario Mense.* This situation, however, was quite different.

"Uh, Ethne, how do I..."

"Remove your night robe, Thaddeus, and step into the tub."

"Oh. All right." He blushed, but did as he was bid, though he took the precaution of facing away from his Mistress of Instruction, gazing instead out the window at the workers toiling in the vineyards.

The water was hot, and he soon felt like one of his mother's stew onions. It was a process that took time. Finally, he was sitting in the tub up to this neck with steam rising around him on all sides. The water proved soothing, however, the smells agreeable and the bubbles pleasing. This new experience mightn't be too bad after all. Suddenly a splash behind him sloshed water over the edge of the tub.

He was no longer alone.

With a cry, he sprang up, then realized he shouldn't have.

"Ethne! Wha—"

"Thaddeus, sit down. You'll catch your death. There is no point in wasting hot water, and I need to bathe as much as you. Well, not quite as much, but still...Have you never taken a bath with a girl before? A sister, perhaps, or a village friend?"

"Well, yes, I mean, no. I don't have a sister. My mother used to take me to the river with her when I was young. And later, some of us would go with the other children while the mothers watched. But that was years ago. Now it's just me and my friends, or just me. But—"

"Would you prefer I leave?"

"No! Never! I mean, please don't go on my account."

"All right, then. Now, Thaddeus, please turn around. It is awkward talking to your back, and I have some things to show you."

He accomplished the complex maneuver, managing to remain submerged from the neck down, though more water was lost over the side in the process. He was nervous about what he would see, but Ethne, too, was up to her chin in the cloudy water. However, his relief was followed by a stab of disappointment.

"Take your ease, Thaddeus. This will not be painful, I promise you. It is, after all, just another part of your education. Now this is called a washing cloth, and you use it in this way..."

Ethne stood, finally, then bent over, holding her long, wet hair back with her hands, and brushed Thaddeus's cheek with her lips. "You are very sweet, Thaddeus. But now I must leave you. It will take me some time to dress this," she said, indicating her mass of black curls. "Now you may get out and dry yourself with the towels, then have some breakfast. Eat sparingly, though. We will be having midday soon, and you will want to save room for that. Morella and Lallie will be back soon with some fresh clothes for you." With that, she stepped out of the tub, wrapped herself in one of the large linens, retrieved her gown and other garments from where they lay on the floor, and left the room.

Thaddeus remained in the tub for a time, all bemused. Something, clearly, had changed—exactly what, he was not prepared to say. But he knew, now, of love. He had lately taken to wondering what such a state would be like, but these speculations, he realized, were as an ember to a forest in full conflagration.

Lazily, he rose and stepped over the rim of the cauldron, picked up a linen, and strolled over to his pallet. After wrapping himself in the towel, he sat on the edge of the bed, pulled the table with the food tray toward him, and removed the cloth cover. Before him was a selection of fresh fruit—including purberries, of course —cheese, crusted bread, and a carafe of fresh goat's milk. He ate without hurry, pausing occasionally with food halfway to his mouth to relive certain moments of this glorious morning. Toward the end of the meal, he was interrupted by the return of the serving women, one of whom removed his tray, while the other laid out several garments for him. He had never before had such finery, although Morella referred to them dismissively as "castoffs."

Recalling Ethne's gentle instruction from the night before, he brushed his teeth with salt, using a twig from the scrub bush, chewed the mint leaf provided, then dressed in his new clothes and spent the intervening time until midday gazing out the window, drinking in the pastoral scene as if it were wine. When called, he followed Annis downstairs to the dining hall, where he was greeted by Master Ormerod and Master Silvestrus, both of whom were solicitous concerning his health. He took the seat indicated by the older servant at the long table adorned by extravagant bouquets of lavender flowers. Within moments, Ethne made her entrance, stunning in a deep-purple gown—in honor of her uncle, Thaddeus assumed. If anyone noticed that both his hair and hers were still damp, none commented on it.

The meal was sumptuous by any standard—venison, pickles, a light purberry vintage, mushrooms, and chicken. A rich pudding and a fresh salad completed the fare. It was all wonderful, even if some items were unfamiliar. He kept his gaze firmly fixed on

Ethne, who shook her head ever so slightly when he picked up the wrong instrument, and nodded when he chose correctly.

The only blemish on the day occurred when Cook came out from the kitchen with a large polished tray, which—with much fanfare and oohs and ahs from the other diners—she placed before Thaddeus. On the silver platter were a large round of white bread, a stone crock of fresh butter, and an entire honeycomb on porcelain.

Master Ormerod beamed as he announced to one and all, "I had it brought up from Beewicke this very morning especially for our guest, young Thaddeus. There's nothing like a taste of home to aid in one's speedy recovery, as I always say."

Thaddeus smiled weakly as his fellow diners offered polite applause. Silvestrus, seated in the place of honor, covered his mouth and turned away as if to cough, but he could not disguise the twinkle in his eye.

As he was finishing his repast, Thaddeus took greater note of the people around him. Though Ethne had favored him with a wink or small smile when no one was looking, it was to Master Ormerod that she gave the majority of her attention. The successful vintner, in turn, hardly took his eyes from her. Clearly his "niece" was the light of his life, and Thaddeus was having trouble with his feelings about the situation. On the one hand, Master Ormerod was his host and had thoughtfully provided him, a stranger and lowly apprentice, with all manner of courtesy, care, and resource. And, the man clearly had first claim on the feelings of loyalty and gratitude the young woman was bestowing on him. On the other hand, Thaddeus's breast was near to bursting with his own feelings of longing and adoration for the vintner's dark-haired beauty. He was also aware of strong emotions of jealousy and resentment at the attention Ethne showed the older man. In spite of the respect for his elders his parents had instilled in him, reconciling this emotional dilemma was beyond him at the moment.

A harrumph from Silvestrus brought his awareness back to his immediate surroundings, and he stood with the others to signal the end of the meal. Silvestrus offered expressions of gratitude to Master Ormerod, and a blessing on the house, its members and lands, and, particularly, on the health and vitality of the current purberry vintage. As the diners dispersed, Silvestrus bade Thaddeus follow him over to their host. The old man personally thanked the vintner for his hospitality, and Thaddeus gritted his teeth long enough to add a few lines of praise, though through a cloud darkly. Master Ormerod appeared pleased and bowed several times in acknowledgment. Now that Ethne had declared Thaddeus fit to travel, Silvestrus made plans to resume their journey. The vintner generously instructed his steward to provision the cart with what remained of the midday. Thaddeus was relieved to note that sufficient passes around the table had depleted the honeycomb to the point that not enough remained to be included in the parcel.

Leaving the dining hall, Thaddeus followed the sorcerer out the entranceway to where Asullus stood, already hitched to the cart. He had been brushed and attended to assiduously, judging from how pleased he seemed to be with himself. Someone had even provided him with a garland of large white flowers that were draped around his neck. Well, it was, after all, almost midsummer. The servants placed several additional bundles in the back of the cart as Thaddeus stood by feeling useless. A wave of melancholia swept over him as he realized he would soon be separated from his true love. He didn't like the feeling at all.

"Thaddeus." The whispered call came from the shadows of the villa's south wall standing next to the winery. He recognized the voice and immediately made his way to Ethne's side.

"Ethne, I—"

She pressed a finger to his lips. "Shh. Dear Thaddeus, I know it will be hard for you for a time, but we must part now. I want—" She stopped abruptly, withdrew her linen from her belt, turned her head, and coughed several times. Drawing a shaky breath, she turned back to him. "I want you to know I will think about you often, and the special treasure you have given me. And I know you will, in time, become a wise and wonderful sorcerer."

"Sorcerer? Why do you say I'm to become a sorcerer? Master Silvestrus is the sorcerer. He said only that he wished me to come with him to his school in order to study a mystery."

Ethne smiled, and the sun blazed forth more strongly than ever. “Thaddeus, Master Silvestrus takes boys to the *Collegium* so he can teach them to become sorcerers. And I know you will make a very good one. Well, it is time for you to go.” She handed him a small packet. “Here, take this. It is to remind you of me, if you wish it. When you tire of it, just cast it away.”

“Never! I would never throw away anything you have given me!”

She smiled again. “It is time now, Thaddeus. Be well always.” She placed her small hand around his neck, drew down his head, and kissed him full on the mouth.

His vision swam.

“Farewell, my sweet Thaddeus.”

The next he knew, the train of her purple gown was disappearing around the corner of the villa.

“Thaddeus! Are you ready, lad? We must go,” Silvestrus called from the portico.

Thaddeus tucked Ethne’s parcel into his tunic and hurried back to his master, trying to compose himself on the way.

Ormerod glanced at Thaddeus, then looked away, his smile fading momentarily. “Ah, here’s the boy now. Well, Master Silvestrus, good days to you. Please call upon me at any time I am able to offer a service. And thank you for your assistance with the press. It’s working fine now.”

“Master Ormerod, my thanks to you. You have performed a greater service this day than you know, I believe. Thaddeus, lad, go round to Asullus and check his bridle fastening, won't you?"

The two men continued their pleasantries as Thaddeus walked up to the mule. "You look very pretty, Asullus, with that garland and all—matches your eyes, I'm thinking." He was immediately sorry to be so sharp with the beast. It wasn't Asullus's fault they were leaving.

"An' ye, laddie," the mule replied softly, "might want to wipe yer mouth on the sleeve o' yer tunic sometime…"

Startled, Thaddeus did so and was surprised at the red smear that decorated his sleeve. Chastened, the boy checked the hitching, found no fault, and returned to his master, who was concluding his goodbyes with the vintner.

The two men shook hands one final time, and Silvestrus urged Thaddeus up onto the cart seat, followed him, and flicked the reins. "All right, you lazy beast, show us a good pace if one like yourself can manage such a thing."

Asullus snorted and leaped forward, throwing his passengers off-balance.

Thaddeus thought he heard the mule's retort, but was not sure. Did Asullus really know such words? The last time he'd heard that kind of language was from a teamster one rainy day on the road home from Figberry.

Thaddeus's eyes, however, were firmly fixed on the balcony of the villa where he'd spotted a slim figure half hidden by a window frame. A small hand waved briefly, and Thaddeus waved back. It was some time before he turned around. This leaving business seemed to hurt a great deal more than it did in the tales he'd been told, and was not at all pleasant.

"I said, Thaddeus, you seem to be *Milibus,*" the old sorcerer observed.

"Oh. I'm sorry, Master, I was just—"

"Thinking of a pretty young girl who has stolen your heart and from whom you are now separated with the experience of much pain and regret?"

"Yes, Master."

"Ah, *Amores.* Believe it or not, I know exactly how you feel, if that helps in any way. Probably not. Usually time is the only remedy—notice I did not say cure."

"Master, may I ask a question?"

"Of course, lad. The man who is ignorant but ignores the opportunity to rectify it when an opportunity presents is twice the fool."

"Sorcerers have great powers, do they not?"

"Well, yes. Some do."

"Have they the power to heal hurts, to restore health?"

"Yes, some more than others."

"Well, then..."

"Is it possible for the young maiden, Ethne, to be cured of her sickness through the use of sorcery, and, if so, can I do it, and, finally, will I? Are those your questions, Thaddeus?"

"Yes, Master." He looked up hopefully. "Can you? Will you?"

"It would be possible, under the right circumstances, but I choose not to. It may be hard for you to understand, and harder to accept. Nevertheless, it is so. I will explain the whys of my choice later, when you are older and able to understand them."

Thaddeus was stunned. How could this until-now wonderful old man refuse to save his beloved? It was her death warrant. Feelings of rage, betrayal—even of being tricked—welled up inside him. For the first time in his life, he was aware of thoughts of violence. He bit his lip until blood flowed in an effort to control himself.

He managed to respond, "My parents used to say that a lot..." The tension was almost palpable.

"The lad ha' asked a fair question, Master Silvestrus." Both started at the mule's interruption. Twitching his long ears, Asullus continued, "An' a fair answer is warranted, I'm guessin.'"

"And you, Asullus? Do you now think to put your two coppers' worth into our discussion? And on what basis, might I ask?"

"On the basis, Master, that just as it ha' fallen to ye to save me bacon on occasion, so it has fallen to me, sometime, to achieve the reverse. It is summat as gives me the right, I reckon. Aside from that, as any can see, she is a sweet lass, in spite o' her earlier callin', an' our Thaddeus here is clearly taken wi' her. Besides which, she it was who wove me this very garland wi' her own pale hands, an' I am beholden to her on that account, as well as some others."

"I see. Well, fair enough. All right, I will give my reasons. I warn you, though, they are selfish in nature. I was intending to offer you a gradual instruction, Thaddeus, and not begin until all our company is assembled, but perhaps it would be better to make a start now. I will not attempt an explanation, however. That must wait for time to pass and effort expended before understanding appears. Knowledge comes, but wisdom lingers, you see."

"I have heard that from my parents as well, Master." It was only his anger that was making him so bold, but the resentment in his voice was clear.

"Harrumph! Very well, then. I will be direct. A sorcerer is born with a certain talent. Once manhood begins to unfold—or womanhood, for that matter—that talent can, under the right circumstances and with the right training, flourish and result in the ability to practice sorcery. However, there is a price. A sorcerer often lives to a great age—illness and accident notwithstanding—on occasion even several times the life span of a normal man. With each use of the Art, however, that span is diminished by a certain amount. If the use is small, the loss is small. If great, however, the loss is likewise of similar magnitude. These deductions accumulate over time."

Silvestrus paused a moment as a bright-blue butterfly fluttered quickly across his path. "Thaddeus, I must tell you, Ethne is gravely ill, and I believe Ormerod may not be far behind her. The illness she carries, she has passed to her master. To rid her of this contagion this far into its course would be tantamount to bringing a dead spirit back to life. Few things take a greater toll from a sorcerer than that, and the effort is not uncommonly fatal. It is a price I am unwilling to pay. Not for her, sweet though she is, and in love with her as you might be. It may be that you will come to understand and accept this in the season of things."

"Ethne said I will become a sorcerer someday. And that is the reason why you came for me and told my parents all those things about a 'mystery.' Well, I will become a sorcerer. A great and powerful one. Then I will go to her and save her. You will not have to trouble yourself, Master! I do not care what the cost is! I will save her!" Blood pounded through his veins. He, Thaddeus, would defy the world, no matter the price.

"All right, Thaddeus. It is your right and your choice. I would only…Well, you have spoken. Perhaps, it is best to leave it at that for now."

For the greater portion of the day, Thaddeus looked out upon a countryside turned bleak. He had no words for his master.

Silvestrus was silent as well, smoking his pipe but seemingly thoughtful and concerned. The creaking of the cart, the groaning of the wheels, and the thudding clip-clop of Asullus's hooves were the only accompaniment.

The party reached Meadsville as the sun was setting. Silvestrus bade them set up camp in a wooded area west of the city.

Thaddeus, sullen and sulky, did what he was told, and only that, without speaking. He was lost in his sorrow, anger, and frustration—and petulance. Once, while clearing the campsite, Silvestrus passed him muttering something about a "distraction." Asullus appeared sympathetic but let him be. Thaddeus had grown fond of the old mule and was grateful for his earlier intervention, even though the mule must have known it would cost him "summat."

After a trip to a nearby stream for water, Thaddeus was returning to camp when he came upon his master sitting on a log, whittling amidst a great flock of brilliant-blue butterflies that hovered around him. He appeared to be listening to something, but shook his head before nodding in Thaddeus's direction and returning to his task.

Within moments, the cloud of butterflies deserted Silvestrus and flew toward Thaddeus. They were soon flitting around him thick enough to obscure his vision. He was dazzled by their radiant color, and his spirits began to lift. However, their activity seemed particularly frenetic, and he had no idea what to make of it.

The butterflies, larger than those he was used to seeing at home, were behaving peculiarly. They would fly pell-mell around his head as if to get his attention, then take off as a group to the northeast of the camp, near the forest edge, where they hovered. As he continued to stare at them, they flew back to him, again surrounded him with their frenzied fluttering, then raced for the forest edge once more. This behavior was repeated three more times before it occurred to Thaddeus to follow them. The next time they rose and flew off, Thaddeus shrugged, set down the water buckets, and followed.

When he reached the hovering mass, they flew down a path into the thickest part of the forest. Thaddeus looked back at the campsite. Silvestrus had disappeared, and Asullus lay napping. He shrugged and followed the fluttering cloud as it led him deeper into the underbrush, where the forest quickly darkened.

Just to the left of the path, the blue cloud stopped and resumed its mad hovering. As Thaddeus approached the mass, it parted to reveal a huge, glistening spider web stretched between two tall birch trees.

Thaddeus approached the web, which was vibrating from the frantic efforts of its captive to free itself. Near the center of the web was a singular blue butterfly, larger than the others. The creature struggled, its wings, torso, and legs caught in the sticky silk, barely able to move. Now, Thaddeus understood the reason he'd been summoned. The larger butterfly bore some important relationship to the others and required his help. Though he understood, it was behavior he'd never seen previously in any butterfly. Very peculiar.

Gently, he held the beautiful creature, which had quieted at his touch, and carefully pulled it clear of the web, thread by thread. At last, it was free. The butterfly sat in the palm of his hand, wings slowly fanning, before it flew up to circle his head several times with the rest of the cloud that now hovered around it. Suddenly, the larger butterfly shot straight up and away, its entourage raggedly following until all were lost to sight.

As he watched the last of them disappear, Thaddeus was aware of a growing sense of serenity. His emotional storm had subsided, and he was at peace. Returning to camp, he found Silvestrus and Asullus in animated conversation. The sorcerer looked up and caught sight of his young charge.

"Ah, Thaddeus, are you all right? We were a bit concerned."

"Yes, Master Silvestrus. I was just walking in the woods for a space, following some beautiful butterflies. I rescued a big blue one from a spider web."

"Good lad. Glad you are safe. Perhaps next time before you go off on a jaunt, however, you will let one of us know."

"Of course, Master. I'm sorry. I promise I will do better." The remainder of the weight that had been pressing down on him disappeared. He couldn't say why, precisely, but he was feeling considerably better—and he was no longer angry. Things seemed much as they had before, before Figberry. He picked up the water buckets from where he'd left them and set them by the other provisions.

"Thaddeus, take Asullus with you and gather some firewood. It will be dark soon."

The boy trudged off with the mule to the forest edge and picked up a night's supply of sticks and faggots, which he placed in the panniers Asullus carried on his back.

"Worried aboot ye, I was—though the old man did no' seem to be so much. An' ye're out chasing butterflies!" He snorted. "This be me last trip, that's fer certain. I'm back to Cobbly Knob after this, an' I'll be lettin' the lovely Lady Lillith tend to me wants 'stead of traipsin' all o'er yonder concerned wi' some young calf-struck, moon-eyed, wet-behind-the-scruntchian doe head who can't seem to make up his mind whether to pick his nose or scratch at his behinder!"

"I said I was sorry, Asullus. It's just that they were so fair. And I—say, where's your garland? Did you lose it?"

"Nay, I slipped it off me neck an' put it inna cart. Dinno' want it to get all crushed or dirty, don' ye know. Well, lad, are ye feeling better aboot things now? Ye've seemed a bit put out lately—no' to say ye've no' a good reason."

"Hmm? No, I'm fine, Asullus. I feel better, actually. I just wish you could have seen those butterflies. And that big one was so beautiful. It was just over there, and..."

It was almost dusk by the time they returned. Thaddeus built a fire, and soon they were enjoying the remnants of Master Ormerod's midday bounty. Following the meal, Silvestrus sat sipping purberry wine from his flask and gazing steadily into the fire, eyes half lidded. Suddenly he straightened, alert.

"Right. Now, Thaddeus, Asullus, I am going into town tonight. I must meet with some people."

"Do you wish me to go with you, Master?"

Silvestrus looked thoughtfully at his apprentice. "Perhaps it would be better if you stayed here, Thaddeus. You have had, all in all, a fairly demanding day or two. I will trust the pair of you, however, to maintain the camp and keep out of trouble. If all goes well, I will return later in the day tomorrow." With that, he stood, took up his walking staff, and set off on a trail leading east.

"Aye, well there he goes, the old ghost. An' leaving us wi' the dishes to do. Quite a surprise there, eh? Sorcerers! Well, come on, lad. Hop to. Ye're the one wi' the opposable thumbs. Me, I'll go scout around a bit. Maybe I'll see me some butterflies, too. Pfah!"

Later that evening, Thaddeus bedded down for the night while Asullus lay nearby. The old mule was of the opinion that the camp was not likely to be bothered during Silvestrus's absence.

"Did somethin', he did. Always does when we camp an' he has to be away. It'd take a troll or some such to get through to us, mind ye. But then, I'd just run away. I'm fast as needs be if I'm properly motivated. Ye—well, there be limits to everyone's luck, laddie. I'd keep ye in me memories, though, I would."

"Why, thank you, Asullus. How good it is to have a true friend in times of trouble," Thaddeus replied dryly.

"Aye, right ye are, me boy. 'Tis indeed. Now try to get some sleep. I expect tomorrow'll be an interestin' day. Although, I'd swear there's summat up tonight. Somethin' in the air, maybe…"

Thaddeus lay on his back on his bedroll, watching the night sky. He mused for some time before turning onto his side. It was then he felt the lump in his tunic. He reached in and pulled out the packet Ethne had given him, a small square of canvas folded over and tied with a leather thong. Inside was a linen cloth wrapped in a bit of bright yarn. Thaddeus opened it and recognized her scent immediately. He carefully folded back the kerchief to reveal a heavy swatch of dark curls tied with a sky-blue ribbon. He held it to his face—so soft, and her smell. Feelings rushed back to him as if from a dream, and damp drops fell on the cloth that she had touched. Eventually slumber overtook him.

Thaddeus gradually became aware it was getting lighter. Slowly, he opened his eyes a crack. It was lighter, but not with moonlight, and certainly not with sunlight. The light was blue—a bright, brilliant blue. He opened his eyes further. The sense of peace he'd felt earlier returned. He sat up slowly, rubbed his eyes, and looked toward the source of the light. At first it was painful, but as his vision adjusted, he could see better.

Something, a figure perhaps only a pace and a half tall, a girl's—no, a small, delicate woman's—figure. A cascade of blue hair fell down her back. She had large, luminous eyes of a deeper blue, and fragile features except for full lips and prominent cheekbones. She wore no clothes. A tiny copy of a woman stood before him, but not really a woman—she was more ethereal Her gaze was steady, her manner regal.

"Thaddeus of Beewicke, I am Caerulea, *Regina Papilionum,* and I have come to speak with you—to thank you, that is. It was I whom you saved from certain death earlier today in the spider's lair. I had foolishly sampled too much of my Lord's nectar, and it went to my head. It always seems to affect my judgment, also my reflexes. My mother, queen before me, often said, 'If you do drink, then do not fly.' In any event, that is how I came to be in my predicament. I sensed your party nearby and sent my courtiers to fetch one of you. I gather the older one, Silvestrus, was disinclined, or, for some reason, thought you more suited to rescue me. Then you came and freed me. My Lord Spadix, *Rex Blattarum*, is away this night—in fact, most nights—so I have come for you, to show you a queen's appreciation. While you are young yet, I sense a great power lying latent within you, like that of the sun. I am attracted to light such as that. Come."

The blue *Faerrae* moved forward and took his hand, and Thaddeus found himself powerless to deny her. Suddenly, great wings unfurled behind her, and Thaddeus was lifted up and borne swiftly over the treetops. As they flew, hundreds of butterflies joined them in a dance of bright blue light. Though all in her court appeared fair, Caerulea was the fairest of them all.

"There." She indicated a small patch in the forest. "My home. You will be my guest tonight. You will find the gratitude of the Queen of the Butterflies is not insignificant."

Once his feet regained the earth, Thaddeus realized he stood naked. He looked around the clearing, noting the house-sized leaves and massive tree trunks—which could have been twigs but for their size—and mushrooms the size of horses. His senses had been clouded since he had first seen Caerulea, so it took some time for him to realize what had happened. His astonishment, however, was muted, as was everything else in what followed that night.

* * *

The embers of the fire slowly died. Asullus's head rested on his crossed front legs. His eyes flicked over to the empty bedroll.

"Ah, laddie, I hopes ye knows what ye're aboot this night. I canno' follow ye there. Butterflies! Pfah!"

On the ground to one side, on a smudged piece of cloth that had once been white, lay a handful of dark curls with a sky-blue ribbon, undone.

* * *

Thaddeus awoke feeling ill. His head felt like it had been rung with a stone cudgel, and his eyes burned fiercely, especially at the back. Covered with dew and shivering, he ached all over. And, he was naked. Again. He struggled to open his eyes, but they were stuck shut. Nausea struck again. He couldn't remember ever having felt so awful—not even with the fevers he'd endured as a child.

His malreverie was broken by a rasping baritone. "Well, laddie, top o' the mornin' to ye! How fair ye, me fine brawny one? Now what would ye fer breakfast? Would a slab o' cold, greasy bacon be to yer tastin'? Or, p'rhaps, some o' that world-renowned Beewicke honey? I ha' saved some extra special just fer ye! Or I can toss some o' that yellow churned, congealed cow curd that we ha' up in the air an' we can see if butter fly! Haw! Haw! Haw! Or, if you're no' in the mood fer a heavy meal o' grease an' lard, how aboot some light entertainment? Ye may not know this, but as a youth, I was champion o' me herd at braying wi' a special award fer volume at a distance. Permit me to gi' ye a wee bit o' demonstration."

Thaddeus lurched to his feet and unsteadily wove his way down to the stream, where he alternately retched and vomited in between thrusting his head under the chilling surface of the water.

Later, the boy sat cross-legged, wrapped in a blanket and shivering violently in front of the morning fire, trying to get warm while balefully glaring at his semi-equine companion.

Asullus, meanwhile, was preening himself, polishing his hooves on a clump of coarse grass and grinning from long ear to long ear.

"I thought you were my friend, Asullus."

"Oh, laddie, but I am. I mean, what are friends fer but to wait up the entire night till just before the dawn, no' knowin' where yer bucko boy might be nor what kind o' trouble he may be in, an' ye no' able to be there to lend a hoof or two? An' then, from out o' the' sky, pretty as ye will, he comes floatin' down, airy as all, in the arms o' an itty-bitty, naked blue lass wi' giant wings. An' him bein' naked as a jaybird himself, an' full up to his scuppers on some kind o' *Faerrae* nectar, three sheets to the wind an' drunk as a skunk into the bargain. Also singin'—off-key, mind ye—at the top o' his lungs, happy as a hamster who's found his hidey-hole, playin' at some kind o' lepidopterist, wi' no word or 'Hi, how be ye? An' his own heart broke into a million pieces no' six hours past, but somehow now forgettin' it all fer some new lass. What's no' to be happy aboot?"

Asullus had gone from a grin to a grimace during his diatribe—a point not lost on Thaddeus.

The mule sighed, "Ah, laddie, I'll no' be blamin' ye—well, no' entirely, anyways. Was beguiled, ye was, as happens now an' then. When ye mix wi' the *Faerrae,* ye must be verra cautious. Ha' their own purposes, they do, an' all yer wishes an' wants mean no more to 'em than a puff in the wind. I saw ye off, I did, but ye was too far gone 'fore I could do much, so I just stood watch, hopin' ye'd come back to us in one piece, don' ye know, an' way before the old man got back. He'd no' be happy aboot such goin's on, mark me. An' so, praise love, ye did."

"You're right, Asullus. It was my own shame, and I did not resist it. It was so strange. I hardly remember any of it. Although, there was one part Caerulea—she's the queen—told me she'd made me a 'Mark.' She said I was now *Amicus Faerrarum,* a friend of the *Faerrae.* She said it'd bring me good luck, make me welcome in certain circles, and provide some protection against evils of one kind or another."

"Well, now, that'd be no small gift, me young *Volans.* Though such gifts usually come wi' a price. Are ye sure ye no' be leavin' anything out o' yer tale as ye might ha' been a party to wi' the lovely young wench, beguiled or no'? The *Faerrae* are well known fer their various appetites, they are."

A scarlet flush suffused Thaddeus's face.

"Hmm. If ye ha' been havin' commerce wi' their likes, then this mark'll usually be one o' two places. One is o'er the heart, an' the other isn't. Slip yer blanket down a bit, an' let me—ah, I thought me as much. Well, as I said, it do happen sometimes, an' ye look no more the worse fer the wear o' it, apart from bein' hung o'er the fence an' not dryin' out verra quick like. Come on, get yerself clad, an' let's go see if there might be summat the old man has in his bag o' tricks as can fix a body up followin' encounters wi' those creatures as be havin' six legs an' such."

Thaddeus got up slowly and dressed. It worked best if he didn't hurry. He joined Asullus, who had his front legs up on the side of the cart.

"Ah, there it is, laddie, the little black bag. Do ye see it? That's the one we'll be wantin.'"

"Asullus, are you sure we're allowed to get into Master Silvestrus's belongings—his personal things?"

"O' course we're no'! On the other hand, how much do ye enjoy yer current state o' feeling? Ye can continue on, if ye like..."

"Well, all right. Here." Thaddeus set the bag on the ground. Tied with rawhide thongs, the pack was covered with a sturdy, stiff fabric that owned signs of many years' use. A large circle with an intricate ***S*** scribed within adorned the cover.

"Go ahead, lad. Open it up. I know what we be lookin' for. Seen 'im do it enou' times."

Thaddeus untied and unrolled the pouch. Inside were rows of pockets holding all manner of items.

"That's it. Now fetch out the green stuff. No, no—not that. That's the weed the old man puts in his pipe sometimes after an especially hard day. He seems to take pleasure in it, but it smells funny an' makes him act silly. Gives 'im quite an appetite, too, I so swear. No, the green powder, three pockets over, in the glass jar with the stopper. Yes, that's the one. Now take it over by the fire."

Thaddeus was not comfortable with this thievery. However, he did feel terrible, and if it would help... He set the jar down next to the fire.

"That's right. Now take that pot an' put in three cups of water. Then add a pinch o' the powder. That's it. Now, stir it round wi' that little stick an' put it on that flat rock near the edge o' the fire. Good, now take that cup an' pee in it."

"What?"

"Ye heard me. Pee in it. It's part o' the cure. Just do it, lad, an' put it in the pot, too."

Thaddeus did as he was told, but he had definite misgivings about this "cure."

"All right. Now take out that little frog sticker ye ha' an' slice yer thumb up along the side. Either one. Good. Then put aboot ten drops into the pot." At Thaddeus's questioning look, he continued. "Well, you suck on it, o' course. It'll stop on its own, Auntie Livia. Now blow yer nose into the pot. Yes, I'm serious. Just do it, laddie. Ye've come this far. So far, so good. Now ye must say the magic words."

"Magic words? What magic words?"

"I swear, do they no' teach the young anything at all these days? Ye must concentrate an' use magic words, laddie, when ye performs magic acts. Sometimes it needs a magic gesture or a magic object, too, an' sometimes no', dependin' on what it is ye be doin'—one's natural strengths an' skills, the difficulty o' what ye be tryin' to accomplish an' so on. With this particular one, methinks only a phrase is required, an' it goes summat like, *Veni, Medice!*"

"But Asullus, I'm not a sorcerer. I'm just an apprentice, if that. And I may never be a sorcerer. I'm not even sure I want to be one, now that I think about it. Besides, you just said the words. Why do I need to?"

"Laddie, ye are the one wi' the inborn talent. 'Tis a gift. Ye ha' it, or ye don'. An' ye ha' it. Denyin' it'll no' make it go away. Ye are the sorcerer here. Meself, I'm just a poor, old, dumb brute tryin' to make his way in the world, beset by..."

"Oh, fine. *Veni, Medice!*" Through his discomfort, a great rush suffused his body, and a deep, distant roaring sound thrummed through his head.

"All right. Now were I ye, I'd stand meself back apace."

Dark green fumes began boiling out of the small cauldron, along with a constantly rising and falling wailing sound that grated on Thaddeus's ears. The smoke began to coalesce as the irritating sound receded, and there, in its midst, stood a thin man, of taller-than-average height, dressed in green robes.

His aloof and disdainful expression alerted Thaddeus as to the man's importance. In his right hand was a skull and in the crook of his left arm a heavy tome.

He intoned, "Life is short, Art is long, the Opportunity fleeting, the Experience fallacious, the Judgment difficult, the..." The man paused. "Wait a moment! Neither of you, obviously, is Master Silvestrus. Where is he, and what is the meaning of this?" The learned one's chin beard waggled as he spoke.

Asullus stepped closer to the fire. "Yer pardon, Honored Physician, sir, but our master could no' be in attendance at this time to greet ye personally, but know he is eager that his unworthy apprentice here, a promisin' lad named Thaddeus, who has been taken ill—poisoned, I believe—be examined by one o' yer stature, as yers is the only true hand wi' the wisdom to cure him that I know."

"Harrumph! You're the mule, aren't you? Yes, I've seen you before. You had...What was it? Oh, yes, some sort of pox, from an Eohippus you'd met in Lippizaria, you said, and—"

"Ah, beggin' yer pardon, Revered Sir, but the lad is sufferin' mightily, an' we donno' wish to keep ye, knowin' as we do that ye have many more important an' weighty matters to attend to than—"

"Yes, yes, yes. Very well." Setting down the skull and book, the doctor squinted at Thaddeus. "Ah, I remember you as well—the human pincushion. All healed up nicely, too, if I do say so myself. Yes. Now step forward, young Tedius, and let's have a look at you. Hmm. Hmm. Now stick out your tongue and say, 'Aesculapius.' Hmm. Nothing there. Hmm. Hmm.

Now turn your head and cough. Hmm. All right. It appears to be nothing more than a common case of post-acute alcohol intoxication *residuae,* though it seems that the original elixir ingested was derived from a nectar, of all things. Interesting."

The medical consultant withdrew two pellets wrapped in purberry leaves from his robes and handed them to Thaddeus. "Here, take two of these with water. Obtain proper rest, diet, exercise, and you'll be right as rain in no time. However, you may call on me again in the morning if you feel no different."

"Oh, thank ye, Learned Sir. Ye're a blessin' to the lad, ye surely are."

"Nothing at all, nothing at all. But that reminds me. Your master has run up a bit of a bill here, and I am certain he would like to see it resolved soon. If neither of you parties is prepared to settle this account, perhaps you could arrange for a third party to—awwkk!"

Asullus, apparently deeming the business concluded, kicked over the pot, and its contents washed into the fire. With a whoosh, the figure and all the smoke vanished instantly.

"Look who be callin' who Tedius. Oh well, lad, the old geezer's a bore, but he usually knows his pharmacy. Just gulp those down, an' I expect ye'll be the happier for it shortly."

By the time the bag of magic ingredients had been rewrapped and replaced in the cart, and the area put to rights, Asullus's prediction had come true. The pair of them decided a short nap was indicated, given the night's exertions. As they were getting settled, Thaddeus rolled over to face the mule.

"Asullus, I have a question. Ever since we met, you've been telling me stories about you and your lady friends, and just now, that doctor made a reference to that, I think. But you're a mule—you said so yourself—so how can you, um...? I mean, isn't there a...That is to say..."

"Laddie, donno' think so much. Ye'll cause yerself a strain or some such. Sure an' ye're right, though. Many—well, most, that is—well, all, really—o' me kind donno' care so much fer the lasses an' the making o' the wee ones an' the like. An' it's summat I've wondered aboot meself. But if I ha' the straight o' it, when the Lady Lillith was doin' whatever it was she was doin' to help me to speak, it also caused me to ha' an eye fer the fair ones, an' I been at it ever since. As it turns out, no' so many there are be expectin' one such as meself to ha' an interest, an' so when I spots me a likely lass, she's sometimes surprised in lookin' o'er her shoulder to see me there, smilin' an' winkin' an' all at her."

Thaddeus propped his head on his hand and listened attentively.

"But let me tell ye, summat, lad. There's few things in this world more frustratin' than bein' in love o' the moment, up on yer hind haunches, an' the object o' yer affection, just like that, decides to saunter off somewhere 'cause she gets it in her head the grass is greener some other place an' so walks off, leavin' ye danglin', so to speak. I'll tell ye, 'tis no' only disappointin', but embarassin'. Sometimes, I do ha' the thought that all this jumpin' aboot an' hair pullin' is no' worth the exertion an' certainly no' the dignity lost in the foolishness. Still, we do keep bein' the moth to the flame, don' we now, in spite o' all that I'm sayin' this minute?"

Thaddeus's long-eared friend finished with a grin, and nothing more was said after that. The sun was three-quarters down before either of them roused again.

New firewood had been collected, water fetched from the stream, and the semblance of an evening meal started when Thaddeus saw Asullus suddenly prick up his ears and turn his head to the east.

"Somebody's comin', laddie—two somebodies. Ah, 'tis the old man an' yer new classmate, I'll be wagerin'."

Within moments, the grass rustled, the underbrush parted, and Silvestrus came striding into the glade wielding his staff. Just behind him trudged a short, pudgy young boy. He was dressed in a white linen tunic and trousers. His leather sandals were laced up, and a leather knapsack of provisions rode high on his shoulders. He squinted and looked down at where he was placing his feet. Shorter than Thaddeus, he had dark-brown hair, apple-red cheeks, and eyes that darted curiously around the clearing.

"Ah, Thaddeus, Asullus, good to see you. All is well, I trust?"

Thaddeus glanced quickly at Asullus, who shook his head slightly, then answered the old sorcerer.

"Welcome back, Master. It has been quiet in your absence—nothing new to report."

"Excellent. The best news days are no-news days. Thaddeus, come here. I want you to meet a future colleague." The old man motioned Thaddeus forward. "Thaddeus, this is Anders of Brightfield. Anders, this is Thaddeus of Beewicke."

"Hello." Thaddeus stuck out his hand as he'd seen his elders do.

The smaller boy hesitantly put out his hand as well. "Hullo."

Thaddeus thought him reserved, but warmed to his self-effacing yet friendly manner.

"Beewicke is a tiny village, and we don't get out much. Where is Brightfield? Is it a town close to Meadsville?"

"Uh, no. Brightfield's near Meadsville, but it's not a town, really. It's just the name of the estate where my family home is. I don't know why they call it that, though. There are fields about, but they aren't really bright. You're from Beewicke? Isn't that where the honey comes from?"

Thaddeus grimaced but nodded. "Oh yes. That's where the honey's from. Is it mead your town's named for?"

"Yes. A lot of the estates around there ferment your honey to use in the mead vats. Also, several of the families grow barley and hops—we do, at our place. Then the brewers turn it into ale and beer as well as mead. They're always testing it to see if it's good yet—and always laughing and falling down afterwards." The boy smiled shyly.

Thaddeus laughed out loud. He liked the new boy very much and could tell they were going to be close comrades.

The sorcerer nodded in approval. "Well, you two seem to be getting on. Good. Thaddeus here will help you get things sorted out, Anders. You boys start a leg on dinner. I'm going to have a chat with Asullus."

After the old man turned away, Anders, his hazel eyes large and round, stared at Thaddeus. "Did Master Silvestrus say he was going to 'chat' with the mule?"

"Yes, he did. You see, the mule talks. Not only that, but…"

For the next hour, questions and answers flew back and forth, each boy perpetually interrupting the other. Anders had much to learn about the group's adventures to date, and Thaddeus had much to learn about the outside world.

"…so he was talking to Mater and Pater, and then they both agreed I should go with him. I couldn't believe it. They usually want me to stay close to home and the villa—on account, I think, of the trouble I have breathing when I exercise or when it's cold. I've hardly ever been out, except to see the vats in the barns during the tapping. And have you noticed the master's blue ring? It glows sometimes, like when he was talking to my parents…"

"…and Asullus is a special mule. He has girlfriends—if you can believe that—and he was raised by an old witch. She's the one who fixed it so he can speak. And…"

"...I always had a lot of tutors. My parents wanted me to know about everything so I could take over the family business, but I never did think..."

"...then we were attacked by bandits. They shot two arrows into me, but I was healed right away. Then a demon came, tall and brown and ugly, and ate them..."

"...that's amazing. I don't know how that could be. But he told me it was a 'mystery,' and I might be a sorcerer, and I was to meet another boy—he must have meant you—who was also, but he never told Mater that, and that's odd because..."

"...and that first night, I took him to an old standing stone, and it glowed blue, just like his ring, when he touched it..."

"...then he showed me an old well that had been covered over ever since I was born, and he told me to look into the water, and I thought I saw a face. It was blue and..."

"Come on, Anders. I'll introduce you to Asullus. He's amazing, and he talks funny. Of course, he's a mule, so I guess he would, wouldn't he? This girl I met when we were in Figberry, Ethne—she's beautiful—she made him a garland, and he's all googly about it."

The boys made their way across the clearing to where Asullus stood, head down, facing the forest. "Asullus! Look, it's the other boy the master spoke of. His name is Anders of Brightfield, and his family makes mead. He's—Asullus, what's the matter? You're standing there like a lump."

Anders stared as Thaddeus addressed the mule.

"Sorry, laddie. I'm no' at me best. The old man ha' some words wi' me concernin' gettin' into his private stocks, he did. He don' care fer it, don' ye know. Donno' worry none, though, I told him 'twas all me idea. Anyways, he gave me a rough-out—deservedly so, I s'pose—an' it's a little slow in gettin' o'er. But here I am going on aboot me, an' we have us a new lad. Anders, do ye say? O' Brightfield? Aye, we been by there before, some years ago. Saw yer folks, I did. Seemed like nice people. Though I would ha' thought they'd be teachin' their son that standin' around wi' his eyes bulging out an' his mouth hangin' open is hardly polite, 'specially on meetin' new folk fer the first time."

"He...he talks!"

Thaddeus chuckled.

"Aye, he do, don' he now. Well, in any event, me name be Asullus. I will no' bore ye wi' all the details, as I'm sure the tall lad here has filled ye in, but aye, I do be speakin', but only as there's summat worth to be speakin' aboot. Which surely has been hard to find in any conversation I've had me so far wi' young honey-knees here. But, if he ever be givin' ye a hard way to go, Anders of Brightfield, ye can probably get yer investment back by askin' him a bit aboot blue butterflies."

"Blue butterflies? Thaddeus, what about the blue butterflies?"

Thaddeus turned scarlet again as Asullus grinned. "Nothing, Anders. Asullus is just making a joke. But come on, we'd better finish getting dinner ready, or we'll get some of what the master gave his pet mule here."

"Ye know, laddie, ye no' be so big as I could no'—"

"Asullus! Boys! What's taking you so long? And where's the fire?"

Asullus turned to trot off. "Oh, me! We'd better be movin', lads. More later."

Following dinner, the group sat around the campfire, full and at peace. The night was ablaze with shooting stars, and Silvestrus told tales of things grand and mysterious, while Asullus related humorous experiences of past travels. Anders was brought up to date on the group's adventures, and he, in turn, related stories his tutors had told him about the days of the Empire. The moon had passed its zenith by the time they sought their bedrolls. As Thaddeus drifted off to sleep, he reflected that his new life seemed much less daunting given that he would now not be facing it alone. He had a friend.

Chapter 3

TERTIUS

* * *

The next day, the party broke camp and placed their belongings in the cart. A heavy drizzle had begun shortly after breakfast, complicating work and dampening spirits. After hitching up Asullus, they clambered aboard and set off north, circling Meadsville, then bore northeast, passing above the tip of the Twin Lakes. Keeping the lakes on their right, they took turns driving the cart, though Asullus kept a steady pace without more than an occasional consultation. The rain gave no sign of letting up.

They rested from time to time, chiefly to stretch and give the mule a respite. But mostly they talked, or rather, Anders talked. He continued his narrative of the previous evening, delving further into the history of the world, a tale that was supplemented from time to time by the old sorcerer, who offered annotation, elucidation, and marginalia. But overall, Silvestrus appeared content to the let the boy speak, being pleased to alternately smoke his pipe, listen, or nap.

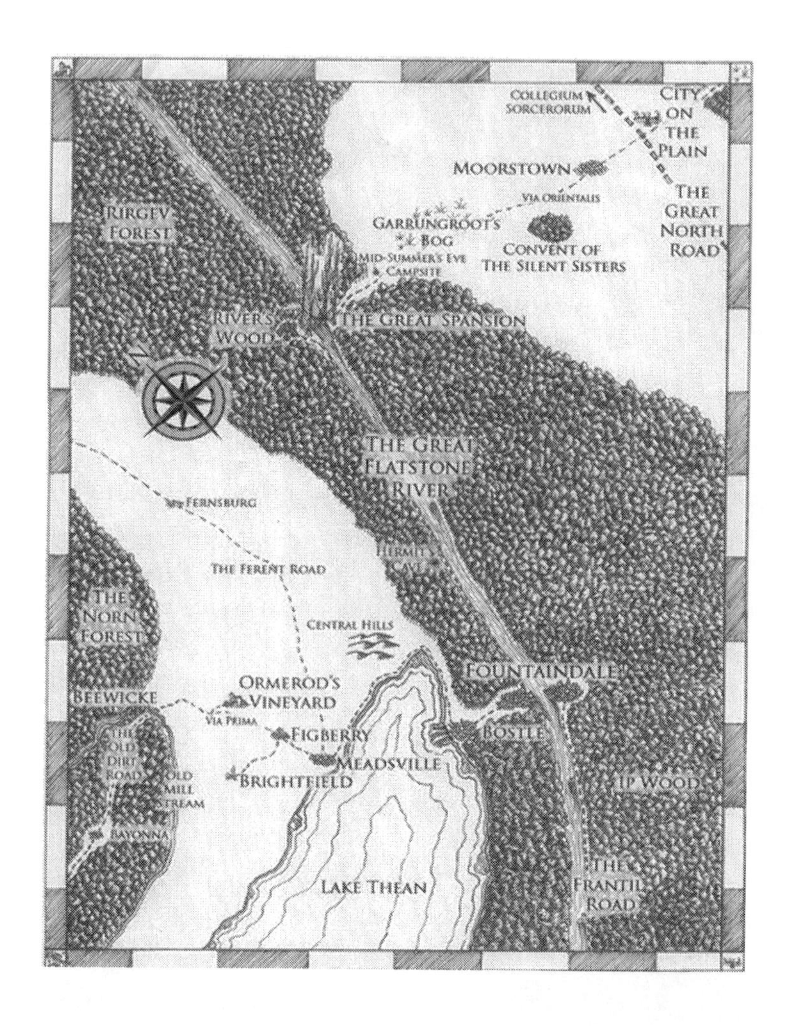
Collegium Sorcerorum
City on the Plain
Moorstown
Via Orientalis
The Great North Road
Garrungroot's Bog
Convent of The Silent Sisters
Rirgev Forest
Mid-Summer's Eve Campsite
River's Wood
The Great Spansion
The Great Flatstone River
Fernsburg
The Ferent Road
Central Hills
The Norn Forest
Fountaindale
Ormerod's Vineyard
Beewicke
Via Prima
Figberry
Bostle
Meadsville
Brightfield
Old Mill Stream
Bayonna
Lake Thean
The Frantil Road

Thaddeus had heard only a limited version of the history and was fascinated by the flow of events starting from before the time of the Empire. His thirst for this new knowledge was like the thirst of sand for water.

"Anders, how do you know all this?"

"My tutors kept at me about it. I do like reading and writing, though. It just comes and is there when I need it. I don't know how. My chief tutor, Primus, always told me I should think of becoming a scholar and, perhaps, teach at the *Lyceum.* I'm not sure now, though. This other business is pretty interesting so far."

As the sun approached the western horizon, Silvestrus cleared his throat. "Well, lads, I wonder. Perhaps you would like to hear the 'official' version of how it was that Man came to be on the Earth?" At their assent, the old man went on. "What I am about to recite is from one of the oldest preserved texts of the Sacred Writings. My own venerable tutor, Master Bede, taught it to me. It goes thusly."

> Everything began with the Sun. It was the Sun who organized everything, and gave form and sustenance to everything at the Beginning, even more so than now. After all was in place, the Sun shone down full upon the land, and the Eldest arose in the South and walked the Earth. They were the First Men of the Sun, and the Sun blessed them, and they multiplied. And they always remained in the South. But the Eldest were small, slight, and

shy. They had no speech, knew not of fire, and were often taken by the wild beasts that lived there.

Time passed, and those Eldest who remained begat the Grandfathers of Man, who were larger, but ill-favored, and also had no speech. And the land remained quiet.

These Grandfathers of Man saw that the Eldest were small and weak, and they slew them and ate them, and what Eldest had survived the wild beasts were consumed by the Grandfathers of Man until none were left living. The Grandfathers of Man did try to live in harmony with the Life around them, but the land was harsh, and the Sun tested them and was set against them because they had eaten the Eldest, who were no more.

Time passed, and some of the Grandfathers of Man decided to journey north to see our lands. So it came to pass, and they spread over our lands and other lands to the East. The Grandfathers of Man came to know fire, but only its beginnings, so they could not shape it fully to their purposes.

More time passed, and those of the Grandfathers of Man who remained in the South begat the Fathers of Man. But the Fathers of Man were great and brutish and fought with the Grandfathers of Man, seeking dominion over them. And the Fathers of Man had the victory and ate all the

Grandfathers of Man who lived in the South till none were left—just as the Grandfathers of Man had, themselves, eaten the Eldest before them.

Then the Fathers of Man took counsel one with another, for they had speech, and the land never knew quiet again. And the Fathers of Man knew fire, more so than the Grandfathers of Man, and they could shape it somewhat better.

And the Fathers of Man decided to go north and pursue the Grandfathers of Man who had gone before them, so they could have the final victory over them and eat them as well. And so they set forth. At first, the Fathers of Man pursued the Grandfathers of Man to the North and slew all they could find and ate them. But the Fathers of Man grew to love the North for itself because it was dark and cold, for the Fathers of Man were strong and hairy. And they stayed in the North and brought the mighty beasts that lived there under their dominion and ate them as well. So it was that the Fathers of Man abode in the North and pursued no longer the Grandfathers of Man, who had gone elsewhere, so that some yet lived.

Time passed again, and the Fathers of Man who had remained in the South came to beget Man. And Man flourished and grew in strength and numbers, and the Sun shone down upon Man with benevolence. And He prospered. And

Man had speech as well—not only the speech of the Fathers of Man, but the speech of Song and Wisdom, which the Fathers of Man had not.

And Man took counsel with one another and found that the Fathers of Man were brutish and repellent and jealous of Man and wished to keep food from Man, and water from Man, and thus keep Man in subservience as a willful child. And Man said, "No! This shall not be!" And so Man rose up and slew the Fathers of Man in the South, but did not eat them, for that was not Man's way.

And when all the Fathers of Man had been slain in the South, Man held further counsel and decided that some of the Men of the Sun—for that is what they now called themselves—would remain in the South and tend to the land there and abide with one another, while others of Man would journey north and pursue the remaining Fathers of Man, for they reckoned that was where the Fathers of Man had gone, for Man wished to have sole dominion over all the land. And so they assayed to slay all the Fathers of Man in the North as well, so that not one survived. And this they did.

Those of the Men of the Sun who remained in the South became marked by the Sun as His own. And those of Man who traveled north became marked by the Moon as Her own. And over time, it was recorded that no little enmity arose between the Men of the Sun and the Men of the Moon, but that is another story.

Man journeyed north and discovered the hiding places of the Fathers of Man, for the Fathers of Man had seen the approach of Man and fled, remembering how they had treated with Man. But the Sun aided Man because the Sun was displeased that the Fathers of Man had eaten the Grandfathers of Man. And the Sun brought light and warmth to the North that it had not before.

And Man made cruel war upon the Fathers of Man and slew them in their tens and their hundreds and their thousands until none of the Fathers of Man were left living. And Man left the Fathers of Man dead in their fields and in their forests and in their caves, and the Fathers of Man were seen no more.

Time passed. Some of Man went further north and abode there and became the Men of the Ice. And some of Man went farther west, until they came to the Sea, where they sought to wrestle with Her and subdue Her. And some of Man went east, and there they found the last of the Grandfathers of Man. But the Grandfathers of Man knew not Man, and were frightened of Man, and so waged war upon Man. But Man was mighty and cunning and now knew fire and wheel and spear in all their aspects and attributes, and Man slew the

Grandfathers of Man unto the very last one, but did not eat them, for that was not Man's way. And thus Man's victories were soon beyond counting. And, in time, he came to sing of them and to write of them.

Then the Sun gave Man dominion over all he surveyed, whether for good or for ill, and thus it has been unto this very day.

The abrupt ending of the recitation caught the boys by surprise, and the giggling that had accompanied their game of faces stood in loud contrast to the quiet that prevailed now that the old man had stopped speaking.

Silvestrus did not seem perturbed but wore a faint smile.

Thaddeus, however, could swear that, if asked, he could now recite the entire lay by heart.

Asullus snorted. "Ah, now that 'tis a bold an' fanciful tale ye tell, Master Silvestrus, an', in truth, I ha' never heard ye tell it previous quite so well. But I'm bound to mention there are significant discrepancies between yer rendition an' 'The Origin of Mule,' wi' which I am more familiar an' does tell the true tale o' the settlin' o' the lands o' the mule with the help o' their servant, man. If I be recollectin' it proper, it do begin, once upon a time, in the green valley, there lived—"

"Peace, Asullus. We are all eager to hear your words, I am sure, but I must have conversation with the lads as we approach Bostle. Now, Thaddeus, Anders, we will likely not reach Bostle much before nightfall. We will stay at an inn I know of. Neither of you is familiar with the larger cities, so I want you to stay close by while we bide there. Perhaps we will find time the following day to see some of the sights. The day after, we will travel to Fountaindale, the Shire Seat, where there will be many more things for you to experience. And one last fish to catch."

* * *

It was twilight when they rode into Bostle. Though some of the townsfolk with torches passed to and fro, most of the twisted streets were deserted at this time of day. Thaddeus, whose turn it was to drive, halted the cart when signaled by the guards stationed in front of the city's inner gate. There followed a brief conversation with Silvestrus concerning the group's business, and they were waved on following a perfunctory inspection. The sorcerer gave Thaddeus directions, and before long, they pulled up in front of a weathered inn, A Friend in Mead.

The innkeeper came out rubbing his hands. He greeted Silvestrus like an old friend and soon had his hostler at work putting up their mule and cart in the stable. Inside, a low-pitched buzz of conversation greeted the group, and a blue haze of pipe smoke hung lazily over the tables and benches. A cheery log fire was burning brightly at one end of the room. It was not so far into summer that they did not welcome the heat from the great stone fireplace.

Doffing their cloaks, the group found seats near the fire and shortly gave the innkeeper their orders for the evening meal. After he left, Thaddeus dug into his leather purse for the gold coins his father had given him and held them out to the sorcerer.

"Master Silvestrus, here is some money to pay for our meal. I hope it is enough."

"Thank you, Thaddeus, but that won't be necessary. Save that for your…tuition."

"May I see those coins, Thaddeus?" Anders asked in a low voice.

"Certainly. Here."

"You know, these are old Imperials. They're pretty worn, but you can tell from the Emperor on the front and the Eagle on the back. Where did you get them?"

"My father gave them to me before I left Beewicke. He thought I should have some money for my travels."

"Thaddeus, these are valuable, especially on account of their age—worth much more than their face value. Keep them to yourself, and don't go showing them about. If a robber were to see them, he might put a knife to your throat just to get them."

"Oh! I see." Hastily, Thaddeus put the coins back in his purse and tied it securely to his belt. "I didn't know cities were so dangerous."

"They can be, boy," Silvestrus said, "but not for us. Here the danger will usually be for others."

"You mean…from sorcery?" Thaddeus whispered.

"Perhaps, but in point of fact—well, here's our fare. Thank you, Bartsome. 'Best stew, best bread, all in Bostle's best.' Dig in, lads. Then it's repose, with some sightseeing tomorrow!"

* * *

Out in the stable, Asullus nuzzled the garland he'd been given. Its fragrance was compelling. As he savored it, a small, faraway voice spoke in his head, *"Watch over him, Asullus. Watch over him…"*

"Aye, lassie, that I will. That I will."

* * *

The next morning, the boys were up early, pestering their master to see the city.

Silvestrus, amused and indulgent, bade them wash first, then all went down for breakfast. Two platters of flatcakes and sausages with a pitcher of cow's milk disappeared with dispatch.

Anders stared at Thaddeus curiously. "Thaddeus, why don't you put any honey on yours?"

Once the platters were clean, the boys left the inn and explored the town, which took less time than they expected. Still, they were wide-eyed at the varied and numerous opportunities for spending their money—tempted, inversely, by what might be practical, long lasting, or necessary. Clearly, the town was built on a logging-and-lumber economy. The smell of fresh-cut timber was forever in their nostrils, and Anders sneezed continually. By midday, they had seen more than enough of big houses, buildings, and strangely dressed people speaking in peculiar accents and, with relief, headed back to the inn. After getting over his initial astonishment at the bustling town, Thaddeus considered that the familiarity and snugness of his modest Beewicke was much to be preferred.

Following midday, the boys took Asullus out for exercise in one of the outlying fields while Silvestrus took his usual afternoon nap. The sun was heading down in the sky as they returned to their room to find the old man waiting for them.

"Well, lads, I think we'll spend another night here and be off to Fountaindale in the morning."

After eventide—game birds this night—they sat on barrels in front of the inn and commented on passersby while their master had a cup and a pipe. After a time, Anders started in again on his history lessons.

"...and so the last Emperor, Tyrannus Superbus—*Imperator Ultimus*—decided to gather together all of the Empire's legions, the entire army, and set out for the East. The Emperor had heard that the wealth and treasure in the land of the Cin were beyond counting, and he wanted it for himself—as if the riches of the Empire were not enough. It took ten years to assemble, equip, and train the Grand Imperial Army of the Invasion. They say a million men were counted, and they marched steadily for nine months to get there. They even took their Gods with them. But after they crossed the Great Rift Valley, they were never heard from again. It was as if they had disappeared off the face of the earth."

"What happened to them?"

"No one living knows. Some of my tutors claimed the Cin came down upon them in a swarm of millions and ate them all. Others say they lost their way in the Sea of Sands, and their bleached bones lie yet on the shifting dunes. Old Secundus told me they became cursed because of the Emperor's pride and still wander the East as neither dead nor living, seeking vengeance—and will continue to do so until the end of time."

"Master Silvestrus?"

"Yes, Thaddeus?"

"Do you know what happened to the Emperor's army?"

"The Legions of the Lost? Well, some truth may lie in all three explanations. Perhaps they came upon magicks—Eastern magicks—things they were not prepared for. The magic of the East is different than what we know here. Very different. And certain of the Wise of the Cin knew well how to wield it. It is said terrible battles were fought, with fire and lightning falling on them from the sky—and demons and dragons. And the dead. It is always hot in battle, and the blood will boil. Death and terror stalk you everywhere. The Cin were prepared. They had spent years preparing. And, yes, Superbus was proud. Overweening pride, he had." Silvestrus's voice dropped to a whisper as he stared straight ahead. "They were all cut down. One million men. All cut down until they were no more. They cried; they screamed; they died. We wanted only to—" Silvestrus shook his head. "That is to say, no one knows their fate for certain, as there is no record of any survivors who returned to tell the tale. All that destruction, all that waste, all that long time ago. Such a pity…Well, boys, it is late, and we will be wanting an early start tomorrow. There is much to do in Fountaindale—and our last fish to catch. I am going up to bed now. Do not be long." The old man stood, stretched, tapped out his pipe, and went inside.

Thaddeus stared at his new friend. "Anders, how long ago was that war?"

"A thousand years, Thaddeus. A thousand years at least."

The following day dawned bright and sunny. After a rushed breakfast, the boys gathered their belongings and brought them down while Silvestrus settled up accounts. Inn Master Bartsome had his hostler hitch up the cart, and the boys stowed their baggage. In moments, they were headed toward Fountaindale. With full stomachs and fair weather, their mood was light, and Silvestrus taught them several traveling songs. Even Asullus joined in, in his own key and time.

Fountaindale lay on a grand river and was the hub and final terminus of the great Western trading route. Raw materials and products from the surrounding regions poured into the city for refinement and shipment down the Great Flatstone River to the Frantilline coast. Finished goods flowed from Fountaindale back to the hinterlands, spreading the artifacts of civilization.

As they rode throughout the long day, fine country villas gradually gave way to stone houses, some two stories high. Then they passed great squares and markets and, eventually, imposing buildings that housed the seat of government for the entire region. They gaped, taking it all in. They had never seen so many people in one place at one time. Crowds were everywhere, rushing and scurrying about. And the sounds—crying, cursing, shouting, laughing—were altogether overwhelming.

Anders cleared his throat. "Master Silvestrus, will we be going to an inn here?"

"Yes, but not right away. We have our fishing to do first. Walk with me, boys. Let us cast our line and see what we catch." The old man led his two apprentices and the cart back and forth in front of the Great Market as if searching for something. In the press of the crowd, Thaddeus was jostled by someone. Recalling Anders's words of caution, his hand went quickly to the purse that held the coins his father had given him. It was gone!

A young voice cried out. "Hey! Let me go! Help! Robber!"

"*Tace!*" Silvestrus commanded.

Thaddeus turned to see Silvestrus's extended arm gripping the wrist of a redheaded boy of medium height, now abruptly silent but violently attempting to break free of the old man's grasp. Clad in a plain, grimy jerkin, both the wearer and the garment looked in need of washing.

"If you continue to struggle, I shall summon the Watch and inform them of your recent activities, young thief. Which of us do you imagine they will believe? And what do you suppose will happen then? The choice is yours."

The youth ceased his efforts to free himself but remained sullen and defiant.

"Excellent. Now give the taller boy here back his purse. And do not attempt to stab me with your knife while you do it." Silvestrus maintained his grip on the boy while the dirty-faced youngster, with obvious reluctance, reached into his tunic, withdrew Thaddeus's pouch—cut strings and all—and tossed it to him.

Thaddeus caught the purse easily with his left hand and thrust it into his pocket. He then angrily advanced on the boy, ready to settle the robber then and there.

Silvestrus, however, held up his other hand in restraint. "Peace, Thaddeus. You have your treasure back and are uninjured. Come. Let us move off this busy street to a more quiet location. That way, we will disturb no one while we become acquainted." Without relaxing his hold, the old man steered the young thief to a nearby alley, while the others followed with the mule and cart. The two or three passersby who had stopped to watch the disturbance turned and went their various ways. Silvestrus leaned close to the boy's ear and murmured a word, then stepped back.

"Now let us see what we have here. Lad, what is your name?"

The boy muttered a short phrase.

"Ah, yes, I am familiar with that word—one from my youth, but hardly flattering. Let us make another effort. What is your name?"

An alternate short phrase was quoted.

"Hmm, I am not sure that is anatomically possible. But perhaps we should try another tack and strive to elevate the caliber of the conversation a bit. *Spumo!*"

Immediately, a gush of white bubbles began spilling out of the boy's mouth as he gagged, spit, and coughed, all the while making a terrible face. Gurgling sounds impeded his attempt to speak. With another word from the old man, the frothing dissipated.

"All right, once more. What is your name?"

"You're a sorcerer!" the boy said accusingly.

"Oh my, yes, indeed. And you are a thief. Do you wish another demonstration of the Art, or are you feeling more cooperative?"

"Are you going to turn me into a dung beetle, then, and keep me in a cage?" the young pickpocket asked anxiously.

"Now that is a very interesting idea. I will consider it. But, meanwhile, one final time, *what is your name?*"

"Rolland. What's yours, old man?"

"Well, it seems we are going to have to add 're-spect' to your syllabus, which is growing longer by the second. Although, you do have spirit—and courage. I will give you that. But to answer your question, my name is Silvestrus. I am a sorcerer and sit on the High Council of the *Collegium Sorcerorum*—the College of Sorcerers—toward which myself and my young apprentices are currently making our way."

Rolland's eyes flicked quickly to Thaddeus and Anders, then back to the old traveler.

"Where do you live, young Rolland?"

"Wherever I choose. I am a Free Man," the boy snapped.

"Are you now? Well, congratulations. And your father? Your mother? Where do they live?"

"They...they're dead. I take care of myself now. I'm one of Faran's Falcons. You've heard of him, I know."

"Not really, but I would venture a guess that he is the leader of the young thieves' guild in this city."

The boy was taken aback. "How do you know that? I never told you. Do you read minds, too, Sorcerer?"

"Signs, not minds. It is almost the same, sometimes, or so the Philosophers say. However, indulge me in some speculation, Rolland." The old man began ticking off on his fingers. "You are an orphan."

A momentary look of pain shot across Rolland's features.

"You steal to stay alive, serving a bigger thief, who, no doubt, serves an even bigger thief, and so on. I would guess you have seen friends caught and lose a hand, an ear, or a tongue, or even their heads. You are often in danger and have few things of value that you can claim for all the risks you take. You can neither read nor write. You cannot recall the last time you were really clean, went without gnawing hunger, or enjoyed sleep without care—or the last time someone told you they loved you. Does that more or less sum things up?"

The boy looked down at the ground in silence.

"Yes, I thought so. Well, I have a better offer. I believe you should come with us to the *Collegium.* There you will be fed regularly, have a warm place to sleep, will not be in fear of your life or the gaol, will not have to do anything particularly onerous, and you will have friends—true friends. Also, you will become literate, and, not incidentally, you will be taught to become a sorcerer."

The boy's mouth dropped open in astonishment.

But his reaction was not greater than that of the other two boys.

"What? Master, are you certain?" Thaddeus said. "I mean, not ten minutes past he was trying to rob us of all we had!"

"All the more reason to give him those things of value we do have—literacy, knowledge, insight, wisdom. Then he will not feel he has to steal from us. Well, what do you say, Rolland of Fountaindale? Are you game?"

Rolland's eyes narrowed. "What's the hook?"

"The 'hook,' as you put it, is that you will have to apply yourself—your will, your mind—harder than you have ever done in your life." He paused and stared intently at the boy. "And, you will have to obey me and the other masters."

"I don't think so, Sorcerer. I've seen your kind before, I have. You are a tricksy folk and never say what you mean right out. I don't believe I trust you."

Thaddeus was relieved. He wasn't sure he liked this brash, raggedy boy anyway—especially after the scofflaw's theft of his three gold pieces.

Anders, however, who had been looking thoughtful, quirked a smile. "It's probably just as well, Master. Asullus would not have wanted to talk with a street urchin such as this in any case."

Rolland turned to Anders with a challenging stare. "And just who is this Asullus, and why should I care whether or not he wants to talk with me?"

"Oh, Asullus, there." The young apprentice from Meadsville gestured over his shoulder at the beast.

"He's a mule. But he's a special mule. He talks to us. All the time."

"What? Are you touched by the Gods? Mules don't talk."

"This one does—but only to people he likes. I doubt that would be likely to include you."

"A talking mule! Ha! Trying to put one on me, are you? Well, I've heard enough. Now if you'll be letting go of my arm, old man, I'll be on my way. A talking mule! Do you really think me that barmy?"

Asullus eyed the scruffy boy critically. "Well, laddie, I'd say ye qualify as well as any other I ha' seen wi' me own eyes. An' you could certainly use a bath, I'm thinkin', though soapin' up the face was a good start, don' ye know."

Rolland's mouth dropped agape. "It's a trick! I saw the like with a talking broom at the Shire Faire one year. Some traveling man did it with his voice, Faran said."

Asullus shook his head mournfully. "'Tis the Gods, indeed, who are personally set against the Mule, I says. First, I'm accused o' no' speakin', then I gets accused o' that very same act, an' now, I'm bein' compared to an everyday household tool. I'm tellin' all who be listenin' that as soon as we're done here, I'm headin' meself back to Cobbly Knob an' the tender care o' Lady Lilllith—no more ungrateful an' misbehavin' boys, no more riskin'-me-neck adventures, an' surely no more o' old men who always be makin' me life a misery at every opportunity."

"I still think it's a trick," Rolland said with a scowl.

"Well, Rolland, I believe there is only one way for you to find out for certain. And that is to come with us. A sharp lad such as yourself should have no difficulty parsing out the truth of the matter soon enough. Then, once you are satisfied with what you have learned, you may return home anytime you like." Silvestrus regarded the boy carefully. "So, what is your decision?"

"Oh, I will go with you—by my own choice, you understand—just to discover your tricks and disprove all the nonsense I've heard about sorcerers and their so-called magicks. Then, when I return in triumph to Faran and the Falcons, everyone will know you and your kind for what you really are."

"Well said, *Magister Furum.* Done! Now walk with me and the others to an inn I know here, and we will talk more of tricks."

Thaddeus fell in with Anders as they walked behind the others. "Why did you bait that thief with Asullus? I don't think he's a very good addition to our group at all. Though I do feel sorry for him a bit, in that he has no parents."

"Hmm, if that's even true, Thaddeus. Well, it seemed to me the master wanted this boy for some reason. So it must be important to him. And I suddenly knew it was necessary the thief make his own choice to come with us. So, I thought of Asullus—he'd make anybody curious. And it occurred to me that if this Rolland was curious enough, he might be more apt to want to come along."

"Well, all right, if you say so, but I still say he's likely to be more trouble than he's worth."

The group traveled several *stadiae* further until Silvestrus signaled a halt in front of what long ago had been a grand old villa, but now, nestled between a smithy and a bakery, was an inn, The Sword in the Scone. The inn's hostler appeared from around a corner and took charge of Asullus and the cart—though Asullus always maintained this was looking at the process backward—while the rest of the party went inside. The interior was dark and cool, with tile floors and great slabs of green marble composing the fireplace, staircase, and half walls, with the rest finished in a warm, dark wood that had been polished smooth over decades, perhaps centuries.

The innkeeper was in vigorous conversation with one of the serving maids, but on spotting Silvestrus and the boys, gave the girl a peremptory order and made a beeline for the group. On reaching the old sorcerer, he immediately grabbed Rolland by the scruff of his neck.

"Ah, Master Silvestrus, good to see you again, it is. So, you've caught one of the street hooligans who plague our fair city. I don't know how they get out and about, bothering innocent travelers and discouraging commerce. But never you mind about him. I'll send Aldo here for the Shire Reeve quick as can be. They know how to deal with his sort. It'll be short shrift for him. Heh heh! Won't be stealing from upstanding folks without hands or neck, will you now, boy?"

Silvestrus let go Rolland's wrist and put a gentle restraining hand on the fat innkeeper's forearm. "Oliffe, it is all right. As it turns out, this boy is with us—an old legacy from another time. Appearances can be deceiving."

The innkeeper looked skeptical. "Not to question, you, Master, but I would swear on my grandmother's trotting harness that I've seen this particular lad before. He sneaks around the clientele, and after every encounter, someone's purse goes missing. Are you certain?"

"Yes, quite certain, good Oliffe. But it is most reassuring that law-abiding citizens such as yourself keep an eagle eye out to protect your town's guests and visitors. I shall be sure to mention it to my brother travelers when next I am come to the College."

The innkeeper relaxed his grip on the redheaded boy, smiled broadly, and added a quick bow. "It is always an honor to serve the Order. Now, I expect you'll be wanting rooms and something to delight the palate from today's menu selection. Our room choice, I'm afraid, is not as it usually is, what with all the logging factors in town for the Solstice, but I'm sure we can find whatever it is you require."

"My thanks, Master Oliffe. Our needs will include your best room facing the courtyard. Are the baths open at this hour?"

"Yes, indeed, Master Silvestrus. I'll send Gertie down with an extra supply of towels, and Aldo will take your things up to our best room. Eventide will be served at the eighteenth hour. Lamb is our specialty tonight. Please enjoy your stay, and send me word if you need anything else. Your rooms are just up the staircase there, but you know the way. Gertie! Aldo! To me!"

Silvestrus bowed and turned to make his way to the upper story. "Just what was the nature of your last misunderstanding with Master Oliffe, Rolland?"

"Nothing of the sort he tells. The man is a notorious liar. He claims his receipts for a week last spring went missing. I happened to be passing by the inn on my way to see my auntie—ill with the dengue fever, she was—and he spots me and draws the wrong conclusion, shouting for the Watch and raising quite a commotion. I think he's the one to blame, actually. I mean, if you're going to leave your treasures out on the table in plain view, walk away to pester the cook, then be upset at their absence when you return, why assign someone passing by the responsibility for your misfortune, when it's your own carelessness that has worked the difficulty in the first place?"

"I understand your reasoning. What was the approximate amount that went missing?"

"Something over thirty Imperials. It had been a slack week for him as I recall."

"I see. Well, perhaps we can make it up to Master Oliffe at some point. In the meantime, I think it would be in everyone's best interest if no more proceeds mysteriously vanished during the time we are guests here. I am certain you grasp my meaning."

The group climbed the grand staircase and turned down the hall, passing several carved oaken doorways, until they came to the last room on the right.

"In here, lads," Silvestrus ordered, opening the door and taking the key from the lock.

The room, elegant and spacious, reminded Thaddeus of the vintner's mansion in Figberry, but more furniture graced the richly patterned rugs—two desks, four padded chairs, a small table, and seven floor urns with stands. Thaddeus glanced at Rolland in time to see his calculating eye as he gazed about the room, lips moving, as if he were summing figures.

"Rolland, what I said about any missing monies also applies to any missing objects while we remain at this inn," Silvestrus said over his shoulder as he stood, hands clasped behind his back, in front of the window overlooking the courtyard.

A frown of disappointment crossed the street boy's features.

"Now, I have a few things to discuss with our host. While I am thus engaged, I think it best if the three of you made your way down to the baths—they are on the lowest level of the inn—and bathe yourselves before eventide. And for you, Rolland, a change of clothes will be provided. Come back here when you are through, but take your time. You might as well relax and enjoy the moment. Besides, you all could use the experience—some more than others."

Silvestrus pivoted and left the room only to be replaced by Aldo, who beckoned the boys to follow him downstairs. The baths, located under the ground floor of the old villa, were faced with green marble up to the cavernous ceiling. Steam rose lazily from the water's placid surface. Two towel-wrapped men—Grecolian merchants by the look of them—were engaged in an intense discussion in a corner enclosed by a ring of heated rocks. Otherwise, the boys had the baths to themselves. Anders, obviously used to this kind of convenience, took a towel from Aldo, doffed his clothes, and stepped into the water, giving a great sigh of pleasure as the steam enveloped him. Thaddeus and Rolland looked at each other and shrugged, then aped Anders, joining him in the hot pool. It was a pleasant experience for Thaddeus, though it caused him to relive the pain of his separation from Ethne—and no little guilt for some of his subsequent experiences. Rolland, however, looked, on the whole, apprehensive.

"I think the heated water must come from an underground thermal spring that they tap into and pipe up here," Anders said, taking a stoppered bottle holding a deep-blue liquid from a ledge near the pool and pouring a measure of it into his hand. "Though at home we heat the water in the pipes themselves." After replacing the bottle, he began rubbing the contents into his hair and soon wore a cap of white bubbles. "Go on, Thaddeus. You, too, Rolland. It's just soap, but it smells good and keeps the bugs off." He passed the bottle to the others, who again imitated his actions. The shared situation and pleasant sensations worked to loosen the boys' reserve.

Rolland, who had heretofore been silent, spoke up. "So the old one is really going to try to make you two and me into sorcerers? Is he on the up-and-up?"

"Oh yes," Anders answered. "He is. He's a sorcerer for sure. I've seen him do things. Thaddeus has, too. Come to think of it, so have you—and not that long ago." He quirked a smile. "How did that stuff taste, anyway?"

Rolland grimaced. "Like *Stercus!* I'd like to pay him back for that someday."

"I wouldn't count on it anytime soon," Thaddeus said. "He seems pretty alert. I don't think much gets by him."

"So, what's it been like for you two since you started?"

Anders worked up more lather in his hands. "Well, Thaddeus was picked first, in Beewicke. That's where he's from."

Rolland nodded knowingly. "Oh, the place they get the honey from."

Thaddeus had a sinking feeling that, for the rest of his life, it would never be possible to separate himself from Beewicke and its apian confection.

"And he was shot by brigands, and a demon came and ate them. Then he was nursed by a princess. Go on, Thaddeus, tell him about that."

"Well, it's not so much, really. I was just getting my staff down from the cart when—"

"Oh, and Thaddeus, don't leave out the part about the blue butterflies!"

Thaddeus shot Anders a combined look of exasperation and mortification, but continued his tale.

After a savoring the steamy water's pleasure, Anders suggested they move to the deeper end of the baths and practice some pool laps.

"You go ahead. I'll wait here," Rolland said, appearing nervous.

Acting on a sudden insight, Thaddeus addressed the thief. "There's probably not a lot of swimming in your line of work here in the city."

"No. Actually, none at all."

"Well, I grew up in the back country, and our parents were throwing us in the creek from the time we could walk. It's taught me a couple of tricks about how to make your way about in the water without swallowing a snootful. Come on down with me. Just hold on to the ledge as we go, nice and easy. I'll stand by you and show you what I mean. Then you can try, if you like, and see what you make of it."

After a moment, Rolland nodded silently and, hand over hand, followed his tall co-apprentice. It wasn't long before he was splashing about with the others. After a time, the boys made their way back to the shallow end.

"Thanks," Rolland muttered to Thaddeus as he paddled by.

Sometime later, the boys emerged from the baths squeaky clean and considerably refreshed.

Thaddeus and Anders decided it was time for Rolland to formally meet the mule. The boys found their clothes folded and waiting for them in the changing room. They hurriedly dressed and headed up and out to the stable yard. But as they were making their way around the back of the building, four rough-looking youths lounging by the fence that marked the villa's perimeter hailed them. The oldest of the group stepped forward and confronted them.

"Hey, Rufus! You'd better leave off from your pansy friends here. Faran wants to see ya, and he don't look much pleased. Want us to gush this lot here for ya? Looks like they might ha' a copper of two we could be usin'."

"Leave off, Sagar. I've got the edge here. I'll be lettin' Faran in on it soon enough."

"Ya know he ain't gonna like this none. An' we'll be sure he hears the tale. C'mon, lads, Puss Lips here has some new marks and don't seem ta wanta share. Give 'em all a kiss for us, Sweet Butt." The ragged group ambled off with exaggerated walks and raucous laughter.

Rolland looked angry, ashamed, and alarmed in turn.

"Boys you know? From before?" Thaddeus asked.

Rolland nodded. "Yes. They're a mean group, and they'll want to make trouble for us if they can. It's strange—until today, those boys were like family to me, but everything seems different now. I can't explain it."

"I know what you mean. I've had the same feeling ever since I left Beewicke. I think we're probably all going to need to stick together and look out for each other now."

* * *

Anders absently acknowledged the commentary. He was preoccupied with an intense study of the grounds, particularly focusing his gaze on the sodden, manure-filled yard in front of the stable, and the daisy-lined fence surrounding it. His attention was drawn to the progress of a sow and seven smaller versions of herself she was leading across the patch, appearing to carefully follow a particular course. One of the litter strayed off the path she'd marked and immediately became enmired to its nose in the tenacious, smelly, and treacherous ooze. The piglet squealed, and the harder he struggled, the more deeply he sank. The mother pig went mad grunting and nudging at her baby until he was finally able to work himself free. One more foot span farther out in either direction from the old sow's track and...

Anders looked thoughtful for a moment. He glanced at the full-petaled daisies, proud in their yellow-and-white finery that lined the periphery of the fence, and nodded to himself.

* * *

Thaddeus grabbed Rolland's arm. "Come on. Let's go see Asullus. You're not going to believe some of the things he says."

The group rounded the corner of the building and entered the gloomy stable. The musty smell sent Anders into a fit of sneezing.

In the last stall, they found Asullus lying on his back, wedged against the stable wall with his feet in the air.

"I've never seen a mule do that before," Rolland observed, "unless it was already dead."

"I'll thank ye to keep yer observations on me postures o' repose to yerself, laddie. Ye don' hear me describin' yer every which way when ye be layin' aboot, now do ye?" Asullus rolled over and got to his feet with what passed for a maximum of mulish dignity, shook himself, then sauntered over to the boys.

Rolland turned a surprised countenance to his new friends. "He does have a lot to say, doesn't he?"

Thaddeus nodded. "You know, Rolland, I said the same thing to Anders not two days ago."

"In me many journeys to all the corners o' this poor planet, I ha' found, wi' remarkable consensus, that there really be little difference from one boy to the next. They all seem to be irritatin' to aboot the same mark, disagreeable, wi'out charity, arrogant an' filled wi' a kind o' unwarranted overconfidence singular in the annals o' civilization. At least ye lot smell better, but by an' large, ye be all the same to my likes. How the greater part o' ye e'er make it to the time when ye ha' at least some utility is a mystery o' *Mater Naturae* o' the highest order an' deservin' o' the most intense study by scholars throughout this land."

Anders offered a mock bow. "Thank you, Asullus, Lord of All Knowledge of Man."

The mule snorted.

Anders continued. "Here, I brought you an apple." He reached into his tunic, withdrew the red fruit, and tossed it to the mule.

Asullus caught it deftly in his teeth, and it disappeared in seconds. "Well now, young Anders. I hope ye be notin' that the above opinion I was offerin' so freely was intended only fer the two louts as ye've charitably brought wi' ye an' in no ways was directed at yerself, a good an' upstandin' lad, as all can see."

"Hmm, Thaddeus, I think they're in love," Rolland offered dryly.

Thaddeus grinned. "I think you're right, Rolland. Perhaps we should be polite and leave them to themselves. I imagine we can find other uses for the apples we brought with us."

"Now in those selfsame travels as I ha' just now referenced, it was befallin' me to also note that mankind, in general, is a hasty species at best, often makin' snap judgments an' actin' on the impulse o' the moment, ne'er regardin' the consequences thereof. I'd wager that, on further consideration, ye likely lads might decide that this poor beast o' burden would—" The mule stopped in midsentence to catch both thrown apples and gobble them down in quick succession.

"I'm findin' that, temporarily at least, I'm fer changin' me opinion o' the lot of ye, subject to further investigations, o' course. That said, why do ye be wastin' me time an' yers standin' around wi'out introducin' me to the third o' yer number? A promisin' addition to our group, I'm sure."

"Right you are, old mule," Thaddeus said. "Asullus of Cobbly Knob, let me present Rolland of Fountaindale, Master Acquirer of Small Treasures such as loose coins and the occasional unguarded apple. Rolland of Fountaindale, here stands Asullus, late of Cobbly Knob, our stalwart and boon companion. Meet and be friends."

Rolland bowed. "Your service, honored mule."

Asullus made a leg. "An' yers as well, young thief."

Introductions concluded, the boys offered to take Asullus out to a nearby open meadow for an afternoon of exercise. Anders, however, excused himself with some comment about flowers and fertilizer, leaving his friends scratching their heads.

"I'll be back in a short while," he called. He rejoined them at a half hour past, offering no explanation.

On their way back to the stable, the three apprentices took an alleyway shortcut familiar to Rolland, only to be confronted by a group of six boys—the four from earlier that day and two new toughs.

The tallest of the of street boys spoke. "Hold on, lads! Here's the group Faran has sent us for. Time for your appearance at the shop, Rufus. Ya got some explainin' to do, Faran wants ya to know. Of course, yer friends here will need to leave all their possessions, includin' their clothes, right here where they stand. With that and a good attitude, we might be lettin' 'em go untouched. But that mule'll come in handy. We can use 'im to haul some of the load across the mountains. Then he's for the gluepot for a penny or two when he's no more use to us."

"Back away, Sagar! These people are friends and have nothing to do with you. I'll go see Faran myself, and you'll soon be taking my orders again."

"Not a chance that's true, Red Dog. Things have changed, and you're in it now. It's high time ya got your comeuppance, anyway, and I been lookin' for a chance to gi' it to ya. All right, me buckos, I'll handle Rufus, here. The rest o' ya bring down Young Treetop over there and get the Short Britches. Stooks, you get the mule. If any of 'em tries to give you a git, use your knives."

The street boys moved to surround the three apprentices and Asullus. A knife flashed in Sagar's hand and one just as suddenly in Rolland's. The two crouched, moved toward each other, and began circling. Two of the larger roughnecks headed for Thaddeus, one with a cudgel and the other with a broken-off shovel handle. Two of the smaller toughs turned toward Anders, while the last thief, a scrawny, acne-riddled boy, moved toward Asullus.

Anders's gaze swiveled between the two advancing toughs. "I hear your mother likes the taste of manure after she spunks it with your brothers!" he said, his pronouncement accompanied by a rude gesture. Then Anders turned and ran out of the alleyway, all elbows and heels. The two thieves gave a howl of rage, drew their knives, and raced after him.

The scrawny boy advanced on the mule, grabbing for his halter. "Come here, ya lousy flea-bag."

Asullus backed up a step. "Donno' even think aboot puttin' yer scabby touch on me, *Pustula.* Ye'll no be leavin' here in one piece, I do so promise."

The thief stopped, confused, and looked warily about. He drew his knife and advanced. "I said come here, you stupid ass. Maybe I'll cut one of your ears a bit. Maybe you'll hear better after that." He reached out again.

"Don'-say-I-did-no'-warn-ye-in-accordance-wi'-all-the-rules-o'-modern-warfare." That said, Asullus brayed loudly and, rising up on his hindquarters, came down full force with both front hooves striking square the young tough's chest. With a sickening crunch, the boy fell to the pavement like a stone. He did not move again, then or later.

Turning sharply, Asullus galloped toward the boy with the cudgel who was threatening Thaddeus, rode him down, then circled around.

"Thaddeus, lad! Get his stick!"

With a quick nod, Thaddeus dodged sideways, grabbed the club from the ground, and whirled to face the older boy coming at him with the shovel handle. The street boy swung his weapon over his head and down at the apprentice, attempting to brain him, but met only empty air. Pivoting around his assailant, Thaddeus hit him in the stomach with all the force he could muster. As the air left the thief, he buckled over in pain and fell to his knees. Thaddeus leaped forward and struck him again on the back of the head. The hapless thief crumpled to the cobblestones and did not move again, either. Breathing hard, Thaddeus looked up to see only Sagar left standing of all the thieves. He'd not yet closed with Rolland but was circling him warily, licking his lips.

"What's the trouble, Sagar—not liking the outcome so far? Asullus! Thaddeus! Get behind him and pin him down so I can carve his tripes out."

The street tough looked around wildly, then broke and fled down the alley.

Asullus trotted over to join Rolland. "Ye ha' a soft spot in yer heart, I see, laddie, fer this here Sagar, lettin' him go an' all."

"Well, he saved my life once. Now, I guess we're even. Next time, though…"

"Aye, Rolland! Asullus!" Thaddeus called. "Did you see which way Anders went?"

"I did see him spool round the corner to 'is left as if the *Furiae* themselves were in pursuit, which they was, in a manner o' speakin'."

"Come on, then, after them!" Thaddeus shouted. Brandishing his club, he ran out of the alley with Rolland at his heels. However, it was Asullus who, galloping past, took the lead and disappeared ahead with the other two raggedly trying to catch up. After turning the corner at the back of the inn, the boys skidded to a halt, barely avoiding collision with the old mule, who was standing there shaking.

"Haw! Haw! Haw! Oh, good at it, me pride an' joy! Oh, me bright, bonny boy!"

Thaddeus looked past Asullus to see Anders at the far side of the lot, near the stable entrance, laughing while chucking horse turds at the two street boys, who were mired to their midthighs in mud and manure, immobile, cursing and shaking their fists. A delicate trail of white petals from the daisies surrounding the stable yard fence wound its way across the offal. The trail was punctuated by footprints just Anders's size. To either side off the petaled path, the larger footprints of the two street toughs became deeper and deeper, until they ended in the middle of the churned and oozing field.

Thaddeus and Rolland jumped up and down whooping in glee, slapping each other's backs, and alternately ruffling the mule's scrubby mane in joy. They, too, soon joined the turd chucking, calling out deadly insults to the young thugs, and their congratulations to Anders, whose flushed face beamed with pleasure.

A shift in the breeze brought the familiar aroma of pipe smoke to Thaddeus's nostrils. Turning, he beheld an important-looking official advancing on them, accompanied by two men at arms, in chain mail, with drawn swords. Behind them, carefully picking his way over the damp ground, was Master Silvestrus with his pipe.

"All right, what's going on here?" the scowling official said.

After all concerned had given their various versions of events, the two young thieves were hauled out of their predicament and taken into custody, while the shire reeve sent one of his men to attend to those left in the alley. The apprentices returned to the inn escorted by the old sorcerer, who seemed to be having trouble keeping his lips from twitching. Once inside, it was universally agreed that a return to the baths was indicated. Amid much boisterous boasting and embroidering of events, the boys relived their adventure. Finally, the apprentices dried off, dressed, and joined Silvestrus in the common room for eventide. The boys ate heartily of lamb, braised potatoes, greens, cheeses, and warm loaves. Near to bursting, the company made its way to the patio, where they continued to talk in subdued tones.

"You know," Anders said, "it's the funniest thing, but I've always had trouble running before today. I'd get so short of breath. Mater always discouraged it, saying it would make me ill. But today, I felt I was flying!"

"I would say you had a certain motivation, my boy," the sorcerer said from the midst of a cloud of smoke centered around a glowing point of light. "But speaking of such things, we had better reconsider our next course of action. I had thought to spend a few days here in Fountaindale, taking in the sights and leaving time for you all to get to know each other before we set out in earnest. But now, after today's attack, it would probably behoove us to leave early in the morning. I am sure we are not currently popular among the local thieves' guild, and I do not wish to be looking over my shoulder every time I leave the inn. So off we go. We have been traveling overland, but now we are going to head straight north to River's Wood." Silvestrus became thoughtful. "Interesting place, River's Wood."

"Master?"

"Yes, Anders?"

"If we are not going to travel overland..."

"We will be renting a barge and heading upstream. We will hitch Asullus to the barge, and he will pull us up the river. I'll see to the arrangements for our travel first thing in the morning."

Anders continued. "Master, doesn't that mean the mule will be obliged to tow us, barge and all, up to River's Wood against the current?"

"Yes. Of course."

Thaddeus cleared his throat. "Master, does Asullus know about this part of the plan? I'm not sure he'll like it very much."

"You know, Thaddeus, I think you are right." The old man grinned fiercely. "I doubt he will like it very much at all. But then, that is why he commands a high rate of compensation. Well now, we will need an early start tomorrow, so I think it best if we all turn in. Boys, before you go upstairs, why don't you go see to our erstwhile mule's comfort? If we are going to require a lot of him over the next several days, then we should at least give him the impression that we are concerned for his welfare." Chuckling to himself, Silvestrus went into the inn and stopped briefly to speak with Oliffe before heading up the staircase.

Rolland took a lantern off a hook hanging from the low porch ceiling, and the boys made their way to the stables.

Asullus rose to greet them, looking expectantly from apprentice to apprentice. "Carrots. Hmm. Well, I'll no' be refusin' 'em, but 'tis well-known in most circles o' the truly educated that fruit o' the red type do seem better fer the general disposition than the orange. An' that I ha' straight from one o' the very highest himself."

"Oh? And who might that be, old mule?" Rolland asked.

"Meself, o' course. Well, now, laddies, what is it brings ye all the way out here to visit me in me bedroom at this time o' the clock?"

"Silvestrus wanted us to check on you and see how you were doing," Thaddeus answered.

"Oh he did, did he now? Then there's something sinister in the mix, an' that's fer certain. That villainous an' parsimonious old horse thief will in no way be deviatin' from his dear-held doctrine o' unenlightened self-interest, mark me now. Hmm, I do see it in yer eyes, lookin' at ye from one to another. Well then, out wi' it, lads."

"You have the right of it, Asullus. Master Silvestrus is going to hire a barge, and he says you're to tow it—with us and our supplies in it—all the way up to River's Wood."

"Really? Well, we'll be seein' 'bout that now, we will! Forced labor, that is. I ha' me rights, I do, an' friends in high places. Meself an' the other mules, all together we'll be formin' a solidarity group, we will, to be seein' aboot what our employers can do to us an' what they canno'. An' then we'll be marchin' on—" Asullus's attention was suddenly diverted by the appearance of the old hostler and his helper bringing a new horse into the stable.

"Aye, Artie, a new arrival. Just came in. She's a pretty dapple, ain't she now? And perky, too. No, the man said to put her in stall seven, next to the mule. No, I don't know why, but that's what he said to do. So those are the orders, and that's what we'll do. Excuse us there, Young Masters, we're coming through."

Asullus continued. "So, as I was sayin', we might be formin' a group, an'—hmm, pretty lass, ain' she now? Where was I? Oh yes, he canno' be havin' his way wi' us all the time...My, she is a frisky one! I, uh, that is to be sayin'...hmm. I tell ye what, lads, this lady looks to be sore alone an' forlorn tonight, no doubt scared an' alarmed at all the goings-on an' whatnot an' in need o' a bit o' comfort, so to say. I'll, uh, get back wi' ye later. Ye'll be needin' yer sleep, o' course, an' we can talk in the mornin', most like."

The stablehand led the mare into her stall, saw to her immediate grooming needs, made sure she had water, turned her around, then left the stable.

Asullus's attention was now focused solely on his new stable mate, all other thoughts and considerations apparently having dissipated into the night air.

Rolland nudged Thaddeus and Anders, and all three exchanged knowing looks.

Thaddeus cleared his throat. "All right, Asullus. We'll check back with you in the morning concerning your rights and all that. Have a good...uh, repose."

"Aye. Thanks be to ye, boys, I...Well, hello there, lassie. Me name be Asullus. Now I know ye may be thinkin' I'm a bit short, an' a mule an' all, but donno' be deceived, missy. There's more here than meets the eye. Fer example, let me be tellin' ye summat concernin' meself, such as aboot the time when I was facin'—just this afternoon, as it turns out—nineteen bloodthirsty villains armed to the teeth wi' swords an' such, who was wantin' nothin' less than to..."

Grinning widely, the boys breathlessly sped back to the inn and up the stairs, making plans for the next day that chiefly involved the mule and his discomfiture.

Chapter 4

FUR, FIDES, VESICA, VESANUS, et CANIS

* * *

Early the next morning, the three apprentices raced to see who could get to the stables first. They found the mule fast asleep with a fixed grin on his face. He was again on his back with his legs in the air. On brief inspection, they found the adjacent stall empty and the dapple mare missing with no clue as to her whereabouts.

After a moment's consultation, the boys each took out a fresh apple and began crunching loudly.

Asullus stirred. "Ah, darlin' Phoebe, ye're a fulsome wench, ye are, but ye ha' done me in entire, an' I admits it freely. But yer fragrance, tho', is to die fer an' be happy in the process, an' reminds me strongly o'—" Asullus's eyes snapped open. "Apples!"

"Good morning, Friend Asullus, on this bright and sunny day!" the boys sang out, grinning from ear to ear.

The old mule snorted, rolled, and rose to a wobbling stance. "Just to let ye all know, I am now fallin' back to me previous-held position regardin' opinions concernin' each an' every one o' ye."

"Oh, Asullus, we're just having a bit of fun," Anders said. "Here, we brought you these. Rolland thought, for some reason, you might want some fruit this morning to help rebuild your strength." The boys each held out an apple, and Asullus harvested them in sequence.

"Well, I'll still no' be forgivin' this particular breach in man-mule relations, but I do ha' some curiosity as to why I am now havin' the pleasure o' ye gargoyles' company at this verra early hour. Sent again from the old man, are ye?"

Rolland adapted a pose of clinical interest. "He is a suspicious sort, is he not, Friend Thaddeus?"

"Aye, that he is, Friend Rolland. What thinkest thou regarding our sure-footed companion, Friend Anders?"

"Why, I am thinking he looks to be a bit tired and tattered about the edges, Friend Thaddeus. Perhaps his sleep was interrupted this past night due to some mysterious influence."

Thaddeus grinned. "This selfsame thought hath occurred to me as well, Friend Anders. Hast thou, then, any speculation as to the nature of what sort of mysterious influence this might be, Friend Rolland?"

"Ye may be wantin' to know that I am no longer feelin' so lonely as bein' the only jackass presently in this stable," Asullus interjected. "What a comfort it is to ha' me some company out o' the same cloth, so to speak."

"As to the nature of such mysterious influences, Friend Thaddeus, it does occur to me that we may even have heard a name put to this phenomenon—'Phoebe,' for example."

"Ye all should be aware that I meself am seein' the direction this conversation is takin', an' am now picturin' how it would look fer that barge to be hauled upriver fer thirty *milia passuum* or so by three young lads wi' harnesses o'er their necks an' bridles an' bits in their teeth. What think ye, young sirs, o' such a scene as that?"

"I think," Anders said, "that this is a good time to be quiet, see to your needs, and help you get ready for the journey."

"Ye have the right o' it, Master Anders. Ye are, wi'out a doubt, the brightest one o' all the candles in this stable. Though I must be mentionin' that it do no' seem an over-significant achievement, considerin' the current competition an' all."

After feeding the mule and seeing to his grooming, the boys returned to the inn for breakfast, where they met Silvestrus in the great room. There, the apprentices gulped down substantial portions of bread, eggs, day cheese, and pork slab. Shortly after, they went up to their room, packed, and came down lugging their belongings. Silvestrus settled accounts and bade good-bye to the innkeeper while the apprentices hitched Asullus to the cart and stowed the group's gear on board.

The party halted near the river crossing, stopping at a local provisions store where Silvestrus found it necessary to address a minor difficulty involving Rolland and a knife that had allegedly disappeared.

The matter was resolved quickly with an apology, the return of the missing item, and a few coins.

Thaddeus was curious, however, as to how this self-proclaimed "professional" could be so clumsy as to be so easily caught. It was only later that he learned that a pair of large, shiny brass lanterns Silvestrus had admired in the emporium was discovered by the master wrapped in a blanket under a pile of clothing stored in their cart. These items did not, on closer inspection, appear to be listed on the bill of sale, however. By this time, Rolland was demonstrating a superior, oh-nothing-to-it attitude, which lasted until Silvestrus, standing by the cart, crooked his finger at the redhead and involved him in a lengthy discussion regarding decision making and property rights. The issue settled, the group made its way to the north end of the city, where the sorcerer sought out one of the barge captains and dickered with him for equipment rental.

Asullus, meantime, adopted a stolid expression—half long-suffering pain and half beatific martyrdom. The day, however, was pleasant and sunny, and Asullus took to his bondage with a certain stoic inevitability. The cart was loaded aboard the small barge, its wheels lashed tightly between blocks, while the boys secured the provisions on deck.

Silvestrus, last on board, gave Asullus the signal to depart and lit his pipe. The old mule began towing the entire assemblage upstream with as much good grace as could be expected, following the well-worn path on the western bank of the river. The four humans settled themselves strategically among the gear so as to achieve the best possible balance for the craft.

The Greater Flatstone River was calm and flowing smoothly. The spring runoff had spent itself by this time of year, and the River Folk—those not directly involved in piratical initiatives—generally kept obstructions and navigational hazards such as sunken boats and submerged trees to a minimum.

Once the novelty of the new mode of transport had worn off, the old man cleared his throat, drew an extra puff, and gestured at the boys with his pipe. "All right, lads, now it is time to get down to the work for which you were chosen. You are to be sorcerers one day, and it is my responsibility to see to it that you turn out to be a credit to us all. Therefore, be mindful that I would not enjoy the humiliation, in the presence of my peers, that any purposeful failure on your part would cause me. And rest assured, I would not take to it kindly."

It seemed to Thaddeus that while the old man gazed at each of them in turn to make his point, his eyes lingered longest on Rolland.

"Bear that in mind and thus apply your best efforts, as I am certain you will, and you will do well. Therefore, absorb what I am about to tell you, and try to stay awake.

"Now, as I was explaining briefly to Thaddeus the other day, the talent of sorcery—and a rare one it is—is bred in the bones. It is a gift one has—or does not have. While a sorcerer may come from a family of non-sorcerous lineage, it is extremely unusual.

Further investigation into such matters typically uncovers either a heretofore unacknowledged talent or, perhaps, some small embarrassment as to the accuracy of parentage. Therefore, if you wish to be a sorcerer, you need a sorcerous parent, grandparent, or great-grandparent. It is amazing how the potency of this particular trait remains hardy for many generations. A sorcerer, for example, might stop at a village, strike up a relationship with a willing partner only to learn many years later that he has a great-grandson—or granddaughter, of course. The ladies do just as well as we, lads. Better, in some areas, come to think.

"On the other hand, contrary to what you might believe, few sorcerers there are who settle down with a lifetime partner and family. A family—father, mother, children, pets—with a small farm is almost as rare in the sorcerous world as are the persons themselves. Much speculation and debate has occurred as to why this might be. Most of the learned will say that since sorcerers are long-lived—and they are, boys, make no mistake—pairing up with a love interest for life is fair to neither party. And I imagine you can puzzle out why that would be. But I have, for some time now, harbored a suspicion that additional, less public, reasons exist. To wit, there may be, among this Brotherhood, a feeling that such a gift should be as widely spread as possible, since its manifestation is so uncommon. Obviously, if you are left-handed—to pick a trait out of the air—and it is your belief that the world would be better served by more left-handers, then you would want to spread your pollen as far from the hive as soon as possible, eh, Thaddeus?"

Thaddeus blinked at the recognition without fully grasping the old man's meaning.

"Now, I mentioned longevity. One of the gifts that accompanies the sorcerous trait is a life span many times that of the non-sorcerous. No one is sure exactly how long this might be, but records suggest the encompassing of many generations. But, as with all things in this universe, what the Gods giveth, the Gods taketh away, without bothering to consult us mere mortals concerning their various whimsies. So, there is a 'hook,' as Rolland would say." The old man glanced briefly at the young thief and winked. "The hook is that the very thing that gives a sorcerer his long years also takes them away bit by bit. That is, each and every exercise of the Art will diminish the hours and days of your life—and this includes any acts you practice while learning at school. The more complex and demanding the use, the more time is shorn from your thread."

The old man paused to relight his pipe and glanced to the port side of their barge. Thaddeus, following his gaze, marked several cut tree trunks drifting lazily downstream past their craft.

"For example, suppose a sorcerer is interested in living the greatest number of years possible. Such a one could accrue an astounding span of decades, even centuries, to himself, but he would be a sorcerer in name only. He could never use his gift. On the other hand, a sorcerer could perform the most advanced and amazing things—challenging even divinity itself—but his flame would die out early with, perhaps, less than the life span of an average man. Yes, Anders? You have something to say?"

"So, Master, it would seem that the best course would be to use the idea of balance. The Golden Mean."

"Right you are, my young *Philologe.* Balance. Use, but don't overuse. Weigh each decision. Employ discretion. Practice self-discipline and self-denial. If you can do it the pedestrian way, then do so. And save the greatest works for times of greatest need. It is, after all, in one's own self-interest to do so. What is the matter, Rolland? You look disappointed."

A frown etched the deeply freckled face. "Well, Master, it just doesn't seem fair—to be given such a gift and not be able to really use it, I mean."

"Hmm. As the wisest of us have said over and over, 'It's not fair!' ranks just under 'Why me?' as the top contender for, first, questions of complaint that have no answers, and, second, examples that are especially irritating for the elderly to hear. But, perhaps, just this one time, I will explain it as far as I understand it. Given your more, ah, 'commercial' background, Rolland, you could think of it as a mercantile transaction. To practice great art engenders great cost. Otherwise, I suppose, we would all be living as Gods in grand palaces in the clouds with a thousand slaves to serve our every whim, slaying all our enemies with only a whisper. And, no doubt, be bored to tears. Not to say, of course, that certain sorcerers have not attempted this very thing. When they do, however, they seem not to last very long. Divine on Sun's Day, dead by Moon's Day—with much frenzy in between. In any case, it is, as I have said, a gift. If you would use the gift, you must be willing to accept the price for it. But I digress.

"No one has, so far, been able to factor out just how much the 'cost' is for each individual practitioner. Some sorcerers, for example, could make a house take wing and fly, losing thirty years of their lifetime allotment. Another, with equal gifts, attempting the same act, would lose, perhaps, only four years. While a third would drop dead on the spot at the first attempt. Also, not only does this cost seem to vary from practitioner to practitioner, but it can vary from time to time in the same practitioner. And no one has yet been able to parse out the whys and wherefores of it. The advantages of youth and vigor seem counterbalanced by the advantages of experience and wisdom."

Thaddeus stirred. "Master?"

"Yes, Thaddeus?"

"How do you decide when to use your power?"

"Now that is a good question, my boy. Let us see what your colleagues would guess. Rolland?"

"Um, for important things, Master?"

"Good. Anders?"

"Sparingly," responded the pudgy boy.

"Ha! Good answers both. So, there you have it. Now, where was I? Oh yes. Although you are born with the gift, that does not mean you can just go out, shout, '*Meretrix!,* for example, and have some sultry siren appear in a cloud of smoke, ready to do your slightest bidding. You have to learn how to do what you wish—what things to say. You see, you must first form the Act in your mind, then release it through your speech. Occasionally, a gesture is needed as well. Also, it depends on how you say what you say. You must, it seems, use the Imperial speech—*Lingua Imperatoria.* No one knows why. But if another language is used, it doesn't work in the same way. It may be that is the reason why the magicks of the Cin—whose speech is very different from ours here in the West—are so alien. Perhaps a cleric could tell you the why of it."

Silvestrus took another long puff and continued. "It is not merely thought, word, and gesture, either. Sometimes an object or objects are required—a bowl with an unfinished leg, for example. Sometimes a powder or potion or certain special ingredients in certain discrete combinations, or, perhaps, feathers, seeds, things from *Materna Naturae* that attract your interest may be necessary."

The boys sat silently, digesting this stew of knowledge. Anders leaned forward. "Master, what you describe sounds very complex and confusing. How is it possible to know those things needful?"

"That is the purpose of the *Collegium,* my boy—or one of its purposes. That is where you will learn what you need to know to answer those questions. But enough talk for this morning. Thaddeus, signal Asullus to pull over, and let us have midday. Then, perhaps, a nap."

Thaddeus stuck two fingers between his lips and gave a shrill whistle. Asullus tossed his head and moved to pull the barge over to the bank near a small inlet. The party disembarked and stretched. The boys unhitched the mule and gave him his ration of oats and a quick rubdown. After making short work of midday, the apprentices suggested exploring inland. Since Silvestrus was already drowsing by the small fire they had built, they approached Asullus. But he declined and lay down on the grassy sward.

A moment later, however, his nose twitched, and he raised his head. "I'm thinkin' there's somethin' funny on the air a bit west o' here. It do no' smell too dangerous, but I'd no' go there, were I ye." With that, he lay back down and closed his eyes.

The boys looked at each other, and Thaddeus mouthed the word "west." The other two nodded, and the group quietly left camp, heading away from the river.

They struck out cross-country and had hiked about two *milia passuum* when Anders called their attention to a flock of ravens circling just north of them behind a small hillock. The boys turned aside and approached cautiously. Drawing close, they peered around the mound to see the voracious black birds at work on a huge manlike body lying supine amidst the scrub. It was not moving. Thaddeus's backwoods upbringing had given him certain useful skills, including tracking. He led the boys several *stadia* farther west, all the while studying the ground. He found what he was looking for and turned back the way they'd come.

"Look. Here a large creature is running—not human. Probably that big lump back there that the ravens are pecking at. I'd guess it was trying to make it to the river. And here's wolf sign, could be a full pack. I'll bet they were chasing it, whatever it was. Looks like it didn't run fast enough, though."

Startled, Rolland glanced at Thaddeus. "Wolves? Here? Now?"

"No. These tracks are at least a day old. Maybe two."

Anders considered the tracks. "Well, they're not around now. Let's go see what it is they were after."

The three made their way back to the carcass. As they closed the distance, however, the stench of rotting flesh assailed their nostrils. The smell was nauseating. Rolland picked up several stones from the ground and heaved them at the birds, while Anders and Thaddeus alternately waved branches and hooted like owls, causing a general commotion. The ravens rose in a mass and flew off cawing curses at the boys. The flies, however, were not so easily discouraged, and paid them no mind as they continued feasting.

The three edged closer to the corpse but had no idea what they were looking at. The body, or what remained of it, was bipedal and had probably stood at least three paces high. It was solidly built. The head was enormous, with large, curving horns jutting out on either side of the skull. Eyes, ears, nose, lips, and tongue were missing. A massive jaw supported two great, upward-curving tusks. The arms would have reached below its knees. A rancid, filthy hide, torn and stripped in many places, partially covered the chest and torso. Dried, clotted blood coated most of the creature, while the remainder had pooled on the surrounding grass. A great brassbound cudgel lay off to one side, beyond an out-flung arm.

"He was right-handed, anyway," Anders observed.

A broad leather strap, slung over the beast's shoulder, draped down the corpse to a small hide pouch, now open, its few contents spilled onto the ground.

Rolland wrinkled his nose. "Well, Thaddeus, what is it? I mean, what was it?"

"It's not human. That's certain. I don't think it was a giant, either. Not with those horns and tusks. And it looks nothing like that demon Charles. What do you think, Anders?"

"I'm not positive, but I think it was an—"

"Ogre," finished Asullus.

The boys whirled to see the old mule standing behind them with the garland around his neck.

"I ha' thought I warned ye lads no' to be puttin' yer nose in this direction. 'Tis a lucky piece fer ye that yer cousin here ha' giv'n up the ghost. Otherwise, ye'd be in a peach fer certain."

Rolland edged closer. "Asullus, Thaddeus says wolves were chasing it and brought it down not that long ago."

"Wolves?" Asullus glanced around quickly. "Aye, I smells 'em, now that ye mentions it, o'er the carnage an' such. Well, I'm sure they're long gone by now, havin' completed their feastin'."

Thaddeus wondered who it was he was trying to convince.

Anders picked up the thread. "So, it's an ogre. I didn't know they came this far south, especially this time of year."

"Usually they do no'. Mayhap he got separated from his clan. Or maybe he was a Caste Out. That's as happens sometimes. Anyway, his roamin' days are o'er, an' now he's fer the daisies, eh, Anders?" The mule circled the carcass as if inspecting it critically. "Young Rolland, come o'er here an' fetch out the sharpest o' the knives ye ha'."

The former thief did as he was told and approached Asullus with his large knife drawn.

"Good. Now cut away that piece o' hide coverin' the place where his legs meet. Do no' be spendin' yer moments lookin' at me, lad—just do it."

The other boys gathered around as Rolland sawed on the stinking pelt.

Anders backed away a step. "Whee-oosh! What a fragrance! Ripe, I'd say—overripe."

"Yes, you have that right, but look at that! *Membrum Sacrum!* I think you've met your match, Asullus, and then some," Rolland said, pausing in his dissection.

"I do no' know how many times I ha' to be tellin' the youth that it's no' to do wi' the size o' the sloop, but yer skills at settlin' it in the slip. But that said, I'll grant ye his missus'll be missin' him presently these long an' lonely nights. All right, me fine chiurgin, cut me a line across his skin there from hip to hip, just above what ye've all been gawkin' at. Good. Now free up the skin. See ye that pale *globulus* there? We're goin' to want that out—in one piece, now, mind you."

Rolland grimaced. "Asullus! This is disgusting! Are you sure there's a good reason we're doing this?"

"Now do no' be gettin' delicate on me, sweet Lucilla. Yer doin' fine wi' yer deft hands. Peel it out—carefully! See there, there's a cord comin' from the upper left, an' one o' the same kind comin' from the upper right. Now, see that bigger cord in the middle goin' down from the bottom there? All right, now cut each o' those cords aboot a hand's width out. Ye got it. Fine work, lad. Now free up the whole piece there an' bring it out here on the ground."

"I'll have to wash for a day and a half to get rid of this stink," Rolland complained as Thaddeus and Anders backed away from him, holding their noses.

"Do no' be such a puss, Rufus. You'll be smilin' aboot it later."

"So, Asullus, why are we doing this? I don't understand," Thaddeus asked.

"Now I'd a thought that a bright lad such as yerself would ha' learned o' the meaning o' 'later' somewhere along the line. But, p'rhaps no'. So, young thief, go back to where ye was carvin' an' cut some lengths o' those remainin' three cords ye had yer hands on earlier—oh, about another o' yer hand's width or so. Good. Now take each o' those strips an' use it to tie off one o' the cords on that *globulus* there. But first, hold it up so it'll drain properly. Oh, don't worry none about that. 'Tis no' poison. Well, not directly. 'Tis just ogre pee. Aye, ye heard me correctly. Tie those cords tight—use triple knots. Now, poke each one o' them stubs directly so that they're all pushed inside o' the sack, to make the outside smooth. All right now, fetch off that strap as is holdin' Sir Handsome's pouch, an' stuff that sweet-smelling orb into it. We might also want to consider searchin' the area a bit more. Ogres are said to carry treasure with 'em now an' then."

Far in the distance, the group heard a faint, mournful howl, immediately joined by another. Asullus looked quickly in that direction, then back at the group.

"O' course, there be no need now to be dabblin' an' dawdlin' aboot, so it's a quick march back to camp fer us. I'm sure the old man'll be wantin' to see what it is we ha' found."

Rolland wiped his blade and hands on the grass as best he could. "But Asullus, how will I get this smell off me?"

"O', I don' know, laddie. It might be considered by some o' us to be an improvement o'er yer usual situation, don' ye know. But if 'tis no' to yer companions' likin', then ye could stretch yer noggin a bit to recall we do be travelin' by a river, if that might mean anythin' to ye. Off we go now."

Another distant howl added an incentive to movement, and the group made it back to the riverbank in a shorter time than they'd used going forth.

At the camp, they were greeted by Silvestrus, who sat on an old log with his pipe in hand. "I saw you a bit back, but heard you farther out than that and smelled you before you had even turned toward the river. What in the world have you got there?"

"Open up the pouch an' show him, Red Rose," the mule barked, grinning.

Rolland spilled the aromatic content onto the ground.

"Ah," Silvestrus said, his eyes lighting up, "an ogre's bladder! How ever did you boys come by one of those?"

The three apprentices began talking at once, and soon enough, the old man had the full story.

"Well, well, Asullus, you remain as resourceful as ever, and you boys are quite clever. We will need to attend to this right away." Silvestrus sprang up and walked to the cart, where he rummaged for a minute or two before extracting his Bag of Sorcery. He laid the bundle on the ground, then untied and unrolled it. After a moment's thought, he selected a purple phial with a cork stopper, a clear crystal bottle filled with a yellow powder and capped with a lead seal, and a small folded parchment. Holding these items carefully, he rose and walked to the campfire. "Thaddeus and Rolland, take the kettle down to the water's edge and fill it to the brim. Then, Thaddeus, return with it here. Rolland, you remain at the river. Oh, and take some soap with you. A fair amount. Anders, bring me my staff."

The boys rushed to do the sorcerer's bidding—Thaddeus and Anders eager and expectant, Rolland, chagrined and resigned.

When the pot was boiling over the fire, Silvestrus added the ingredients in select proportions and order and motioned with his staff. He picked up the ogre bladder with a stick and said, "*Inverte!*" The bladder now appeared to have been turned inside out. It was then deposited into the kettle. "This must cook for a while—to cure it."

A little later, a dripping Rolland came back to the camp, looking like a drowned cat but much less fragrant. Thaddeus and Anders filled him in on the proceedings up to that point.

As they waited, Thaddeus turned to the mule, who had doffed his flowers. "Asullus, why do you still keep that garland? And how is it that it remains so fresh? And why did you put it on earlier, anyway?"

"Hmm, quite the *Quaestor Quaesitor*, are ye now? Well, no' that 'tis any o' yer business, but just to be sociable, I ha' kept it because 'tis special to me, considerin' who gave it an' all. Fer example, why do ye still have those curly locks ye carry around in that packet so close to yer heart? Secondly, I don' know why it's persistin' in its freshness, but I'll no' be complainin'. Smells pretty as the lass herself, don' ye know. An' thirdly, 'tis no' o' yer concern. There, are ye satisfied now?"

Thaddeus, who had been steadily turning redder, nodded and glanced around before changing the subject. "Think we might get rain tonight?"

Silvestrus prodded the boiling bladder from time to time as he enjoyed his pipe. When the dottle went out at last, he stood, hooked the mass with his stick, and drew it out of the boiling mixture.

"*Reverte!*" he commanded, and the bladder turned back outside in, except it was cleaner. "We will let it dry overnight. Then we may have some use of it tomorrow. Rolland, you could probably use another soak, or two, but the afternoon is getting on, so let us resume our journey and see how much farther Asullus can tow us before it is time to set our camp for the night."

The mule snorted, muttering something under his breath.

"What was that, Asullus? I did not quite catch it," the sorcerer said sharply.

"I ha' said, I thought it would probably be clear tonight, though we could ha' rain on the morrow."

"I see. Well, good enough. Come, boys, get to it. We have many more *mille passae* to cover before we rest."

The barge was quickly reloaded. Asullus was hitched to the towrope, and the party proceeded upriver. Once under way, Silvestrus returned to his instruction.

"I have told you all a little about how one comes to obtain the gift of sorcery. But it occurs to me that you may be curious as to how each of you, specifically, was selected. The answer to this is simple—I do not know. That is to say, I cannot tell you precisely how because I do not really know. I can tell you, however, that as I have traveled from place to place looking for likely lads, which I do from time to time, I get a nose for who might do and who might not. Each of you I have seen before."

The boys looked at each other, startled.

"Though you likely will not recollect it. Nor would your parents. What draws my attention is that each of you radiates a natural energy field of sorts. Anyone with a gift for the Art would know another who has it—if they were looking for it. Of course, it helps if one has had experience. In addition, a special link between a searcher and a likely prospect is useful. At the request of our *Princeps Academiae,* the leader of our Order at the College, I myself journey about, casting my net, so to speak. I enjoy it, and it is good exercise. Additionally, it is nice to see the country and meet divers and interesting folk. And, though I am, by nature, much too modest to admit it, I am rather good at what I do."

Asullus snorted again.

"Though not all may feel so," the sorcerer added.

Asullus brayed a warning. "Low-hanging branch coming up. Guard yer heads an' hats—them as has 'em."

The barge company ducked and passed safely under the threat. A moment later, the sorcerer resumed his gentle instruction.

"So, we now have set the scene, introduced our actors onto the world stage, and it is time to posit our main thesis. To wit, the key to all this business—the 'critical element' as Brother Barnabas would put it—is, simply, Belief. To put it plainly, if you are born with the talent, obtain the training, and have the Belief, then you are able to practice sorcery—*sine qua nihil.* Belief is the third, but most important component in our tripodal equation. The magic words, gestures, and objects exist only to abet the Belief. But Belief is the key, the cornerstone. During your time at the

Collegium, you will hear this phrase repeated endlessly by your instructors, myself included. So, be prepared, and know that I speak truly. The stronger you Believe in what you are doing, the more you will accomplish, and the more likely you are to accomplish it—'it' being any miracle of one's choice."

Anders half stood in his excitement, causing the barge to rock. "Master, how can this be? I mean, how can merely believing in something cause it to happen?"

Talking over his companion, Thaddeus interrupted. "Master, do you mean to say that if—"

To which Rolland added, "But, Master, that doesn't make sense. How does a person…"

The challenging questions continued, and the more explanations and examples the old man gave, the more questions were asked, and the demand for knowledge grew.

After a time, Asullus, who always had one ear cocked to the rear, began to smile, then grin, and finally to whistle.

At a distance Master Silvestrus announced was just past the halfway point to River's Wood, the party grounded for the night. Silvestrus finally put an end to his apprentices' constant badgering by glowering sternly at the demanding, skeptical group until they fell silent. The boys, obliged to accept the admonition, did so with ill grace, resulting in an almost surly display of attitude that lasted until well past eventide.

After the utensils were cleaned and stored and the camp put back in order, Silvestrus directed his apprentices' attention to the task at hand.

"Tomorrow, boys, we will arrive in River's Wood, which I've always considered a rather unusual place. The town's economy is based on timber. However, unlike Bostle, where the lumber is prepared and shipped out, here it is centered around the taking of the trees themselves. It is said that, in the distant past, a monastery stood at River's Wood where lived a brotherhood of Druids—a farrago of tree sorcerers, if you will. They claimed to draw their power from the Earth's trees and, in turn, devoted themselves to the protection of those selfsame trees, as well as all living things, from the ravages of civilization. However, *Commercium* itself is a powerful God and not so easily thwarted or diverted. These days, however, the population of River's Wood is comprised, by and large, of tree cullers. They are, by some divination, able to deduce which trees to cut and which to spare. The cut trees are sent downstream—you have all seen the great trunks floating by us here on the river—and, in return, they receive certain items from outside their world they consider important to their needs."

Thaddeus stirred. "Master, do all the folk harvest trees? Are there none who raise crops or milk cows?"

"Most, but not all. It is a bit of a mystery, but what farms there are, are few—subsistence, primarily—and scattered. As near as I have been able to determine, most folk in River's Wood are remarkably gifted in working with wood. Almost all the artifacts you will find there are wood based. Little metal—beyond woodworking tools—is available. Even their coinage is made from wood, although they will accept our money in certain of their stores and shops. The work of their carvers and artisans, by the by, is generally of an excellent quality and demonstrates high craft."

Silvestrus rekindled his pipe, drew a draft, and continued.

"While you are in River's Wood, you must be cautious. As a rule, the people there do not take kindly to strangers, whom they view as wishing only to take financial advantage of them or to harm their forests. The townsfolk are a little less likely to trouble a sorcerer, chiefly because we have never given them any reason to distrust us. But on the whole, they are a suspicious lot. It is best to be polite, respectful, largely silent, and to quickly conclude any business you have with them and move on."

Rolland appeared anxious. "Will they try to harm us, Master?"

"No, I do not believe so," the old man replied, "especially if you give them no reason to. Now, it is late, and we will need an early start in the morning. Oh, and Rolland, I should probably mention that the last time I was in River's Wood, I did happen to see what was surely the remains of a man nailed to one of the trees leading into the village. Above his head was a meticulously carved sign reading, 'THIEF.' Well, good night, boys. Rest well." Silvestrus rose, tapped out his pipe on the heel of his sandal, and walked downstream a piece. A few minutes later, he returned, unfurled his bedroll, and lay down to take his rest.

The boys, meantime, were involved in an animated discussion concerning the dangers inherent in mixing with lunatic tree worshippers. By the time they sought their sleep, they were favoring Rolland's strategy, whereby harm done to any one of them would result in the survivors setting fire to the entire village and surrounds and watching it all burn to the ground.

The next morning, travel resumed until around midday, when Silvestrus signaled another stop. "We are nearing River's Wood, but rather than pull right up to the dock, perhaps it would be prudent to scout first the surrounding territory. I do not wish to walk into any unforeseen difficulties through ignorance when effort might have prevailed."

The party disembarked and tied the barge to an old willow tree. After partaking of midday, they prepared to set off. However, on returning to the barge, Asullus nudged Silvestrus and nodded to the north.

"Ye ha' asked me from time to time to tell ye when we might be in range o' some o' that medicinal herb ye find so useful. Well, unless me snufflin' tool is off, I'd say there'd be a good stand o' it just into the forest field o'er yonder."

"You know, old mule, I am indebted to you once again for your keen olfactory perception. I think we should break out the panniers and go see if there's enough to justify a harvest." The old man turned to the boys. "Lads, Asullus has detected what must surely be a patch of a rare plant that we use in our sorcerous rituals from time to time. He and I are going to investigate. I want you to remain by the barge and protect our belongings."

In short order, the sorcerer and his mule were off exploring, and the boys were left to chuck stones into the river.

Rolland skipped a flatter for seven jumps. "Thaddeus, what are we going to do if some of those mad sylvans come down here wanting to know why we're 'defiling' their land?"

Thaddeus skipped his stone for eight. "That's a good point. I don't much like sitting on this barge like a nesting loon. We have no idea who or what may be lurking around these woods."

"Well, if it's information we need," Anders replied, "then we'll have to go get it. It surely won't come to us—until it's too late, of course."

Rolland looked over at his friend. "What do you mean, 'go get it'?"

"I mean, good thief, we should form a scouting party and go see for ourselves."

Thaddeus scoured the ground for another flat stone. "Hmm. I'm partial to that idea, but Master Silvestrus told us to stay here, to make sure no one bothers our possessions."

"Well, if anyone is going to bother us, they'll be coming from the north, correct? So, if we head north—quietly and carefully, of course—we should see and hear them long before they see or hear us. Then we can run like the Hells back to the barge, jump in, shove out to the middle of the river, and paddle around in a circle, yelling, 'Help! Help!' until the master returns and sends that demon you keep talking about after them."

"Right. Good plan, Anders," Rolland said. "You know, Thaddeus, I think the trouble is, he just doesn't look that smart."

Anders made a rude retort.

"Aye, go on, short 'n' sweet, you don't even know what that means."

"I do so!"

"Come on," Thaddeus said, interrupting the exchange. "We don't have much time, and we've no idea what we're going to run into. We'll leave the barge here—it's too heavy to tug along, and we'd only see what's by the shore—and go overland."

"Right," Rolland said. "Let's go."

The boys set out due north, parallel to the barge path and keeping close to the forest edge. After they'd gone a good distance, Thaddeus stopped and sniffed.

"Hold on. Smell that? It smells like a cook fire. There might be a camp of those River's Woodsmen around here. Let's spy them out. Be especially careful—no noise, now."

Stealthily creeping forward, the boys came to a thicket and, peering through, saw—not fifty *passibus* away—a dilapidated cabin with smoke coming out of its chimney. But it wasn't what they saw that riveted their attention, but what they heard—a man's angry voice cursing and a dog yelping and whimpering in pain, followed by the repeated staccato sound of a stick or strap.

Thaddeus breathed deeply, passion instantly aroused. "Somebody in there's beating a dog! Come on!"

Charging the cabin, he banged open the door and rushed into the one-room hut with Rolland and Anders at his heels. A small, skinny man, slovenly and unkempt with several days' growth of stubble, was holding a thick length of willow branch. As the boys watched in horror, he brought the switch down rhythmically on the back of a pale-colored, slat-ribbed, long-haired dog, whose body was already covered with welts and sores. Patches of fur were missing and scabbed out. It cowered from the man and yelped, crying pitifully at every stroke.

Thaddeus's fists clenched white. "You! Stop that! Now!"

The man whirled around, obviously taken aback at the interruption. "Who in the Hells are you? What do you think you do, breaking into my house!" he roared, brandishing the branch as he advanced on Thaddeus.

Anders and Rolland stepped from behind Thaddeus, ranging themselves on either side. One had a wooden cudgel, and the other a knife held low in each hand.

The man hesitated.

"I know this is your house, but it isn't right for you to treat an animal in that way." Thaddeus paused. A quick glance at the only table in the room showed an open stone crock tumbled on its side, its amber liquid dribbling into a puddle. "Especially when you've had too much to drink." Thaddeus didn't know how much that was, but the swaying man was red eyed and slurred in his speech.

"How much I drink is my business, damn you! And this is my house, where I do what I want! And this animal"—he paused, thrusting an outstretched arm at the dog—"is for beating. Yes, for beating!" The dog lay shaking, pressed against the far wall of the hovel. The man peered at Thaddeus and adopted a crafty look. "Who sent you? Madigan? Well, you can tell him to orff himself. I know what I'm dealing with." He paused, calculating. "But you don't, do you? Who are you? Just boys from the river? You have no idea what you got yourselves into. That's not a dog. She changes! Yes, she does. And she's the Devil! And it's up to me to beat the Devil out of her! And I will!"

The man spun around and raised his arm to strike the cowering dog once again, but the boys jumped forward and tackled him, knocking him to the floor. Anders swung his club, catching the man on the side of the head, stunning him. Thaddeus grabbed the willow bolt, while Rolland brought his elbow down hard on the man's privates. The drunk lay unmoving on the floor for several minutes, until he stirred and moaned in pain.

Thaddeus stood over him, displaying the whip. "All right, you. Explain yourself. We are the apprentices of a mighty sorcerer, and when he comes here and sees this, you'll be lucky not to be blown to bits on the spot!"

The man stared at them in silence before speaking. "Well, it might be better at that. You don't understand, you know, barging in here. I tell you, she's a Daemon! She comes on all sweet, but there's something she wants. And she'll have her way."

The man's eyes bulged, and froth appeared on his lips. "You can tell she's thinking it over. You can tell. And she won't stop until she gets it. And then she'll change for sure. Oh yes, young lads, and that will be it for all of us. She must be stopped. And I will do it! Yes, I will be the one to do it if it is the last thing I do!"

The man struggled to all fours and, pulling a knife from his boot, lunged at the dog.

Thaddeus stared as if frozen to the spot. His gaze grew distant as a strange thought surged into his mind—then a command. "*Fiat Canis!*"

A peculiar roaring rush overtook him as he looked at the man on the floor—except that now it was not a man. It was...blurring, changing. The man's jaws began to lengthen, as did his ears. His arms grew longer, and he began to grow fur. A tail appeared. The boys' mouths hung open. Where the man had been crouching, now stood a dog, a cur of mixed breed.

Rolland's eyes glazed. "*Vermes Venite!*" he roared.

Suddenly the dog retched and vomited. A great mass of wriggling worms with bloody suckers and hooks spewed from its mouth.

"*Impetus Pulicium!*" shouted Anders, with an identical look.

A swarming cloud of biting insects abruptly materialized above the man-turned-dog and descended upon it. The dog gagged again and vomited more worms. Howling at the torment from the insects, it shook its head from side to side and ran out of the cabin toward the woods, pursued by the biting cloud. The pitiful yelping grew fainter and fainter until the boys could no longer hear it.

"*Mehercle!*" Rolland cried. "What happened? What did we do?"

"I think," Thaddeus replied softly, "we just used sorcery. What a strange feeling." Suddenly he shook himself. "The dog!"

The boys rushed to kneel around the abused hound, which initially flinched from their touch, then lay still, whimpering.

"Anders, get some water," Thaddeus ordered.

The nearsighted boy jumped up and looked around the cabin.

"Try outside—a rain barrel. Take a cup, or pot."

Anders nodded and rushed outside. He was back in a moment with the water. Thaddeus held it close to the dog's mouth, but the dog seemed too weak to take it. Thaddeus wetted his tunic soppy and squeezed water onto the dog's tongue. The dog, with great effort, lapped it up.

"Poor, poor dog. Good dog, now. Good dog," Thaddeus intoned, gently stroking the dog's neck. The pale head, with large and trusting eyes that were rheumy and filmed over, swiveled slowly to gaze adoringly at the boy.

Rolland turned to the Beewickean. "Well, what are we going to do? We can't take her with us, and we can't leave her here."

Thaddeus looked over at his friend. "Why can't we take her with us?"

"I can think of about twelve different reasons, all beginning with the words 'Master would not...'"

Anders knelt beside the dog. "Hmm. Are you so certain, Rolland? My guess is that Master Silvestrus likely has a soft spot in his heart for animals. That's just my impression, mind you. I think if we approach him in the right way, he won't object. We'll have to be the ones to look after her, though."

Thaddeus turned toward the distiller's son. "Anders, have you ever taken care of any animals—had any pets?"

"Well, no, not really. Mater would not allow any large or rough animals to be around the estate. We had cats for a while, though. But they don't require much care. And to tell the truth, they really don't do much with you, either—unless they want something, that is. After a while, however, I started sneezing every time the cats came around, and that was that."

"How about you, Rolland?"

"No. How I was raised, well, it just wasn't a good situation for a dog, rabbit, or any animal. It probably would have been skinned, cooked, and eaten. I always wanted one, though."

"Well, a dog is a lot more work than a cat, I can tell you. I have—or had..." Thaddeus sighed, then continued, "a dog. His name's Argus. And you have to do a lot for them, sort of like with Asullus. Water and feed them, groom them, exercise them, and so on. This poor dog is in a wretched condition. So she'll need a lot of special attention. If we take her with us, we all have to agree to help bring her back to good health. Then, we all have to swear to take care of her on a regular basis. Otherwise"—Thaddeus's tone grew stern—"I will take the dog out back, slit its throat, and bury it here."

Rolland blanched. "What? You wouldn't!"

Anders quirked a smile. "You're a hard-hearted thief, you are, Rolland of Fountaindale. But I think Thaddeus has the right of it. And I think he could—and would. And I would have to agree with him on this. All right, count me in. I'm for perpetual dog-care duty."

The two boys looked to the city lad.

"Well, I'm not going to be a party to any dog murder, that's sure," Rolland said. "All right, I'm in, too. But we all have to agree to do our share of the work. No shirking."

"Agreed."

"Agreed."

Thaddeus extended his hand, which Rolland grasped and was then covered by Anders's own. "Done!"

To the boys' amazement, the beaten dog slowly, and with what appeared to be a great deal of pain, raised its head and turned to where the boys' hands were clasped. She gave the three hands a brief lick, then fell back, exhausted and panting.

Thaddeus swallowed, cleared his throat, and assumed a businesslike attitude. "Right. Now we have work to do. Rolland, why don't you get that ax down from the wall and go find a couple of saplings from the woods? We're going to have to make a travois to lay her on so we can move her back to camp. Anders, look around the cabin to see if there are any supplies we could use for the dog—or for ourselves, for that matter. Load anything you find on one of those blankets over there. We'll use the other one to stretch between the poles. I'll examine her to see if I can find anything else wrong." He addressed the dog. "Lie back, girl. That's right, take it easy now. Don't worry, I've got you. No one will hurt you now—or ever again."

Soon a small pile of assorted goods lay on one of the grimy blankets. The golden-haired dog lay on the other. Rolland returned with two stout stripped saplings, which he placed on the cabin floor beside the dog. The redheaded thief eyed Anders's collection.

"Hmm," he said, then went efficiently around the cabin looking in a variety of out-of-the-way places. After a few minutes' effort, he contributed two knives, a tooled leather belt of good quality, several *passae* of rope, a length of harness strapping, and three small purses of coins, one containing thirteen gold half Imperials.

Anders looked at the pile from the second collect and bowed to Rolland. "I salute you, *Furis Magister.*"

Rolland made an airy wave of dismissal. "Nothing anyone couldn't do with a bit of practice."

Thaddeus cast a glance at the clinking purses and acknowledged a nagging sense of discomfort. "Uh, Rolland, are you sure we should be taking that money? It's not ours, you know."

Anders smiled again. "Thaddeus, you have an interesting sense of comparative morality."

"Excuse me?"

Rolland barked a laugh. "Well, Taddy, considering we just turned its owner into a be-pestered mutt who wouldn't be up to using money again in any case, I agree with Anders. The point's moot—look at all the goods we've collected. Besides, if you wish, you can consider it my contribution to the Perpetual Dog Care Fund—of which, I am Chief Reeve, by the way. We'll eventually have to buy supplies for her, and this should come in handy. Consider it as compensation."

"Not to mention it lends an ethical justice to the whole proceeding," Anders added.

Thaddeus rocked an outstretched hand back and forth, as he'd seen his father do, then sharply clapped his hands together. "Points given, good sirs."

Anders continued. "But how will we carry her? Toting her several *Millae Passae* is going to be tiresome."

"That's what the belt and ropes are for, to make straps to bind the poles for slinging over our shoulders and making a cradle to carry the dog," Thaddeus explained patiently. "Good work. Now let's get the—you know, we can't just keep calling her 'the dog.' She needs a good and proper name. Any suggestions?"

"*Bellis. Bellis perennis*, to be precise," Anders said. "I don't know why, but I was thinking that underneath all that filth, blood, sores, and bruises, she does have a bright yellow coat. It reminds me of the color of those flowers by that fence at the inn the other day."

"Bellis! Perfect. Bellis it is."

Rolland nodded. "Yes, that fits. Good choice. All right. Well, let's get this litter put together, get Bellis aboard, and get back to camp. We don't want to walk in and find the master sitting there with a meticulously carved sign reading, 'EX-APPRENTICES.'"

Thaddeus and Rolland rolled the blanket with precision around the poles and tied the rope straps to make the litter. With Bellis lying on the travois, they slowly raised it to their chests, ducking their necks under the strap loops and gradually letting the weight settle on their shoulders. After setting out, it took some time for them to coordinate their gait to offer the least jostle to the dog while minimizing their own fatigue.

Anders brought up the rear, dragging the treasure from the cabin—an ax, a length of rope, a shovel, a small pouch of nails, and the knives and belt.

Rolland carried their newfound financial resources in the stoutest of the three purses tucked deeply inside his tunic as carefully as a mother would carry her baby in a pooka.

They'd gone only a short distance when Anders cleared his throat. "You know, in our rush to tend to Bellis, I think we're forgetting the significance of what went on back there."

Rolland twisted his head to look at Anders. "How do you mean? What was so important?"

"I know," Thaddeus replied. "I said it earlier. We've just used sorcery."

Rolland stopped midstride, swaying the litter. "You know, you're right! I hadn't thought of it, but that's the first time I ever did anything like that."

"Me, too. How about you, Thaddeus?"

"I think I used it before. Asullus had me say some magic words and use a powder when I was feeling sick—you know, to summon that old green physician I told you about."

Anders smiled. "Oh, you mean that time you were hungover from the blue butterflies?"

Thaddeus shot his short companion a look of irritation. "Yes. That time. But I was...prompted then. This time, it just seemed to come. What did it feel like to you?"

"Strange," Anders said, his smile gone. "All of a sudden, I just knew I had to say something. Then it came to me what to say and how to say it. I just knew. I've never had that feeling before. All this energy just rushed out of me. It was almost as if someone else were doing it."

"Me, too," Rolland said. "I had to say something. Then *Vermis Venite* came to my mind. Even to shout it. Odd."

"We'll have to tell Master Silvestrus about this. He'll want to know," Thaddeus said.

"Yes. Maybe he'll be pleased with us."

"For a change," Rolland added.

The short scholar paused, then added, "And I can't wait to tell Asullus."

Rolland slid a finger under the strap for a moment to ease the weight. "Hmm. Speaking of Asullus, what do you think he'll be making of Bellis? He doesn't seem to fancy wolves very much, now, does he?"

"Oh, I think once she's healed up and has her strength back, they'll be good friends," Thaddeus said forthrightly.

Anders smiled again. "Yes. Once her diseases are all cured up, only her bark will be worse than her blight."

Rolland groaned. "You know, Anders, that was really pitiful. You'd think some priss from the bookworm factor'd know better than to make such a stupid joke."

"Oh really? Well, speaking of pitiful, I remember seeing you when we were in the baths at Fountaindale the other day swimming and..."

The discussion continued in this fashion until they arrived back at the barge, relieved to find it and their belongings untouched—and their master still absent.

It was near sunset when Silvestrus and Asullus returned with the mule's panniers filled to bursting with the special herb they'd been seeking. Thaddeus thought he recognized it from the sorcerer's pouch. The foraging must have been particularly enjoyable, as both the old man and mule were given to much hilarity for the rest of the evening.

The boys were somewhat disappointed at Master Silvestrus's reaction to the news about their first use of sorcery.

"Really? You don't say? Isn't that remarkable? Did you hear that, Asullus? Well, what do you know..."

The apprentices were more reassured by the old sorcerer's response to Bellis. He immediately went to her and petted her, offering soothing words. Even Asullus appeared mildly interested, then made a number of silly comments, repeating a theme of "all the animals in an arc," which he brayed in self-amusement that made sense to no one. When Thaddeus asked his master if he had any powders or potions they could use to heal the dog, Silvestrus said something regarding "time" and "best healer." Both the mule and the sorcerer ate heartily at eventide, then went immediately to their night's rest.

The boys were initially puzzled by this behavior, but Thaddeus watched with interest when Rolland, adopting a shrewd look, strolled over to the panniers, now propped against a tree. He knelt and picked up some of the herb, examining it carefully. He tore off a small leaf, crushed it, rolled it between his fingers, then smelled and touched his tongue to it. Nodding, he stood and tossed the sample aside before rejoining his companions.

The boys gently cleaned and fed the dog and tended to her wounds as best they could. By the time they were ready for sleep, they had all remarked that Bellis did seem to have perked up a bit, even in the short time they'd had her.

Chapter 5

PILAE et PUELLAE

* * *

When Thaddeus next opened his eyes, it was late morning. A low murmur of voices reached his ears, and he swiveled his head in the direction of the sound. Silvestrus was in earnest conversation with the verdant physician who had assisted Thaddeus with his postnectar ills. They were bent over Bellis, who looked a little brighter, appearing to mark the to and fro of the old men's conversation by first gazing at one, then the other, a worried expression on her muzzle.

Wanting to alert his fellow apprentices but avoid bringing undue attention to himself, he closed his eyes, passed a bloop of gas, then snorted as if restless in his sleep. The low conversation stopped briefly, then resumed.

At a kick on his leg, he opened his eyes again, turning to catch the attention of Anders of Brightfield, whose own eyes held his. Anders wrinkled his nose but smiled and surreptitiously nodded in Rolland's direction. Thaddeus turned his head and caught Rolland's gaze. The young thief pinched his nose with his fingers and winked.

THE
GREAT SPANSION

Thaddeus held his forefinger to his lips. Both boys nodded and carefully turned to regard their master's negotiations with the powdery *Medicus*. The conversation was difficult to hear, and occasional gusts of wind made it more so, but with concentration, they could just distinguish what was being said—at least by the sorcerer.

"...and that is what I told the boys last night. I am certain her injuries will heal well enough with time, but I am more interested in how this adventure came about in the first place. I was not entirely at my best last night, a temporary indisposition, but it—no, no, I'm fine now. Thank you for inquiring, but it is not the physical I am concerned with. There seems to be more here than meets the eye. So, you are certain you found nothing else of note in your examination? No, I do not mean to question you. It is just that I must be sure. Well, then, that leaves but few other explanations. I mean, why would these normally sensible lads—yes, yes, I know, but they have seen only fourteen summers—intercede the way they did and in that particular manner? And look at the result. This is unusual. I am afraid we will have to seek out some of the Elders in River's Wood and ask their opinion. I dislike this, but I see nothing else for it. Very well, thank you again for your assistance, Doctor. Your ministrations are always of the greatest value. Ah, unfortunately I do not have that precise amount with me at this moment, but perhaps I can find something here in my robes..."

The boys watched as the old man reached behind him. Instantly, a small leather pouch materialized in his hand, which he then gave to the waiting physician. "You are welcome, Learned Sir. Yes, I will have the balance for you very soon. *Ave!*"

With that, the medical apparition vanished in a cloud of smoke.

Silvestrus sat thoughtfully for a moment, then turned to the boys. "Come over here, lads—seeing as how you are all awake. We have a puzzle on our hands that requires a solution."

The boys, chagrined at having been found out so easily, hastily scrambled to join their master.

"My nose tells me there is more to this dog—what is it you call her? Oh yes, Bellis—than presently meets the eye. Consider, for example, your response to her situation and to what lengths you went to defend her. And, lest we forget one modest detail, for all of you it involved the use of sorcery, with two of you employing it for the first time. Does not that strike you as odd? And all for a dog? Not to demean her obvious sweet nature—I am quite taken with her myself—but you threw yourselves into a perilous situation, and you cannot account for what prompted you to take the actions you did, except for a 'feeling.' Lads, that is most imprecise and requires further study."

The old sorcerer glanced at the sun's position in the sky, then turned his gaze back to his charges.

"Since it is too late for breakfast in any case, tell me, each of you in turn, exactly what you recall of the circumstances, what you thought and what you felt. Be sure to leave nothing out. Thaddeus, you begin."

There followed several hours of discussion, but no further light was shed on the situation. Silvestrus allowed that Bellis could accompany them but cautioned the boys to remain alert for any further peculiar behavior.

A rumble from Rolland's stomach signaled it was time to trade the discussion for midday, which was efficiently prepared and consumed. Afterward, Silvestrus instructed his apprentices to make a place for Bellis in the cart, pack up their possessions, clean up the campsite, and move everything onto the barge. Bellis appeared a little stronger and was taking to the ministrations on her behalf with a mixture of good grace and apparent gratitude, at least as much as her strength allowed. The boys had devised a plan of frequent watering and food preparation that she was, so far, tolerating. Careful brushing had removed all but the most stubborn of the dirt, crusts, tangles, and inhabitants.

Asullus was hitched up and again harnessed to the barge. The old mule had been strangely silent this morning. Thaddeus and Anders wondered if it had to do with the dog's condition, but Rolland ventured the theory that Asullus might be suffering from the aftereffects of yesterday's herb use.

"You know, we may have a problem here. Those herbs the old man and the mule brought back last night are from the green lotus plant. People chew it or smoke it, then talk and act stupid. I've tried it myself, but I don't like it because I found it affected my judgment. It made me careless once, and I almost got caught during a chase. And sometimes people start using it and can't stop. I think we should keep an eye on those two and be wary of anything they tell you to do after they've been using it."

The other two apprentices nodded in agreement and vowed to be alert for any problems with their master or their Minister of Transport.

The last leg of the trip upriver was short, and, rounding a broad bend, they beheld River's Wood. All the buildings, which Silvestrus had described as "quaint," were constructed of wood. Some hung out over the edge of the bank, but none of the structures stood taller than two levels. The sound of working rough-cut saws was continual. Many tree trunks were already floating slowly downstream past their vantage point, and more were stacked in loosely organized piles along either side of the river.

Several townsmen were walking about, talking or tending the cut trees, but no women were among them. All the men wore similar garb—tanned hide breeches and tunics, some with rows of fringe at cuff or hem. Their feet were shod in soft leather slippers, and they had gloves of the same material. All affected beards and wore their jet-black hair long, tied back with rawhide thongs. No elderly were on the streets. An uncommon number of dogs were running loose, however, most with a significant amount of wolf in them. Thaddeus found the surroundings eerie and more than a little unsettling.

Asullus towed the small barge to a docking area, then stood stock-still, eyes rolling, while their craft was made fast to the dock. The old man waded ashore to supervise the boys as they disembarked, unhitched the mule, unloaded the cart, and rehitched Asullus to it. Bellis was placed in the tumbrel and made as comfortable as possible, with her head propped over the cart's side so she could see the town and all the goings-on.

Asullus looked around nervously. "I'll be lettin' ye know, I'm no' fond o' such cities as are full o' carnivores."

Silvestrus came and stood by his mule. "Be at peace, Asullus. None here will harm you as long as the boys and I have breath in our bodies."

The boys nodded reassuringly, looking as fiercely determined as their master.

"All right. Then I'm thinkin', let's conclude our business here an' be off, quick as yer clever red fox jumpin' o'er any lazy brown dog—no offense to our Bellis, o' course."

Silvestrus fetched his staff from the cart. "Anders, come and take hold of Asullus's bridle while we walk. Thaddeus, Rolland, grab your walking staffs from the cart and place yourselves one on either side. I myself will lead this parade. Now, all of you remember your manners, and smile for the citizens."

With that, the old sorcerer led his small cadre up to the transport factor's office at the head of the docks, where he made arrangements for the barge's return downstream at the next running. From there, the group wound its way up the crooked mud-and-woodchip streets, heading toward the largest building in town. No sawmills were evident, but the populace all carried axes or crosscuts, and the sound of chopping wood came from every direction.

As they passed the various stores and dwellings, Thaddeus became aware that the townsfolk stopped what they were doing and stared as soon as they came into view. Then a look of recognition dawned, and they looked down deferentially as the company passed. Several gave brief bows. The odd behavior was puzzling.

Soon enough, the group arrived in front of what Thaddeus took to be the town hall. Silvestrus faced the building and spoke softly to his apprentices out of the corner of his mouth.

"Wait here. Do nothing. If the people want to stare, let them stare. I do not believe I will be long. Perhaps you might feed the dog again." With that, he disappeared into the imposing timbered structure.

The boys stood steadfast around Asullus and the cart. Bellis seemed curious about what was transpiring and appeared to note the proceedings with interest. Thaddeus dug out a small portion of leftover meal for the dog and offered her more water, which she accepted with enthusiasm. A good sign—clearly, Bellis was beginning to mend. Thaddeus gently stroked the dog's head, and she gave his hand a quick lick, then resumed her perusal of the town's activities.

The River's Wood folk who walked by continued to behave strangely. None spoke to them or seemed friendly, but their reactions were essentially identical to those they'd passed earlier. All eyes were immediately drawn to the little group. They'd stop and stare, then lower their heads as if in respect before passing on their various ways.

Every villager they saw was accompanied by one or more of the large, dark, wolfish dogs, each of which nodded at them in ways similar to that of their masters. Thaddeus looked at Rolland, who shrugged. Asullus remained silent throughout their vigil but glanced around frequently, his eyes rolling. No one felt like talking. It was as if a weight pressed down on them, enforcing silence.

Presently, Silvestrus emerged from the timbered Town Hall. "Well, boys, I am not certain how much I have learned, but this is clearly an intriguing place. Did anything curious transpire while I was inside?"

The boys told him about the behavior of the townsfolk, which he seemed to find of interest. "Well, well, and well. This deserves much thought." The old sorcerer's gaze shifted to Bellis, who gazed back. "Well, well, and well."

"Master, where do we go now?" Anders asked.

"We, ah, will cross the river over the Great Wood Spansion, uptown a ways, then stop at a supply store I know of on the other side. Originally, I had thought to spend the night here, but something tells me it would be wiser to get some miles behind us before sunset. There is, however, an inn close by the general store that has a rather good bear stew we might try. I don't mind a last full belly before heading out into the wilderness for a time. Come, lads. Follow me."

Rolland looked at Thaddeus and mouthed, "Bear stew?" Then made a face.

Anders caught his look and whispered, "You know, back at Brightfield about this time of day, Mater would be setting the cooks to making some of that soft bread and raisin pudding I told you about. Something tells me it might be wise for me to reconsider the *Lyceum* after all."

The party made its way farther up the twisting dirt-chip roads until they reached the Great Wood Spansion. A toll master turned out of his watch station and approached the group. On gazing at the wagon, he behaved much as the other townspeople had and stood mutely looking at Silvestrus.

After a moment's hesitation, Silvestrus produced a pouch from his robes and passed two coins to the man. The toll master regarded the money briefly, then nodded toward the other side of the bridge. He bowed in the direction of the boys and cart before returning to his watch station.

Silvestrus signaled his charges to proceed, and they crossed the great log arch, which, at its highest point, rose some thirty strides above the surface of the river. The apprentices stared in awe at the towering log structure. They kept in close formation, artificial smiles stuck across their faces while remaining silent, their eyes continually scanning the surround. Thaddeus had such a grip on his staff that his hand began to ache.

As soon as they cleared the bridge, Silvestrus guided them to the supply store. At the entrance, he turned to the boys. "Thaddeus and Anders, you stay here and look after things. Rolland, you come with me to help carry—oh, and Rolland, we already have enough brass lanterns for now."

Reddening to his roots, the former thief said only, "Yes, Master."

Thaddeus walked around to the front of the cart to check on Bellis. The dog, with, effort, extended her neck for a scratch, which the boy was glad to supply. While continuing to pet Bellis, Thaddeus turned to the mule.

"How are you doing, Asullus? You've been awfully quiet this morning."

"Aye. Well, I canno' say as I'm entirely comfortable here, but I'll manage, soon as we are shut o' this place. How is our queenie doin' now, think ye? Seems she looks a little less peaked."

"She's better, I think. She's starting to eat, and she doesn't seem as scared. In fact, she seems very interested in all that's going on."

"Aye, I ha' noticed, so I have. Interestin' behavior in a beat-up dog, would ye no' say? I ha' to speak me piece, though—ye three lads did well by her yesterday. Had I been there, I'd ha' no' stopped with just transformin' that no-father into a cur but probably would ha' killed him dead. 'Tis fortunate fer him he was only transformed—or maybe no', all things considered."

Just then, two townsmen came out of the store speaking quietly to each other and carrying supplies. They stopped abruptly when they saw the boys by the cart, and repeated the same action of obeisance the group had witnessed previously, before going on their way.

Anders looked after them as they walked down the street. "I wish I knew what all that meant. Just what, or whom, are they acknowledging? Master Silvestrus is inside, as he was at the transport factor's and the town hall, so those bows can't be for him, nor for Rolland. I don't think this cart is a Holy Relic of any sort, so that leaves just you, me, and Asullus—and Bellis, of course."

The pudgy boy's speculations were interrupted by the return of Silvestrus carrying his staff and Rolland carrying a bulging mountain of goods, staggering under its weight. Thaddeus and Anders rushed to give him a hand. He was pink-faced, and appeared about to share his opinion of his maltreatment, when Anders stepped on his foot and whispered, "Later, Friend Thief. This may not be the best time."

Rolland glared at Anders, then nodded and made his way to the cart, where he and the others stowed the supplies.

The boys resumed their strategic positions and followed the old sorcerer as he set out up the street and took a left turn at the first intersecting road. Two *stadia* farther brought them to a plainly built planked inn, the *Quercus Antiqua.* Silvestrus, under the guise of inspecting the positioning of the goods in the cart, spoke in a low voice.

"Now, we are going in for eventide. The cart is positioned so we may observe it through that window there, assuming we will have the right table, which I believe we will. Asullus, keep your eyes peeled, and bray if any trouble arises. Pay especial mind to Bellis.

Boys, behave yourselves, and keep your wits about you. This is our last stop in River's Wood, so let us not stir up any bee's hive, eh, Thaddeus? Oh, by the way, I really do recommend the bear stew."

The party entered the inn and waited for their eyes to adjust to the gloom of the drab interior. The beamed ceiling, rough-hewn tables, and woodchip-strewn floor did nothing to dispel their first impression. The room was immersed in a blue haze, which Thaddeus at first attributed to the pipe-smoking patrons, but his nose detected a different, more pungent aroma Silvestrus identified as emanating from the numerous bear-grease candles flickering smokily on tables and ledges.

The low hum of voices suddenly stilled, and a hush fell over the common room as all eyes turned toward them. Thaddeus noted Silvestrus's interest in a bearded local with a tankard sitting at the desired table with a quill in his hand and various parchments scattered about. Several crumpled pieces of composition littered the floor. The man, concentrating on his writing, did not seem to be in any hurry to leave.

"*Alvis Defundas!*" the sorcerer said under his breath. The man at the table sat bolt upright with a look of distress on his face. He quickly gathered up his writing materials, threw a few coins on the table, and bolted for the door. The old sorcerer watched the author assay his exit. "I regret doing that. However..."

The group headed toward the now-empty table, but the bartender reached it first, scooped up the coins, gave the table a swift wipe with his shoulder towel, and silently indicated they should sit.

Silvestrus, Thaddeus, and Anders opted for the bear stew, while Rolland ordered only cheese and bread. Though their meal was not interrupted, they were acutely aware of the quiet and the surreptitious glances directed their way by several of the buckskin-clad patrons.

Thaddeus had to agree with his master concerning the stew and even ordered a second portion, which he and Anders shared. Rolland, however, was immune to suggestions he sample the ursine cuisine, asking if next they could expect portions of badger or, perhaps, panther.

When they finished eating, Silvestrus signaled it was time to leave. He left a half imperial on the table, much to the bartender's delight. The man's shift of attention from the group to the money was the first time in the course of the evening he'd taken his eyes off them.

Once outside, the master and his apprentices resumed their order of march and turned onto a street with the grand name of *Via Orientalis*, which, however, soon ended in a faded trail once they were past the outskirts of the town.

Silvestrus continued to lead them away from River's Wood, speaking over his shoulder. "Our next stop is not until Moorstown, some distance from here. We will be going cross-country until we reach it. So place yourselves in a hearty woodsman's frame of mind for the next several days. Off we go."

The boys exchanged resigned looks but dutifully followed the old sorcerer's pace.

As time passed, Bellis gathered more and more strength and soon was getting around under her own power. Although she appeared to like all the boys, she was particularly attached to Thaddeus, perhaps because he'd had the most experience with dogs. Bellis's relationship with Asullus was more formal, with what Thaddeus thought of as a growing mutual respect. Asullus refused to speculate further on the dog's situation, and the boys soon wearied of asking. Silvestrus's response was to acknowledge the uniqueness of the encounter, but he also refrained from any helpful conjecture. The boys were thus forced to mutter among themselves until they, too, tired of the topic. With no further odd demonstrations concerning Bellis, they soon turned to other topics—one being *Pila Ludere.*

Following breakfast on the day after their interlude in River's Wood, Silvestrus went to the cart, rummaged about, and pulled out the ogre's bladder. He addressed the apprentices, who gathered around him, anxious to understand the mysteries concerning magical micturation.

"Rolland, take an ax and go chop down four goodly saplings of about three strides in length while your colleagues finish cleaning up. Asullus, join us, please. I think this is a good day for us to have some fun."

Puzzled, the boys did as they were bid and reassembled when their tasks were completed.

"Ah, good. Now, Thaddeus and Rolland, you go pound two of those poles upright in the ground about five *passae* apart. Anders, help them sight up the configuration. The second is to stand due east from the first. Then mark off about thirty *passae* due south of an imaginary line connecting the two poles. There, set up the other two saplings in the same manner opposite each of their northern brothers."

As these tasks were accomplished, the old sorcerer moved to a point roughly midway between the two sets of upright poles and summoned the boys and mule to him. Unbidden, Bellis walked quietly over to lie down on the outskirts of the new playing field, again appearing to show great interest in the proceedings.

Silvestrus continued. "All right. Now you are going to learn to play *Pila Ludere*—an activity involving a different kind of sorcery, that is, one of speed, endurance, effort, skill, and competition. For this exercise, our goodly beast of burden and I are going to form a team, just the two of us. We shall call ourselves the *Maximi.* You three shall form a second team, the, um, *Minimi.* Now, stand in a line—you, Thaddeus, there next to Anders, and you, Rolland, over there—between myself and those northern poles facing me. Yes, that's good."

Silvestrus held up the drooping bladder in one hand, passed his other hand over it in an arcing motion, and intoned, *"Inflatus Sis!"* The bladder instantly inflated into a globular shape, approximately three hand spans across. "This, gentlemen, and mule, is the *Pila.* The object of this contest is to see which team can kick this ball through the opponent's two poles the most times within a certain passage of the sun."

Anders gazed at his mentor intently. "Master, which two poles are we supposed to kick it through?"

"It will vary, but for today, you and your confederates will want to kick this ball through the poles to the south, behind Asullus and me. My companion and I will try to prevent that accomplishment by kicking the ball away from you. We will then endeavor to kick the ball through the poles to the north, which you will try to prevent. Each time the ball passes between either of the two sets of poles, the team that has done the kicking earns one point. The team with the highest number of points by the end of the time—usually an hour—is declared champion of the match, and the losing team must then perform some bidding decreed by the winning team for the remainder of the day."

Anders spoke up again. "Master, is it permitted to pick up the ball or throw it?"

"No. You may kick it only. There is no use of hands."

Rolland reviewed the instructions. "Master, you and Asullus are going to run and kick the ball over there, while the three of us—Thaddeus, Anders, and myself—try to stop you? And you will try to stop us from running and kicking the ball down there? And the ones who lose must serve the winners for an evening?"

"Yes, that is correct."

The boys nodded to each other and grinned.

"All right, Master. We are game, I think," Thaddeus said.

"Oh," the sorcerer said, "I should mention there are a few unpermitted movements that draw certain small penalties. I will point them out as we go along in my role as *Arbiter*. Any questions?"

"Um, no, Master." The boys were openly smiling now.

"Good. Now, Asullus, come stand behind me." Silvestrus hitched up his robes, which showed his thin white legs, then bent down to untie his sandals. He threw these to the side, well away from the field of play. "I run better in bare feet, as it were," he offered by way of explanation. "Are you ready, then? All right, let us commence." He gave a shrill, piercing whistle and tossed the ball roughly halfway between himself and the line of apprentices. *"Incipe!"*

Immediately, Silvestrus ran up and kicked the ball bladder forcefully between Anders's legs, then ran swiftly past him, turned, and kicked the ball back over the boys' heads, where it dropped close to the waiting mule. "Asullus! *Calcitra!*"

The ball rolled to a stop in front of the mule, who turned around and kicked it squarely with both hind legs. The ball sailed back high over the boys' heads in the opposite direction, bounced several times, and rolled straight through the poles the boys were defending, splitting the distance precisely down the middle.

"One to nothing! Good shot, old friend!" the sorcerer chortled. He retrieved the ball and spoke to his apprentices, whose mouths were hanging open, as he passed. "Let us show a little more effort, eh, lads? Do try to make a game of it, will you not?"

The remainder of the morning followed suit, with the final scores of the two games 12–0 and 9–1. Thaddeus scored the only goal for the *Minimi.* This occurred when he broke into the open after Anders contrived to faint from exertion directly in front of Silvestrus, who tripped over him. The tall Beewickean tore down the field to come face-to-face with Asullus, defending the south goal. Thaddeus feinted to the right, then went around left and scored. But, in retrospect, he felt he'd scored primarily because the mule's heart wasn't really in stopping him.

The boys were chagrined to have been bested by a beast of burden and a crotchety old codger. Silvestrus swore on Holy Orders he had not used sorcery—"There was no need," he said. Rather, his strategy appeared to revolve, in part, on the employment of his shrill whistle on all occasions of game violations. However, his opponents felt it would have been better had he applied his rules more universally.

Following their humiliation, the boys collapsed in despair until revived by midday. The replenishment offered by the repast rekindled their spirits and generated a thirst for revenge. Putting their heads together, they manufactured several plans of strategy. Although Thaddeus and Rolland were in top physical form, Anders was not. After due consideration, they agreed that experience and treachery were more often likely to triumph over youth and energy than the reverse. The answer, therefore, pointed to the employment of such useful devices as deviousness, misdirection, ganging up, likely-to-be-undetected cheating, out-and-out perfidy, and the like. They vowed that the next time, victory would be theirs.

Both Silvestrus and the mule took longer naps than usual, so it was midafternoon before the party was ready to continue the journey east. The trip was relatively uneventful, and when they made camp that evening, the boys walked over to a nearby open area to practice some of their new stratagems. Only later did they discover that proximity leant itself to informal observation.

While even Rolland had to agree that Master Silvestrus showed a fair degree of restraint in the appreciation of his victory, nevertheless, the boys were required to spend the night in watch shifts, rather than rely, as they had previously, on the sorcerous warding of the camp. They were unused to interrupted sleep and, as a result, were unusually surly the next morning in spite of the fact that the night had proved uneventful.

After breakfast, the boys quickly completed their chores, seeing to the needs of both the mule and the dog. Bellis was making good progress and now walked most of the way, usually at Thaddeus's heels. She was gaining weight, her sores and bruises were healing, and a new golden coat was emerging. Everyone loved her, and she had the attention of any of the group whenever she wished. Not uncommonly, these demonstrations of affection were accompanied by various treats, which supplemented her weight gain regimen in complementary fashion. Silvestrus proved noncritical of these indulgences and, in truth, was one of the worst offenders.

The group strode along, ranged alertly around the cart. Silvestrus had taken to perching on the cart seat, holding the reins, with Bellis keeping up as best she could afoot. The hiking toughened the boys, and even Anders had increased his stamina. Whether this was by chance or design, Silvestrus made no comment. His rationale was simply that the extra weight of the new supplies stowed in the cart placed an additional strain on the mule.

Asullus, however, was wont to complain to anyone who happened to be near him. He and Bellis did not converse with each other, but Thaddeus had the feeling they communicated on some other, more archaic, level.

Silvestrus did not continue his formal instruction, stating that was the task of the *Collegium.* On any other topic, he was open, sensitive, and flexible, unless it concerned *Pila Ludere.* On that topic, he was adamantly mute.

That afternoon, the boys made their second attempt at the game, employing several of their new strategies. These were chiefly contrived from the combined inventive efforts of the crafty and duplicitous brewer's son and the treacherous and amoral redheaded street thief. Their success was not worse than their first trial, resulting in further humiliation. At a strategy session afterward, they realized a practice area at some distance from the camp was in order. It was not that they thought Silvestrus would purposefully use any information he might gain from casually spying on them to his advantage—such as they suspected he had done earlier—as much as that it would be very difficult for him not to do so.

Since a good portion of the afternoon remained—it had not taken very long for Silvestrus to administer his educational chastisement—the boys asked permission to explore a bit farther east. After receiving the familiar admonitions to be careful, the young apprentices set off with Bellis at their heels. The bright, sunshiny day lifted their spirits. Soon they were striding along, alternately discussing combat strategy—Rolland had secured the ogre's bladder with no one the wiser—and rehearsing various traveling songs.

The trail, essentially a deer track, led into a forested area. Shortly after, they were under a thick copse of trees. Thaddeus, in the lead, raised his hand to signal a stop. He pointed up and to the left. A cloud of flying insects was hovering about one of the trees off the path, emitting a low buzzing sound.

"They're swarming," Thaddeus said. "The hive is getting ready to split."

"What's swarming?" Rolland asked.

"Bees. Right, Thaddeus?"

"Yes. That's right."

Anders nodded. "Primus told me, in my studies on natural philosophy, that when a beehive is ready to split, it's because the Princess of the hive is in rebellion against the Queen, each having her own adherents, to see who will rule between them. And the one who loses must take all her loyal subjects and leave to establish a new queendom elsewhere."

"Well, yes, in a manner of speaking, but—"

"And when that happens, the hives are left temporarily unguarded, and it's easy to get the honey."

"Well, I'm not so sure about that, Anders. I—"

"So, Thaddeus, can we get some honey? You would know how."

"Well, I don't really—"

"Shh!" hissed Rolland. "Look at Bellis!"

The boys turned to see Bellis standing frozen, her tail sticking straight back, her right paw elevated, and her head held forward.

"She's pointing," Thaddeus whispered, "but look—not at the bees."

"Yes, I was taught about that. They say when certain types of dogs point, it means there is some danger nearby they have detected and they are alerting you to where it is. Secundus said—"

"Anders!" Rolland interrupted. "Will you be quiet for once about everything you know? We need to figure out what to do."

The pudgy boy looked down, obviously stung by the rebuke. "I was only trying to say—"

"It's all right, Anders," Thaddeus said. "You can tell us another time. For now, let's see what this is all about."

Slowly, carefully, and as quietly as they could manage, the boys crept forward in the direction Bellis was pointing. Ahead was a small clearing. As they closed the distance, the sound of growling reached their ears.

Thaddeus parted the last bush, and the three apprentices peered through. At the far end of an open space, a young tree was barely supporting the weight of three older children clinging to its upper branches. Directly beneath them, three *passae* down, two forest lions—young females—paced with upward glances at their cornered prey. The lions could clearly not climb high enough to get to the three, nor could the three leave their perch. The lions growled and snarled in frustration at the impasse, while the treed trio gave them peremptory commands.

"Shoo!"

"Scat!"

"Go away!"

"You're not wanted!"

Thaddeus turned to his companions. "We've got to help those children!"

"Thaddeus"—Rolland's eyes were narrow and shrewd—"those aren't children. Those are girls!"

"*Iovis!*You're right! What are they doing out here?"

Anders peered ahead, squinting. "Are any of them short?"

Thaddeus's head was down, his brows knitted together in concentration. Then he straightened. "Hah! I've got an idea that just might work. Rolland, you and Anders wait here and keep watch. Those girls seem safe enough for now, so don't do anything to draw the lions' attention to yourselves. I'll be right back." With that, the tall apprentice slipped back into the woods, retracing his earlier path.

Within a minute, Bellis joined the two boys. Her hackles were up, and she issued low growls.

Rolland stroked her head and urgently whispered, "Shh! Bellis! Be still!" while Anders put his arm around the dog and began speaking to her in low tones while they waited.

Then, from behind them, came a steadily increasing buzzing sound along with cracking noises, as if someone was not watching where he was stepping.

Anders turned and let out a yelp. "Yow! Rolland!"

Rolland spun around to an apparition coming straight through the brush. It was tall and covered with a furry, undulating skin. The boys backed away in alarm, but Bellis cocked her head at the new arrival, then sat back on her haunches, her tongue lolling.

Anders gasped. "Look, Rolland, it's Thaddeus! Those are his sandals!"

As the figure made its way past them into the clearing, the sunlight illuminated the figure, whose every square thumb span of its body was covered with swarming bees, all buzzing loudly.

"Make some noise," Thaddeus rasped at them through clenched teeth.

Anders and Rolland whooped and shouted, and Bellis joined in, barking and growling. The bee-coated Beewickean shuffled on. Distracted by the uproar, the two lionesses turned to stare at the figure approaching them. They appeared confused, as if undecided what to do. The three girls in the tree were pointing at the lurching apian and gesturing excitedly.

Overcoming their timidity, the lions began to move stealthily toward the man-form, crouching low and swishing their tails. When they were ten *passae* away, the figure stopped and slowly raised its extended arm, pointing at the lions. In a rush, the bees sprang off Thaddeus and dove toward the pair of hunting cats. Within seconds, the lionesses were in an agony of snarls and yelps, stung dozens of times from nose to tail. They could not stand against the onslaught and bolted for the woods, hotly pursued by their angry attackers.

Thaddeus, unharmed, watched the lions' frantic retreat with no small measure of satisfaction.

Anders and Rolland burst from the bushes, whooping with delight, and ran to their comrade, nearly knocking him down with their slaps, cuffs, praise, and congratulations.

"Um, it was nothing," Thaddeus mumbled, both pleased and embarrassed. "Just something I picked up tending the little buggers for *Magister Apiarius* back home."

Suddenly, Anders slapped his forehead. "The girls!"

The three boys dashed toward the tree, only to find the last of the group scrambling down from the lowest branch.

Thaddeus strode forward. "Are you all right?"

The shortest of the group, a pale girl slightly rounder than the others, with two dark braids curled in a circle at the nape of her neck, stared at her erstwhile deliverers with a haughty demeanor. "Of course we're all right! What did you expect? And what possessed you to interfere? We had the situation well in hand and were about to begin our conjuring when you interrupted with your silly trick and threw everything off!"

Of midheight, the second girl wore her brown hair in a single braid that fell to her waist. She nodded with dignity, but her solemnity was given the lie by the glitter in her eyes and the spattering of pale freckles that danced across her nose.

The third girl, a tall honey blonde, did not nod but gave Thaddeus a shy smile. Her hair also fell to her waist, but was tied by a leather thong and rippled in the gentle breeze.

Without the courtesy of any warning whatsoever, Thaddeus was abruptly engulfed in a slough of confusion.

Rolland spoke up with some heat. "Excuse us, but the last time I saw you, you were yelling, 'Scat,' at two lions, who, by the way, seemed not at all impressed with your 'conjuring'—distracted by their plans for dinner, no doubt."

The short girl took a step forward, fists balled at her sides, but the middle girl placed a restraining hand on her arm. "Perhaps we are forgetting our manners, Nannsi. These boys do seem to have come here to help, whatever the flaws in their plan, and it's not polite to dismiss them so uncharitably." Having finished her speech, the girl smiled—not a shy smile, but a radiant smile that lit up the clearing.

"Wait a moment," Anders said. "Did you say conjuring? You can't be sorceresses—hmm, that's hard to say, you know—but you can't be they…them… those…"

The middle girl stepped forward, hands on hips. "And why can we not? Are you, perhaps, referring to some long-forgotten and obscure Law of Nature? But it's unlikely the three of you, um, country gentlemen would know much about that."

Rolland also took a step and leaned forward. "Well, not that I enjoy pointing out another's ignorance, but we are sorcerers, you know. We are traveling with our master, the Great Silvestrus. Furthermore, be advised that the last person to really annoy us will now end his days as a cur with fleas and worms for companions."

The short girl, Nannsi, jumped in. "The Great Silvestrus? I'm sorry. I did not realize you were members of a traveling troupe. What time are your performances? Are any to be starting soon? As for your flea-bitten and worm-infested cur, I presume you refer to the bitch at your feet. My advice to you is that you should take better care of it."

The hackles rose along Bellis's back, and a low growl issued from her throat.

The tall girl strode forward. "Now, Nannsi, I'm sure this is a wonderful dog. She reminds me of my Daisy back home." She knelt before Bellis and put her hand out, palm up, for her to smell, then gently stroked the golden coat. Bellis stopped growling and wagged her tail at the girl's ministrations. "Though it looks like she has had a hard time recently." The girl threw a stern glance at Thaddeus. "Not your doing, I assume."

Thaddeus flushed. "No. We found her being beaten by a crazed man in River's Wood. It was he whom we changed into a cur. This is Bellis, and she's one of the sweetest dogs you'll ever know." He knelt on Bellis's near side and scratched her behind her ears. "My name is Thaddeus, by the way." He regarded the tall girl on the other side of the dog hopefully.

She responded, "My name is Marsia. You have met Nannsi already, and my other companion is Sonnia. It is true, we are familiar with the Art. We ourselves are traveling with our instructress, Mistress Geanninia. Actually, we are on our way to the *Ludia*—our school—for training. We had just encamped for the day when Mistress Geanninia went into one of her spells—"

"Ssst! Marsia! We should not tell them about our mistress's gifts!" Nannsi said fiercely.

"It is all right, Nannsi. These boys appear honorable and are themselves of the Art—or the Sisterhood, as we call it." The girl ducked her head to hide a smile. "In any case, after she came to herself, she said she had to meet someone, mounted Bucephalus, and headed southwest. She bid us stay together in camp. But it is such a beautiful day…Anyway, we were enjoying ourselves and became inattentive, until those two lions bounded out of the brush and gave us a start. We were able to get up that tree, and were preparing to use our skills, when your timely intercession saved us the trouble. A rather clever intervention, that." The girl looked probingly into Thaddeus's eyes. "Where did you learn to control bees?"

"He's from Beewicke," Anders explained immediately. "He knows all about bees!"

* * *

In truth, there were only a few times in the course of the long history of the steadfast relationship of Thaddeus of Beewicke and Anders of Brightfield when Thaddeus had a definite impulse to punch his shorter friend in the nose. This was one of them.

* * *

"Ah, Beewicke," Sonnia replied sagely, "the small village that produces such excellent honey. It is harvested by the peasants there. It is said that those who live with bees have a sweet disposition. Is that true, do you think, Thaddeus of Beewicke?" The girl gazed smokily at the tall apprentice.

"Well, I—"

"Sonnia, Marsia, we have business to attend to," Nannsi said, interrupting. "Perhaps some of these boys may have a modicum of intelligence and know what they are about." Her eyes swiveled briefly to Anders. "But our need now is to find our mistress. Standing around gibbering on over honey will not accomplish this."

"If I may suggest, um, Nannsi," Anders said deferentially, "if your mistress is indeed traveling to the southwest, then she will run directly into our camp.

If you like, we would be pleased to guide you there so you may be reunited with her."

"A good suggestion, Friend Anders, if I may call you that. However, our belongings are back at our own camp, and we should really not leave them unattended any longer than necessary."

"We could go to your camp with you," Thaddeus offered, "and help you pack everything up so you can carry it to our camp."

Sonnia smiled again, dazzling the apprentices. "That's a very sweet suggestion, Thaddeus of Beewicke. We accept."

"But—" Rolland began, then winced as Anders's foot came down on this instep.

Thaddeus nodded. "All right, but let's be quick about it. Master Silvestrus will not like it that we are gone so long, and sooner or later, those hungry lionesses will recall they're still wanting supper."

"Very well," Marsia said. "Follow us."

As the group made its way to the girls' camp, Rolland caught up with Thaddeus. "Do you think we should go back to our camp first and get the cart? These frilly types are likely to have nothing but dresses and fancies without number and have undoubtedly made no serious provision to carry them—probably some old goat and a wagon. They'll just slow us down, complaining all the way, while they carry all their things."

"Let's see what the situation is first. It is getting on. Perhaps they won't want to take much."

When the group arrived at the campsite, the boys were surprised to see three small silk tents blazing with bright colors that faced a larger multihued tent. Placed outside each tent was an oaken chest. The camp was laid out in a regular order, while off to one side, a taut line stretched between two trees, to which were tethered three of the most beautiful horses Thaddeus had ever seen—with nary a goat nor wagon in sight.

Sonnia waved a hand. "This is our camp. We've been roughing it for a few days, so please forgive the mess."

Thaddeus was curious as to what "mess" she was referring. Anders and Nannsi were in deep discussion, apparently concerned with the logistics of packing and travel. Marsia moved to stand by Thaddeus. She came up to his eyes—quite tall for a girl. While Sonnia's smile burst forth to engulf the entire surround, Marsia's smile was more demur, close, intimate. Anders's recitation of his old tutor's declamation about the two horns of a dilemma flitted across the tall boy's mind.

"Bellis seems to care for you," she said. "She walks at your heel, and her eyes seldom look elsewhere. You must have made a good impression."

"Uh, thank you. I grew up with a dog, and I like them. How long have you been practicing the Art?"

"Oh, I'm fourteen. I'll be fifteen next month."

Now why had she answered that way? That wasn't what he'd asked—was it?

"All three of us are the same age. The mistress came and collected each of us this past spring, and we've been with her ever since, learning the Preliminaries of the Art. Now, though, she says it is time we went to the School. So here we are, trekking across the country. Our academy is on the Great Sea Coast, due west of here. A rainy climate, alas." She made a face. "Do you also go to a school? Is that where your master is taking you?"

Thaddeus found himself willing to answer any questions the tall girl asked, even if it took all afternoon. Or longer.

Their conversation was interrupted by Sonnia, who glanced sideways at Marsia. "Nannsi and Anders say to join them with, um, Rolland. It's about our traveling arrangements."

The two followed Sonnia back to the middle of the camp.

Anders stood in front of the little group like a fussy chief scribe at a document factor's appraising his staff. "Thaddeus, Nannsi here says she and the other girls can compact some of their gear. Also, they each have carry packs, which will fit on our backs while we walk. Their horses can take some of their really heavy things. Isn't that a good plan?" Despite Anders's silly grin, his companion, the dark, formidable Nannsi, nodded earnestly in approval.

Rolland sputtered, looking as if he'd swallowed a pear whole, his face matching his hair within seconds.

Thaddeus glanced at Marsia, who gave him an encouraging smile. Then he addressed the group. "All right. We'll follow that plan—for now," he added as Rolland's mouth flew open to protest. "We can't spend the rest of the afternoon arguing. It's getting late, and we need to head back to our campsite. Let's go."

It was only afterward that Thaddeus realized he'd been giving orders as if he were the leader. He had no idea what possessed him to think he was in charge, but no one had raised any objections. They went about their assigned tasks quickly and without complaint, even the erstwhile street thief.

Soon, the party of six was on its way back to the young sorcerers' campsite—three riding, smiling, and chitchatting, and three trudging, grunting, and cursing. The ladies had described to their male counterparts the interesting spells their mistress had worked for compacting their possessions, gear, and luggage into bundles small enough to fit each girl's grip. However, though the size was smaller, the weight remained unchanged, as the boys learned soon enough. The mistress's possessions were likewise compacted, but these were parceled out among the three horses.

As they came into the clearing of the men's camp, they found Silvestrus sharing a cup and pipe with a handsome, slender woman. Her sleek black leather riding habit was partially covered by a forest-green cloak that sported an intricate golden brooch at the shoulder. Her rich midnight hair, with a white blaze at each temple, was tied up in a bun. As they were introduced, Thaddeus noted her eyes—one green and one brown, just like his master's, but the other way round. She sat easily on the log but radiated great dignity. And she spoke with the old sorcerer in a way that suggested familiarity. She seemed neither surprised nor concerned at the group's sudden appearance and greeted each of the boys warmly. The old man was likewise gracious, charming, and welcoming toward the girls.

The woman spoke in a rich contralto. "Thank you, gentlemen, for rescuing my girls from such dire circumstances." The girls, standing directly behind their mistress, rolled their eyes. The older woman glanced briefly sideways before clearing her throat. "Though, perhaps, such efforts might not have been necessary had they followed their instructions a touch more literally. On the other hand, I suppose, had they done so, this, um, chance encounter and the opportunity to make new friends and renew old acquaintances might not have come to pass."

The lady's eyes flicked to Silvestrus, and Thaddeus marked the small flush that sped momentarily across her features.

"Mistress Geanninia and I are old friends, lads," Silvestrus announced, "and our students have often gotten together from time to time over the years, despite the great distance between the *Collegium* and the *Ludia.* All the more pleasure to be taken in these chance meetings, as she has said. In any case, we have been talking, and, given the fact that this is the day before Midsummer's Eve, she has agreed to share our humble camp for the next half week. I am delighted for her acceptance and expect that every courtesy will be extended to both herself and her young charges. That said, Mistress Geanninia, perhaps you will allow me a moment with my apprentices so we can best organize our camp to accommodate you and your students with as much comfort as possible."

When Mistress Geanninia smiled and gave a nod of assent, the old man signaled the boys to accompany him over to where Asullus was tethered, craning his neck to get a better look at the new equine arrivals.

Bucephalus stood off to one side, seemingly interested in neither the girls' horses nor the sorcerer's mule. He exuded an aloof air and had a decided curl to his lip, as if he held the entire proceedings in disdain, which, being Mistress Geanninia's mount, the chestnut stallion probably did.

As Silvestrus talked, the boys and mule listened. The lecture consisted chiefly of admonitions regarding good behavior, with threats of reprisal should the admonitions be ignored—standard fare by now to Thaddeus's mind. The next instructions concerned preparations for eventide.

Master Silvestrus turned the boys over to Mistress Geanninia's care, as, with guests present, an extra effort in hospitality was expected. Both apprentices and apprenticiatrix were divided into work teams. Thaddeus and Sonnia were dispatched to the forested area north of the camp and advised to look for, identify, and return with several varieties of foodstuffs—herbs, as well as garnishes and condiments. Nannsi and Anders were assigned to menu planning and preparation. This left Rolland and Marsia to see to the needs of the horses and mule, as well as grounds cleanup, camp logistics, and sleeping arrangements.

Thaddeus attributed Rolland's surliness to his delegation as large animal caregiver and domestic servant, roles for which the worldly urbanite had never expressed any enthusiasm whatsoever. Marsia glanced at the thief, sighed, then squared her shoulders and went about her duties, uncomplaining. Thaddeus was unsure what her reaction signified.

Sonnia, on the other hand, did not seem in the least bit discomfited by her task assignment. Rather, she appeared to demonstrate a degree of enthusiasm for it.

Thaddeus strapped the wicker panniers to hang astride Asullus and walked into the forest with Sonnia. Obeying an internal impulse, he looked back over his shoulder at Marsia, receiving for his effort a smile and a wave.

As Thaddeus and Sonnia walked, they talked.

Thaddeus learned she was from Frantillia, the country to the south on the Sun Sea. Thaddeus remembered that Anders had mentioned Frantillia—the capital and region bore the same name—as a commercial fishing and trading port on the Frantilline coast during one of his geography recitations. Sonnia was the only daughter of a successful merchant there and had an older brother. She resembled her mother, and her father could deny her nothing. Always fascinated with the sea, the girl was an excellent swimmer, regularly beating her brother and his friends in local competitions. Sonnia also studied various forms of sea life and was considered the family scholar. Thaddeus judged her quick, clever, humorous, and interesting.

Then, she had that radiant smile. He made sure to say things he hoped she'd find amusing just to see that smile.

For her part, Sonnia seemed openly curious about him. He began to imagine himself as one of her sea creatures stretched out on a cedar plank in her study, with a pin in each limb holding him down while she regarded his internal organs one by one. That Silvestrus had picked him first of the three boys seemed to impress her. Conversely, the activities of Charles and the bandits drew no more than a noncommittal "Oh? Do you say?"—as if demon summoning was an everyday occurrence. She was puzzled about their experiences in River's Wood, the next destination for the girls and their mistress. She ventured an opinion that Thaddeus might be part of the mystery in some way.

Thaddeus found her stimulating and up to any challenge. Comparing Sonnia with Marsia was like comparing a lively dancing tune to a slow piece for moonlight—which to choose if choosing only one?

Asullus was uncharacteristically quiet during the trip. After the initial shock of witnessing the mule's gift of language, Sonnia assumed the role of *Scientia* and fired a barrage of questions at him. Once her curiosity offered by this diversion was satisfied, however, she resolutely turned her attention back to Thaddeus.

It was late afternoon by the time they made their way back to camp. Marsia spied them first and called out to the others. Many changes had been made to the grounds in the interim. The amenities now included neatly erected tents, a roaring fire, horses that had been fed, groomed, and tethered for the night, and a large, bubbling cauldron promising culinary delight.

Seeing the ongoing preparations for eventide made Thaddeus's stomach growl and his mouth water. He hadn't realized he was so hungry.

Nannsi and Anders, their heads together, stood conferring on the far side of the fire. They waved when they caught sight of the forest foragers.

"Ah, our last ingredients," Anders declared, heading straight for the panniers. As he rummaged through the containers, he called off the various items to Nannsi, who replied aye or nay as to which were needed. Having completed their inventory, the pair toted their bounty to the pot.

To Thaddeus's raised eyebrows, Sonnia responded with yet another smile. He unburdened Asullus, while Sonnia went off to speak with Marsia.

Master Silvestrus and Mistress Geanninia were still in conversation, strolling about the grounds, taking their ease.

Asullus looked in the direction Sonnia had gone, then looked back at Thaddeus, speaking softly. "Ye'll be wantin' to watch that one, laddie. She strikes me as the type as is lookin' fer the best vessel available in which to be placin' all her wants an' ambitions. Ye goes in that direction, an' ye'll be an important fellow, no doubt, achievin' quite a résumé, an' the giddy heights o' courtly society an' all. But I do no' think ye'll be havin' any lastin' warm an' cozy times by the fireplace, dandlin' yer greatchildren on yer knee while growin' old together—if any o' that be important to ye. But that's just me opinion. Best do as seems wisest to yerself."

Thaddeus stared intently at the mule before speaking. "Thank you, Asullus. You're a good friend."

"Donno' be mentionin' it, me bucko. I know ye'd do the same fer me was we to be reversed. An' it happens summat' that an old mule's eyes do see a bit more o' the pot than the lad as is in the soup already," he said with a wink.

"I think that deserves an apple," Thaddeus said over his shoulder on his way to the food sack.

"Now ye' be talkin', laddie!" Asullus called after him.

Thaddeus rummaged in the rucksack and tossed an apple to the mule, who caught it in midair and began munching contentedly. Thaddeus walked over to where Rolland sat on a log looking as if he'd been working over his spleen recently.

"This is ridiculous! A man of my talents shoveling manure! 'Friend Rolland, go here, do this. Friend Rolland, go there, do that.' And that's just Nannsi! And even Anders has turned! I've a good mind to—"

"I, ah, hate to be the one to bring this up," Thaddeus said, suppressing a grin, "but if I remember correctly, you did agree, when you came with us, to do what you were told."

"Well, yes. But how was I to know it would include servant's work? What has that got to do with learning sorcery, anyway?"

"Hmm, you do have a point. Though I believe Master Silvestrus has us all doing a lot more for ourselves lately. Have you noticed we do everything by physical labor, and we're now standing watches—with no wards? I'm beginning to think it's all part of our training in some way."

"Well, maybe. But maybe it's as he said—why reduce his years further by casting spells just to make us comfortable?"

"Those things aren't mutually exclusive, Rolland."

"True enough, Taddy. By the way, I think you have yourself a person of interest in our new company."

"Oh? Really? You must mean Bellis. Marsia told me she thinks the dog is particularly attentive, even devoted. But I told her it's just that I'm used to dogs. That's it, I'm sure."

"That's not who I meant, you backcountry dolt. I mean the tall girl."

"Marsia?"

"The same. She looked in the direction you'd gone for five minutes after you were out of sight. Then, all afternoon, 'How long have you known Friend Thaddeus? What does he like to do? Has he used any sorcery yet? Does he have anyone special back home?' And on and on. Frankly, after an hour, you become a very boring subject of conversation." Rolland lost his sour face and grinned.

"Oh. Well, I think you're overplaying it a bit. I barely know her. She's been pleasant, I suppose. And she does have those dimples, you know. But that hasn't got anything to do with anything. She's just one of the girls."

"Hah!" Rolland guffawed. "*Stercus Tauri!* Oh, and is that the only finger you have, Thaddeus of Beewicke? By the by, how is that Sonnia? She looks kind of interesting."

"Well, she's got that great smile, but I don't know. Asullus told me she's ambitious and might want to use one of us to advance herself and her position."

"Asullus told you? Is he now a *Homo Iudcare,* knowing humans so well?"

"Well, he has kind of a different perspective, but what he says makes sense. I was glad of the counsel."

"That accounts for the apple, then." Rolland sighed and stood. "Uh-oh, here comes our side switcher."

"Hullo, Thaddeus, Rolland," Anders said, coming to a stop before them. "Thanks for your help in getting those herbs and garnishes. Well, what do you think of her? Isn't she wonderful?"

"Mistress Geanninia?" Rolland replied. "Well, she seems nice enough, but she's a little old for you, don't you think?"

Anders glanced disdainfully at his cutpurse friend. "Even you are not that thick, Rolland. No, I mean Nannsi, of course. She's quite intelligent and knows a great deal about sorcery already. And, she seems to like me!"

"Well," Rolland replied, "there should always be at least one person in your life who remains oblivious to your obvious faults—excepting your parents, of course."

Ignoring the redhead, Anders turned to Thaddeus, an unspoken plea on his face.

"Anders, I think you two might have been cut from the same bolt of cloth, so to speak. You both seem to have a like approach to things and a similar manner. You even resemble one another. I mean, except for the fact she's a girl, of course."

"They do look a bit alike, now that you mention it," Rolland said, cocking his head to one side, considering. "Anders, is it true your father traveled widely?" He held out two hands, palms outward, to forestall Anders's advance. "Peace! Peace! So where is this Goddess of Organization from anyway? Bossyville?"

"For your information, she's from Zorbas, in Grecolia, in the East. Her father's an important figure in the government there. She has seven brothers and sisters, if you can imagine, but they're all tall and fair. She says she's the runt of the litter. But she's the only one who practices the Art. She told me Mistress Geanninia came to her father's guesthouse and met the family this past spring. She seemed interested in Nannsi right away, as if she'd known her before, though Nannsi says that was the first time she'd ever seen her. I guess her parents didn't really want her to go, but they suddenly changed their minds after Mistress Geanninia spoke to them privately."

"You know," Thaddeus said, quietly intent on Anders's tidings, "there's something familiar about all that."

"Yes, I think you're right. Hmm. Anyway, we are really getting along. So, what do you think of her?"

The unguarded petition in his friend's eyes was compelling. "I think she's just right for you—perfect, in fact. I think you should pursue her. Don't you think so, Rolland?" The look he directed at the redhead was impossible to misinterpret.

Rolland nodded and managed an encouraging smile. "Oh yes, indeed. Just the girl for you. Made in the Heavens, for certain."

"Good. I think so, too. Well, you both may want to get washed up. Eventide will be ready soon. I think you'll like it. It's a stew Nannsi and the girls thought up for us just for this occasion. Isn't that clever of them? And it doesn't even use any meat, just rutabagas and some of the things you found in the dirt and leaves in the forest. Isn't that interesting?"

Rolland looked hard at Thaddeus, while Thaddeus mouthed, "You promised."

At eventide, the contents of the steaming cauldron, with its unfamiliar smells, were dished out into wooden bowls. While the girls and Anders ate easily and Thaddeus ate bravely, Rolland ate sparingly and failed to ask for seconds. If Master Silvestrus had any hesitation about what he was being served, he did not show it. Midway through the repast, Thaddeus got up as if to relieve himself, leaving the others chatting around the fire pit, and headed for his pack for the dried cheese he'd stashed earlier. On his way back, he noted Asullus off by himself and joined him.

"Aye, Asullus, why the long face?"

"Ye'll be notin' that I ha' heard that particular joke now near on a thousand times, yet every new boy thinks he's the Paraclete o' Wit an' Wisdom in bringin' it up. So, what can I do for ye, Bee Master?"

"I saw you standing here all alone. Why aren't you mixing with the horses?"

"Ah, well, as a rule, yer purebred's here donno' care to mix wi' the likes o' meself, though things are sometimes different when it's one-on-one. Besides, 'tis no' all so interestin' being 'mongst a bunch o' hay munchers. The conversations do seem to be a bit limited, so I say, leave 'em be. No' nearly worth the effort."

"Well, if you're free, then, why don't you come back with me and dazzle all the two-legs with your displays of ready wit and mulish charm?"

"H'rumph. Well now, donno' mind if I do. Beats standin' here as a target fer them early summer bugs as does bite an' itch, even if it do mean sharin' me evenin' with humans."

Thaddeus made his way back to the campfire with Asullus ambling behind. Though dark by now, the setting sun had turned the entire sky a deep red. Tomorrow would be a beautiful day. A few more steps took him to the ring of logs, where he cleared his throat.

"Master, Mistress, everyone, I hope you don't mind, but I have asked Asullus to join us. He looked lonely and bored over there, and I thought he might brighten up our evening a bit."

Asullus snorted his hellos.

Of the group, only Nannsi and Marsia had not spoken with him at any length. The two girls' reactions differed. Where Nannsi seemed to regard him as an interesting oddity and looked for practical uses for his talent, Marsia appeared to warm to him immediately and began looking for a brush with which to groom him.

Mistress Geanninia greeted him by name. "Hello, Asullus. It has been a while. You are in good health, I trust?"

"Aye, Mistress. Master here ha' been seein' to me every want an' whim, don' ye know. I must say, though, that ye looks as ravishin' as always, an' as I ha' tol' ye on occasions previous, were I no' o' the mulish persuasion…"

Mistress Geanninia's smile deepened. "And were I of the mulish persuasion, dear Asullus, I would take you up on it at first chance."

Everyone laughed, Silvestrus most of all.

Asullus sat back on his haunches and easily joined in on the give-and-take. After a time, however, members of the party began to pair up. Rolland, odd man out after having been rebuffed by Sonnia several times, had little to say to the others. Sonnia herself continued to focus her attention on Thaddeus, while Thaddeus, meantime, found himself sitting on a log next to Marsia, a plate of food on his knees, a cup in one hand, and assorted utensils in the other. It was a juggling act, trying to eat and talk at the same time without spilling and making a buffoon of himself in front of her. Perforce, the talking part worked out better than the eating part, which seemed all right, overall.

Eventually, the conversation turned to *Pila Ludere.* "I hear from Nannsi that you have invented a game of bladder kicking," Sonnia said, breaking into Thaddeus's and Marsia's exchange.

The group fell silent and looked to Thaddeus for a reply. "Um, not exactly. It's ball kicking, really, and it's a game our master taught us. In this case, the ball was made from an ogre's bladder, but I think a proper ball could be made of almost anything and would do just as well."

Sonnia leaned forward. "Oh, an ogre's bladder. You had to have killed it, of course. It must have been dangerous."

Rolland suddenly smiled and leaned forward eagerly. "Well, now, as to that. There's a tale, indeed. We came upon it all unexpectedly. It was running hard, straight at us, roaring defiance, when—"

Thaddeus sighed and interrupted. "The ogre was dead already, Sonnia. Asullus told Rolland how to carve the bladder out of the beast, and Master Silvestrus prepared it so we could use it. Then he explained the rules and showed us how to play. We've even had a couple of games. In fact, we were on our way to practice today when we met you."

"A couple of games? With whom did you play?"

"Uh, well, Master Silvestrus. And…Asullus."

"You played against your mentor and the mule?"

"Yes, that's right."

"Just you?"

"No. Rolland, Anders, and I all played."

"So, you three boys played against your master and Asullus?"

"Yes."

"And what was the outcome of these games?"

"We've lost four times out of four tries, so far."

"You lost all?"

"Yes."

"I see. This sounds like a very interesting game. Would it be possible for Marsia, Nannsi, and I to play?"

Thaddeus was confused. "You want to have your own game?" Surely, she couldn't mean…

"No. We want to play your game."

"You want to play with us against Master Silvestrus and Asullus?"

"No, silly. We want to play against you three boys."

"What? I don't think that would be fair. I mean, you're just girls, and—"

All at once, Nannsi, as if conjured, was standing two thumb lengths from him, her hands planted firmly on her hips. "Excuse me?"

"Well, I mean—"

"Do you think we will do any worse against you than you have done against an old man—oh, your pardon, Master Silvestrus!"

"Not to worry, sweet one. I have taken no wound."

"And a mule?"

"Well, I, that is—"

Rolland stepped forward. "It's all right, Thaddeus. We'll be happy to play against you girls. But, you know, we ought to try to make it a little more interesting, don't you think? Add some incentive for fun's sake? How about this—we'll play our game with you with all glory and praise to the winners. But the losers must do all the meal, horse, and ground chores around the camp for as long as we stay together. Unless, of course, you would feel uncomfortable taking this wager for some reason?"

"Done!" the three girls cried out in unison.

Mistress Geanninia leaned over and whispered something to Master Silvestrus, and they both chuckled.

Asullus shook his head, muttering under his breath. "I hates to say this meself, but ye young lads may be ruin' the day ye made this particular wager. I ha' no good feelin' aboot it at all."

Rolland, however, was elated. "Now, finally a chance to set things to rights!"

Thaddeus was less sanguine but still confident. He was conflicted over the thought of beating the girls, particularly Marsia, in front of the entire group. His concern, however, seemed as nothing when he saw the anguish and soul-searching Anders was going through. The youth was actually wringing his hands.

Rolland patted Anders on the shoulder. "Don't worry, Friend Anders. By this time tomorrow night, we'll be sitting pretty, taking our ease and enjoying the day's outcome. Mark my words—you can count on it!"

Chapter 6

SUB DIEM MEDIA AETATE

* * *

By the time Thaddeus awoke the following morning, the girls were up and gone. He finished his morning wash-up, using water from the large goatskin bag hanging on the brass tripod near the fire. Even though they were almost two-thirds the way through *Iunonius*, the water was cold. As he dried his face with a linen, first Anders, then Rolland stumbled up from their bedrolls, made their way to the verge of the nearby forest, and returned.

"Morning."

Anders yawned. "Morning. Say, where are the girls?"

"Gone, I think. Maybe they're out looking for flowers."

Rolland nodded. "Aye, Thaddeus, the ogre's bladder is missing from where I left it last night. Could they have taken it?"

"Hmm. Possibly. Could be they were serious about wanting to play us in *Pila Ludere,* after all. Let's go ask Asullus. Maybe he saw them go."

The boys picked their way through the dew-laden grass over to where the mule stood, tethered separately but equally from the horses. Asullus himself had asked to be tethered, though, of course, it wasn't necessary. His point of view was pragmatic.

"Well, now, ye know there's ne'er been an animal as skittish or sensitive to class an' so on as yer basic horse types. An' ye'll also be notin' as to how they feel aboot the lowly mule. So, should they be seein' themselves tied up to a rope an' meself standin' free to come an' go as I please, they'd be apt to get a mite uppity aboot the entire matter an' take it out on us all. Besides which, lads, as Thaddeus knows quite well, I can slip me rope anytime I needs to, should the occasion arise."

As the boys talked, Thaddeus noted that Bellis was missing, too. Their golden dog was, by now, almost completely recovered from her ordeal and spent most of her time seeking hugs and treats, in no particular order. The recent advent of four extra pairs of willing hands had clearly sent her into *Caelum Caninum* and caused Rolland to remark that all the extra tail wagging might cause that particular member to fall off one day soon.

"'Lo, me lads. Ye are all up early—fer boys, that is. I don' suppose ye brought any—"

The mule's stream of conversation cut off abruptly as he deftly snapped an apple out of the air that Thaddeus had lofted his way. The boys clustered around, stroking him and producing yet other apples after the first had disappeared.

"Asullus, did you happen to see Nannsi and the girls earlier?" Anders asked. "They might still be in their tents, but we don't want to disturb them if they are. Also, we're looking for our ogre's bladder. They wouldn't have taken it, would they?"

"Aye. Nay. Aye. Any other questions, laddie?"

Rolland's mouth dropped open in surprise. "Those girls took our ogre's bladder? What on earth for? Is it some sort of trick? Ah, maybe they're trying to get out of that bet they made with us by hiding the ball."

"Eh, I do no' think that be the way o' it, me young thief. The lasses rolled out at first light, dressed as if they were to be spendin' the day on the plains. They seemed plenty cheerful, gabblin' 'mongst themselves, an' they took special care to lay ahold o' yer bladder. I believe I did hear more than one o' 'em mention the word 'practice,' should that mean somethin' to ye. They first considered saddlin' up their 'mounts,' as they calls 'em—interestin' use o' the word there—but decided to walk out instead an' headed up the northern pathway yonder. Yer sweet golden queenie went wi' 'em as well, don' ye know, trottin' along as pleased as can be."

Rolland laughed. "Well, that's something. They actually intend to take the bet seriously. But why take Bellis? Anders, what do you make of it?"

"Hmm. I think it's as you've said. They do intend to take it seriously. Bellis probably went along because they were the only petters vertical at that hour. You go where the sesterces are, as my Uncle William of Suttonus used to say."

Rolland snorted. "Pfah! I am truly amazed they would go to all that trouble just to be beaten and make themselves look foolish in front of everyone. But I certainly intend to enjoy a little service around here after they've lost the wager. Yes, indeed."

"Ah, Rufus, ha' ye ne'er heard o' the ol' chestnut concernin' pride comin' previous to a fallin' down? I ha' seen me summat o' the world o'er the years, lads, an' I be here to tell all who be listenin' that unwarranted overconfidence ha' lost more contests than lack o' skills an' adverse refereein' taken together."

"But Asullus, they're just girls. They're no fair match for us," the redheaded boy persisted.

"As to the former, aye, an' be thankin' yer lucky stars fer it. As to the latter, I am inclined to agree wi' ye, though p'rhaps not as ye're intendin'. Well, no matter boys –whatever will be will be a pickle, howe'er ye wants to slice it, as I always says. An' if ye're lookin' for an extra piece o' advice, ye might be considerin' gettin' a fire goin' an' seein' to breakfast. Will no' hurt any o' ye to do it, an' pleasin' the master an' mistress is ne'er a bad idea, neither."

The boys concurred and returned to the fire pit to begin morning preparations. Soon thereafter, Master Silvestrus rose from his bedroll, and Mistress Geanninia emerged from her tent. The two shared a quiet moment of greeting, then went separately to wash and prepare. By the time they returned, the boys had a good start on the morning meal.

Silvestrus sat down on his log to eat. After a bite or two, he cleared his throat. "This Midsummer's Eve will be a lovely day and an interesting night. A shower of stars appeared in the west last evening just at midnight. Later, a chorus of three frogs sang their dolorous song in unison and in harmony. Then a boulder from that foothill just south of us rolled gently down the slope—and rolled back up again."

At this last statement, all eyes were upon him.

"Master," Anders spoke up, "what do these strange things mean? Are these portents or forewarnings of great or terrible events?"

"I have not the faintest idea, boy, but it is certainly interesting, is it not? I think tonight will be the—ah, Mistress Geanninia. Please join us. I was just telling the boys we should be having a splendid Midsummer's Eve this night."

"Good morning, gentlemen. Oh my, yes. Myself and my three charges all have 'maiden's signs' this day, and that's unusual all at once. I was awakened at dawn by a baaing sound, and when I looked out the back of the tent, a bloodred goat was eating the grass into the shape of a perfect circle. And when he had finished, he walked slowly into the forest until I could see him no longer. I fell back asleep, but when I awoke an hour ago, one of the *Pixae* was sitting on my hairbrush, grinning at me, and braiding several of my loose strands. As soon as she saw I had seen her, she vanished."

The hair on the back of Thaddeus's arms stood up. "Mistress Geanninia, do you think these events have a special meaning?"

"I do not know, dear boy. But I agree with Master Silvestrus. It certainly bodes for an interesting day and night. And I wouldn't miss it for the world!"

Anders took a step forward. "Mistress Geanninia, when we woke this morning, the girls were already gone. This doesn't have anything to do with the odd day, does it?"

"Ah, Anders, your concern for others is a credit to you. However, I believe you may rest your mind about this, young sir. The girls told me last night they wished a little exercise this morning. They have not gone far, I believe. And I am sure they will be safe."

Silvestrus cleared his throat again. "Lads, I have a thought. It is possible, as you have suggested, these peculiar happenings have some purpose connected with Midsummer's. It is also possible they are just ordinary, everyday, random magical occurrences, and we are only paying more attention to them because of the time of year. But perhaps not. What we need is more information. I propose you three, after you clean yourselves and the camp from breakfast, take Asullus out with you and scout the area widely—the woods, hillocks, and all around—looking for any further signs of import and report back to us here at midday. Perhaps we will have some answers by then."

The boys agreed this was an excellent idea and soon completed their chores after seeing to Asullus's needs. Anders proposed they begin sweeping the area in an expanding spiral, starting from camp—that way they would miss nothing. The boys were excited about the prospect of something mysterious and possibly dangerous and proud of their master's confidence in their ability to carry out the task.

After the apprentices and mule set out, their steps light and their hearts full of the morning, Asullus spoke. "Well, now, that was easy, was it no'?"

Anders glanced at their companion. "What was easy, Asullus?"

"Why, the ease o' gettin' ye lads out o' the way, o' course."

"Getting who out of what way, old mule?"

"Are ye deef? Ye boys. Gettin' ye boys out o' the way, away from camp, don' ye know." He was greeted by three blank expressions and rolled his eyes heavenward. "I'm no' sure why I keep meself tryin' so hard these days. Me years is gettin' longer, no appreciation is ever shown, an' the lads is gettin' denser. It's Master Silvestrus. He was wantin' ye out o' the way."

"Why would Master Silvestrus want us out of the way?" Thaddeus asked. "I don't understand."

"It is, p'rhaps, because they all be innocents. Aye, that must be it, I am sure. It canno' be that they're struck stupid. No soul can be so limited an' yet be livin'—so, it's innocence is all. Good. Now I do feels better meself. The master wants ye out o' the way, lads, so he an' the mistress can be together, cordial like."

Thaddeus's eyes widened. "What?"

"No!" Anders exclaimed.

Rolland remarked confidently, "That's nonsense, Asullus."

"Oh, now, fourteen years each, an' they all knows so much! Remarkable. I takes it all back aboot the stupidity an' such. Must ha' been thinkin' on some other three apprentices I be knowin' at this time."

"Asullus, are you serious?"

"Quite so, laddie. Like I'll be tellin' ye, soon as ye puts yer eyeballs back in their sockets an' yer tongues back 'tween yer cheeks. Master an' Mistress ha' been wantin' as to ha' some time together, just they two. Ye ha' surely noticed that they be friends o' old, aye? Well, 'tis true. They goes back a ways. Was real close at one point, as I ha' heard the tale. Then summat happened. I ne'er did hear the what o' it. No' me business anyways. An' then they drew apart. But every now an' then, they runs into each other—like now, by p'rhaps no accident at all—an' I suppose the old flames be comin' back from the embers, don' ye know. An' at such times, they puts a high priority on their privacy, which even ye can surely understand, limited tho' ye are. So, here it is, Midsummer's Eve, a beautiful day wi' the same kind o' night predicted, an', like any old couple as has a history, they wishes to be alone fer as long as might be. Now, if ye still do no' understand, then I'll be callin' on our revered Medico to dose ye wi' some evil brew 'cause ye must ha' some sort o' serious brain fever that warrants immediate attention, I dares to say."

"Oh."

"Oh."

"I see."

"Oh, an' they see! Praise be, vision is restored! So as I was sayin', we ha' us a little hikin' to do whilst the two old friends is renewin' their friendship."

"That's all this trip is, then?" Rolland said with a cynic's frustration. "We have to go tramping through the grass and bugs and burrs all morning just so those two can—"

"Whup! Watch yerself, Young Master. Let us be respectful an' all. Ye niver know when, as yer life unwinds its coil, ye might be findin' yerself in the exact same position an' such."

The boy reddened. "Well, all right, but honestly—"

"Besides which, I do no' think 'tis all subterfuge. I would no' be surprised at all that we find ourselves summat o' interest. 'Tis Midsummer's Eve, after all, an' on this day, any manner o' curious thing can occur. Why, I remembers me once, when as a youth, I happened to find meself down on the Frantilline coast on this very day wi' this young filly just come to country, who was black as midnight, 'ceptin' her tail, which was itself striped. And therein lies a tale, so to speak. Y'see, her uncle on her mother's side had a hag fer a mistress, an' she herself used to..."

It was a hairsbreadth from midday when the group returned to camp. Having approached the camp singing and thrashing about loudly, they found Master Silvestrus and Mistress Gcanninia as they had left them—sitting on a log, talking. Their trip, they reported, had, disappointingly, uncovered nothing of note, except the usual scratches and bruises that beating about the bush always produced. Thaddeus had easily found the girls' trail, and the group debated briefly about whether to sneak up on them. Asullus seemed to feel such an act was beneath them. Rolland added that it was unnecessary, anyway, given the inevitable outcome of the afternoon's game. Thaddeus was for looking for *Faerrae* sign and letting the girls be. Anders's was the only vote for spying on the girls, but Rolland said it was only because he hoped they would be playing without clothes, and he wanted to see Nannsi. An immediate and violent denial from the shorter boy only seemed to confirm the redhead's suspicion.

Moments after the boys had settled around the campfire, the girls returned, laughing among themselves. Each had a sheen of sweat from exertion. Nannsi carried the ogre's bladder casually in the crook of her arm. Bellis detached herself from the group and sauntered over to Thaddeus for some attention—and treats. Thaddeus wondered briefly if it was her affection for him, returning after a morning's absence, or whether she had wrung the ladies dry during her time with them and was now looking for a new resource.

"Ah, so that's where our ball got to. You've been carrying it around all morning," Rolland said, an impudent grin on his face.

"We were doing more than just carrying it around, as, perhaps, you will learn later this afternoon," Nannsi responded loftily.

The boys grinned. "Ooooh!" they said in unison.

Rolland snorted. "Well," he said disdainfully, "it's good luck you have so much spirit left. That will serve you well as you prepare our midday. It's only good sense to begin practicing something that you'll have to be doing over and over in the near future—honing your skills, so to speak."

Sonnia lifted one eyebrow in a challenging gaze. "How interesting that you use a sentence with the words 'good sense' in it. One would think—"

"Ah, ladies and gentles all," Silvestrus inserted, "how good it is to see both groups back from your morning exertions. I have no doubt you have all learned things of great interest to you this day. We eagerly await the recitation of your reports, but first, as to midday, in acknowledgment of its being Midsummer's Eve's day—my, that is a clumsy phrase, is it not?–Mistress Geanninia and I would like all of you to be our guests at a small feast we will be preparing. But first, why don't you wash up and rejoin us as soon as may be?"

A short time later, the group reassembled.

"Excellent. Now, are you ready, Geanni? One, two, three—*Convivium Sit!*"

"Epulae Sint!" Mistress Geanninia added, accompanied by a clap of her hands.

A long wooden table flanked by stout oaken chairs appeared before the assembled group. On the large snowy-white linen that covered it were set matching earthenware plates, crockery, and flatware—enough for eight, with pewter mugs for all. Steaming platters piled high with a variety of hardy foods were sitting at intervals, interspersed with plates of cold cuts, warm loaves of various breads, and sweat-beaded terra-cotta pitchers of what smelled like mulled cider. Unexpectedly, Rolland found what appeared to be a large bowl of bear stew in front of his place, while at Thaddeus's setting, a dripping honeycomb nestled in a wooden bowl.

"For you, dear boy," Mistress Geanninia said, smiling.

Minor issues aside, the group attacked the feast with good will and good humor. Thaddeus's appreciation of the cost of the banquet for his master and the mistress added a solemn note, which was ultimately folded into his trove of experience.

A pleasant time later, the group, one by one, pushed themselves back from the table and enjoyed the afterglow of a satisfying meal. Cleanup duty was shared, and a temporary *Pax Mundana* between boys and girls was decreed by Master Silvestrus. Conversation reigned as the sun passed its zenith and began its descent toward the horizon. Almost imperceptibly, a level of excitement laced with anticipation spread over the group. Soon it would be time for the game.

At last, Master Silvestrus rose, cleared his throat, and announced, "All right, we are present on this fine day to witness a significant contest of will and stamina with fell fate hanging in the balance. This afternoon will see a championship contest of *Pila Ludere* matching the fair *Virgines* against the stalwart *Minimi,"* The old man bowed deeply and swept his arm wide, acknowledging each team. "Our *Arbiter* for this afternoon's laurel wreaths will be Asullus, late of Cobbly Knob. Mistress Geanninia and I will comprise your attentive, appreciative, and enthusiastic audience. We will now repair to the playing field, and may the better team end up administering an educational and heartfelt drubbing to its opponent. Ladies and gentlemen, if you please."

Mistress Geanninia walked to the field on Silvestrus's arm, and they took their places on the sidelines, each producing a chair to sit on. The two teams gathered in the middle of the field. Lastly, Asullus appeared, wearing his white garland and dribbling the ogre's bladder on alternate hooves toward the waiting players.

"Right. Gather 'round, ye lot. Now I knows ye all be familiar, generally, wi' the various ins an' outs o' the game, so I'll no' be wastin' me time on that topic. Master Silvestrus has well instructed me in terms o' what's a foul an' what's a mere bendin' o' the path. So do no' be tryin' yer tricksies wi' me, or it'll go ill wi' ye. Now, the master has promised me fifty apples after the game fer me work, unirregardless o' who wins, so no tryin' to influence me unduly. I will gi' ye fair callin' an' show ye no discernible bias or neglect. If ye hears me brayin', that's the signal to let ye know I saw what it was ye did, an' it's goin' to cost ye. Otherwise, keep playin' till I says stop. The ladies will defend the goal to the north an' the louts, the reverse. Oh, an' do no' forget, no hands may be used, so none o' ye will be pickin' up the ball. All else, help yerselves. The game will end at the settin' o' the sun, unless I calls it previous. Now, assume yer positions."

"What do you think Master Silvestrus was going on about?" Anders asked as they walked to a spot several paces back where they could talk without fear of listeners. "He was laying it on a bit thick."

"It doesn't matter," Rolland replied. "Besides, I think he knows we'll be the ones doing the drubbing. Speaking of drubbing—Anders, so help me to all the Gods above, if you buff off a play so Nannsi can get an advantage, I'll skin you within a thumb's width of your life, and I'll use my dullest blade. *Intellegis?*"

"Oh, all right. But—"

"No buts, Anders. I'm serious."

"Very well. Thaddeus, how do you want us to play this?"

"Rolland and I will play close to the line. That way, we can get the ball away, kick it down to their goal, and score. Anders, you guard our goal, and don't let anyone through. If anybody gets close, use that body tackle you put Master Silvestrus down with the other day."

"I didn't tackle the master! I wouldn't do that! I fell."

The redheaded thief snorted. "Of course. Anders, never try to lie—especially to me. You're terrible at it. All right, let's show these sugar bosoms why men rule the world!"

He clapped his hands, and the other boys followed suit. They took their positions, confidently ready for the worst the girls could offer.

Asullus's gentle kick nudged the ball slowly forward. It came to rest midway between the two sides.

"Initium!" Asullus called.

* * *

Sweating from the late-afternoon sun and the load he was carrying, Thaddeus made his way behind Mistress Geanninia's tent toward the fire pit via the shortest distance from the wood. A large straw hamper, jammed to overflowing with kindling and small sticks, was slung over one shoulder, the strap digging in uncomfortably. He had purposefully overfilled the basket, hoping a second trip wouldn't be necessary. Several steps later, he spied Rolland sitting on a log, head in his hands, cursing softly to himself.

Thaddeus slipped quietly up behind him. "Aha! Slacking off on the job, Friend Rolland!"

Rolland jumped as if stung and looked around wildly. "Thaddeus! Don't ever do that again!"

"All right. But you did look funny. Why are you back here hiding out?"

"Because I'm back here hiding out. Why else? Those girls have been riding me mercilessly—especially that Sonnia. If it isn't fetch and carry every little thing, then it's stupid questions. 'Oh, Nannsi, what did you think of the game, dear? Do you think the boys may actually appear for our next game? They didn't seem to have been here at all for today's.' It's been going on like that all bloody afternoon. I can't stand it! So I'm taking a break. I still can't believe they beat us. I just can't believe it."

Unbidden, the scene paraded through Thaddeus's mind—the three girls spread out in formation, dancing in place, their short tunics allowing them to run fleetly up and down the field with ease. None wore sandals. As soon as the ball was released, they took control and began passing it back and forth as if they had been practicing for weeks, which, he afterward discovered, they had. *Pila Ludere* had apparently been a staple activity on their journey west immediately after Mistress Geanninia had introduced it, though their ball had been made of fabric rather than an ogre's bladder. They slipped lightly and swiftly around their heavier, slower opponents all afternoon, showing no mercy.

As Rolland raved on, other images replayed in Thaddeus's mind—Sonnia bowling him over from behind while he was dribbling the bladder, only to fall heavily on top of him, smiling her wonderful smile and running a muddy finger down his nose before jumping up, laughing, and running off with the ball. Then later, Anders bravely throwing himself in front of Nannsi to block a kick, only to receive the ball full force in the face, resulting in a fountain of blood gushing from his nose. This led to the kicker briefly abandoning the game to carefully tend to the young distiller's battle wound with gentle hands, dabbing cloth, and soothing words.

On the field, Rolland was compelled by the sharp-eyed mule to sit out the game for three hundred heartbeats after being caught tripping his opponent for the third time.

Later, Marsia streaked down the field with Thaddeus right behind her. In the heat of the moment, he'd been torn between catching the ball and catching the runner. Just after she scored, he'd hoped, from her flushed face and lowered eyes, that she might be harboring a similar notion.

He remembered glimpsing Master Silvestrus and Mistress Geanninia gazing into each other's eyes and speaking earnestly.

After the initial onslaught, the boys were steadily able to recover their balance and tie the score toward the end of the game. Then, with the sinking of the sun, came the critical moment—a face-off in front of the boys' goal with neither side able to gain an advantage as time was running out. At that moment, Bellis, who had been lying quietly at Master Silvestrus's feet, watching the game intently, leaped up and dashed into the midst of the melee. With both sides yelling, she snatched up the ogre's bladder in her bared teeth and dashed straight between the apprentices' goalposts, tail streaming behind, as the last remnant of the sun's red disc sank beneath the horizon.

"Heus!" Asullus barked. "*Debellatum Est!* Girls win!"

Pandemonium ensued, with the three girls jumping up and down, whooping in triumph, and hugging each other, while the master and mistress laughed and toasted their frosted wineglasses together. The three boys descended on the mule in a rush, waving their arms and shouting while Asullus stood sturdy and staunch, remaining impervious to all pleas, threats, and exhortations. Calmly surveying the chaos, the golden dog, Bellis, sat on her haunches at the far side of the goalposts panting, ogre's bladder at her side, tongue lolling, and looking very pleased with herself.

The boys, shaken and outraged, accosted the mule.

"That wasn't a fair goal!"

"Why not, laddie?"

"She's a dog!"

"None ha' said the game was limited to humans."

"She can't come in at the last moment like that!"

"No rule aboot when somebody can come in or no', don' ye know."

"She can't play for them!"

"She's a girl. 'Tis a girls' team."

"She's an extra—that makes it three versus four!"

"None ha' said the numbers fer each team must be identical, Rufus."

"But she picked up the ball with her teeth!"

"I ha' said only ye could no' use yer hands. Ne'er said a thing aboot teeth, did I now?"

"That's unfair!"

"Pfah! Ye be confusin' unfavorable outcome wi' disequity."

"I thought you were our friend!"

"I ha' heard this before, methinks. I ha' gi'en ye fair judgements, Young Masters. P'rhaps ye're disappointed that ye ha' been outfoxed. Should ha' asked more questions, ye should. Although ye'll be remembrin' I did tell ye I had a bad feelin' aboot this to-do from the beginnin'. No' to say I told ye so, but I did tell ye so. Now, if ye be lookin' for another piece o' free advice, I say, go swallow yer gorge, give the ladies yer congratulations, an' start doin' their biddin' per yer arrangement. Probably time to start that sort o' thing, anyway. After a while, they'll leave off their crowin' an' be nice again. Ye'll have learned some valuable lessons, an' ye'll like it when next they treat ye well. Besides, 'tis Midsummer's Eve, an' ye niver can know what's goin' to come o' that."

By the time the game was declared, all objections addressed, and all celebrations endured, it was dark. The group slowly made its way back to the campsite, some hearts lifted to the sky, some sunk in the depths of despair. Once back at the camp, Silvestrus turned and addressed them all.

"That was a wonderful display. Good job from all of you, winners and, um, others alike. Now, as it happens, this being Midsummer's Eve, Mistress Geanninia and I have certain sorcerous rituals to perform to mark the occasion. We shall, therefore, have to take our leave of you for the duration of the evening. Enough provision remains from midday to make you comfortable. We, however, must fast as is required by the rites. We shall make the camp secure before we leave. If you do fall into extremity, pray solicit Asullus, who will know how to reach us. Now, I understand you boys have made a wager with the young ladies. I am sure everyone will steadfastly fulfill any oaths and obligations they may have made. Otherwise, I bid you good evening and—"

Mistress Geanninia turned her head to whisper in his ear.

"Ah, yes. Thank you, Geanni. I am reminded to advise you concerning things you may experience tonight.

> Some may be real, some may be fey,
> Some tell tomorrow, some view today,

Some show the past, some are those last,
Some you may hear, but only if near,
Some need your act, but only post fact,
Some are to see, so attention's the key,
Some may alarm, but none will cause harm,
Any fogging your senses, will just confuse tenses,
These visions a-borning, hold power till morning.

"Hmm. I think that's it. Farewell!" With that, he and Mistress Geanninia walked north into the woods.

The rest of the group looked at each other, puzzled and uncertain. Then Nannsi strode up to the apprentices. "Very well, you three, now here is what you are to do. First, Friend Thaddeus, you will..."

* * *

A strident voice broke in on Thaddeus's musing. "Thaddeus! Pay attention! I said, what do you think we should do about this?" Rolland demanded.

"Um, nothing, I reckon, Rolland. It's as Asullus said. The game's over, and we've learned 'summat.' I guess it's time to 'make honey from bitterflower,' as my father used to say."

"Pfah! It's always honey with you, Thaddeus! You're too easy. We've got to do something! Let me think. There must be some—" The young thief's voice broke off as a peculiar look appeared in his eyes. "Ah...you go on, Thaddeus. Tell the girls I'll be along to slave more for them shortly."

"Rolland, I've been with you long enough to recognize that look. What are you on about?"

"Never you mind, Taddy. Nothing terrible. Besides, I think you'd really rather not know."

"Be careful, then. You don't want the master coming down your throat searching for your tonsils when he gets back."

"Not to worry, Bee Master, I'm always careful."

Shaking his head, Thaddeus resumed his trek to the fire pit with his burden.

It was on the return from his third trip to the woods—at Nannsi's insistence—that he found Rolland dressing the fire. One of the larger panniers lay open on the ground beside him, its contents unceremoniously dumped onto the burning logs. The fire, roaring several moments previously, had now abated to a smoking heap. Rolland tossed more kindling and sticks over the layers of greenery, hiding it from view. The ex-thief looked up at Thaddeus's approach and grinned.

Thaddeus eyed his friend dubiously. "Rolland, what are you doing?"

"Evening the score, Taddy. Just evening the score."

Thaddeus started. "Say, that's not the master's special pipe weed, is it?"

"Not yet. I'm saving the master from himself. I told you he goes funny and may not be able to stop using it. So now, we'll get rid of it for him."

"Uh, have you thought this out? I mean, he really doesn't seem to like it when one of us gets into his supplies. He almost took Asullus apart last week for that very thing."

"Thaddeus, you worry too much. This is a service to our master. It may also have some beneficial effect on the girls' attitudes as well, 'don' ye know.'"

"Just exactly what beneficial effect do you mean?" Thaddeus asked, suddenly feeling protective of the tall girl who had come to occupy a large portion of his thoughts lately.

"Oh, nothing serious. If anything, it'll just make them giggle. They're in Mistress Geanninia's tent preparing for Midsummer's Night Eve's ceremonies—whatever they are. Oh, and Thaddeus, my lad, a word of advice. Were I you, I'd stand back a little from the fire tonight, out of the smoke. You see, it's—uh-oh, here they come. Shh."

The mistress's tent flap was thrown back, and the three girls emerged, dressed in robes the color of sable with belts of white rope. All were barefoot in the emerging evening. Nannsi carried a small lute and pick, Sonnia a small wooden flute with a silver bell, and Marsia a tambourine with black silken streamers. The girls walked in single file to the fire with great dignity of purpose.

Anders—looking like a raccoon following his bludgeoning at the game and sniffing repeatedly into a cloth—returned from burying the garbage left from eventide and joined his two fellow apprentices as Nannsi strode up to them.

With the slightest of smiles for the short scholar, Nannsi turned and addressed the group. "As your master said earlier, this is a special time—Midsummer's Eve. It is paramount that certain rites and ceremonies take place to acknowledge the importance of this day. After all, should the summer fail, the harvest will fail. Should the harvest fail—well, I'm sure even you can puzzle out how disastrous that would be. In any event, just as your master and our mistress have their parts to play on this occasion, so, too, do the three of us, though in a smaller way, of course. Our mistress has given us strict instructions concerning the rituals to be performed this evening, and that is why we have these instruments and why we are dressed thusly."

Rolland gave his diminutive friend a dig in the ribs. "Sorry, Anders," he whispered, grinning, "looks like it's clothes tonight, too." In return, the street thief received an undisguised look of venom, causing him to grin even more broadly.

"Though there may be changes later, depending on how our rites are received, we will begin tonight's celebration with solemn music and dance. We will call upon the *Igenium Ignis* and invoke their wisdom to guide us. You would be well advised to stay clear of our work. And please do not interfere. You may, however, observe the ritual if you wish. Just do not interrupt, ask questions, or make any noise. Once we begin, it is imperative that we complete the rite as prescribed. Sonnia, Marsia, come. Let us take our places."

The three boys obediently stepped back several paces but remained observant and curious as the girls formed an equilateral triangle around the fire, instruments at the ready. Bellis, who had walked over to stand by Thaddeus, sat down on her haunches and placed her head against his leg. He reached down absently and scratched her behind the ears. The dog whimpered, and Thaddeus found Bellis looking beyond him to the sky overhead. He gazed upward and gasped.

"Anders, Rolland," he said softly, "look at the sky."

The boys gazed heavenward into curtains of iridescent blues and greens dancing across the nighttime sky, filling the North from horizon to horizon. The eerie light shimmered and wavered, never still, like a clothes-lined blanket on a windy day.

The girls began their ritual with odd, haunting music that rose from each instrument before blending together in subtle phrase and form. The music spun and wavered as they wove a stately dance with a measured pace around the fire—which was now smoking in earnest.

Anders sniffed. "Say, what's that funny smell?"

"Oh, just some scraps and trash from around the campsite," Rolland said in an offhand manner.

"That's odd. I never smelled anything like that before."

Thaddeus looked hard at Rolland, who winked.

The tall boy looked skyward again to see the veil of shimmering light parting down the middle as if it were a curtain opening. The tempo of the girls' music increased. Overhead, a few, next a shower, then a storm of shooting stars issued from the dark vault between the parted banks of lights. As the boys watched, the streaking stars, initially all white, gradually burned in colors Thaddeus could not describe. Stunned, the boys were transfixed. None had ever witnessed such a sight before.

Without warning, a loud detonation and retort sounded off to the left.

"Did you see that?" Anders asked. "One of those streaking stars flew into the woods and exploded! Look at those sparks!" His eyes were round with wonder.

More streaks flew by and crashed, the bright explosions lighting up the landscape. Thaddeus flinched violently as a tiny one shot by just in front of his nose. As it zipped past, parting the fire's fragrant smoke, time froze for the tall apprentice. Thaddeus gasped involuntarily as he gazed at a little man perched atop the star, riding it down in slow motion. But it was no sort of man Thaddeus had ever seen. This little creature, no more than two thumb lengths tall, sat astride a fireball half the size of Thaddeus's fist. He was scrawny with outsize bat wings, clawed hands, and feet and a nose and a chin so long and narrow that they met in front of his face. He wore a crazed expression, and flames from his burning mane shot out behind him. A high-pitched cackling followed him down until the star collided with a large oak, tearing a sizable hole through the tree trunk before exploding with a deafening roar into a million fiery fragments.

Thaddeus had bunched his muscles, ready to shout for them all to run, when, just as abruptly as the celestial storm started, it stopped. The boy returned his gaze to the girls' dance to see sparks issuing from their fire as well, but these sparks were looping and twisting, spiraling out of the fire, higher and higher, wider and wider. It was as if they were keeping time with the accelerating tempo of the music.

Thaddeus's concentration on what he was experiencing distracted him from the others, and he began to lose track of his friends. One particularly large spark captured his attention as it flew out of the fire, bowing and weaving in a dance. When it flew near him, he held up an outstretched hand, and it settled on his palm. Looking down, he beheld a fire *Pixae* sitting astride a minuscule winged salamander. The *Pixae* looked up at him and smiled. He thought it might be female but could not be sure. The next second, the *Pixae* and the enkindled amphibian leaped from his hand and soared off into the night.

Thaddeus, bemused, stared after them and marked the odd events of the night. Despite the evidence, one part of his mind was convinced nothing was unusual or remarkable about any of it.

Suddenly, something tugged at his leg. He looked down in surprise to see, not Bellis, but a small blonde girl with large brown eyes smiling up at him and raising her hand for his. She was so sweet looking, he could not help but smile back at her.

"And who are you, little one?" he asked.

"You know me, Thaddeus of Beewicke," she said in a very formal tone, "though, perhaps, not exactly like this. I have come to take you away with me."

"You have? Away to where? What's your name?"

"Yes. You will see. Luperca," the child replied. "Come. Take my hand." He hesitated, and she gazed at him directly. "What? Are you afraid?"

"No, I don't think so. It's just that it's all so odd. Where did you come from? Why are you doing this?"

"From very nearby. Because I can, of course. After all, it is Midsummer's Eve. Come, Thaddeus, *Amicus Faerrarum,* come with me." The little girl clasped his hand firmly and began tugging him toward the wood. "We will go in there."

Thaddeus stopped. "Wait. What about the others? Where are they?"

"They will each have their own experiences. Some may be shared. Come."

The pull from the small girl's hand was insistent—and irresistible. They followed a winding route, and within moments, Thaddeus had lost all sense of direction and had no idea where he was.

"You know," she said conversationally after they had walked for what seemed a goodly distance, "it's at times like this people always ask, 'What will become of me?' You haven't, however, so I thought perhaps you'd like to know. You'll have to count backward, though." She grinned mysteriously. "Starting with me."

Thaddeus was confused, and nothing made any sense. But it was interesting. So far. He stopped abruptly when the path opened out onto a small plain.

"Wait here," she said.

Thaddeus waited. Within moments, his attention was drawn to a tiny figure moving toward him through the tall grass. As it advanced, it grew in size. Thaddeus stared as the figure resolved into a towering man shape, though it was not a man. It was tall—as tall as two men standing one atop the other—and broad, with yellowed, upturned tusks protruding from its lower jaw, and great curved horns jutting out from either side of its head. It was dressed in skins and carried a massive brassbound club. An ogre! Thaddeus turned in alarm, concerned for Luperca, but the girl was nowhere to be seen.

The ogre advanced, but it was soon obvious it neither heard nor saw Thaddeus. It was, instead, searching the immediate area, its gaze sweeping back and forth until it stopped by a small outcrop of boulders. It put down its club and knelt, its snout sniffing vigorously, apparently tracing a scent on the ground. Then it reached a massive arm into an opening in the earth between the rocks. After feeling about, it withdrew its arm. In its grasp were two wolf cubs, one black and one yellow. The ogre casually dropped them and reached back into the den—for a den it surely was—and dragged out three more pups, then three more after that. When it seemed satisfied that it had all of them, it stood, then took the great cudgel and smashed all eight cubs, one by one.

Thaddeus stared in horror, but found he could not move, not even a twitch.

The ogre's chest convulsed rhythmically in what might have been a coarse laugh. It reached down, picked up one of the dead pups, sniffed it, licked its muzzle, and opened its mouth as if ready to eat it. Then it unaccountably paused and looked sharply over its shoulder as if listening. It snuffed the air, glanced around wildly, and, dropping the dead cub, sprang into a lumbering run, heading away.

A few minutes later, a pack of wolves came on the scene, led by a great golden female, her jet-black consort right behind her. They went immediately to the bodies of the pups, frantically nuzzling and licking their dead whelps. After a moment, the leader threw back her head and uttered what Thaddeus knew must be a long, keening howl, though he heard no sound. The rest of the pack joined in the eerily silent concert. Moments later, she stopped abruptly and started circling the area, nose to the ground. She howled once more, though Thaddeus surmised it was a different kind of howl, and rushed off at full speed in the direction the ogre had taken. The rest of her pack arrayed themselves on either flank, and the entire group swept off and vanished in the long grass.

Without warning, Thaddeus abruptly found himself to be one with the wolves running the ogre's trail. He knew what they were after and why—and how it would end. He rushed over the uneven ground, hatred pounding in his heart, shoulders jostling against his pack mates and bloodlust rising in his gorge. Within moments, the pack caught up with the desperately running creature, which stopped and turned to face them, a look of inevitability writ large upon its heavy features. The huge club rhythmically described a large figure-eight arc.

The golden female and her coal-black mate flew through the air, lunging directly for the ogre's throat, one on either side, while the others dashed in to hamstring it and bring it down. The ogre swung his club, catching the black wolf on the side of its head and sending it sprawling. It did not get up. The ogre got no chance for another swing, as Thaddeus surged forward and bit through one of its knees. It toppled to the ground, thrashed briefly, then lay still.

After a time, the wolves had taken their fill.

Thaddeus found the taste of blood both exciting and satisfying. Suddenly, the wolves were gone, and Thaddeus was standing again, looking down at the ripped and bloody corpse. A shudder ran through him, but he could not tear his eyes away from the monstrous form and the havoc worked upon it. As he stared, however, the creature clambered slowly and laboriously to its feet. It looked directly at Thaddeus for a long moment, then reached down, put its hand into its lower body, and ripped out what looked like a fully cured and inflated game ball. It rolled the object toward him, where it came to rest at his feet. The ogre sighed, lay back down where it had fallen, and closed its eyes. A moment later, a pair of curious crows landed lightly on its chest.

Thaddeus looked sideways as a movement to his left caught his eye. A procession of wolves had emerged from the forest and made its way toward a great boulder that stood in the center of the meadow. On top of the boulder, with great dignity, stood the yellow-haired pack leader. Thaddeus blinked as the golden female gazed directly at him. The grass rippled with the slinking forms until the entire area was filled—first with wolves, then with dark, wolflike dogs like those in River's Wood, and, finally, members of the other dog families. All seemed to be paying homage to the golden one, standing regally on the rock as if on a throne.

The young boy blinked again, and the scene faded and shifted. He looked around for Luperca, but though he called her name several times, the little girl did not appear. Shrugging, he found the forest path, which was shimmering now in the light of the full moon. He glanced back over his shoulder, but the plain had disappeared, and only a few tufts of long grass were left among the trees.

Thaddeus followed the downward-sloping path until it opened onto a wide expanse of rocky, boulder-strewn shore lined by waves that stretched toward the horizon. Thaddeus had never seen the ocean before—just heard of it from itinerants passing through his village—but he knew it, nonetheless. He breathed in the salty tang as flocks of gulls wheeled and soared overhead, calling loudly.

A deep, rasping noise, followed by a low-pitched roar, startled him. Curious, he peered cautiously around a large rock. Down at the edge of the shore, two strange creatures faced each other. Considering the descriptions he'd heard from Asullus, the immense beasts could only be...dragons. One, smaller and more petite, was sea green—a female, he guessed. The second, larger and more robust, was bloodred. The red male seemed to be pressing his suit to the green, but after a time, it was clear he was being rejected. With a final toss of her magnificent head and flowing mane, the proud green dragon turned about and strode away with great dignity.

The male, however, appeared enraged by her action and, roaring a challenge to the heavens, began to transform. Within seconds, a giant red warrior holding a cruelly bladed crimson spear stood where the dragon had been. Suddenly, he rushed forward, hurling his weapon toward the retreating female's arched back. The green, not sensing the danger, took the fell lance directly between her shoulder blades and reared up, clawing at the pointed shaft protruding from her chest. Thrashing about, growing weaker by the second, she fell onto to her side with a reverberating crash, where she, too, underwent a transformation. Now a comely woman's form lay grasping the spear with both hands.

For an instant, he thought she called to him—"Thaddeus!" He felt it would only be a matter of time before she died if no one came to her assistance. He rushed forward to her aid, but a large wave welled up and swept onto the land, obliterating everything in its path. Backing hurriedly away from the incoming wall of water, Thaddeus found the coastal scene had changed back to the more familiar forest, and the *Dracones* were gone. Nonplussed, he resumed his journey, judging nothing was to be gained by standing still. He was also uncertain that he could find his way back to where he started, even had he wished to.

Continuing to follow the path around a great curve, he came upon a scene that looked more familiar. Between two tall, moss-covered trees stretched a huge web made from a shimmering substance thick as ropes or vines. In the center of the net, an enormous black spider, clearly angry, was lashing out with its several legs at a myriad of swooping, darting winged men and women, all blue, who were teasing and taunting it. Surprisingly, Thaddeus was able to hear the exchange.

The largest of the the troop detached itself from the azure mass and fluttered down to Thaddeus, landing on a fallen tree trunk lying in front of him. Even with this advantage, she barely came up to his chest.

"Thaddeus of Beewicke, welcome. Behold your Queen."

He recognized the figure at once—Caerulea. She had changed, though, since he'd last seen her. Her abdomen was now swollen and protuberant. He feared she was ill. He remembered when he was a small boy, his mother's only sister, Aunt Auricia, had developed a growth like that and had come to live with them for a while. Later, she had become more seriously ill, turned yellow, and died in the spring. Caerulea, however, did not look sick. In fact, as far as he could tell, she glowed with health—for a great-winged blue person.

She took his hand in hers. "I know you have not much time this night, fair Thaddeus, so I will tell you that all is well, though My Lord Spadix has, of late, been in a right state. Well, that is his fault, is it not? Perhaps he should not spend so many evenings away from his Queen, chasing about all night with common moths. It may be possible that even a Lord can learn a lesson." The regal blue lady smiled and, standing on tiptoe, kissed Thaddeus firmly on the mouth. Thaddeus became aware of several of his "new feelings," as he called them.

"I know you must go, brave Thaddeus. Worry not. I will send word when all is complete." With that, she leaped into the air and resumed her circling flight around the spider, with her court in tow, as the entire company bared their wiggling bottoms at the enraged but impotent arachnid.

Thaddeus waved to the *Lepidopterae* and continued his journey. "It's like a big circle," he said aloud as he moved away from the woodland scene. He stole a look back over his shoulder to see the web, spider, and butterflies shrinking in size, growing rapidly smaller and smaller. "Or is it that I'm getting bigger?"

Presently, the path opened up into a broad meadow where a riot of blooming flowers covered every inch of the broad expanse. It struck him as strange—what flowers remained open at night? The bright, vivid colors were a counterpoint to the heady fragrance wafting across the field to him—intoxicating, transporting. In the midst of the meadow, a slight, blossom-bedecked figure faced away from him, her white, gauzy raiment fluttering lazily in the light breeze. He gasped at the sight of the long black curls trailing down to her waist. He knew her.

"Ethne!" he called.

The figure turned and rushed toward him, smiling and laughing. She flung herself into his arms. "Thaddeus, my beloved! I hoped you would come!" With that, she drew him close and pulled his head down for a long, lingering kiss.

This was no pale, sickly girl from a city's back alleyway, but a vigorous, mature woman full of strength, energy, and the fire of life. He pushed her to arm's length to drink in the sight of her. Her cheeks were rose blushed, and her eyes sparkled. She did not cough.

"Ethne! How did—I mean, what's…?"

"Oh, my dearest, I am as you see me this night—as you would wish to see me. As I would wish to be seen by you. I am a dream come to you. Shh, don't speak. We have moments only." She again pulled him to her. "Oh, if only it could go on like this…"

Suddenly, her body began to change, to grow smaller, thinner, turn in upon itself. She coughed.

"Oh, my love…" Her abdomen began to swell, but, unlike that of the Queen of the Butterflies, it did not cause her to look flushed and vibrantly healthy. Rather, it was as if some giant worm were gnawing on her insides, consuming her from within. "We have—we have no more time, my sweet." A spasm of coughing racked her now-frail body. Blood trickled from her mouth. "I have no more…time. All my strength is… gone. I have given it to…another. I managed to do it, my love—for us…for us all. You will see…You will…"

Her color bleached. Her skin stretched, thinning. Her bones protruded. Her skin became transparent. She grew thinner and thinner until she dissolved into mist and was gone. The flowers from her hair, her neck, her gown fluttered slowly to the ground.

"No! No! Ethne! Come back!" Thaddeus sank to his knees, put his hands to his face, and wept. Great racking sobs shook his body. He cried until he was spent. His first love was lost to him. There would be no other.

Chapter 7

SOMNIA et NASUS CAERULEUS

* * *

After a time, Thaddeus opened his eyes. The meadow, once green and fecund, was now brown and sere. Dun-colored rocks poked raggedly through the ground, while dust plumes swirled by on random gusts of wind. He stumbled forward, dead leaves and twigs crunching under his feet. Just ahead, a flash of alb caught his eye. He lurched forward and found a single white flower—a rose. He bent over and picked it up, inhaling its fragrance. Cradling it carefully in his left hand, he sighed and strode away with only the moonlight for a friend.

When Thaddeus came to himself, he was walking along a dusty road, a weathered fence keeping him company on one side. He glanced about uncertainly. Lost in thought, he had been unaware of his surroundings for some time.

He passed an ancient willow, its gnarled roots sunk into the bank of a small, gurgling creek. At a bright peal of laughter, he glanced up to see a lithe young girl disappear behind the tree only to peek out at him a moment later from the other side of the trunk. Her olive-colored hair and bark-like skin marked her a dryad, and the willow, her tree. He did not stop, however, but walked on.

An hour had passed, by the course of the full moon, when, coming around a bend, he spied an old barn standing at one end of a field. The fence curved gradually away from the road to end at the far corner of the ancient structure, inviting him to follow. A lane marked the path leading to the barn. In front of the yawning entrance, a man with a wooden pitchfork was heaving piles of hay from the ground onto a sturdy wagon. A mule's harness hung on a peg outside the barn with a wooden plow parked beneath it. Thaddeus wondered fleetingly why a man would be working a farm by moonlight.

As Thaddeus approached, the man speared his fork into the ground and, leaning on it, took out a handkerchief and mopped his brow. He fetched an apple from his tunic, polished it for a moment on his leather vest, and took a bite.

The fellow was short and bowlegged but solidly built. He moved with a plodding strength born of practiced toil. His dark-gray hair and short beard accentuated his long face. Particularly arresting were his large brown eyes that appeared to miss nothing. Though Thaddeus had never seen the man before, he nevertheless seemed familiar.

"Hello," Thaddeus said, raising a hand in greeting.

"'Lo, lad. Care fer one?" The farmer held out a second apple while taking another bite of his own.

Thaddeus shook his head, and the extra apple disappeared back into the man's vest. "Is this your barn, sir?"

"Nay. It belongs to one R. Loxley. But I tends to it fer 'im. What do ye here, Young Master? An' by the by, ye need no' be callin' me 'sir' an' the like. Will no' know to whom ye're speakin.'"

"I've been walking this road for…a time. Do you know where it leads?"

"Aye, that I do, but it might depend a bit on yer destination. Do ye know where it is ye're bound?"

"Well, not exactly. It's all so strange. First I was with…" Thaddeus's voice trailed off. "Your pardon, I don't mean to be rude, but have we met before? I feel I should know you."

"Aye, well, that would no' surprise me, 'specially at a time like this. 'Tis true enough, though—I ha' been around, I has. An' sometimes it may depend upon the light. Ye know, someone may look different than what ye're expectin', though 'tis still the same one on the inside."

Thaddeus's thoughts drifted off again. When he came back to himself, he was staring at the white rose in his hand.

The farmer cleared his throat and gestured toward the flower. "I note ye've been to see the Lady. More to her than meets the eye, an' that's certain. Has a powerful strong love, she does. Would no' startle me to discover something verra grand comin' from all that."

The farmer shifted his weight from the pitchfork. As he did so, a stray shaft of moonlight glinted off a necklace he wore. Thaddeus had not noticed it before, but now he found it spellbinding—white globes of fire on an intricately worked chain. Why would a farmer be wearing such a necklace? Especially one like that?

The farmer caught Thaddeus's stare. "I see ye're admirin' me garnish. 'Tis the Lady herself as has gi'en it to me. Well, 'tis a pretty one to be true. An' ye niver knows when such a thing might come to be quite handy on down the line. But me wager is ye did no' come so far as this to be discussin' me personal choices in raiment. So, laddie, how is it I may help ye, fer I am inclined to do so, I vow?"

"I, um, I think I'm lost. I'm looking for my master. I've not seen him for some time. He said if I needed help, I should ask..." Thaddeus gazed at the ground. What was it the old man had said?

The farmer nodded, a twinkle in his eye. "I believes I knows what ye're sayin', lad. An' I believes I can show ye to yer master. Around here, he is, methinks. But 'tis best no' to disturb him outright. Let's sidle up to him quiet like. If he's no' preoccupied, he'll deal wi' ye, all right. But should he be distracted an' all, then ye may ha' to wait to see 'im another time. But we'll no' know that until we tries it—like wi' most things. Come on, then, lad, an' follow me."

The laborer led him around behind the barn to where the fence opened onto a large worked field, beyond which was a densely wooded area. They headed toward the trees. As they passed through the gate, Thaddeus noted a figure sitting on a stump off to the side apparently eating his lunch—probably a farmhand.

As they passed the figure, however, Thaddeus's impression changed drastically. The man was huge, with brown, bulging arms and chest. He had talons for fingers. The figure was dressed in a simple field hand's smock and tattered straw hat. The old farmer nodded to him, and the worker held up a hand in return. It was holding a half-eaten arm. Thaddeus blinked and looked again, but the stump, creature, and arm had disappeared, vanished.

"Pay it no mind, lad," the old farmer said over his shoulder without looking back. "Once ye ha' seen one, ye ha' seen 'em all."

Thaddeus and the older man continued across the recently turned field until they came to the edge of the forested area. "Now keep close by me, boy, an' exercise the greatest quiet. We'll no' wish to scare off our quarry."

The ground again sloped down until Thaddeus smelled water. But this time, the smell was of freshwater, not salt sea. The loam gradually gave way to sand, and the tree cover grew more sparse.

At last, the old farmer raised his hand to signal a halt and turned to Thaddeus. "What ye seek is on the other side o' the last tree, lad," he whispered. "Be cautious in yer lookin', though, or ye'll miss it entire. I must leave ye now, ha' others to attend to, I do. But fortune go wi' ye. If it ha' any meanin' to ye, know that ye are well favored in this place. Ne'er before ha' I known such a rankin', an from the old man himself—but do no' go aboot wi' yer head gettin' bigger'n yer bottom. 'Tis still a chancy thing, an' none there be who can say how it'll come out in the end. *Vale.*"

Thaddeus nodded in acknowledgment, though he took little meaning from what the farmer had said, and glanced toward the sound of gently lapping water. When he looked back to ask a question, however, the man was gone. Only a discarded apple core lay on the ground where he'd been standing.

Thaddeus took a careful step toward the last tree, a large sand pine. He carefully pushed aside an obscuring branch to disclose a placid lake surrounded by a white beach. Near the water's edge, a couple stood facing each other, holding hands. The man was young and robust with black hair and beard. He was dressed only in his short clothes, which were wet as if he'd recently been wading. The woman's hair, dark and straight, hung to her waist and clung to her figure. The lower half of her tunic was wet as well. Her head was tilted up at the man, while his was bent down to her. The man drew the woman to him and embraced her. Thaddeus's cheeks burned. As he prepared to let the branch fall back and leave the two to their privacy, the couple turned and stared directly at him. The man raised his hand, and blue light flashed from it.

Embarrassed at his discovery, Thaddeus beat a hasty retreat back up the path and mulled over what he had witnessed.

Walking briskly, he left the sound of the lapping water behind but soon realized he should have reached the field by now. He kept walking, hoping to see something he recognized. Nothing. Without knowing when it started, Thaddeus became aware of a humming—no, a buzzing—growing in intensity with each step he took. Though much louder than what he was used to, he recognized it. Within minutes, the sound was so loud as to be painful to his ears.

Thaddeus pushed through the last screen of bushes and tree limbs and came to a stop at the edge of a large glade in which there were thousands of milling bees. These were not just any bees, though. These bees were huge, the size of horses. He blinked and surveyed his surroundings to make sure his perspective hadn't changed, but everything seemed as it should. The leaves were the right size, the twigs were the right size, and he was the right size. Only the bees were out of proportion.

The buzzing sound steadily increased in volume until it became deafening. He looked up to see hundreds of the great creatures flying around in an intricate pattern he recognized as the signal for danger and opportunity. He craned his neck and stared into the maelstrom as far up as light and distance allowed. They all seemed busy. Without warning, one of the larger bees flew down and hovered in front of him, surveying him with its multifaceted eyes, its wings beating too rapidly to see. The chittering sounds it made constituted speech, a language he understood.

It spoke. *"Thaddeus of Beewicke, I am Princess here. We know you of old. For ten generations in our reckoning, you have gently tended our sisters. And we have reciprocated by fighting for you these days past. I am come to tell you not to tarry here. Your time is incomplete. Therefore, proceed through our glade. Affairs of great importance—some to you, some to us—await you on the other side. None will hinder you. Farewell."* The giant form abruptly lifted and flew upward in ever-widening circles, followed by her entire retinue, until she was lost to sight.

Intrigued, Thaddeus made his way to the center of the glade, now eerily empty. Several paths crossed. He could not tell one from the other. He chose the one just to the left of center, as it seemed the most inviting, and followed its twists and turns, which sloped upward.

For the third time this night, the young apprentice smelled water, and for the second time, it was the Sea. But on this occasion, the trail dead-ended on a high cliff overlooking a rocky shoreline where gray-flecked black waves crashed against the cliff base in never-ending succession. A sturdy stone tower, altogether striking to his eye, rose five stories if he'd counted the lighted, spaced windows correctly. It was the tallest building Thaddeus had ever seen and sat close to the cliff edge. A bare thread of a path wound its faint way up to the base of the structure.

Squinting, Thaddeus made out a small door that appeared to be open from the pale glow emanating from it. Striding purposefully brought him to the tower entrance. The salt tang, very pronounced here, made him lick his lips. He looked about but saw no one. He called out several times but received no answer. Shrugging, he entered.

The silver moonbeams stopped abruptly at the massive doorway, replaced by flickering light shed by torches set in sconces at intervals along the wall. Several doors led off the entry room, and a stairway curved upward. All the doors he tried were locked. He hesitated, then sighed and headed up the stairs. The stairway wound round and round, up the inner aspect of the outer wall. At each level was a small landing with a door leading to the interior, but they, too, were locked—except for the last one, which stood ajar.

Thaddeus gently pushed the door back and found himself in a short hallway with several more doors on either side. Only the last one was open. He walked cautiously down the hall and peered into the room. The large, airy suite was apportioned with fine, comfortable furniture, rugs, and accouterments, clearly suitable for a lord's estate. His eyes swept the room and stopped at the far end, where a solemn tableau was taking place amid the shadows.

Standing out from the far wall, a huge bed of some rich, dark wood was illuminated by a single large candle burning brightly on the headboard. Only one figure, the bed's occupant, was fully visible. The bedridden form, a frail and wasted elderly woman, lay unmoving, her mouth open. Thaddeus feared she was dead, but with concentration, he detected slow, shallow breathing. Her arms, outside the fine white linen coverlet, framed her body. One of her hands was grasped by a shadowy figure off to one side, whose own arm was clothed in dark green with a swatch of thick fur bordering the sleeve. The man's hand, though strong and firm, was also aged. A large gold ring, set with a glinting green stone, encircled his fourth finger. Her husband,

Thaddeus knew of an instant, though he could not say how. The man to whom the arm belonged was kneeling by the bed, his face in the crook of his other arm, his body racked and heaving.

As his eyes adjusted to the dark, Thaddeus became aware of twelve other figures gathered at the deathbed vigil, men and women in equal number. All were tall—some dark, others fair—and in their middle years. As a group, they were fine of feature and elegantly dressed. All but one of the men wore medallions, ribbons, and sashes and carried swords of various descriptions. The remaining man wore a dark robe. The comely women were likewise dressed elaborately in colorful gowns. The most senior looking of the men stood next to the kneeling lord with a hand placed comfortingly on his shaking shoulders.

A moment passed, and the elderly woman's breathing slowed further, then ceased. As one, the men and women ranged around the bed bowed their heads.

"She has died," Thaddeus said in a whisper and offered a brief Prayer for the Dead. When he looked up, however, he was shocked to see the old woman's head turned toward him and, eyes open, staring at him intently. A smile spread across her face.

The ring of mourners remained immobile in their grief, seemingly unaware of the dramatic change in the deceased's condition. The woman released her hand from the man's grip and, gazing at him tenderly, brushed his beard-covered cheek with her hand. She then sat up and pushed herself off the bed. After standing for a moment in her night shift, she walked across the floor and came to a halt in front of the gaping apprentice.

The woman was tall, yet looked up to Thaddeus. Her smile was somehow familiar, and, after a moment, she spoke. “Be not alarmed, Thaddeus. I know you, though you know me not. I wish none but the best for thee. My time with you this night is limited, though, and I am constrained from speaking with you concerning all I know. This is very difficult for me, but I would give it all up again to see you as you are now. Follow me closely. I have something of great import to show you.”

The woman turned and left the room, heading confidently down the circling stairway with Thaddeus following obediently. They made their way out of the tower and traced the path back to the woods, where more paths branched off the main trail than Thaddeus remembered. As they passed by one, the sound of raucous laughter caught his attention, and he paused to stare. A short distance down this path, a roaring bonfire blazed, in front of which three figures—young women, none of whom had on so much as a stitch—were gyrating wildly in time to the pulsating flames, flinging themselves about and laughing hysterically.

Behind the group stood an ancient beech tree, to which was attached a short young boy, bound chin to ankle with ropes, suspended halfway up the trunk in an inverted position. This circumstance did not seem to trouble the boy, who was grinning and laughing along with the women, keeping time to the dance by bobbing his head rhythmically—all this while constrained upside down.

Thaddeus laughed. "Well, Anders, you finally got your wish."

Thaddeus turned away to find the tall lady looking at him, quirking a smile. "And do you wish to join them, then, Thaddeus of Beewicke?"

Chagrined, Thaddeus's cheeks flamed. "Uh, no, no. That's fine. Um, we should probably press on. I'm sure it's getting late." Not for all the sage in Calumnia would he have admitted that the thought had, briefly, crossed his mind.

The two walked on silently. Thaddeus noted the elderly woman had an easy, though mysterious, grace about her. Regarding her more closely, he guessed she'd been bewitchingly beautiful in her youth.

Soon, the forest gave way to a more rocky terrain with, at first, large stones, then great boulders littering the landscape. The air grew steadily warmer and arid. Thaddeus's nose began to burn. Finally, the lip of a huge rocky ridge reared up, blocking their path.

The woman turned to face her charge. "I must leave you now, young Thaddeus. Proceed on up just over the edge of this ridge. There you may receive enlightenment." She did not move to leave him but stood gazing at him quietly. Tears welled in her eyes. Of a sudden, she reached up and gently stroked the side of his face in the manner she had the man at her bedside. "It is so hard," she whispered, then turned and walked away into the shadows. Within seconds, she was gone.

Thaddeus stared at the spot where she'd stood, then squared his shoulders and climbed to the edge of the rock formation. Mounting the crest of the ridge, he looked down upon an immense circular crater spread out before him. He could barely make out the far rim. Great stone spires, like giant spikes, rose from the floor of the basin at irregular intervals. Hot gases and vapors vented from cracks and fumaroles in the tortured surface. At the center of the depression, a huge pool of bubbling molten rock, in violent reds, yellows, and whites, was punctuated by great gouts of fire that leaped skyward every few seconds.

Without warning, the night grew darker, and the moon faded as if a great cloud had passed in front of it. Even the fires died down.

Thaddeus, unsure of what to do, recalled that he was to receive enlightenment, so he sat down on a small boulder near the edge of the crater and gazed at the center of the pit. As he stared, an outline of a tremendous figure began to form, hazily at first, then sharpening and solidifying. The figure was that of a demon—at least, it reminded him of Charles—but huge, vast, blotting out the moonlight, then the entire sky.

It reared up and up, with massive ribbed wings and talons, yellow slits for eyes, and a sinuous forked tongue that flicked in and out. The immense demon seemed unaware of Thaddeus's inconsequential presence, for which the boy was profoundly grateful.

As the figure filled in and became even more solid, its attention focused on its tightly closed left fist. After a time, the demon slowly opened his clawed hand. As he did, an intense, brilliant white light spilled out between his fingers. The glare was so bright, Thaddeus could not bear to look directly at it.

The demon gazed down at the blaze resting in his palm, regarding the light for a long moment. Then, as if having made a decision, he raised his right arm in a great arc and smote it down on the light in his palm with all the force at his command. The result was instantaneous, spectacular, and cataclysmic, as if the entire universe was exploding. Thaddeus started so violently he fell backward off the boulder. Regaining his seat, he discovered the explosion had shattered the demon himself, who, with a terrible bellow, was torn asunder into an infinite number of bits and pieces. These fragments flew apart in all directions, filling the night sky from horizon to horizon as they streamed outward at speeds faster than Thaddeus could comprehend.

He stared as each dark speck grew in size and brightness, forming different shapes—some a globe, others an ellipse or spiral. Occasionally, at the very center of each, black pits began to distort and grow into miniature replicas of the Great Daemon himself, which gobbled up the small fiery balls nearest them as fast as they could dip them up with one clawed hand after another. They never stopped eating.

Smaller demons were present as well, zipping away to the edge of a spiral, which grew in size at incredible speeds.

A movement caught his eye. One of the globes, a flying rock, was speeding toward the center of the nearest cluster in the spiral. It was a deep red-orange with cones of fire spouting flames from its surface. But what drew his attention were yet smaller demons—the globe was covered with them. As he watched, the demon rock headed toward one of the circling globes greater in size than itself by a factor of four.

The bright red ball, growing larger as it neared, appeared to be the demons' intended target. The orb was starkly beautiful, hanging in the black, velvety space as if magically suspended, though fiery cones erupted from its surface as well. It was solitary and, unlike most of the other globes in this system, displayed no other globes circling it.

As the intruder sped closer, a name rose in his consciousness—*Bellona.* The demons riding the smaller ball grew more agitated as it sped toward the larger solitary globe. The impact, Thaddeus knew, would be catastrophic. He held his breath.

The orange-hued demon ball struck the larger red globe at an angle. In a cataclysmic explosion, the surfaces of both bodies began to crumble and explode outward as the remnant of the demon rock swung back around, held in the grip of some unseen force, and smashed into the red rock again. A second titanic explosion occurred with flames shooting out from both bodies. The smaller orange rock vaporized, and the detritus from the collision thrown off from the surface of the larger rock came to form a ring around the remaining red globe, made up of bits of dust swept into a great circle around the larger body.

Unless his eyes were playing tricks, the demons on the smaller orange rock had all been thrown into the boiling center of the larger body by the force of the impact. Before any of the maniacal survivors could escape, they were sealed beneath the raging fires by a mixture of molten rock and iron.

"Like honey poured over ants," Thaddeus said aloud.

Clearly, the demons were now trapped inside the center of the larger red globe. Had that been their plan, the boy wondered, or had something gone terribly wrong?

The encirlced red rock gradually cooled, and more changes occurred. The flotsam and jetsam from the tremendous impact that formed the ring began to coalesce into a new, smaller pale globe that gradually pulled away from the red rock, coming to orbit its large red partner with one face perpetually turned toward it.

The greater change, however, occurred to the red ball itself. As the globe cooled, storms scoured its surface. With time, the color of the rock changed. What had at first been a tortured red ball turned into a shining blue globe, layered over with wisps of white. It was truly beautiful. But not all was peaceful. Every so often, an eruption took place on the surface of the azure globe.

Thaddeus nodded. "It's the demons. They don't like being trapped inside there—they want to be free."

"Aye, lad. It's the way o' things, ain' it now?"

Startled, Thaddeus whirled to face the laborer, who stood in a casual pose, chewing on a blade of grass.

"Sorry, boy. Did no' mean to surprise ye, but 'tis late, an' it occurred to me that ye've seen a great deal tonight an' liked to be tirin' in the process, p'rhaps wishin' fer yer covers an' whatnot. If I ha' the right o' it, then come along, an' I'll be seein' ye safely back to yer camp."

Thaddeus, bemused and tired in body, yawned and fell in behind the older man without speaking. The path continued its gentle arc, and, passing by a grove of red maples, Thaddeus caught sight of Rolland. At least, the person he spied had red hair.

A large blanket was laid out on the grass by a copse of trees, and a generous open hamper attested to the remains of a hearty luncheon. In the middle of the blanket, Rolland sat with two others. One was a middle-aged woman with fiery red hair who kneeled behind him, smiling and massaging his neck in a maternal way. The other figure, also middle-aged, was a dark-headed man sporting several nautical tattoos on his exposed arms. The resemblance among them was obviously more than chance. Rolland and the man were gazing down at a playing board with little carved figures upon it that lay on the blanket between them. From time to time, one or the other reached down and moved a figure on the board.

In the distance, a rooster crowed.

"Aye, lad, we'll be needin' to pick up the pace a bit. I got to get back, meself. I'm sure there'll be no one o' the party wishin' to see me in this fashion, an' that's the certain o' it."

Thaddeus followed with only half his mind, the other half mulling through a myriad of feelings and sensations, all jumbled together. The melange included fatigue, racing thoughts, hanging questions, new ideas, revelations, prophecies, and hidden dangers. He was unsure if he'd ever be able to sort them all out.

Moments later, the farmer stopped at the edge of the forest and pointed out the campsite. "There ye be, laddie. Now try an' get some rest. 'Tis niver a good go to expect to work marvels when ye be at the point o' physical collapse. Good repose to ye." With that, the older man turned back toward the wood and vanished.

The apprentice, however, did not immediately move to find his bed but sat down on a nearby log by a stand of walnut trees, still considering the evening's events. Small *Faerrae* folk—field *Pixae* by their appearance—danced and gamboled amidst the morning dewdrops by his feet, but he paid them no mind.

A trumpeting birdcall off to the west caught Thaddeus's attention as a large black swan with rider came winging into the meadow next to the camp. After the beautiful sable bird glided to a smooth landing, a small figure slid gracefully off its back, stroked the bird's neck affectionately, then headed for the tents. It was one of the girls. Judging from her height, it had to be Nannsi. The girl turned at her tent flap and waved as the swan leaped into the air and flew back the way it had come. Staring after the beautiful bird, she nodded once and entered her tent.

The tent flap had just dropped shut behind her when, from the east, a thudding of hooves heralded a brilliant horse-drawn carriage, bright with lights and flowers. The glowing conveyance slowed to a stop at the edge of the camp, and a uniformed footman hopped down to open the carriage door, where he handed Sonnia down. He then bowed gracefully and hoisted himself onto the rear of the carriage, which turned in an artful circle and swept out of sight. Sonnia was dressed in an ornate *Stola*, her hair piled high atop her head in an intricate coiffure set off with a glittering tiara. She smiled wistfully as she watched the carriage depart. Then she, too, sought her tent.

Thaddeus peered into the distance, wondering how Marsia would make her appearance, and was therefore startled to hear her voice behind him.

"Hello, Thaddeus. Oh, I'm sorry. I didn't mean to take you unaware. I just left the forest and saw you sitting here, so I thought I'd join you. How was your evening? Did you see anything strange? I certainly did." She seated herself beside him on the log.

Thaddeus's heart began to race, and his mouth was suddenly dry. The moonlight was fading, and the rose of dawn tinted the eastern sky. He was pleased she'd sought him out.

"I-I, oh, I don't know. It's all been very strange. I'm not sure I even know where to begin."

"That's all right. I feel the same way. It was interesting, though, wasn't it? Part dream, part smoke, I think."

Thaddeus nodded, gazing into Marsia's eyes. And for a moment, he thought he saw...

The rooster crowed for the second time.

"Well, I expect we'd better get to bed. Good repose, Thaddeus. I'll see you in the morning."

"Good repose to you, too, Marsia. We didn't have much time to talk, though," he added hurriedly.

"Ah, it's not the number of words, is it?" Marsia gave him a smile, rose, and headed for her tent. At the entrance, she turned and, with a wave, ducked inside.

Thaddeus stood, stretched, and yawned. Without volition, his feet turned and tracked toward his bedroll, when the distant sound of blaring trumpets rang out over the campsite. From around one of the hillocks to the south emerged a great procession with a magnificent golden chariot in the lead drawn by four matched emerald-green firedrakes, each roaring and belching flames every few steps. All manner of fey folk accompanied the chariot, including nymphs strewing rose petals in its path, winged *Spritae* blowing elaborate fanfares on long polished-brass horns, and *Aelvae* choristers following, raising silvery voices on high, declaring for the celebrants. Standing at the reins was the strong-sinewed man with black hair and beard Thaddeus had seen at the shore, but he now wore a golden coronet upon his brow and was dressed in robes of white samite. The dark-haired lady standing proudly at his side was similarly attired with a golden diadem circling her forehead. One arm was locked in her escort's, with the other gracefully poised on the chariot rail.

Thaddeus watched transfixed as the stately procession crossed the short plain until it vanished behind the last hillock on the far side of the camp. Moments passed before a movement at the other side of the hill caught his attention. But only two people emerged, and he knew them instantly. They walked slowly, as befitted their age. A tall older man in a worn traveling robe, and a just-past-middle-age woman in black, leaning on his arm, made their way to the campsite. At her tent, Mistress Geanninia bade Master Silvestrus good repose. She disappeared inside, and the old sorcerer went to his bedroll. Turning, he caught sight of Thaddeus and gestured, pointing to the boy's blankets.

Neither Anders nor Rolland had returned, but he didn't fear for them. Sighing, he made his way to his bedding, pulled the covers up around his ears, and plunged into a deep and dreamless sleep. Just before he dozed off, he thought he heard a rooster crow a third time.

* * *

A light wind brushed Thaddeus's face, and he awoke to the low murmur of voices. He opened his eyes lazily. The sky, a wonderful translucent blue, was interspersed with fluffy puffs of brilliant white clouds. Turning on his side, he observed Master Silvestrus in conversation with Asullus, but of his fellows, there was not a trace, and the ladies' tent flaps were still closed.

Stretching languidly, he rose, strolled over to the bushes, scratched himself, then walked back to join the others.

"Good morrow, lad. Slept well, I trust? Intriguing night, do you not agree? On another matter, Thaddeus, could you tell me what went with that hamper of green weed Asullus and I gathered the other day?"

The old sorcerer's eyes danced with mischief, but Thaddeus was unsure of his mood or exactly how he should respond. "Well, Master, that is to say, I..." he stammered.

"Ah, pay it no mind, Thaddeus. There is always more of everything in the forest. But, you know, I do believe I will ask Rolland about it more specifically. Perhaps he will have an idea. Speaking of Rolland, I have a task for you. I would like you to go and scout about for your two comrades. They seem to be lost. I do not fear for them, certainly, but boys your age should never miss a good breakfast following a long night in the woods, as it were. Asullus will go with you."

"Yes, Master. Right away," Thaddeus said, grateful for any diversion. He walked over to the mule.

Asullus jerked his head toward the north, and they started off.

"Ye know, laddie, if an' when we e'er get to the *Collegium*, ye'll be arrivin' replete wi' legends concernin' yerselves already in place, methinks."

"I don't follow you, Asullus."

"Oh, don' ye now? Well, 'tis simple enough. How many o' yer friends from back home would ye say ha' fought robbers, seen demons, wooed lassies, courted butterflies, killed street villains, rescued wolf dogs, transformed religious madmen, played ogre's bladder, an' made off wi' a hamperful of yer master's own smokin' narcotic at yer age—an' all in a few days' time? No' so many, I'd be wagerin'." The mule snorted with laughter. "No, no' so many at all. They'll be tellin' tales aboot this trip fer years to come. Heh heh heh. Course I ha' to be sayin'—an' 'tis a surprise to me entire—the old man is takin' it all in good stride. He seems to ha' a tolerance fer yer bewilderin' gaffes an' gaws like might be expected o' a proud an' dotin' greatpa, don' ye know. Quite amazin', it all is. I ha' meself seen him flay a man alive fer much less. Much less."

"Well, I hadn't thought of it like that. But, you know, these things just happened. I mean, it wasn't as if it was all of a purpose, just..."

"O' course. No one there'd be who'd plan such an itinerary. But all the same, this be no common series o' events, e'en on trips such as these. An' as I told ye in the beginnin', I ha' been on a fair few o' them o'er the years meself. No, laddie, there's summat special goin' aboot, make no mistake. Further, let me add, in spite o' what ye usually be used to hearin' me say, this ol' mule be havin' quite a time wi' it all. Quite a time indeed. Well, enough aboot that. Let's be lookin' out fer the other two young masters. Elsewise, we'll just ha' to go back, get two more, an' start all o'er again. Way too much work fer an old servitor such as meself. Here, let's try this trail."

The pair headed into the woods and took the path Asullus suggested. Thaddeus had always felt close to the old mule and had developed an affection for him over their time together. On impulse, he reached out and patted Asullus's shoulder. The mule glanced sideways, winked, and returned to scanning the forest path. Farther on, in a small clearing, they came upon the smoldering remains of a bonfire and found Anders fast asleep at the foot of an ancient tree. Rope burns marked his wrists and ankles, but, otherwise, he seemed to be in one piece. He was smiling.

Thaddeus knelt down and shook his friend's shoulder gently. "Anders. Anders! Wake up! Nannsi's here, and she wants to see you!"

The pudgy boy's eyes flicked open. "Wha? Who? Oh, it's you, Thaddeus. I thought you said—oh, um, hello, Asullus. What are you two doing here? Where is everybody?" Anders rubbed his eyes. "I was just... just...hmm..."

Asullus prodded him with a hoof. "Quick as a snake, as I ha' said on many occasions. No wonder he's to be a sorcerer. Come on, lad, 'Tis time fer ye to put yer cobwebs away an' come wi' us in lookin' fer that thievin' an' purse-snatchin' partner o' yers. If ye're here, he's bound to be around an' aboot as well."

Thaddeus gave his young friend a hand up.

Anders kneaded his back as if getting out the kinks, then looked at his fellow apprentice, all manner of questions in his eyes.

"Later," Thaddeus mouthed.

Anders nodded, and the three set off back down the path.

Soon they came to another clearing, where they found Rolland, also asleep under a tree. He, however, had a different reaction when awakened. As Thaddeus knelt down to stir his friend, he noted tear tracks running down the boy's face.

At a shake, the former thief opened red, swollen eyes, glanced quickly around, then whispered, "Thaddeus, a moment. P-Please."

Thaddeus blinked but stood up quickly and turned to the other two. "Anders, Asullus, follow me over here while Rolland is getting his wits together. I want to show you something really important. You see, last night I saw a Great Daemon. It was the biggest thing I've ever seen, and it filled the entire sky. It was just over here in this depression, I think. Did either of you see it? There were showers of other demons, too, all over, and..." Thaddeus, still talking, led the two down the path.

Anders, looking concerned, stopped. "Thaddeus, what was that all about? Is Rolland not well? Is there something we should do?"

"Ne'er ye mind, laddie, yer thief'll be right as rain in no time flat," the mule interjected. 'Tis lucky fer all o' ye that ye ha' each other. 'Tis a rare thing, indeed, an' perhaps one o' the few areas in life where ye boys are excellin' o'er the common sticks an' stones as always is to be found on the ground, I must say. 'Tis proud I am o' ye all. Well, that is fer now."

Rolland joined the group after a few minutes, his usual jaunty smile in place and all trace of any other state vanished away.

Thaddeus led the way back to the campsite at an unhurried pace as the apprentices shared portions of their adventures from the previous night.

When they returned, Mistress Geanninia and the girls were up and had begun preparing a combined late breakfast and early midday. Without discussion, the boys joined in, fetching wood and water and performing whatever tasks seemed needful. The master and his mistress sat on their usual log and smilingly watched their charges willingly work together.

The conversation among the young workers was initially tentative, then increased apace as if the participants couldn't wait to tell of their night's experiences—and perceptions. Each tale was different from the others.

Thaddeus talked chiefly about his vision of the Great Daemon, while Anders spoke shyly of being at a prestigious center of learning where, at a relatively young age, he became a respected master, and, later, a beloved one as well. Concerning upside-down bonfires, he was altogether silent. Sonnia regaled the group with a vision of an assignation with a wealthy and powerful noble, court intrigues, and the subtle wielding of vast political power. Nannsi was a bit more reluctant to describe her experiences, but did say her time was spent in pursuit of the fine arts, such as singing and dancing. Strangely red-faced, Anders looked away whenever she spoke of these things. She later added details concerning sensations of flying and observations of bird lore. Marsia said little other than noting scenes involving close family ties. She seemed alternately sad, then blushed whenever she looked at Thaddeus. Rolland was the least forthcoming, though after Marsia acknowledged material concerning families, he was able to say he, too, had felt, "something like that." Otherwise, he kept his own counsel. The master and mistress would only say it had been an extraordinary experience, much had been learned, and if a similar opportunity presented itself again, it would be all right with them.

The rest of the discussion centered around whether the various personal visions were prophetic, historic, idiosyncratic, allegoric, or hallucinatory in nature—or, perhaps, some combination. The subject of burning weeds was not broached.

The midsummer day was pleasantly warm, and after cleaning up, an impromptu game of *Pila Ludere* was unanimously endorsed. Asullus was prevailed upon to reprise his role as *Arbiter*, and everyone participated. One difference, however—the players in this game changed sides regularly, depending on the score. Earnest alliances and black-hearted betrayals occurred with equal frequency. Even Master Silvestrus and Mistress Geanninia participated, the latter showing a measure of leg with her skirts hiked up.

"I could run a pace or two when I was a slip of a girl at school, you see." After one particularly close call, she even had it out nose to nose with Asullus.

"Tsk-tsk. Such language," Rolland said, grinning for once, while the three boys stood casually with their arms folded, watching the theater.

"So that's how you pronounce it," Anders observed clinically. "I'd always wondered."

The mule, however, was unmoved by any profane threats involving dog food or glue.

Amid much laughter, Bellis raced in and out among the players, scoring at will for either side whenever she could steal the ball. Anders cheated shamelessly and, on one occasion, assisted Nannsi in scoring a dramatic goal against significant odds. He was rewarded with an enthusiastic buss from his partner in front of everyone, causing him to turn progressive shades of red. He failed, however, to lodge any complaint with the referee, though the mule asked slyly several times if Anders would rather institute a penalty.

For Thaddeus, the highlight of the day was the opportunity to again run down the field with the tall honey blonde, but this time, they were on the same side, scoring together.

That evening, after eventide, Thaddeus and Marsia sat next to each other on their log, smiling, stealing glances, and exchanging small conversation. Rolland smiled as well but seemed preoccupied, his thoughts elsewhere and his tongue uncharacteristically quiet. Sonnia was impatient with the proceedings, as if she wanted to be off and about the rest of her life-to-be. Nannsi gave Anders a list of what she considered categorical dos, don'ts, and cautions to steer him through his next several years of study.

"He's only a boy. I'm sure he can hardly strap his sandals," she said to no one in particular.

The master then stood and, with the leaping fire at his back, declared that the evening would be dedicated to wondrous tale spinning and other diverse entertainment. To set the mood, he offered up a harrowing adventure concerning a spotted troll, a mermaid, and a mad centaur. The mistress, in turn, told a story of a tragic love triangle among a virgin, a knight's squire, and a nymph, which resulted in much eye dabbing toward the end. Thaddeus gave an amusing account of a lost forest-cave bear cub and a village beehive, while Rolland casually walked his way around the circle of the audience making lighthearted jests and performing sleight-of-hand displays while methodically, and without notice, relieving his audience one by one of their valuables—displaying them at the end to the astonished group. Anders spoke from his store of historic lore, and the girls performed an intricate pageant of song with dance. Thaddeus thought they were very good and, along with Anders, clapped loudly.

Eventually, Silvestrus again rose and gave a benediction to the evening. "All good things must run to their natural conclusion, and we are now at ours. Tomorrow we must sunder our glad company and go our own ways, according to our appointed tasks. As solace, I can only say that our retained memories will stand in for true experience until we may next meet. But I have always found that the more vivid and wonderful the memories, the more often they can be reexperienced. And, sometimes, a measure of the original pleasure can be retained in that way." He cast an intimate glance at the mistress. "As for myself, I will now drag my weary bones to a well-deserved rest, and I imagine the lovely Mistress Geanninia will wish to do the same. Rolland, I would ask that you and Sonnia clear up the grounds here at the campsite before turning in. Anders, Nannsi, perhaps I could prevail upon you two to make a sweep of the south side of the camp and around the nearest hillock for any possessions overlooked there or back at the playing field. Thaddeus, Marsia, if you both would be so kind as to check on Asullus and the horses before you retire and also see to the north side and the near forest area. Something may have been left there inadvertently. Now, thank you all and good repose."

* * *

Thaddeus and Marsia walked side by side along the tree-lined path that was dappled gray and black in the bright moonlight. Almost by accident their hands brushed and gently clasped. After a moment they slowed, then stopped, facing each other.

"I, um…It was wonderful meeting you, and I hope, I mean…maybe…" Thaddeus's heart pounded in his chest, and his pulse raced in his ears. He savaged himself for sounding an utter fool. He expected the tall girl to turn on her heel and walk away in despair at his backcountry clumsiness, and he wouldn't have blamed her if she had.

Against all logic, however, she smiled, moved toward him, and kissed him full upon the lips.

He was transported.

She then stepped back a pace and reached into her robe before taking a deep breath. "Thaddeus, I have come, in this short time, to feel toward you in a very special way. In my family, when we have met someone we like especially, it is customary to give them a gift. I have something that would please me if you would accept it." She opened her hand, upon which lay a small greenstone. "I do not know if it is so, but my greatmother has told me this greenstone has been in our family for many years and is said to have certain felicitous powers when used by someone with the Talent. I am unaware of just what these might be, but I think this stone may sometimes influence how people regard us. I would like you to have it."

"Oh, Marsia, I can't take something that was given you by your greatmother. It's a priceless gem, I'm certain, and should be kept in your family."

"Well, perhaps it will be. But, please, do not spurn my gift. I greatly desire that you have it—for a remembrance."

Thaddeus could only stare at the ground while waves of shame welled up inside him. "I-I have nothing of any value to give you in return."

"Yes, you do, Thaddeus. More than you know. And perhaps you already have." She smiled again, then moved toward him and gave him another kiss.

His head swam, and he could hardly stand up—honey knees, indeed.

After a moment, Marsia stepped back again. "We should probably be getting back. I would hate for them to have the bother of looking for us." Nevertheless, she did not move away immediately but stood looking deeply into his eyes. She then reached up and gently stroked the side of his face. A roaring began in his ears, not the roaring of the sorcery so recently learned, but that of a far more ancient and powerful magic.

* * *

The small, golden-haired girl stood in the shadow of one of the old oaks watching the young lovers kiss. Luperca sighed. What was her future mate doing with that tall, gangling girl? She knew the answer to her own question, of course, but that didn't make it any easier to accept. Once Old Mattom the Wise of River's Wood, Chief Druid Madigan's father, had told her about the stranger who would one day rescue her, and by whom she would birth a High Priestess, it had been just a matter of waiting. But she'd made too many assumptions and hadn't asked nearly enough questions. For example, she'd assumed her new mate would come to her rather than the reverse. Also, she'd assumed she would have her new mate to herself rather than have to share him. And, she'd assumed that once they met, he'd know her for whom she was, and they would never be parted thereafter. Well, none of this was working out the way it should, and she wasn't very pleased with any of it. But that wasn't his fault—or at least, not entirely.

She sighed again. He was clearly going to go on to the *Collegium* and remain for his years of training. True, she could go there and stay with him as Bellis—how she'd come to treasure that name!–but it was always cold, windy, and dark that far north, and winter was coming, which would make it even worse. Not that she couldn't abide the frozen wastes—she'd been born in that setting—and not that she wouldn't be spending most of her time snuggled up by the fire in the apprentices' quarters, but she'd still have to go outside sometimes, and the back-and-forth of such climatic extremes was almost worse than the constant winter.

Also, she was positive the masters there would be as intolerant of her true wolf form in the dormitories as they would be of her tawny-braided siren form.

Of course, the boy would have to leave the College eventually, and what were a few years to a wolf? She would be waiting for him, but not right at his doorstep. She would know when the time was right, and she would find him, just like she'd found him the first time—but this time without a madman beating her nigh to death. That had not been pleasant, but Corrigan had now reaped a richly deserved reward. That she'd allowed herself to become careless in her excitement and had to suffer the consequences constituted what Mother would call "an education."

Her thoughts returned to the tall, freckled boy. He was so handsome, so brave, so gentle—and so powerful. He reminded her of Father. What a story they had already experienced—ogres, maniacs, *Pila Ludere*, and all the rest. He made her current consort, Blue Tooth, seem rather humdrum by comparison.

Well, there was nothing for it but to wait. She needed to have another litter soon, in any case, to replace the one she'd lost to the ogre. Maybe she'd have two or three. It would give her something to do while waiting for her Thaddeus. And if she had to share him after they had their daughter, well…she'd have to think about that.

In an instant, the little girl vanished, and in her place stood the great golden pack leader. Sniffing the air one last time, she turned and made her way westward. It was long past time to return to her den and be about her lupine business. Her pack needed a keen nose on their courses if they were to continue their current prosperity. It was her responsibility, after all.

* * *

Thaddeus was aroused by the sound of activity and rolled over to discover packing preparations were already proceeding apace. The apprentice jumped up and kicked Anders and Rolland awake, then went to see what he could do to help, joined shortly by his two sleepy-eyed friends.

The horses were fitted out and made ready for travel. Tents were folded and belongings packed. In between tasks, the group stopped to grab bites of cold leftovers.

Thaddeus and Marsia had time for only snatches of conversation—most of their communication occurred visually. Once, when he was sure she was looking, he patted his purse holding the greenstone so Marsia would know her treasured gift was being kept safe.

Nannsi continued to add to the list of admonitions she'd given Anders the previous night and occasionally stopped to fuss over him and brush off a stray blade of grass from his tunic. He listened attentively, endured patiently, and offered no protest.

Sonnia paid absolutely no attention to Thaddeus. She was the first packed and arrayed by her horse in her traveling robe, pacing back and forth and impatiently slapping her riding gloves against her palm.

Rolland was even more quiet and withdrawn than he had been the night before. Thaddeus asked him several times how he was doing and if all were well with him. He always gave an affirmative answer, which seemed, however, less than heartfelt.

At last, all was in readiness. Mistress Geanninia made amends with Asullus, then lined up her girls, after which Master Silvestrus marched down the row pressing hands and presenting a whiskered cheek to each in turn.

For her part, Mistress Geanninia embraced the boys warmly one by one, offering comforting words. She spent a longer time in earnest discussion with Rolland and, after leaving him, reflected a look of concern.

When she came to Thaddeus, she kissed his cheek warmly and whispered, "People to whom we are important never forget us, dear boy."

The ladies mounted their horses and turned them to the west, setting off in single file with Mistress Geanninia in the lead. Nannsi kept glancing over her shoulder at Anders and dabbing her eyes, while Anders seemed totally miserable. Sonnia rode line straight, head held high, but Marsia looked steadfastly back, waving and smiling bravely until distance took her. Thaddeus waved his arm in great arcs until it ached as much as his heart.

When the party was out of sight, Thaddeus turned and went to his pack for a final inspection. He was in a black pit of despair, with an empty hollowness gnawing at him from within. Although he knew if this meeting had never taken place he'd have no pain at all, he still would not have forgone the experience, the heartache of deepest melancholy notwithstanding.

Tying a final knot, he looked up to witness Rolland, his pack slung over one shoulder, disappearing north into the wooded area. Seeing that Master Silvestrus and Anders were involved in a discussion with Asullus, he sprinted after his friend and soon caught sight of him.

"Rolland! Rolland! Wait! Where are you going?" As the thief did not respond, he increased his pace and soon overtook the redhead, grabbing him by the arm.

"Get off me!" Rolland cried, shaking off Thaddeus's grip.

"Rolland, what are you doing?"

"I'm getting the Hells out of here, you backcountry turdhead! What does it look like?"

"Yes, I can see that. But why?"

Rolland stopped and turned toward his fellow apprentice. "It's no good! It's not going to work! I don't belong here! Faran was right—I belong in the gutter!"

Thaddeus was shocked at the intensity of his friend's pain and certainty. "Rolland, wait. I don't know what any of this is about, but I think I should tell you—last night, I saw you with…some people. A lady and a man. They sort of looked like you. I was thinking they were your family. Does that have anything to do with it?"

Rolland had been staring at the ground when a familiar voice intruded on their tableau. "Thaddeus, Rolland, good. I was looking for you both. Thaddeus, please return to the campsite and assist the others with the last of the preparations. We leave shortly. Rolland, I would speak with you."

"Yes, Master." Thaddeus gave his friend a last glance, turned, and ran back to the camp, a wild jumble of emotions coursing through his heart. On arrival, he immediately hailed Anders and told him what he'd witnessed.

Anders whistled. "I'm not surprised. I was talking with the master when, all of a sudden, he looked past me toward the woods and took off in a line like one of your bees. So, Rolland was that upset? It's too bad he and Sonnia didn't get on better. It might have helped distract him. You know, though, I think you're right. It must have something to do with his family. You remember when we first met him and how he looked when Master talked to him about those things?"

"Yes, that's right. Has Asullus said anything?"

"Only, 'Ah, no' to worry, laddie. The old man knows what it is he's aboot,'" Anders said in a perfect imitation.

Thaddeus glanced over to see the mule standing stock-still, gazing northward.

"Psst! Thaddeus. Give me a hand getting these cook pots and supplies into the cart, will you? I think it would be good for us to look busy when they get back."

"Yes, I think you're right."

Soon enough, Silvestrus came striding out of the woods with an impassive expression on his face, but it was some moments before they caught sight of their urban friend. Rolland emerged from the wooded area, head bent, not looking up. He was walking slowly and had some sort of blue scarf dangling down his chest.

After a few more strides, Anders gasped. "*Iovis!* Thaddeus! What's that thing on Rolland's face?"

Thaddeus gulped. "Oh, Anders, that's not a thing. That's his nose!"

Coming closer, it was clear Rolland now sported a foot-long bright-blue proboscis. The boys immediately looked to their master, but he'd gotten out his pipe and was smoking while he checked the cart contents, seemingly oblivious to any external concerns. Their eyes swiveled back to their friend, but just as they stepped forward, Asullus bolted for the boy. Eating the distance in no time, he skidded to a halt just in front of the redhead, turning his body so it was interposed between Rolland and the rest of the camp. He talked rapidly to Rolland in low tones, then listened. Suddenly, Rolland threw his arms around the old mule's neck, burying his face in Asullus's shoulder and crying out in loud, heart-racking sobs. Asullus turned to fix Silvestrus with a baleful stare. The boys had never seen the mule look so angry. Then he turned back to the crying boy and resumed talking softly to him.

Thaddeus was unsure what to do. "Come on, Anders," he said finally. They had covered half the distance when the mule gently separated himself from the young thief and trotted toward them.

"Come to comfort yer friend is the name o' the plan fer this day, lads. But should any o' ye say one disparagin' thing or be makin' one jest at his expense—well, I'm just blowin' me smoke. Neither one o' ye would e'er do such a thing, I'd bet me tail. I am, howe'er, goin' this minute to be havin' me piece out wi' the old rooster o'er there. Ye go on, now. Yer thief'll be needin' yer kindly words, an' more, yer kindly ears."

* * *

"...and I really don't remember them at all. I was just a babe." Rolland sat on the grass facing his two friends, plucking grass stems aimlessly, twiddling them in his fingers for a moment, then discarding them. His azure nasoid hung down his chest. Casual observation suggested it might be prehensile.

"The only thing I had of them was two small portraits my mother had had made—miniatures, they call them, little oval paintings in pewter frames about the size of an egg. A street artist had made them for her. I know, because Faran showed me the pictures once I was older. He'd sold the frames but thought I should have the pictures—or maybe he just wasn't able to flog the portraits. I tore them up a couple of years ago one time when I was angry, but that's how I know what they looked like.

"My father was a sailor and my mother a 'flower girl'—at least, that's what they called it. But I learned what that meant later on. I was told he shipped out on a merchantman in *Plutonius* and was lost at sea when I was about one. My mother was stabbed to death by some drunken 'customer' one night a year or so later. Faran had been her...business manager. He told me once she'd said the few months with my father were her happiest ever until I came along and that I'd made her life worthwhile." Rolland did not cry. He was all cried out.

"After she died, some of the other ladies raised me up along with their own brats. It was the way things worked. When I was old enough to run fast and keep secrets, Faran took over my training. It was a fair amount of hard times, but there was a bond amongst us outcasts. We always stuck up for each other. No one ever thought of leaving. At least not till the old man and you clowns showed up. It's funny, that. I was as loyal to that bunch as any ever in my life. They were my family. But I meet you, and in the space of five minutes, I was ready to chuck it all to follow some dream. That's not natural, you know. I'd just never thought about it till now."

Anders nodded. "It was the same for each of us, Rolland. We were in our homes, reasonably content with our lives. Then all at once, those we love suddenly said, 'Oh, it's all right. Go with the nice man. And good luck to you.'"

"The ring!" Thaddeus said. "I think it has something to do with that blue ring of his. I'd bet my staff on it. Each time we, or those we were with, needed convincing of something, that ring glowed." Thaddeus reached into his tunic and brought out his pouch, dumping the contents on the grass—three old coins and a small greenstone. He held up the last for the others to see. "Marsia gave me this last night. She said it was old and had been in her family for a long time. She said stones like this could influence people. I wonder if that's what our master's ring stone does?"

"That's an interesting idea," Anders said. "Let me see it, Taddy."

Thaddeus passed his gift to his friend, who held it up to the sun, squinting at the greenstone.

"Hmm, I can't tell anything about it one way or another. It's a little warm, but that could just be from your body heat."

He passed it to Rolland, who peered at it closely, then shook his head and handed it back to Thaddeus. The young beekeeper scooped up his coins and put his treasures back into the pouch and into his tunic.

"He can be a sneaky old crust, that's for certain," Thaddeus said. "Say, um, Rolland, you don't have to tell us if you don't want to, but why did..."

"Oh, that's my comeuppance, he called it." Rolland gestured at his bright blue rhinoid. "For taking his smoke weed and burning it. He said this would teach me to keep my nose out of another's business. But I don't think he was all that angry with me, really. Actually, I think he did it to make sure I'd stick around."

"How so?" queried Thaddeus.

"Well, I'm not about to go skipping into town dragging this thing between my legs, am I now? He's got my feet nailed to the floor, he does."

"Is it...I mean...does it come off...sometime?" Anders asked tentatively.

"He said, when the time is right—whenever in the Hells that's supposed to be. Meantime, I got me a bright blue flycatcher."

Anders's eyes widened perceptibly. "Really? Can it do that?"

Thaddeus and Rolland looked at each other and burst out laughing.

Rolland snorted, the sound echoing hollowly. "Anders, never go to a city market without me. You'd just come home with nothing but your fingers sticking out of the hole in your pants where your purse and your pickle used to be."

"Well, I don't see how'd I'd be going to market with you, in any case, Blue Nose. Somebody'd just want to catch you up and mount your member above their mantel, anyway, if not dice it up for stew."

The three boys laughed, and Thaddeus was relieved things were returning to normal—if not exactly like they used to be.

Abruptly, he looked around the campsite, hand shading his eyes. "Say, have either of you noticed Bellis lately? I don't think I've seen her since the game."

"No," Rolland said.

"No, I haven't either," Anders added. "But don't worry. She'll show up in plenty of time for the next meal. She's not missed one yet."

While they awaited the order to leave, Thaddeus cast his thoughts about for anything that would take them off the sadness of loss. Of a sudden, his attention was drawn to the grass between the campsite and the forest, which had been trampled down by the constant comings and goings of the past few days. Now that the grass was flattened, it was easier not only to see where the forest path started but easier to follow it, too. There was nothing in the way…

"Anders! You said once in one of those history lessons you're always giving us that the last Emperor—uh, Superbus, was it?"

"Yes."

"Right. Tyrannus Superbus, *Imperator Ultimus.* Anyway, you said when he marched east, he took the whole Imperial Army with him—a million men."

"Yes. That's right. At least that's what Primus told me."

"And they were all lost, right?"

"Yes, right."

"A million-man army. Anders, how many men were left at home then? I mean, to defend the Westlands? Couldn't have been that many, could there?"

"No, not many at all. In fact, Primus said there was great privation for many years afterward on that account. What are you getting at, Thaddeus?"

"Well, just this. I mean, if I were the Cin and an army had come to my homelands to try and annihilate me, but I had figured out a way to eliminate them instead while keeping all my troops from harm and in one piece, I think I might want some revenge. I believe I would surely give some thought to giving something back to them—especially if I knew their lands were now empty of defenses while I still had my entire army hale and healthy."

"You know, Thaddeus, you're right. I hadn't thought of that before."

"Anders, is there any record of the Cin coming west—coming to attack us?"

"No. Not at all. In fact, for the thousand years since Superbus went east, we haven't heard one peep from them."

"That's sort of strange, don't you think?"

"Yes, it is. It is indeed."

"What made you think of that, Taddy?" Rolland asked.

"I was looking at the trampled grass between here and the woods. It was standing tall when we first came, and you couldn't really see anything at all. Now that the grass is beaten down, you can see clearly where the paths begin. It's an easy walk. So, if there's nothing standing in the way, it would be easy as pie to just march in. So, why haven't they?"

Chapter 8

ANUS ARBOREA

* * *

Asullus cantered over to where the boys were sitting, flicking his tail—in part at the flies, in part at the irritation. "Well, lads, Master *Spiritus Duri* over there is indicatin' we're to be up an' aboot our business an' on our way. An' no more of this layabout idleness an' more o' the same, don' ye know. I tell ye true, that old crow can be the most exasperatin' bein' on this firmament when he's a mind to. Oh well, I canno' see no point in arguin' any further wi' him—probably just get us all turned into newts o' one kind or another. So, ye lot, get yer last bits together, an' if one o' ye'll fetch me my harness, I'll meet ye o'er by the cart." With that, the mule turned and made his way, slowly and deliberately, over to the conveyance, where he stood waiting patiently.

Rolland rose. "Well, let's get at it. This was an interesting stop, that's for certain, but I'm not sure I'd care to repeat it."

Within a short time, they broke camp, but Bellis still had not returned.

GARRUNGROOT

Questioning the master and the mule brought no answers. Apparently, no one had seen her leave. Anders ventured the opinion that now she was fully healed, she had decided to return to her family. While Thaddeus accepted the logic of that argument, he found he missed the dog and suggested they search the area thoroughly just to make certain. The master, however, reminded the group that time was fleeting, and denied further time for search.

Rolland walked over to his tall friend and threw a comforting arm around his shoulders. "When she's ready, she'll come back. She's quite the tracker, you know."

Thaddeus nodded but, all the same, felt at a loss without his canine companion.

The group headed east again, greeting the sun. In spite of the trying events of recent days, it was not long before their spirits had risen, and they broke into one of their traveling songs.

After a few bars, however, Thaddeus stopped singing and stared at Rolland in surprise. His friend, heretofore an indifferent tenor, had suddenly become a resonant baritone.

Anders, who also appeared to have noticed the difference, caught Thaddeus's eye, winked, and made a curving motion from his brow to chest, indicating Rolland's new nose, silently positing that the additional volume accounted for the improved sound.

Thaddeus nodded.

As the day was warm, the boys walked, mindful of Asullus's burden, and only Master Silvestrus sat upon the cart seat. Rolland moved to take his usual place in their treks, walking last in order. He had changed into a hooded jerkin, pulling the hood down over his face as far as it would go and still allow him to see the road. It wasn't very effective as a disguise, but it seemed to make the blue-nosed thief feel better. They met no fellow travelers on the road, however, so such precautions turned out to be unnecessary.

Thaddeus, who had been looking over his shoulder for their missing golden hound since they began their march, finally stopped. "Good-bye, Bellis," he said softly. "Take care of yourself, and be safe."

Aside from the occasional rest stop, they didn't pause for midday but traveled on till near dusk, when they camped near a clump of trees off the road. The land was changing as low wetlands and the occasional bog began to replace old-growth forests and rolling hills.

After stopping for the evening, the boys prepared dinner from several unwary rabbits and local forage—which they'd learned from the girls. Master Silvestrus had hardly spoken two words all day other than giving instructions, and an uncomfortable silence fell around the eventide fire. The master had brewed some tea for himself, with his usual dollop of Beewicke's Best, and was sipping as he stared into space. Asullus was munching the local grass somewhat apart from the group, and the three lads were eating quietly.

Finally, Thaddeus broke the silence. "Master?"

The old sorcerer started and looked at his first apprentice with raised eyebrows. "Yes, Thaddeus?"

"I was just wondering. I know you said we would be receiving further instruction at the *Collegium*, but I have a question."

"You may ask it."

"Back near River's Wood, when Anders and Rolland used sorcery for the first time, then earlier with the blu—I mean, when I first used sorcery—how was it we were able to do that? I mean, neither I, nor the others, had ever done any sorcery before. How could we do it then? Was it something you did to us? Or something you said that made it so?"

"How could you come to practice Sorcery when you did, and why then—not earlier, not later—those are the questions?"

"Yes, Master."

"All right, fair enough. Well, let me see…Very well then, allow me to ask you a question in return. How was it that your father decided to give you your first knife when he did?"

Thaddeus thought a moment. "I was old enough. I could handle it."

"Very good. And what was it about you that had changed, something that, perhaps, wasn't there, say, the year before?"

"Um, well, I had grown. I was able to handle it. I could control it safely."

"So, physically, you were ready. Your body had passed a certain threshold. And mentally and emotionally, too, I'd wager. You were ready for the experience, the responsibility?"

"Yes, Master."

"It is the same thing, Thaddeus."

"But what threshold had I passed, Master? I can't think of any."

"Oh yes, you can. What had you done then that you had never done before?"

"Nothing. I mean, nothing that I know of."

"Oh, I believe I know," Anders said quietly. "I had been thinking about this before, but I hadn't mentioned it. Master, does it have anything to do with... death?"

"Go on, Anders," Silvestrus prompted.

"Well, Thaddeus, do you remember those street toughs in Fountaindale?"

"Yes. What about them?"

"Well, you killed one. And, Rolland, if I'm not mistaken, has mentioned that he had, too, back in his old life."

Rolland looked up. "Yes. I'm not proud of it, but it's true. I killed my first man when I was nine. But he was trying to take me to his room, secret like, and I didn't want to go. Put a knife in him, I did, then ran like the Hells and never looked back. It was a good knife, too. I hated to lose it."

"Wait a minute, Anders," Thaddeus interrupted, suddenly disquieted. "How do you know I killed that boy? I thought I just knocked him unconscious."

"I overheard the Shire Reeve mentioning it to Master afterward. But I knew, anyway. On our way back to the inn, they were loading him and the boy Asullus fought onto a hurry-up wagon, and they pulled a canvas over them. They don't usually do that for people who're still breathing."

"I killed that boy? Oh. I didn't think I had. I don't know. I thought..."

"Troubled by something, Thaddeus?" the sorcerer asked.

"I, well, it's just...taking a life. It's something to think about. I hadn't meant to. I was just—"

"Defending yourself, Thaddeus," Rolland interrupted. "I knew that boy. Gladitoris, his name was. He was stupid and a bully, like the others that day. I never cared much for him. I tell you true—he was meaning to kill you, and would have, too, if you hadn't got him first. I've seen him do the deed before. I promise you, the world is a better place without him in, it if that helps."

"Well, yes. I guess." Thaddeus looked up sharply at Anders. "But wait a moment. I see a problem with your theory. If we are going to use death as our criteria, then just when and where did you kill someone?"

Rolland snorted.

"Kill someone? Me?" Anders blinked, surprised. "Oh, no, I never did that. Hmm, I see what you mean. Well, I guess that couldn't be it then."

"Very good, boys. What you three have worked out so far is correct—death is not a criteria for sorcery. Have you any further thoughts?" Silvestrus asked.

The boys looked blankly at each other.

"Thaddeus," the old man said, "you started to mention something, something that started with 'blu.' Does that call anything to mind?"

"Oh, the blue butterflies? But what would that—oh..." Thaddeus's face flushed.

"Yes. Precisely."

Rolland nodded in understanding, a smirk playing across his lips.

Anders, however, seemed perplexed. "I'm sorry, but I don't understand."

"It takes sparkin' to make the spark, so to speak, my boy," Rolland offered.

Anders continued to look confused, his head swiveling between his two comrades.

Rolland made a crude hand sign and smirked again.

Anders gasped. "What? You're not serious!"

"Anders, for all your alleged brilliance, I think you've spent way too much time near the ale vat fumes. Your wits are as addled as the hops. Of course I'm serious. It's what the master means. It appears you have to have been with a lady before you can practice sorcery. I remember my first time. It was three years ago. Molly o' the Willows, her name was. I never learned why they called her that. She was the sweetest girl I ever knew. She took it upon herself to look after several of us in the crèche in the early days, but then when I was older...well, we became special to each other. Just last year she was bought by some greasy Grecolian merchant, but she later escaped, someone said. It was hard to lose her. I've not heard anything of her since."

Both boys were gazing steadily at Anders, who looked down, his cheeks aflame.

"Well, Anders? You already know about Thaddeus and the blue butterfly lady. I've just told you about my Molly. We all know you've done sorcery. So...?"

"I-I had a governess, Carolle, who had a niece, Nyree. She—the niece—came to visit her aunt every summer at Brightfield. Had for years. She's older, actually a bit older, and..." The young historian ground to a halt, unable to continue.

"Ah, well," Silvestrus intoned, "everyone has things to be held close for a variety of reasons. The point, lads, is that you cannot practice sorcery without the necessary ingredient of *Amor*. Why Love is chosen over Death, I cannot say, though I think it a wonderful asymmetry. As for what the Wise think, who can say? There are many, many theories, of course, as you might expect. Some so ludicrous as to be downright silly. Perhaps one of you will be able to search it all out someday.

"In any event, inborn talent and native intelligence, your birthrights if you will, combined with your experiences—this one in particular—along with a little training for leavening, and, of course, Belief, and there you have it, a recipe for a sorcerer. Take away any single component, and you have an ordinary man. Take away any two, and you have a village fool. Take away three, and you have a tax collector, as my master was wont to say." Silvestrus laughed heartily at his own jest.

"Master!" Anders's eyes had suddenly grown large, and his call was both plaintive and insistent. "Does it work the same for gi—I mean, would Nannsi have to have...I mean..." Anders floundered.

"Master, I think Anders means, do the ladies require the same experience as well in order to practice their sorcery?" Thaddeus stepped in, trying to remain calm, though his heart was racing with concern as well.

"Why, of course. Why would it not? Goose and gander, you know," the old sorcerer replied airily. "Why? Does it matter? That which binds us both to the Earth, binds us equally. Property may be owned by either gender. Both sexes bleed when cut. The list goes on."

Anders looked truly miserable.

"However, if it is any consolation to you, my recollection of our visit with the young ladies recently is that, while they related numerous accomplishments and achievements, that particular history was not revealed. Nor do I recollect any claim for the use of sorcery. References, perhaps, but no solid evidence. In addition, my—that is, Mistress Geanninia—made no such reference, and I am sure she would not have failed to note that particular accomplishment."

Anders sighed, letting out the breath he'd been holding, and Thaddeus unclenched his fists.

"There are some differences, however. The girls have the added benefit—a miracle, actually—of being able to harbor life growth afterward, depending on the circumstances. And while that may be the crowning achievement for most, for others it may be a disaster. Especially if the girl is too young. So certain precautions are put in place, I believe, by the Heads of their

Orders. Alternate paths may allow the ability to use sorcery without that specific requirement.

"However, it seems that may not be the exact point of the distress to which you are responding. You boys may wish to examine this element within yourselves and try to discover some better understanding of why this should trouble you in the way it apparently does. Introspection is a valuable endeavor and well worth the effort, though few things of import reveal themselves at the beginning—or easily." The old sorcerer returned to his tea, sipping it slowly until he was finished.

"Well, boys, I am for repose. Please do not remain astir too long. We will be wanting an early start in the morning." The old man went to accomplish his preliminaries before seeking his bedroll.

The apprentices were tired but not yet ready for sleep. As they sat around the fire talking in low tones and speculating on issues concerning the mysteries of the female reproductive cycle, Rolland, midsentence, stood and gestured toward the east.

"Say, Thaddeus, do you see that patch of light over toward the horizon? Any idea what it could be?"

Thaddeus followed Rolland's gaze. He could see something—several pale, luminescent lights that hugged the ground and seemed to move and shift about in the distance.

"Yes, I see. I don't know what it is, though."

"Let's go look. It can't be that far."

Anders shook his head. "I don't know, Rolland. I don't think Master would want us to go traipsing about the countryside, especially at night. It could be anything at all, a Will-o'-the-Wisp or even a Boogus."

"All right, *Ignave*, stay here and guard the empty camp from the empty countryside. Then you'll be here to explain to the master where we are when he gets up in an hour to check on things. Meanwhile, Thaddeus and I will be out in that *Aelvae* light, looking for enough sacks to bring home all the treasure."

Anders glanced up in astonishment. "Treasure?"

"What treasure are you talking about, Rolland?" Thaddeus asked.

"Well, my good Beewickean, there's bound to be treasure out there. I mean, those lights are obviously Fey, and the *Faerrae* always have treasure, you know." Rolland warmed to his subject. "And Marsia will certainly love the baubles you find. Too bad Nannsi won't be getting any." He turned a sly face to his studious friend.

"All right! I'll come. But I know we're going to get in trouble for this. Just a minute."

"Where are you going?"

"To get some rope, so when we get lost and Master finds us near death, having ruined everything, I will be able to show him how you dragged me off with you against my will." He paused at the thief's gesture. "Oh, really, Rolland? Well, the same to you."

Thaddeus was also a trifle leery about this adventure, but as the three of them headed off, the feeling slid back down into the turgid emotional pool from which it had emerged and was replaced by excitement!

The boys carefully made their way eastward. Each carried a torch, though only Thaddeus's was lit. The yet-full moon was bright enough. Wisps of fog began to rise from hollows in the terrain, which soon turned the ground damp and slippery. They steadfastly followed the lights, however, but were unable to close on them, as if the lights continually receded as they walked.

After an hour of traveling, which Anders estimated by marking the moon's path, they seemed no nearer their goal of dancing lights. Straight ahead, however, Thaddeus glimpsed a dim shape on the squishy ground.

"Hold. I think someone's out there."

"Is he moving?" Anders asked anxiously.

"No. He seems to be waiting."

"Well, he's sure to have seen our torch by now. Is he alone?" Rolland asked.

"I can only make out one," Thaddeus replied.

"I don't know. What do you think we should do?" Anders asked.

"Well, we might as well go ahead. I agree, he must have seen us. Doing anything else would seem suspicious. Now stay close to me. If it gets sticky, make your way back to camp and get the master. Come on." Thaddeus once again found himself giving orders as if he were the leader but shoved that thought down to mull over later. They had work to do.

Several more paces brought clarity and uneasy laughter.

"Ah. Our stranger is an old scraggly tree. Long dead by the look of it. See how the branches flare out? Makes it look as if it was reaching for us. Someone should have taken a torch to that thing a long time ago."

A thin, quavering voice spoke out of the night. "Well, that's hardly friendly, considering the circumstances."

The boys started as a second shape emerged from behind the first as if from thin air. But the second shape was short with bony hands, hunched shoulders, and dressed in a swath of dark robes. As it stepped nearer, they made out the form of an old woman.

"Your pardon, Mistress," Thaddeus said, recovering quickly. "We didn't know anyone was out and about at this hour."

"Hah! It's a long time since I've been called 'Mistress'—although once, long ago...But speaking of being out and about, how is it three likely lads such as yerselves are here at this hour mucking about in the moonlight?"

As the boys drew closer, they beheld a time-ravaged, pockmarked countenance with milky eyes that stared sightlessly past them into the distance.

"I'm sorry, Mistress, but...that is, can you see us? I mean no offense."

"Oh, none taken, Good Master. And my name is Merriwhiddle. Never fear, I see right well enough, Young Master. I see many things—more things than ye can imagine, I'll wager. Smell them, too."

Thaddeus was startled by the odd comment. "Excuse me, ma'am?"

"I said, I smell them. Ye lot, for example. Let's see." The old woman tested the air, circling around the group and sniffing each apprentice in turn. She halted in front of Rolland. "Ye did not get that nose from yer mother, boy. That's sorcerer's work, that is. Did ye offend one of them, then?"

"Yes, I did, Mistress. Stole his smoking narcotic, I did."

"Ha! It's lucky ye still live. That trumpet, though, is not going to get ye very far with the maidens, I imagine. At least, not with most."

She continued her circuit, stopping abruptly in front of Thaddeus with a sharp intake of breath. "Ye, boy, what is that ye have on yer chest?"

"I don't know what you mean, Mistress."

"I said, what is that on yer chest, lout?" She grasped the front of Thaddeus's jerkin and, with a quick snap of her wrist, tore it down the middle, exposing his skin.

Thaddeus grabbed the old crone's wrist, but to his astonishment, he could not move it more than a hairsbreadth even with his best effort.

The old woman stood in front of the boy, sightlessly staring at his chest. "*Amicus Faerrarum*!" she spat.

In a blur of movement, Rolland was suddenly behind the old hag with a knife at her throat. "Now, now, Mother. You'll ruin my friend's finery if you keep on that way. Why don't you release your hold and stand away? Then we can talk and get to know each other more peaceably."

Merriwhiddle let go her grip, allowing her arm to fall slowly to her side.

Thaddeus sprang back, rubbing his neck.

Rolland's attention remained fixed on the old woman. "Very good, Merriwhiddle. Now tell us, Mistress, what do you mean by all this?"

"It is uncomfortable for me to speak with steel at my throat. Perhaps ye could imagine the same?"

"Yes. Of course. You are right." Rolland sheathed his blade and stepped away. "Now let's hear your story. But do not bother with invention. I have the Gift of Hearing and the fastest reflexes in Fountaindale. I can make the knife reappear in a gnat's wink."

"Such a polite boy, though thief is nearer the mark, I'll wager. Very well. It is nothing disparaging, Young Master. It is just that I was once on the bad side of some *Faerrae* tricks, and I did not relish the experience. I harbor some resentment toward them to this day—and toward those they favor. Ill reasoned, I'm sure. And it is true, this young master has done me naught of harm, though his Mark did give me a turn. But my adventure with the *Faerrae* was long ago, and I did forget myself. It will not happen again, rest assured."

"'Tis naught," Thaddeus said. "I was just taken off guard, that's all. You are incredibly strong, Mistress, I must say."

"It comes from years of toil, my boy. Years of toil. Now, how may I help ye, Young Masters, for I trow ye are not out here because this land is all that familiar to ye?"

"Well, that's true enough," Anders said, relaxing. "Actually, we were trying to find some lights we saw glowing in the distance and—"

"Ah!" the old woman said. "Yes, the Lights of Calling. Fey, they are. Only occur at certain times of the year, they do. It is said if ye follow them to ground, ye'll find something of great value."

"Ha!" Rolland interjected. "Treasure! I knew it. So, how may we find them again? I don't see them now."

"Easy enough, Young Masters. I'd accompany ye myself, but old Merriwhiddle has got a touch of the grippe, and her bones complain on these damp nights. But I'll be glad to point ye in the right direction. There. See ye that fork in the path? Just bear to the right. Ye'll come across them soon enough, like as not, if they can still be seen. Then follow them to the end, wherever they may lead. Most importantly, make sure ye keep them in sight, and don't stray from the path, or ye could wander the moors forever. I had an uncle once, a Lord Basker—kept hounds, he did, at his villa. He went out on the moors one night chasing those lights, and we never saw him again."

"Wait," Anders spoke up. "If they lead to treasure, why are you here like this, Mistress, instead of warm and dry in your own manor with servants to look after you?"

"It is a smart one, ye are, darling. Well, ye have delved the truth. These lights do yield up treasure, that's certain. But only once to each petitioner. I chose me treasure many years ago when I first came here. But I spent me wealth foolishly, as the young are wont to do, and now I have only a pittance remaining." The old woman abruptly drew back, looking alarmed. "Ye'd not take what little Merriwhiddle still has to her name, would ye now?"

"Oh, no, Mistress!" Thaddeus reassured her. "We're not robbers. We'll have our desserts from the lights of our own efforts."

"Well, ye have the right of it there, I'll wager." Merriwhiddle uttered a small laugh and seemed to relax. "All right. So it's as I've said, lads. Follow the fork to the right, and all will be made clear. Good hunting, Young Masters!"

The boys thanked the old crone, turned, and followed the path to the right. Thaddeus glanced back over his shoulder, but the woman was gone.

"Now, she was a strange one for certain. You know, she never did say why she was out here this time of night. Do you think we should—Ow!" Anders slapped at the back of his neck. "I've been stung! Oh, it's like fire! What's a hornet doing out at nighttime? I thought—oh, I don't feel so good. I think I'd better stop...for a minute." The young historian wobbled a step or two, then dropped where he stood.

"Anders! What's the matter with y—Damn! One just got me in the neck! How many of these things are there? Thaddeus...Oh, misery, I'm sick. I..." Rolland slid to the ground in a slow spiral.

"Ow! Hornet! What do you do? I am a *Bee Keeper!* Anders! Rolland! Hold fast! I'm coming!" Thaddeus lurched toward his two comrades, but the world began to swim, and he knew no more.

Thaddeus's senses returned to him slowly. If he hadn't known better, he would have sworn he was being dragged along the ground by the back of his jerkin. A few minutes more, and he knew he was being dragged along by the back of his jerkin. All he could do, however, was make note of it, since he could not move any of his muscles by so much as a whisker.

"Big oaf!" a voice above and behind him muttered. "Yes, old Merriwhiddle is strong, but that does not mean I have a liking for yanking an overgrown boy-man half a *mille passae* because I'm enjoying the experience. Why did I save the biggest for last? What was I thinking? Pfah!" The old woman spat and fell silent as the strange journey continued, her breathing unlabored for all her complaint.

Thaddeus had a thousand questions, but try as he might, he could utter none of them. He was only able to hear, see, and breathe.

"Ah, awake, are ye? Fancy the view from down there, do ye? Ha! Well, ye'll be joining yer friends soon enough. A puzzle ye are, though. My little stingers didn't seem to want to bestow their kisses on ye. They're usually not so reluctant. I must talk to them about that. I can't imagine why they'd—ah, here we are. All right, me boys, all together again. Happy about that, are ye? Ye, the short, scholarly one, too bad ye couldn't tell the difference between swamp gas and *Faerrae* lights, eh? And ye, Blue Beak, ye should have considered exchanging the Gift of Hearing for the Gift of Listening. When I bade ye follow the lights, ye believed I said 'treasure,' but what I really said was that ye'd find 'something of great value.' What I meant, of course, was knowledge. That's always of great value, don't ye think? Of course, there's also timing, as, for example, when it is that ye actually receive that knowledge. But that's often the way of things—nothing is perfect. Hee hee! Hmm, ye don't say much, do ye? Ha! Not now and not later, either, I think."

Merriwhiddle dragged Thaddeus over to a rock outcropping facing the old, gnarled tree. He was dumped unceremoniously next to Rolland and Anders, who, like him, appeared only able to note their circumstances, not interact with them.

The old woman stepped into Thaddeus's line of vision and addressed the group. "Now, ye lads are an unlikely lot, it appears to me. One *Amicus Faerrarum*, one blue nose, and one just plain nosey. And all with the Power—at least a fledgling power. And I doubt ye're all here by chance. Mayhap your master, if you have one, will be looking for you shortly, as soon as he sees ye've run off. But by that time, ye'll all be shriveled husks lying at the bottom of this bog, I vow. Sorry I am to waste good flesh, but I don't want the bother of questions and other troubles. At least me pets and the Old Mister"—she jerked her head at the tree—"will have their uses for ye. But why am I maundering on so? First rule of Dark Acts—shut up and just do it. Must be getting old."

Meriwhiddle sniffed the air, turned away from the boys, and called out in a keening drone. A high-pitched humming sound commenced, and several mosquitos alighted on Thaddeus's arms and face. The humming escalated and intensified as first hundreds, then thousands joined them. They were biting him everywhere—every thumb's breadth of skin, inside his ears, up his nostrils, on his eyelids—and he could do nothing. As soon as one flew away, engorged and swollen with his life's blood, another ten took its place as wave after wave of them descended. He began to feel drowsy, sleepy, weak. All feeling had left his face and limbs. All sound had been reduced to a droning and humming that went on and on without end.

"*Sphaerae Ignis!*" A voice from behind Thaddeus boomed with a loud retort.

A bright stab of yellow flashed, and a brief lick of heat moved out and away from Thaddeus in an ever-expanding globe, then was gone. He became aware that the droning had stopped. The mosquitos he could still see on his arms were now nothing but burned grit lying lifelessly on his skin. He felt a soft, velvety tickling as a rain of charred insect bits gently drifted down on him from the sky.

"Nooo!" Merriwhiddle wailed. "My pets! Ye're all killed! Who—?" The old woman sniffed the air frantically, then stopped. Staring at a space behind Thaddeus's line of vision, she smiled cheerlessly. "Ah, Silvestrus, my old love."

"Hello, Merriwhiddle."

"Oh, I see. Ye've come for your brats, have ye? And do they know they're yer brats, old man, if only a little removed?"

"No, Merriwhiddle, I have not told them yet. I was waiting for a certain time in the future—different from this one, though."

"I'm sorry to have spoiled it for ye." The old woman had a faraway look on her face, and when she spoke again, her tone was almost girlish. "How…how are ye? Are ye well?"

"I am well, Merriwhiddle. And you?"

"I am as ye see me. Bound in chains to this place and to me Mister here. But ye knew that, already, didn't ye, old man? It was ye as put me here!"

"You came to this of your own free will, Merriwhiddle. You know that. Your eyes were wide open when you struck your bargain."

"Yes, I know the bargain. Knowledge and power. Enough power to hurt even one of the Great, even one who sits on the Council of the Wise. Do they still call it that, Silvestrus, when ye meet?"

"Yes, they do."

"Wise, ha! A gaggle of old farts, I say!"

The sorcerer chuckled. "As tactful as ever, Merriwhiddle, but I must confess, I have little to argue with you there."

"But we do have our arguments, don't we, Silvestrus? Concerning prophecy, for example."

"Merriwhiddle, we have been over that ground a thousand, thousand times. I felt I had no choice—"

"One always has choice! Ye taught me that! No, I do not blame ye, at least not entirely. It was that slut of a teacher at the school—Geanninia!" The old woman spat again. "She it was who turned yer head. Ye left me for her! And I seven moons gone on me time with yer sprigs in me!" Merriwhiddle's voice rose in timbre, full of passion.

"I am sorry, Merriwhiddle. I truly am. But you knew I had to go. The Prophecy—"

"Don't talk to me of prophecy! I don't care a fig about those four whores who came to ye! It was easy enough to cry prophecy, when all they really wanted to do was enslave the gullible. They forced ye to leave yer black-haired mistress and thereby create a false sense of a chasm that ye thought only she could fill. So when ye had done their bidding with me, back to her ye crawled, leaving me…me! Of them all, I was the only one who ever truly loved ye for *who* ye were—not for *what* ye were. And there I was, abandoned, two months later having our daughters, our lovely twin girls. And where were ye? In the arms of that trull!"

"Peace, Merriwhiddle. It was, you remember, many, many years ago."

"It's like yesterday for me. It is a pain that will never leave me."

"Yes, I heard they were lost. I am truly sorry."

"Lost? Oh, yes, that's what ye were told, weren't ye? Ha! It wasn't exactly like that, ye know."

"No, I don't know," Silvestrus replied, his voice suddenly becoming stern. "What do you mean, old woman?"

Merriwhiddle's face turned sly, and her voice took on an icy edge. "Ah, the truth. The truth at last. Yes, ye have it right. To obtain this knowledge and this power, I became bound. But that wasn't the only price. There was another, some would say a higher, price. Did it never occur to ye to ask what the cost of this kind of power would be?"

"No. Never. It is a power in which I have no interest."

"No interest? Yet ye are interested in the fate of yer daughters, are ye not? Little Fabia and Fabrica? Yes, I thought so. I can smell it on ye."

"What are you saying, Merriwhiddle?"

"Only that it was an exchange, an exchange in which I willingly partook—as ye so gallantly pointed out. I obtained a life span with no foreseeable end, physical invulnerability to all external threats, true power, and in return, I gave something of value. Great value."

"Merriwhiddle! What are you saying? But you cannot have done such a thing. They were your children!"

"Only half, old man. Yers was the other half, and ye were the one I wanted to hurt. More than anyone else has ever been hurt before. Ye and yer arrogance, yer infidelity, yer haughty power, so casual in its use. I wanted ye to feel as I felt, and now, at long last, I've achieved my goal as my Prophecy said I would."

"Oh, Merriwhiddle. You sacrificed our children and threatened the Prophecy just for spite? So I would feel what you feel? But I do not feel what you feel, you know. That is, unless you feel pity."

"Pity! Don't you throw the word 'pity' in my face, ye old fool! Ye're in no position to pity anyone except yerself. It was here I stood that night—right here! All that time ago, shushing them while I slit their soft little throats and watched his greedy tubers suck up every last drop that fell upon the ground. After a while, they were still and cold, and I buried them among his roots, where he told me to. I never thought about them aga—" Suddenly overcome, the old woman began to weep. "And now ye know. Now ye have the pain. And now yer precious Prophecy lies in ruins, and it is I, Merriwhiddle, who did this. It is I who have interrupted the chain. Yes, I can tell ye remember. Ye told me of the Prophecy. *Circuitus Octipes Magnus!* The Great Compass, the Eight-Pointed Star, four Cardinal and four Ordinal. Ye have the four *Cardines* by now, I presume. I can smell the signs. But the four *Ordines,* where will ye get them? Perhaps two. But I have interrupted that line. Two of the *Ordines* were to have come from us, weren't they? He told me that, the old Mister. Yes, I know it from yer sweat. But they are no more. All your scheming and treachery—all for nothing. Ha! It's no more than what ye and yer wretched Prophecy deserve!"

Silvestrus let out a long sigh. "Ah, poor Merriwhiddle. But has no one ever told you there is more than one way to pluck a goose? True, a pair of the *Ordines* were to have been descended from us. Originally. But there is another way. Consider the *Cardines...*"

"What about them?" she demanded in a voice now grown shrill.

"Well, there is nothing to say that the *Ordines* cannot come from one of the *Cardines,* you know."

The old woman stood in stunned silence as the import of Silvestrus's words washed over her. "But... ah, wait. Yes, I see it! The *Ordines* could, indeed, come from the *Cardines.* But they would not be human—at least not entirely human. They would have to couple with...others. And who'd it be who'd do that?"

"Stranger things have happened, Merriwhiddle. Do you not recall that verse from our youth? 'The flower, the insect, the serpent, the beast / who, indeed, can encompass them all / in tomorrow's song today?'"

"Gibberish, old man. But even if it weren't..." The old woman's sightless gaze suddenly shifted to where Thaddeus and his fellow apprentices sat paralyzed. "There is still a way to end this once and for all and be certain of it this time." She whipped around to face the tree. "Master and Mister of Old, I call on ye now..."

"Merriwhiddle! Stop! Yes, you have sinned, but that can be addressed. With a heartfelt repentance and the correct rites, there is—"

"Heartfelt repentance, Silvestrus?" the old crone laughed scornfully. "I am a ways beyond that by this time. But now I will show ye *my* power. The power I have purchased at such great price!"

"Queen of the Midges, do not provoke me further! I would not wish to harm you, but—"

"Harm me? Hardly, old man—or weren't ye listening? Ye cannot harm me. That was a part of my bargain. Attempt to slay me if ye will—arrow, sword, poison, lightning, choose. I will yet abide."

"Yes, I know, Merriwhiddle. But when I said I might harm you, I did not think to strike at you directly. I—"

"It does not matter what ye think. I have the power now, and now ye are a dead man, and yer precious brats with ye—and the Prophecy after that! Old Master and Mister, attend to me and rise up! Yer enemies surround ye! Rise up and slay them now!" she ended with a great cry.

Thaddeus forced his eyes open further. Unless they were betraying him, the old, gnarled tree was moving and growing in size, reaching out.

"*Arbor Incendat!*" Silvestrus's voice thundered, reverberating over the land.

Instantly, with a powerful boom, the ancient tree was engulfed, root to crown, in a great red-orange tongue of flame. A roaring scream erupted from deep inside the trunk, and the massive tree writhed as if in pain. But the tree's screams were nothing next to those now issuing from the old crone.

Thaddeus watched in horror as she began to smoke, then burst into flame, fire pouring from every orifice. She ran in a circle, arms flailing, crying out in a piercing wail, flames trailing her like a ragged garment. Both flames climbed higher and higher. Finally, overcome, Merriwhiddle collapsed and burned at the foot of her old tree—or what was left of it. Eventually, only smoke and embers remained.

"Ah, Merriwhiddle. I did love you, you know. Once, I truly did." Silvestrus sat down with a sigh, his head upon his knees, lost in thought.

After a time, the sky, at last, began to lighten in the east.

Thaddeus found he could again move. "Master? Are you all right, Master?"

Silvestrus looked up. "Ah. Sorry, my boy. My thoughts were wandering. Yes, I am well. How do you fare?"

"Only a little worse for wear, Master. A little stiff. But it's nothing—except for the itching."

"Good lad. I will see what I can do about that later. Well, this was a night to remember and think about, was it not? Ah, I believe your comrades are coming round as well. Perhaps you could help rouse them. It has been a long night, and I think we would be well served to return to camp and take what ease we may."

Thaddeus, light-headed, rose with some difficulty. He put a hand to his swollen face. It was as bumpy as the pebbled path that led to the hives back home. It was also wet, as some of the lesions had begun to weep. He tottered over to his friends and helped them up.

"Is it over?" Anders asked. "I feel awful."

"Not as awful as Merriwhiddle," Rolland murmured under his breath.

"Save your strength, you two. We've at least an hour's hike back to camp. Time for talk then. And don't scratch. Master said he has some salve that will help."

If Thaddeus thought the walk back to the camp would clear his head, he was mistaken. Far from feeling better, he felt much worse. By the time they made the camp, the boys were having to support each other.

He was uncertain whether Silvestrus, lost in thought as usual, was even aware of their condition.

Asullus greeted the party, his eyes full of concern, but kept his peace once he'd seen the boys' faces.

As soon as they gained the fire ring, the boys collapsed, asking only for relief from the itching. After applying the master's salve, they hardly moved until eventide. Silvestrus plied with them with conjured foodstuffs, but one and all claimed they were not hungry. He had to browbeat them to get them to drink something.

Afterward, Silvestrus poured himself some tea and attended to the boys, who lay scattered around the fire pit at odd angles, having dropped where they stood.

When he next awoke, Thaddeus mustered sufficient energy to struggle to a sitting position. The others soon followed suit. "Master?"

"Yes, Thaddeus?" A small smile played across the old sorcerer's lips.

"I, that is to say, about the old woman, Merriwhiddle, she said something about a Pro—"

"—phecy. Yes, she did. She said a great many things, actually. And, yes, a prophecy was among them. All right, to save time—you all look wretched and in need of a good night's sleep—I assume you were about to ask me about said Prophecy and, perhaps, several other matters she alluded to. Am I correct?"

"Yes, Master."

"Well, I will tell you, though it will take some time, and we, all of us, ought to be sleeping to regain our strength. However, since you have asked...This story is a dreary one and is as yet without any resolution."

* * *

"Prophecy, you say. Well, prophecy, as an entity, is highly overrated. These days, every single scroll you read appears to require a prophecy in it somewhere for validation. It is a hackneyed and sorry story device, if you ask me—not to mention that the majority of it is suitable only to wrap fish innards in. This, of course, is because we are only able to look into an event after the fact and check to see if a prophecy concerning it can be identified. That is, after all, the only way to know a prophecy to be correct—to see how it all ended up. The whole matter begs the question, what good is a prophecy if you only know whether it was accurate after the events it has prophesied have transpired? That is an excellent query with no satisfactory answer.

"Nevertheless, occasionally a prophecy comes along that seems to have some substance behind it. Such a one, I believe, is the Prophecy to which Merriwiddle and I were alluding earlier. This Prophecy, a very old one, was given me some years ago by a group of ladies who called themselves the *Intelligentiae.* They were four in number—*Ingenia, Argutia, Sapientia,* and *Providentia.* They told me a great danger lay ahead in the future. That was safe enough, I suppose, as there is always some sort of great danger lying ahead in the future. They were quite insistent I pay attention to their warnings. However, they said the key to defeating the danger once and for all was through the use of the *Circuitus Octipes Magnus*—the great eight-pointed compass."

Thaddeus leaned forward. "Excuse me, Master, but what is a compass?"

Anders looked eager. "If I may, Master? A compass, Thaddeus, is a device made from the clinging iron. It always points north. Navigators and explorers use them a lot. North, and the three other directions inferred from it, are known as the *Cardines*, or Cardinal Points. In between each pair of major compass points is a lesser compass point, an *Ordinis*, or Ordinal Point, four of them as well, so it is the eight points together that comprise the Eight-Pointed Star. Is that correct, Master?"

"Of course, my studious Anders. To continue, the Great Compass is an object, certainly, but it is also like a simile—almost a metaphor, actually. In the case of the Prophecy, it is believed to have a specific meaning, to refer to eight living persons who, acting together, will somehow be able to stop this great danger before we all join the ranks of the Eldest, that is, *Extincte!*

"It was made clear to me that, for some reason, I had been selected to discover the Eight Points and use all my power to orchestrate their working together to achieve this end. They even compelled me to go through a particular ritual with them to initiate the process. Merriwhiddle was correct on that point. However, preceding the visit of the four ladies, I had met Mistress Geanninia, and we had become...close. To underline the seriousness of the situation, the *Intelligentiae* foretold I would need to put aside this new relationship for a time and start my search for the *Cardines.* This was extremely difficult, as Geanninia and I had become quite fond of one another and had planned to become one. She did not take the news well. Perhaps you have, at some point in your lives, seen a woman put off or thwarted in a relationship? They generally do not favor this and often act accordingly."

"Yes, Master," Rolland said. "Once, a couple of years ago, a girl staying at Faran's, Floria of Copperville her name was, got jilted. After, she knifed three women, killed her ex-beau by slicing off his scuppers, and tore the place apart."

"Yes, quite so. Now imagine a similar situation but with a fully trained and powerful sorceress."

"Oh, I see."

"So did we all. Fortunately, I am not without resources, so most of the damage was repaired, but I digress. I came to discover through my researches that it would be necessary for me to strike up a series of relationships with a variety of people over time. The *Intelligentiae* foretold that some of these relationships would necessarily produce offspring." Silvestrus paused to sip his tea.

"Pursuant to this plan, it occurred to me that I might be able to accelerate the pace of this process by using my powers to cause a twinning. This was my own idea—a shortcut, if you like, so I could return to my Geanninia. It was my attempt at tweaking Destiny. Well, it did not turn out so favorably, as you have witnessed.

"I took it into my head to make the acquaintance of Merriwhiddle, who seemed to me a likely candidate. As it turned out, she had been a student at the *Ludia,* where Geanninia was an instructress. But poor Merriwhiddle had experienced a difficult first three years and eventually decided to leave the school and return to her home. I followed her there—to the countryside near Moorstown—and struck up an acquaintance. She was a shy girl, but I persisted, and, well, you heard what she said. Afterward, the *Intelligentiae* appeared to me one night, and they made it quite clear they were not well pleased with my efforts to circumvent the natural order of things. They said my duty to her was done and recommended I return to Geanninia forthwith. In fact, they strongly advised it with little room for dispute. I was deeply torn. I had come to care for Merriwhiddle by that time, loved her after a fashion. And she was pregnant—with our twins as it turned out." The old man's eyes misted. "But the four Ladies were adamant. I went to Merriwhiddle, and we talked for a day and a night. She was hurt and angry—with reason, it is true—and we were getting nowhere. Then, while I was sleeping, she arose and put a sorcerous spell on me."

"A sorcerous spell, Master?" Anders cocked his head to one side and stared at Silvestrus intently. "Of what kind?"

"It is not important. The problem was, she had not enough knowledge and power to do it correctly, and it turned out badly. It took me some effort to get back to my proper self, and by then, I had decided to leave.

Merriwhiddle was unbending in her wrath and made all manner of threats. But by that time, my heart had turned, and I knew she was not the one for me. So one morning, I left her a long note and a heavy bag of gold and headed west. Well, you know the rest."

"Not my business, Master," Rolland said, "but after all that, I'm thinking that getting back into Mistress Geanninia's good graces might have posed a problem or two."

"You have no idea. Now, boys, you look even worse than before. So get yourselves to your bedrolls and sleep the sleep of the justly weary."

The boys did not stir until midday. They got up slowly, tended to their ablutions with no great enthusiasm, and again refused any food. Silvestrus regarded the group solemnly as they packed and resumed their journey toward Moorstown.

The pace was slow and plodding, as if they were ascending a mountain, though the land was comparatively flat. Silvestrus called an early halt, and again the boys refused anything but water.

"I feel like a cart-and-eight just ran over me, swung around, and did it again," Rolland said to no one in particular.

Anders and Thaddeus nodded dully in agreement. Discussion that evening was limited to essentials, and the boys sought their bedrolls early.

Silvestrus made rounds during their sleep, checking on his charges at intervals throughout the night, his look of concern transforming into a frown of concentration.

Again morning came and went, and again the boys remained abed. Silvestrus now marked that they took turns sweating, then shaking—first throwing off their blankets, complaining of burning up, then clasping as much cover to themselves as they could, complaining of freezing. They were all weak and barely able to leave their bedrolls, all the while clamoring for water. Silvestrus rotated among the group with the water bag, noting that as soon as one's thirst was slaked, another called out.

Asullus paced the campsite back and forth in a frenzy of worry. "Master, what is it as has taken our bonnie boys? I ne'er seen a group o' young'uns no' already dead so discomposed."

"Ah, Asullus, I think I know, but I hope I am wrong. Well, there is nothing for it but to summon the good doctor."

Within moments, Master Celsius was standing in a cloud of green vapors, gazing at each of the apprentices in turn, his hand stroking his beard in thought. "Well, Silvestrus, it is the Singing Sickness for certain. It is just that I have never seen such a virulent course of it—and in three at once. You say they were on the moors and were bitten by the mosquitos there? Ah, yes. Thousands of bites? Well, that accounts for it, I suppose."

Asullus stopped pacing. "Excuse me, Learned Sir, but did ye say the Singing Sickness? I confess, I ha' ne'er heard o' such a contagion."

"Well, I would not be surprised. Firstly, it is confined only to this area of the world. Secondly, you are nonmedical, and, thirdly, you are a mule as well—all of which might help to explain this island in the sea of your knowledge. But, the Singing Sickness is known in the Literature as Mallia's Aria. Mallia, for whom the illness was named, was a woman of the Coast who obtained medical training with Relso of the Order around two centuries ago. How she contrived to become a physician in the first place is, of course, a mystery. I mean, women in Medicine..." The figure spread his hands, rolled his eyes, and shook his head. "In any case, she it was who first described this malady and its cure. A fine piece of work, I must say, though perhaps she had help with it. As she retired from medicine some time afterward to join an operatic touring company, the disease was so named.

"Now, as to the cure, that is problematic. I will require the bark from a local willow tree, amongst other ingredients, to make a potion for the boys, but the course of this illness typically waxes and wanes, exacerbates and remits. Even given the fact that these lads are young and healthy, it will be touch and go. I will prepare the medicine and leave you with instructions, but I must recommend you interrupt your journey and seek, without delay, the Convent of the Silent Sisters—the *Sorores Silentii*—close on to Moorstown. They stock an excellent vintage in their cellars, by the by, and, of course, they really do maintain silence—another blessing in any commerce with the ladies. Primarily, though, they have had extensive experience in dealing with this malady. Mallia herself is said to have resided there during the last years of her life, instructing the Sisters in the treatment of such stricken unfortunates."

Celsius busied himself with the preparation of his medicinals. Obtaining the willow bark, indigenous to the area, proved to be no difficulty, and soon three beakers of a gray-green, foul-smelling brew stood on a rock by the campfire.

"This should do it, Silvestrus," Celsius said, staring at the sorcerer for a moment before continuing. "I will, of course, be happy to check in on the boys from time to time to note their progress, but it's now mostly a matter of dosing and waiting. On another topic, I hesitate to bring this up at such a delicate time, but I don't suppose..."

Silvestrus gave the physician a hard stare.

"Yes, well, of course, I understand. Another time. *Vale!*" And the healer was gone.

Asullus moved to stand by the old sorcerer. "Master, our Medico did no' seem all so confident to me regardin' his current poison, especially concernin' its efficacious effects. I'm wondering if it would no' be wiser for ye to use yer powers to bring the lads around?"

"Yes, Asullus, I have been debating that very question this recent while. But I run into the same dilemma as I described to Thaddeus regarding Ethne. To heal one apprentice of this deadly disease would take a good part of my reserves, but all three at once? I must weigh this against conserving for the time of need that's coming soon, according to the writings. And yet, my boys, my boys..." The old man turned away and began pacing back and forth, hands locked behind him.

The potion, which the apprentices took only with much gagging and sputtering, seemed to ease the boys' symptoms. After a time, Silvestrus, having come to a decision, left off his pacing and approached the mule.

"Asullus, we must get the lads to the Convent of the Silent Sisters as soon as may be. However, as you can see, they are in no condition to walk. I know it is warm here, and the journey long and difficult, but..."

"Ye pay it no mind, Master Silvestrus. I see the direction o' yer wishes, an' I ha' me no objections. Ye load the lads in the cart, an' seat yerself up there as well to do the guidin', an' I'll see we get there. I ha' me the remains o' me youth, more or less, an' me strength, which is considerable. The goin' will no' be so speedy, but it'll be sure an' steady, an' we'll all be arrivin' in one piece."

"You're a good friend, Asullus, and I know you have the best interests of the boys in your heart. No one could ask for more."

"Well, Master, thank ye fer yer kind words, but ye just be puttin' off the inevitable. So get off yer lazy behind an' put on me harness, then get those worthless collywobbles up in the cart, an' we'll be on our way 'stead of talkin' the day away."

* * *

Thaddeus remembered little of the next few days. He was sick, and the bouncing back and forth only made it worse. He had an incredible burning thirst and headache that threatened to split his brainpan open. The persistent bouts of nausea and vomiting were debilitating. Additionally, the insult of the warm water, thin, sour broth, and the truly vile-tasting potion was sufficient to make him vomit repeatedly. He could control neither his bowels nor his bladder. Every so often, the Physico appeared, looked into his eyes, and murmured something meant to be reassuring, but wasn't. Once, or perhaps twice, it rained, which offered some relief from the heat. Mostly, though, it was a misery of alternately shivering and sweating—*rigor et calor*, as Master Celsius said often enough.

After what seemed an eternity but was, in fact, only a few days, Thaddeus woke up to sounds that were different than the usual jingling, jouncing, and bumping of the cart. Night birds called, a bell rang, and women talked in whispers, their tones full of concern. Gentle hands grasped him, and he was let down from the cart and placed on a litter. Moments later, he was inside a building where it was cool, quiet, and dark. Dazed, he was carried up some stairs and placed in a room that smelled fresh, like a spring meadow. His clothing was removed, and he was placed in a tub where he was washed carefully. Lifted once again, he was dried and moved to a bed with clean sheets. He wondered if Ethne were nearby and called out for her. He was given more broth, but this time it was fresh and flavorful. It grew dark, and after a time, the voices withdrew, and a door closed.

Finally, he slept.

Chapter 9

CONVENTUS et CASTRA

* * *

The *Mater Amplior* peered over tented hands, elbows resting on her desk. The middle-aged woman, prim and thin lipped, brushed a miniscule bit of lint from her bleached burlap *Palla* and straightened her *Mitra,* tucking a wisp of gray hair back under the lining. She adjusted the golden *Insignia Matris* dependent from its heavy gold neck chain, moved a teacup slightly closer to her inkwell, and regarded her guest. It had been a ten-day since he'd first darkened their door, and much had happened since then. She remembered that first conversation...

* * *

CONVENT OF THE SILENT SISTERS
(SORERES SILENTII)

The old man seated across from her was taking his ease, neither disrespectful nor, in truth, all that respectful. His attitude was similar to that of the Arch Abbess when she came to pay a call—indulgent, socially correct, and faintly mocking. Yet he was neither angry nor hostile. And he definitely seemed to care about his charges. He had hardly spent a moment out of the boys' room—unless chased out—since he had brought them some two days previously. And what charges! The Warrior, the Scholar, and the Blue-Nosed Ferret, as she'd dubbed them in her mind. The last boy was a study in facial anatomy to be sure. Where had he come by that bright blue proboscis? Sorcerer's work for certain, but which sorcerer, and for what reason? Was it this old man? Subtle, she thought him, and unlikely to suffer fools, she imagined. But all in all, he appeared to regard his sojourn at the convent as an unexpected, though not unpleasant, interruption in his journey. He clearly had bigger fish to fry.

Catching herself woolgathering, she pulled back to the moment and continued her inventory. His dress was careworn, indeed, but fresher now than when he had been pounding at the gate with his staff that wind-whipped evening, urging haste and care all at the same time while ordering her nurses about as if they were his personal body servants. Harrumph! And how they had all jumped to obey him without question! A neat trick, that. She would need to give that matter more thoughtful study.

His silver hair and beard suggested several things, including the need to treat him with deference but also with caution. And those eyes—one green, one brown. Now where in the world had they come from? They twinkled easily enough but also proclaimed power and a manner quick to anger. It would have been a mistake in the extreme to dismiss him as a mere vagabond. She did not need to be told she sat across from a Sorcerer of Power—one of the Council of the Wise, if she was not mistaken. And usually she was not.

Still, he had been civil, courteous, caring, even charming—for a man. On more than one occasion, she had found herself wondering what would have happened that day thirty years past had she been one hour later to her Novitiate Adorning. Tardiness on that day would have meant expulsion, and expulsion would have meant Kenneth, a house, and children... Well! There she was, forgetting herself again, like some silly novice first-time to Parnassa, all wide eyes and no brains.

"Master Silvestrus, I appreciate your coming in response to my invitation on such short notice." She indicated the serving tray. "Please help yourself to the tea. I have taken the liberty of obtaining some honey from Beewicke, as I understand it has become your preference of late. I hope it meets with your approval."

The old man smiled, and she had to suppress a thrill. Stupid girl!

"You are just as kind and thoughtful as you have been since our unlooked-for advent on your doorstep, *Mater Amplior.* I shall attempt to repay you for your more-than-generous hospitality in any way within my power."

"That, as they say, Master Silvestrus, is a bargain! What I desire from you is information. You are of the *Collegium Sorcerorum,* are you not?"

Silvestrus nodded.

"And the three boys who accompany you are your apprentices?"

"That is correct, *Mater Amplior.*"

"Oh, please, do not call me that. I've heard nothing else for the past ten years, and it has become a wearing weight over that time. Call me, instead, Melior."

"It would be my pleasure, Melior..."

* * *

Yes, pleasure. That's what she had felt then, and not for the last time. That is, until Sister Orbis had searched out that dusty scroll in the library concerning the Sorcerers of the College—the one that mentioned Rings of Resonance. Following this, it was a simple matter of the correct phrase and so...Her guest had been much less smug after that, she was here to say!

"Silvestrus, your charges appear to be responding well to our humble ministrations and are growing in strength daily."

"It is only through the efforts of you and your dedicated staff that this has been possible, Melior."

"Thank you. But they are young and full of the healing energy. However, perhaps as a consequence of this transformation, certain unusual occurrences have transpired here at the Convent which I feel duty bound to call to your attention—in the, um, unlikely event they are at all related to your apprentices."

"Pray tell, Melior, to which occurrences do you refer?"

The *Mater Amplior* picked up the scroll sitting by her hand, unrolled it, and began to read to herself. After a moment, she addressed her guest.

"Silvestrus, please understand in what follows that I'm not proposing that you or your apprentices have any connection whatsoever with the peculiar happenings we have lately experienced. However, the timing of these events following the arrival of your group suggests a series of otherwise fascinating coincidences. To wit, you and the young lads arrived here the night of six Septembris in rather desperate straits, if I remember correctly. Since then, a twelve-day has passed, and it's now the eighteenth.

"At first nothing seemed amiss. We tended your boys, burning up with fever one minute and in rigors the next. We concurred with Master Celsius's diagnosis of Mallia's Aria. As I'm sure you know by now, Mallia herself was with us for an extended time prior to her passing—taken by her own eponym, as it were, in the end. We applied our knowledge of ministrations to your boys, and, thanks be to the Gods, they've all turned the corner, clinically. Their speech soon began to make sense. They first accepted soft food, then full meals. Their functions returned. All was proceeding smoothly until we noted the beginning of a series of mysteries.

"Cook was the first to bring it to my attention. Of a sudden, over a period of days, small food items began to disappear—buns, apples, tarts. No one was seen. All foodstuffs are under the watchful eye of the kitchen staff from the time the raw produce is brought into stores from the local farms until it enters the Sisters' mess. Yet items continued to disappear. After the passage of another day or two, entire pies went missing, and now, only yesterday, a whole roast pig! We are baffled, Master Silvestrus. Can you think of any conceivable explanation for these amazing events?"

"Normally, Melior, I'd tend to look hardest at the three lads. But I assume this must have crossed your mind as well. And, since you are querying me beyond that, I have reason to believe you have ruled them out as major suspects?"

"Yes. But whether fortunately or unfortunately, I cannot say. They, as you know, have been most closely watched since their arrival. Initially, of course, they were too ill to do aught but moan. Now that the crisis has passed, all of them have been able to make their way to the commode and back. You have been with them as much as we, and together they do not own an unchaperoned moment. I assume that, while they may have made some initial steps toward the Art, they are not yet anywhere near to being competent Transpositioners? No? I thought not. So that takes us back to where we began."

The *Mater Amplior* took a sip of tea and paused before consulting her scroll again. "You know, that honey is really quite delightful. However, back to the matter at hand. Not all occurrences involve food items, though it seems they constitute the overriding majority of them. Some of the items missing are items of...comfort. We, as you have no doubt observed by now, are a rather austere order. Our pallets are straw, our walls bare, our feet unshod, our bowls and plates are of stone, our utensils wooden, and so on. While items of comfort are not specifically prohibited here, they are, let us say, discouraged. Chastisement of the flesh can lead to greater enlightenment of the mind, we are taught. However, we are also of the human race, and its failings are our failings. It is not unknown, for example, for a footstool or a wall embroidery to be discovered among the possessions of a Sister recently gone to her reward. And those items apparently disappear as soon as they are uncovered, or so I understand.

"Lately, however, our cunning *Spiritus* has apparently taken a liking to your apprentices. Several items of comfort have turned up in their possession—down-filled pillows and comforters, tooled doeskin slippers, fine linen nightshirts, to name but a few. The Sisters watching the boys have come to feel that a Presence beyond their reckoning is taking a part in your lads' healing process, and they refuse, therefore, to interfere or confiscate this contraband."

"Amazing news, Melior. Quite amazing."

"Yes. Quite. Let me hasten to add that not all items of mystery are those gone missing. Several relics we had feared lost forever have suddenly appeared at the foot of the *Statue of Silence* in the vestibule. Arconia's Girdle, for example, missing since the sixth century, was suddenly found there. The *Scrolls of Antoninus,* lost these many decades, were there in their original leather casings. And the *Prepuce of Persephone,* a truly unique artifact, was rediscovered after all this time!" The *Mater Amplior* shook her head. "But I fear that is not the worst of it. The most serious concern has been the effect upon the Sisters themselves. They all seem to be distracted lately, almost giddy. They forget the words of the prayers and homilies and are negligent in rituals they have practiced since they became novices. And, most disconcerting of all, Sister Ardens and two others of her cell came to me this very morning, seeking absolution regarding their vows and asking permission to leave the Order! All Sister Ardens could speak of was the lovely soft skin and fine long limbs of your three boys!"

"Well, Melior, I would hardly hold that against them. The boys are handsome-enough rogues as those things go, and the Sisters are still women, come to that."

"Master Silvestrus, Sister Ardens is seventy-eight years old! And the two others not that far behind her!"

"Oh. I see."

"Yes, I'm sure you do." Melior sighed. "I am at a loss to explain any of it. Therefore, I thought I should advise you. You, I believe, are one of the Wise and likely an Initiate of the Mysteries. I was hoping you would be willing to turn your considerable gifts to this problem so the rest of us can return to more mundane pursuits, such as understanding the difficulty in the plumbing of our Fountain of the Grove, dry these past fifteen months."

"Of course, Melior. It shall be as you say. I will begin my investigations at once. By your leave." With that, the old sorcerer stood, smiled, and gave a deep bow before making his exit.

Melior stared after him, absently regarding the small bare room with its single glowing candle, scented this time, though the *Mater Amplior* could not recall why she had chosen it for this interview. She let out the breath she hadn't been aware she'd been holding and turned to the next scroll on her desk, squinting, suddenly irritated at the crabbed handwriting of the missive's author.

* * *

Silvestrus strode down the corridor from Melior's office and passed by the infirmary, from which several voices issued. He recognized them as belonging to several of the Sisters—and Celsius.

"…meant nothing by it. It is just a phrase. I—"

"And what sort of phrase is it, Goodly Physician, that mocks women in the role of the healing arts, might I ask?"

"Well, I dare say, that is not precisely what I—"

"Did you not know that Mallia herself spent the last few years of her life instructing us in the Art? And yet you belittle the entire matter?"

"No, no. You misunderstand. I was merely—"

"Being rude, I would say! And where would you be without a woman, eh? Green cloud or not, your foundation is physical, and some woman went through the Pain to bring you into this world!"'

"Of course. I do not dispute that. I was only—"

"Discounting the value of our Profession! And undermining the importance of the contributions of generations of our gender stretching back into the mists of time! Was that your goal, then, oh, Wise Tutor?"

"Ladies, please, it was only that—"

Silvestrus smiled to himself as he strode along. Some things in life, he reflected, were deserved. And some well deserved.

He paused by a sunlit alcove in which sat a large two-handed floor urn. It was glazed in deep orange with rows of naked black figures chasing about on it engaged in some activity requiring shields, spears, helmets, and bulls. Next to the urn, a small purple-winged *Spritae* was sound asleep on a ledge, drool trickling out of the corner of her mouth.

"Morphia! Awaken! What news have you?"

The small winged creature sat up with a start, wiped her chin, then yawned and stretched, gazing lazily at the old man.

"Oh, Master Silvestrus, I thought you might be coming this way, so I waited here for you."

"A fortunate choice, little one. Now, what news have you?"

"Concerning your charges, I assume you mean? They are healing well. I myself have seen them up and about, though they detected me not. They are farther along in their recovery than they seem. I believe they are playing yet at being invalid, perhaps to coax further favors and kindnesses from the Sisters. These women appear to be quite taken with them, even the blue-nosed one—rather especially the blue-nosed one. You have not, by chance, given any of them a Ring of Resonance, have you? No? Well, in any event, the boys have commandeered the lion's share of attention. Not all of the items suddenly vanished are the work of the redheaded one who flits about reaping as he wills so that even I am pressed to keep up with him. Additionally, several of the Sisters conspire to spoil the lads with divers gifts. It you want my advice—and you should—best get your apprentices out on the road again soon, before the whole convent is either in a riot or abandoned entirely."

"Hmm, I think you are right. I believe I will go have a talk with them."

"They're all in the south courtyard, taking their ease."

"Thank you, Morphia. Now if you will make your way to our cart in the stable shed, you will find four slightly sticky stone crocks. You may take one of them for yourself and your sisters by way of my thanks."

"Ah, the honey! We were hoping…Thank you, Master! Call on us again, anytime!" With a jaunty wave and thrumming of wings, the little sprite launched herself out of the window and was gone in a wink.

Silvestrus resumed his trek. Taking the next left, he passed through an arch that led into a sunny atrium where he stopped to survey the scene. There he found Thaddeus under the branches of a great oak, carefully pushing a two-seated swing that was suspended by vines. A pair of giggling Sisters rose higher and higher into the air with each shove, their black-bottomed feet protruding from their long smocks, kicking in delight.

On the other side of the ancient tree, Anders sat on a small marble stool with several scrolls spread out before him on a low stone table. Three of the Sisters sat at his feet on the grass, two considering scrolls of their own, while the third appeared to be engaged in gentle disputation with the young scholar. But it was Rolland who drew the greatest part of his attention. The blue-nosed apprentice lay propped on one side, full in the sun, on a soft blanket with a pillow under his head and a smaller one next to it for his azure nasoid. Two of the four Sisters around him were busy kneading his back, while another peeled what looked to be ripe purberries, plopping them into his mouth one by one as the fourth sang a melancholy lay, accompanying herself on the lyre. She had a lovely voice.

Yes, Morphia was right. Time to be gone from this place. Long past time.

"Sisters!"

The women jumped as if stuck from behind with toothpicks.

"Ah, if you would all be so good as to excuse us for a time, I would speak with my apprentices. In private, if you please."

The Sisters scattered, vanishing within seconds.

"Lads, I..." Silvestrus scanned the boys' expressions. Thaddeus, attentive and eager, was trying one-handedly, but unsuccessfully, to stop the recently vacated swing in its course. Anders, looking a little guilty, quickly rolled up one of the scrolls, which, judging from the illustrations, appeared to concern itself with matters of anatomy. And Rolland, challenging and irritated as if a treat had been unfairly snatched from him, was rapidly stuffing the remaining fruit in his tunic for later attention. Without warning, the old sorcerer tossed his head back and began laughing aloud from pure joy. It was some time before he regained his composure.

Nine days later came a farewell of many tears and flowers. The laden cart, pulled by the bedecked and well-groomed mule, and accompanied by the laden young men, was sent off with earnest and heartfelt waves. Even *Mater Amplior*, standing near the gushing Fountain of the Grove, shed a tear, quickly wiped away by a pocket linen as the party passed by. With a deep boom, the brass-banded gates swung shut behind them.

* * *

Melior surveyed the scene around the courtyard critically. The Sisters were now standing quietly as if not knowing what to do. Some let the bouquets they had but moments before been waving wildly slip from their fingers and fall to the ground. Smiles and tears steadily changed back to somber expressions portraying the possibility of a future without hope. Eyes once bright and shining now turned dull and downcast. The close-knit groups of Sisters recently chirping and buzzing dispersed inexorably into individuals as each walked woodenly away in her own direction, silent with arms folded in her habit, touching nothing. The world had gone from a festive and colorful fair time to a gray and impersonal existence once again.

The *Mater Amplior* sighed deeply. Something important had been lost, she judged, perhaps never to return.

* * *

The group took the dusty path leading southeast from the convent, circling south of Moorstown. The footpath became a trail, which joined a lane that emptied onto the main West-East road that would eventually intersect with the major North-South Way at the Great Crossroads. At that juncture, they would turn due north and embark on the last long leg of their journey to the *Collegeum.*

Silvestrus calculated as they walked. They had lost almost a month in their most recent adventure. The moon was lacking a day of being full once again. If nothing else interfered, they would be arriving at their destination in good time. However, even one more interruption would make it a close thing. Time constraints or no, he refused to set a faster pace. It was true the boys were doing well, but they still needed their rest. They would make frequent stops and take the road in four or five easy pieces.

The party reached the Great Crossroads by the evening of the next day. The boys had walked throughout the morning but had dozed in the afternoon in the back of the jiggling cart and awakened refreshed. They seemed energetic as they prepared the evening meal and asked many questions concerning the Crossroads.

Anders swallowed the last of his bread and cleared his throat. "Master, how is it that such a large and important place is abandoned? We've seen no sign of habitation for hours. I would have thought an intersection of that import would have a sizable town or even a city."

"Well, one would think so, but none there are who will live here anymore."

"Anymore, Master?" Thaddeus asked.

"Yes, once, long ago, this was as bustling a thoroughfare and center of government as you might wish for. It was called Terminus. But it has been essentially deserted these past thousand years—since the Invasion, as a matter of fact. This was the staging area and mobilization point for the Imperial Army's Eastern Campaign, the one Tyrannus led. It was here that the commands from all over the Empire converged, joining together before heading east. But after, well, it just withered and died."

Rolland's brow furrowed. "Why was that, Master?"

"No one knows exactly. Not one stone has been left standing upon another. All right, lads, try to get some rest. I would say you are very nearly back to normal. One more repose should do it, I believe."

* * *

After their master retired, the boys sat around the dying fire contemplating the curious fate of Terminus. The moon shone down fully for the first time since midsummer.

"Thaddeus, Anders, I know you'll not take me seriously, but look to the east. It's the Lights of Calling again."

Anders squinted. "By the Gods, you're right. Well, we know enough to stay away from them now, I'd say."

Thaddeus gazed east intently. "I'm not so sure about that. Those swamp lights danced and moved. And they had a green cast. This light is steady and blue."

A familiar look stole across Rolland's features. "I think we ought to investigate. There might be—"

Anders stood. "No! Absolutely not! Are you mad? Have you learned nothing? We stay put. I don't care if all the treasure of the Cin is out there for the taking. We stay put. Besides, Master would skin us. Slowly."

"I think he has a point," Thaddeus concurred. "Fool me a first time, shame on ye. Fool me a second time, shame on me."

"You know, you two pedestrians lack all the essential ingredients for the enjoyment of adventure and intrigue. With that view of life, you're going to miss out on any number of fine opportunities."

"Such as almost being turned into compost by an old, irate tree hugger? No, thank you. My Nannsi will still care for me without a bauble or two."

"Very well. Stay here, then. I'm going to have a look. I may—or may not—share my portion of the treasure when I return." Rolland leaped to his feet and slipped into the moonlit shadows.

After waiting ten minutes, Thaddeus threw down the twig he'd been twisting back and forth. *"Stercus!* All right, Anders, come on. I'm going to need some help dragging the remains back here." The tall apprentice stood and headed resolutely after Rolland with his shorter companion muttering expletives, trying his best to keep up. Thaddeus was aware Anders thought cursing to be coarse and that he strove to avoid it whenever possible.

They had not gone far when the thief, gray headed in the moonlight, materialized in front of them.

"Come with me," was all he said.

A few more minutes took them down into, then up out of, an arroyo.

"Behold!" Rolland commanded. "The City on the Plain."

It was not so much a city, however, as it was a fortress built entirely of logs, the

largest structure any of them had ever seen and easily dwarfing the Great Spansion in River's Wood. It was huge—perhaps a mille passae or more on a side—and appeared to be a military encampment. The tall trees constituting the stockade's bulwark must have been dragged in from a great distance, for the boys had seen no forests for days. Timber walls the height of three men were reinforced with cross works, and elevated guard towers were spaced at regular distances along the entire length. A series of three concentric moats with sharpened spikes sticking out at random intervals comprised the perimeter. A wide avenue paved with flat stones that Anders identified as lava, worn smooth by passage and time, led down from a massive double gate. The avenue ended abruptly a hundred paces from where the boys stood. The entire periphery of the structure sat within a haze of blue whiteness. The sheeted light extended vertically to a height several paces beyond the highest tower of the fortress. The boundary of the haze was sharply demarcated, though Anders pointed out that they could see the moon rising over the encampment through the blue-white glow.

As the boys cautiously drew closer, they discerned glowing figures marching back and forth, patrolling the wall and, through the open gate, rows of identical tents. Others walked in and out of the gate in twos and threes, all of them outfitted in antique armor. A patrol paraded in front of a tall pole topped with a pennant bearing the image of an eagle with several unfamiliar markings below it.

Thaddeus nudged Anders. "What's that insignia on the standard? It says SPQI"

"Why, that's the initials for the old Empire. I think it stands for *Senatus Populusque Imperatus*—the Senate and the People of the Empire."

"What about the flag?"

"That's the pennant, I believe, for the *MI*st Imperial Legion."

"What number?" Rolland asked.

"The Thousand and First."

"*Iovis!*" Thaddeus exclaimed. "I didn't know the Imperial Army had that many legions."

"They didn't. There were only nine hundred and ninety-nine legions. The Thousandth was an honorary legion left at home in Fornia, the Imperial capital, to guard the homeland—mostly toothless old veterans and scullery lads. There never was a Thousand-and-First Legion. But that's not half the problem."

CITY ON THE PLAIN : TERMINUS

"Oh? What do you mean?" Thaddeus asked.

"The last Imperial legion marched east a thousand years ago, Thaddeus. So who are those men, and what are they doing there dressed like old Imperial legionnaires? And what is the meaning of that blue-white haze encompassing the whole encampment?"

Rolland leaned closer, his voice low. "Maybe they're actors putting on a play, or revelers in some sort of theatrical hoax?"

"I don't think so. It seems a bit elaborate for that," Thaddeus said. "Besides, I don't think people usually attend plays in the middle of the night, hoax or no."

"Well, all right, my tall friend, points given. Who do you suggest they are?"

"I don't know."

"I think I know," Anders said, glancing up at the moon.

"Oh, who then, Bright One of Brightfield?"

"Mortui. The Dead."

At his words, a group of four soldiers who had been patrolling the glowing blue perimeter stopped and pointed to the boys. The soldiers made no sound but gave the universal gesture for "come forward." The apprentices looked at each other and shrugged.

Thaddeus squared his shoulders and led the way.

The boys halted within hailing distance but were bid forward to the boundary line with another imperious gesture. Rolland, his scarf around his face, stood behind his two friends.

One of the glowing figures strode forward. "Who are you to disturb the peace of our night?"

Though the man spoke Common, his dialect was nearly impenetrable. It reminded Thaddeus of the old farmers from the South who periodically came to Beewicke to trade for honey. They were just as difficult to understand.

Thaddeus took a deep breath and stepped forward. "We are apprentices traveling with our master, gone exploring. We saw the light and thought to come and learn its source."

"You are hard to speak. From whence do you live?"

"We are from…Fountaindale, sir."

"Ha! No need to 'sir' him, lad. He is only Marcellus. No makings of an officer there." The man at the patrol leader's elbow guffawed at his own jest, while the leader cast him a we-will-talk-later look.

"Fountaindale? I've heard naught of it."

"It lies in the, um, Western Provinces, sir, on the Great River," Anders added quickly.

"The Western Provinces. I see. Well, that may account for it, but this matter requires investigation. Bernardus, Franciscus, Horatius—you three remain here with these boys. I will go fetch Helveticus. He will sort this out, I'll wager." With that, the soldier turned on his heel and strode back up the avenue and through the gates into the fortress.

The older balding man Marcellus had called Horatius stepped forward. "Young one, you have an accent, true, but also the tongue of a scholar on you, should I not miss my mark. Where have you studied?"

"I have only had my tutors, sir, Primus and Secundus. When I was younger, I even had Tertius, but he left after some trouble with Cook, I think."

"Ah, yes. Well, it is often so. In any case, we are an isolated outpost, and I thirst for news of the outside world. Many there were who came at first, but now, well, it is a mystery. One of several, as it happens. I can't quite seem to remember—"

A new voice broke in on the conversation, a voice used to command. No doubt this was Helveticus. "What you can't seem to remember is that you're on parade duty, Old Bookworm. Now be gone, all of you. Back to your posts! I'll handle this crew fair enough."

The new arrival was broad and strapping, with close-cropped iron-gray hair. His slitted eyes were cautious rather than piggish, clever rather than cruel. His armor, dressed full, though bright and spotless in the moonlight, had the used look of a professional. He sported a tattoo of a black eagle, wings spread, on his forehead above the right eye. The four soldiers struck fist to chest in salute, turned, and marched back to the parade ground. The older man looked the apprentices over thoroughly, taking his time.

"You, in the back, uncover your face. 'Tis no benefit in conversing with one as likes to have something to hide."

Rolland, obviously reluctant, let down his scarf. His nasoid, the blue turned to gray in the pale light, hung limp to his chest. The boy, who had been staring at the ground, gradually raised his gaze to regard his inquisitor.

"Sister to the Mother! What's that you're sporting, young one, instead of a nose?"

Anders interceded quickly. "It's a sorcerer's curse, sir. He offended one of their Order."

"Ah. Well, we have that in common, don't we now. We"—the large man's arm swept the entire camp—"are under a sorcerer's curse as well. Though I expect we've been at it longer than you three. I judge you all to be mid-young, fourteen or fifteen, is it?"

The boys nodded.

"I have some of the same at home—at least I did…"—here the man looked away quickly, then back again—"who would be your age about now. Put me in mind of them, you do." The legionnaire straightened his shoulders. "Now to business. I am Helveticus, *Centurio Prior* of this command. Your names, lads?"

"Thaddeus of Beewicke, sir."

"Anders of Brightfield. That's near Meadsville, sir. I mean, if you know where Meadsville is. That is—"

"And I'm Rolland of Fountaindale, as you've heard, Centurion Major," Rolland, now recovered, interrupted smoothly, "at your service."

"I don't recognize those names, but then, there's as many towns to the Empire as stars to the sky, as my father was wont to say. A centurion he was in his time as well—decorated by the old Emperor himself. But what is it brings you lads out this night?"

Thaddeus cleared his throat. "We're making our way with our master to the *Collegium Sorcerorum,* sir. He's back at our camp now."

"Ah, so you're to be sorcerers yourselves, then? Good lads. 'Tis a noble calling, however fraught with hazard, I hear tell. How is it, though, that one of you who is cursed by a sorcerer is traveling with a sorcerer?"

Rolland explained quickly.

"Ah, I see," was the man's only comment.

Anders interjected with obvious interest. "Excuse me, sir, but I believe you said you were under a curse as well. You seem to have a high opinion of sorcerers, nonetheless, for one who has suffered at their hands."

"Bright lad, to pick that out. Well, yes. But you see—um, Anders, is it?–we've all had some time to think on it, and sometimes a man gets to regretting what it is he's done. In any case, we've come to the conclusion that we had more the blame in this. That sorcerer—Silvestrus was his name—he and his colleagues were only doing what the Emperor had commanded them to, cursing us for our cowardice, and—" The Centurion Major stopped, peering at them intently. "What's the rub here? You all jumped when I mentioned the man's name."

Thaddeus stepped forward. "It's just that our master's name is Silvestrus, Centurion Major—though I'm sure it must be a different man, just one with the same name."

"Well, I don't know, boy. It'd have only been about forty years ago, and those sorcerers are a long-lived lot as I hear it."

Anders's eyes widened. "Excuse me, sir. Forty years ago?"

"Yes. It has to be at least that long since we first marched east in the spring."

"Marched east, sir?"

"Yes, east. Now don't tell me the news has managed to miss your Meadsville, wherever that may be. Yes, the Imperial Army of the Invasion. It's been twenty years in the making, boy. Everyone knows of it. We were going east to take back the Treasure of the Cin."

"Take back treasure, sir?" Rolland asked, eyes alert.

"Yes, of course. The reason they have so much treasure is that they've been robbing us by foisting their cheap goods on us all these years and charging exorbitant prices for these trinkets. Now we're going to get back what is, after all, rightfully ours." He paused and added with a wry grin. "Well, plus a little extra for the aggravation. I've heard the Emperor himself say this when he addressed the troops."

The boys looked at each other. Finally, Anders turned back to the soldier.

"Centurion Major Helveticus, if I'm understanding you correctly, you are saying that your company was part of the Grand Imperial Army on its way to invade the Land of the Cin?"

"Yes, lad. What else could I mean?"

"Um, Centurion, I don't quite know how to put this, but that was a thousand years ago. Your army and your Emperor are...long dead."

"What? That cannot be! We count only thirty-six years since, well, since the Army crossed into the Eastlands."

Anders pressed on. "How do you reckon your time, Centurion Major?"

"Like any other fool alive on this Earth, boy. One day each moon."

"Moon, sir?" Rolland asked.

"Yes, moon. Although we've discussed it much among ourselves, we still do not understand it entire, but each day—or night, rather—is marked by a full moon. Thus we have counted. Horatius, our scholar, the bald fellow here earlier, thinks it part of the sorcerous curse somehow. The moon now shows full, and full only, each night."

"In truth, sir, the moon has not changed," Thaddeus supplied. "It shows the four phases as it always has."

Anders furrowed his brow in concentration. "I think I'm beginning to understand. But Centurion Major, you mentioned a curse. Why was it you were cursed?"

For the first time, the stalwart figure looked down, plainly uncomfortable. "Well, lads, I am sorry to say it—sorry indeed. But this company, you see, is made up of, well, deserters. None of us are proud of the fact," he hastened to add, "and we'll all regret it till the day we die. But there it is. We're all marching east, and word gets around—you know, nothing good's to come of this. We're here only for the Emperor's greed, the Eastern Magickers will have our souls, all those things. Well then, we melt away, one by one, you see. Then one night, a bright light came upon us, and here we are. So we organized ourselves against attack as we've been trained to do, built our camp and patrolled it, doing the things soldiers do. At least we try, nowadays, to do well by the Army. No officers, though. Perhaps there were none who left early, but I don't know about that. Or perhaps they're in a different place. But we're here, and we made our company the Thousand-and-First Imperial Legion, the Leopard Legion. And here we sit awaiting our orders. But like I said, it's been thirty-six years, and each night's the same—full moon and empty news. It's begun to get discouraging."

"That's it! It has to be!" Anders broke in, pounding his fist into his palm. "Centurion Major, each night your moon is full, and you never see a different face of it. That suggests that your nights really occur only once every one of our months, so a night for you is thirty days for us. So, your thirty-six years is really—let's see, twelve times thirty-six times thirty. That's, um, twelve thousand nine-hundred and sixty full moons, so that's—yes, that's one thousand years! Give or take. Centurion, you are in this world only once each month, only at the full moon. You and your men have been encamped here for a thousand years!"

If the figure before them had looked surprised before, now he looked stricken.

"One thousand years? That means, that means… we're…all…dead." The crested helmet slipped out of his hands and fell to the ground. He bent his head and soon great tears began to fall upon the glowing land. After a moment, Helveticus looked up, wiped his eyes on his forearm, and took the kerchief from around his neck to blow his nose.

Helveticus swallowed hard and spoke again. "My poor Marta and the little ones. And they say the dead don't cry. Ha! You know, boys, I suppose 'tis not so much a shock to me as you might think. Over the years, we have been trying to puzzle out what has happened to us. We wake up every night—or what to us is every night. There's always that full moon, and we're always in this blue-white light. We haven't seen the sun since, well, since then. Horatius is the one who's always asked the questions. I think he thought as much. We used to have plenty of visitors. At first. Though it seems they were just looking to loot the camp. It's a strange curse. You come in easily enough, but you can't ever leave. Those looters came in, took what they wanted. Sometimes we caught them, sometimes not. The ones that got away made it all the way to the border. But if they took one step over, they vanished! Just like that." The centurion snapped his fingers. "Then the next night, we'd wake up, and we'd have us a new recruit. Had to arm him, teach him soldiering—they don't like that very much at first, but you can get used to most anything, I believe, given enough time.

"So our numbers have increased over the years. We started out with just a thousand or so. Now we have close to ten thousand, last count. Of course, that's a fair amount more than should constitute a true legion, but we decided, what the Hells. It's our legion. We'll do what we want. Besides, what could they do to us, eh? After the Imperial Army left Terminus, the town remained bustling for a time. And we had many new recruits. But as the people who had depended on the

Army for their livelihood moved away after the troops left, the numbers dwindled. Now'days, people avoid us. I believe I understand why now—they must take us for haunted. Another odd thing. These new ones don't remember much of their previous lives, either. Just their names and the names of their towns, maybe something about their families, but that's the most of it. So, we're hungry for news." The clean-shaven professional raised his hand to stroke his chin and looked expectantly at Anders.

"Yes, sir. Your man Horatius said much the same thing. Well, there may not be much I can tell, but I can think of some things. May we sit down? It could take a while."

"Of course, lads, make yourselves comfortable." The centurion squatted on the glowing blue grass while the boys aped him on their own green sward. "I'd invite you to my tent, so you could take your ease, but, well, unless you were looking for a lifetime of military service…" Helveticus let his hand fall in a gesture and chuckled at his own jape. "And I can't leave this area, either. Believe me, we've tried. But we're stuck here, as I've said. So, lads, what can you tell me of the last thousand years?"

Anders took a deep breath and began his recitation, with Thaddeus and Rolland breaking in with commentary from time to time. None of the boys had traveled widely, but they knew their own areas well, and all of them had heard stories of the greater world. The centurion was told what the scrolls had said and what Silvestrus had let slip concerning the Imperial

Invasion. Toward the end, they added personal bits about themselves—their hopes, dreams, aspirations, and fears. The centurion was an avid listener and appeared to absorb all he was told. He asked many pertinent questions, understanding military matters well but with a contempt for politics and those who practiced it. He seemed most interested in the lands that were new since his encampment, their names and boundaries. And he was intrigued by Thaddeus's speculations concerning the Cin coming west.

"You know, young Thaddeus, I think you're onto something. It is a strange thing that you haven't heard from these *Orientales* in all that time. I tell you true, if it were up to me to advise, I'd get to searching for a likely young man to rebuild and restore the Empire and get all in readiness. The Cin are bound to come west sometime, especially having had all this time to prepare. And when they do—well, it'd be best to be ready."

Thaddeus grew thoughtful. "Centurion Major Helveticus, what was it like, sir? I mean, when you set out for the East. A million men—what a sight that must have been."

"You have the right of it, lad. It was a sight indeed. Columns of soldiers, row on row and rank on rank, in burnished arms farther than the eye could see in every direction. All the Eagles, all the pennants! Nine hundred and ninety-nine legions, all at full strength. That's a picture you don't see every day. The horns blaring, the drums beating time, the citizens yelling and throwing bouquets and kisses. You see, in over the ten years of preparations, Terminus had grown into a sizable town. Not all military, mind you—that wouldn't have worked. Many, many supporting staff, logistics, blacksmiths, coopers, ferriers, fletchers, farmers, their families, and, of course, the ladies. Well, the list goes on and on. Then that first day of spring, all the auspices were right, they said. And there was the Emperor, Tyrannus Superbus himself. A handsome man, lads, pepper-gray hair, back stiff with pride, golden laurels around his brows, Imperial purple cloak of the finest weave draped from his shoulders and rippling in the wind, standing tall in a chariot of ivory, chased with gold and pulled by four of the most perfectly matched whites I've ever seen. Then came the speeches, exhortations, priestly blessings, and all manner of rigmarole. At last, the Emperor raised his Imperial baton and lowered it, pointing forward toward the East. The command was given, and we stepped off smart and lively. What a sight! It took the Imperial Army an entire week to evacuate the area. All those brave lads with their hopeful faces. All those..." The centurion turned his face away as his voice trailed off.

Thaddeus was suddenly aware the sky had grown lighter with the false dawn. He looked eastward wondering what would happen now.

Helveticus caught his gaze and nodded toward the east. "Well, lads, I'm guessing it's time for us common foot to sink back into the earth, or wherever it is we go, until next moon. I must thank you boys for the kindnesses you've shown me. I will tell the others what I think best for them to know. Be assured you are always welcome here at the Thousand-and-First Leopard Legion. I don't know why your sorcerer chose to curse us so, but perhaps he has something special in mind for us down the line. Until then, Thaddeus, Anders, Rolland, know you can count Helveticus as your friend among the dead, and if you are ever in need where we can render assistance, you have but to come here at the full of the moon, and any aid you ask will be given."

The centurion extended his hand through the bluish glow to shake each of theirs, but when the boys looked down, they saw only dried, rotted wisps of flesh falling from protruding bones of fingers and wrist. Helveticus followed their gaze. He looked sad and, nodding to himself, started to withdraw, but Thaddeus swallowed hard and reached to grasp the skeletal hand and shake it. He then nudged Anders and Rolland to do the same.

Helveticus smiled. "Thank you, lads. Just remember, ask for Centurion Major Helveticus..." The old soldier's form grew dim as he waved until it just faded away, leaving Thaddeus with a feeling of loss he couldn't explain.

Soon, the sun broached the horizon, and light flooded the area. Of the grand encampment of the Thousand-and-First Imperial Leopard Legion, no trace remained.

Rolland's mouth, which had been hanging open, snapped shut, then opened again. "Aye! That was something! We've got to get back to camp and tell Master Silvestrus!"

The apprentices set a good pace back despite fatigue from their recent illness. They expected to find Silvestrus waiting expectantly, Asullus by his side, but instead, only a rolled-up scroll in a felt case dangled from one of the camp's tripods to greet them. Rolland reached it first.

"Read it to us," Anders said.

"Read it yourself," the thief replied, proffering it to the scholar.

"Rolland!" Anders said, exasperated at his friend's behavior.

The thief looked down, coughed, and let the hand holding the parchment fall to his side.

"I, um, can't read."

"What?" Anders's eyebrows shot up in disbelief.

"I said I can't read, damn it! Are you deaf?"

"Wha—I mean, how can—"

Thaddeus placed a restraining hand on his short friend's wrist. "Anders, don't you remember, when the master made a list of Rolland's situation in Fountaindale when we first met him, he mentioned that? It's all right, Rolland. Here, let me read it."

Rolland handed over the scroll, and Thaddeus glanced at the note before addressing his friends. "It says here the master has taken the cart with Asullus and gone into Moorstown for supplies. We're to wait for him, get some rest, and perform—let's see, here's a list of chores. He says the camp is warded, we're to take our medicine, not leave the camp again, and—well, it goes on in the same way."

Rolland snorted. "Oh, that's nice of him to be so concerned about us. Here we were out all night—he had no idea where or what kind of danger we might have been in. Then we get back, dead tired, having had a truly great adventure with plenty to tell, and he's left us all alone and gone off shopping."

Thaddeus straightened, cocking his head to listen. "We may not be all alone, though." He dropped his voice. "Listen, do you hear that? It sounds like heavy breathing, and it's coming from over there." He pointed. "Come on," he whispered.

A muted, rhythmic buzzing was emanating from behind a large rock lying just west of camp. Thaddeus put a finger to his lips and motioned for the others to follow him. Quietly rounding the rock, the boys spied an open honey crock on its side, a portion of its contents pooled on the ground, and a small figure sound asleep beside it, snoring softly.

The *Spritae*, for Thaddeus could think of nothing else it could be, was very short—an infant's height only—and slim, dressed only in a breechclout. A young girl, he thought, given that the creature had small breasts and puffy nipples. A pair of violet wings lay akimbo beneath her, one folded, one pointing outward. Thaddeus was reminded of an old man he'd once seen sleeping off a drunken stupor outside a tavern in Fountaindale.

"What should we do, Thaddeus?" Anders whispered, peering more closely. "She's beautiful," the scholar added, captivated.

"Anders, she's too short, even for you," Rolland observed, then went on slyly. "Besides, what would Nannsi say?"

Anders appeared to struggle in his attempt to ignore the former street urchin. "What do you think, Thaddeus?"

"Well, she's not here by accident. All the honey crocks are in the cart, and the cart's with the master. I don't think he'd let one go missing, given as how he's come to like it so much. So he must have given it to her. I think we should give this small one a shake and ask her what's going on. Maybe she can tell us more about where the master has gone and what's been happening."

Rolland nodded and started forward, sticking out his foot to give the tiny *Faerrae* a nudge, but Anders grabbed his arm.

"Wait. If we startle her awake, she'll just fly off, and we'll have nothing. Let me think. We need something to hold her here until we can find out what's what. Let's see, what would hold a *Faerrae* folk?"

"How about cobwebs?" Thaddeus offered.

"What?" Rolland asked.

"Cobwebs. I don't know if that would work with this creature, but they worked with Caerulea, and she's Queen of her folk."

"And where are we supposed to get cobwebs this time of day, Lord Bee Master?" Rolland asked.

"I know," Anders spoke up. "Look around you on the grass. See all the dew? Now look closely. Notice the patches of webs stretched across the blades—you can see them glistening in the sunlight."

"This is ridiculous. Who ever heard of..." The thief's voice trailed off at the looks from his two friends. "Oh, all right, but this is stupid."

However, working quietly, the boys harvested and carefully applied the delicate bindings to their snoring prey in a relatively short time. The *Spritae* did not stir.

"Now give her your nudge, Rolland," Thaddeus ordered.

It took three attempts, but the small figure finally opened bloodshot eyes, closed them again, smacked her lips, then opened them again in consternation.

"Oh! Oh! Oh! Let me go! Let me go!" the *Spritae* cried, desperately struggling against the shiny silken threads.

"Peace, small one," Thaddeus spoke reassuringly. "None will hurt you. But your presence is a mystery. If you will give your oath to stay, answer our questions, and not fly off until we are done, we will release you without penalty."

"Oh! I do give it! I do! Now loose me, please!"

Rolland was at her side in an instant, his hand casually caressing his knife hilt. "Oaths so easily given are oft so easily broken. Look you, little sparrow, one false step and you'll not get above two men's height before this point finds your vitals."

The small figure quieted but regarded the redhead archly. "You may live to regret that threat you make to me, Blue Nose."

Rolland smiled an evil smile and made a quick gesture, drawing his thumb across his neck.

The *Spritae*, in turn, grasped the air two handbreadths in front of her own nose and, with her other hand, made a downward slicing motion as if severing something she was holding. Mustering what dignity she could, she turned her attention to Thaddeus.

"Lord in Beewicke, hear me! I height Morphia, *Spritae* indentured to Silvestrus, Vice Master of the Council of the Wise of the *Collegium Sorcerorum.* As long as your questions conflict not with my sworn obligations, I will answer what I can. If I like you, that is. Now loose me."

Thaddeus suppressed a smile. "All right, Morphia. Fairly spoken." He pulled away the restraining fibers until the *Spritae* was entirely free. He held his breath, but she sat quietly, wings slowly fanning, making no move to escape. "Very good, miss. Now tell us, please, what do you here?"

"Your manners match your stars, Lord in Beewicke. The lady Ethne has taught you well. And I think I like you, after all, *Amicus Faerrarum.* Therefore, I will tell you. I am spy to Master Silvestrus. I have been set to watch you all and have reported back to the master everything you've done since the very beginning. Everything."

Chapter 10

DISCERE LEGER et IUDICARE LIBERI

* * *

"Spy! I knew it! I knew we couldn't trust him! I told you so!" Rolland shouted, pointing an incriminating finger at the diminutive *Faerrae.*

Anders rolled his eyes. "Rolland! Calm down! You never said anything of the sort about trusting the master at any time. Now take an even strain and let me think. Thaddeus, I'd like to know if Morphia's agreement with you to be straightforward might apply to me, too."

"I'll ask." He turned to the *Spritae.* "Morphia, will you extend our agreement to Anders as well?"

"Well, all right," she replied after a moment's consideration. "But do not ask me to include—what is it the mule calls him? Ah, yes—Rufus. I will not speak with him! Ever!"

Rolland took a step forward. "Really? Well, you can go put—"

"Rolland! This is not useful. Please allow me to continue."

"Oh, all right, but if there's one falsehood—"

"Your pardon, Morphia." Anders gave the thief a hard look before turning back to the winged Fey. "You say you're indentured to the master. How did this come to be?"

"It'sonaccoutofthehoney," she mumbled in a low voice.

"I'm sorry, I didn't quite hear you."

"I said, it's on account of the honey. My sisters and I, we have developed a, um, liking for the honey—just like the master!" she stated defensively. "And we knew Master Silvestrus of old, of course, and he learned of our…attachment…to it. Especially that elixir from Beewicke. And he, um, said he could provide some for us if we might be willing to do little favors for him now and then. At first, we saw no harm in this. After all, to have it given to us saved us the trouble of having to steal it from our cousins, the *Pixae,* or those stupid humans who harvest it—no offense, Lord in Beewicke!" She hiccuped and ran her tongue over her lips. "What we didn't know, however, was that it has a much different effect on us than on you selfsame humans. To wit, once we acquire a taste for it, we can't do without it. I mean that literally. After a day or two without, we begin to feel ill. We become nauseated; our tummies cramp up terribly; we loose bad air. Next we break out in sweats, feel grievously sick, and are afraid we will die. Then we must have it! It is a plague. I don't know if Master Silvestrus was aware of that or not. He has never refused us in our need, but we feel we dare not leave him now or refuse any bidding of his for fear of losing our delectable nectar. It is a dreadful dilemma!"

"I know what you're saying," Rolland broke in. "We had this trouble crop up in the thieves' guild in Fountaindale from time to time with the red *Papaver Orientalis.* It's the one thing Faran was strictest about." Rolland adopted a serious tone. "You know, if you or your sisters ever want to rid yourselves of its grip, I've seen it done. I know how to do it, and I would help you."

Morphia gazed at him in amazement. "You would do that for us?"

"Yes. I don't think anyone should be beholden to another on that kind of basis."

Thaddeus glanced at Anders and nodded, a new level of respect growing in his eyes.

"I should tell you, however, that it will not be pleasant. You will not die, but you may beg for death before you're done, I vow. But afterward, you will be free."

"I-I shall think on it and tell my sisters. Thank you."

"You needn't mention it." The thief was silent for a moment. "Of course, there might be a time one day—and that day may never come—when I would wish for—"

"Rolland!" Thaddeus and Anders said together.

Immediately, Morphia's wide-eyed gaze was replaced by a calculating, slitted look. "Humans! Of course!"

"Every time Rolland jumps out of his saddle, he lands on his head," Anders observed. "In any event, Morphia, what was it Master wanted of you concerning us?"

The *Spritae* sniffed dismissively at the redhead, then returned her attention to the scholar. "To spy on you, as I've said. He told us of his advancing years and that his stamina and powers were changing with time. He said he was going out to recruit three new apprentices—to join one other, I think—who would be vital to some prophecy he knew of. He said that should ill fortune befall any of these apprentices, the consequences would be beyond reckoning. Therefore, he wished us to keep an eye on the three of you. But he stressed we must never be detected for fear the knowledge of being watched would begin to change your responses—or something like that—and that would be bad. So, my sisters and I were to follow you, unseen, and report back to him regularly on your whereabouts and circumstances. You recall the street brawl in that place called Fountaindale? And how it happened that Master Silvestrus arrived with the Shire Reeve at just the right moment? Well, I had flown to him with the news. And then on Midsummer's Night—what an experience that was! You must have your thief friend tell you sometime just what it was he put into the fire that night."

Anders looked at Rolland quizzically, but the thief only shook his head.

"So, I kept him abreast of all the happenings. Then, when that Merriwhiddle witch caught you out—well, I've never seen him so worried."

"I see," Anders said. "Did he say how long this scrutiny was to continue?"

"Yes. Until you were safely at the College."

"Interesting." Anders tugged at his ear. "Well, Thaddeus, what do you think we should do?"

Thaddeus shook his head. "Nothing."

"What?" Rolland said, astonished.

"Nothing. We go on about our business. Consider, tomorrow we turn and head north. Master has said there are no real towns or villages between the Crossroads and *Arx Montium*—the Mountaingaard. And once we're through the pass, we're within spitting distance of the College. So, we'll just go on our way, doing our apprentice best. To do anything different would only reveal our discovery and place Morphia in jeopardy."

Anders nodded. "All right. I agree that makes a certain amount of sense."

"Rolland?"

"I'll agree, too, but I'd like to know what our little bottle fly will run and say to the master when he asks for her report on this morning?"

"Replying only to you, Lord in Beewicke, and ignoring Surrounding Unimportants, I will say you arrived back safely from the Terminus encampment, and after you took to your bedrolls, I fell asleep as the consequence of a small indulgence."

"Good enough, Morphia. Now go as you please and with our thanks."

The little *Spritae* smiled and jumped up, wings buzzing. She made a dash at Thaddeus, but only to kiss his nose. She then turned and, sticking out her tongue at Rolland, laughed and flew off into the forest.

"Peckish little *Faerrae.* Don't count on her keeping her word," Rolland warned.

"You just be sure, Rolland, that you keep yours with her," Anders said sternly.

Thaddeus stretched and yawned. "I don't know about you two, but I'm exhausted. I think we should get some sleep and save the chores for later."

Rolland nodded. "That's the first sensible thing you've said all day."

"Perhaps a quick nap would be good. Then we've work to do." Anders stared briefly in the direction the *Spritae* had flown before lying down to seek his rest.

* * *

At first, Rolland was enjoying his dream. He was being held snugly and fed the sweetest liquor. He almost called out, "Mother?" But the dream faded, and the elements seemed different. The holding seemed more like binding, and the sweet taste had turned sticky and sour in his mouth. Waking further did not improve the situation. Moving only confirmed he was being held in restraints, and the sticky substance smeared over his mouth also covered the rest of his face and hair, plastering it down.

The thief struggled to open his glued-shut eyes, then wished he hadn't. Resolutely, he opened them again. A quick inventory revealed he was tightly bound in crisscrossed vines. The harder he wrestled, the more tightly he was held. Biting flies buzzed about his face. He couldn't move his arms to swat them, and he could barely move his head. He gazed around frantically, seeking assistance. A foot's pace to the left, a small stick was thrust into the ground at an angle. Impaled on it was a scrap of parchment with a few words scratched on one side. He saw the note, of course, but could not understand its meaning.

Voices on his other side proved, on twisting around, to belong to Thaddeus and Anders. Relief flooded him. Judging by the sun, it was midafternoon, and in moments, he would be free. He was hungry, in any case, and tired of this stupid game and whoever had—oh, yes. He now knew who had bound him. He also knew what he was going to do to that small personage.

"Aye, Thaddeus, Anders! Over here!"

The pair of stalwarts glanced at him, smiled, waved, then went on with their conversation.

"Aye! What are you two playing at? Come get me free!"

Thaddeus waved again, nodding at something Anders said, and, carrying two empty buckets, headed toward the small creek that flowed by their campsite. Anders then headed toward Rolland with several rolls of parchment under his arm and two or three sharpened sticks blackened at one end.

"What in the Hells are you grinning at, Anders? Untie me, you little prick!"

"My goodness, such language. Yes, I will untie you—against my better judgment—but eventually rather than immediately. First, we have some business to transact."

Rolland strained at his bindings, thrashing futilely. "What? What are you talking about? Anders, loose me! Then I'm going to carve that little purple peahen stem to stern and—"

"Rolland! Will you be quiet and listen for a change? Master Silvestrus has not yet returned. You were still sleeping when Thaddeus and I awoke and found you thus. I have an idea who might be responsible, as I imagine you do as well. Thaddeus was going to set you free at once. However, I pointed out an opportunity to him, and he agreed to wait."

"You convinced Thaddeus to leave me tied up? Anders, I'm going to slice—"

"You are not going to slice anything. At least not for a while. Not until I release you, in any case. Now stop sputtering and listen! You are a danger to our group."

"What? What are you talking—"

"Silence, knave! You are a danger to us. Rather, your ignorance is a danger. And by that, I mean your illiteracy. There may come a time when our survival will depend on your ability to correctly interpret the words of a message. For example, when we were ill recently, what if Master Celsius could only leave written instructions for our care with you? What if Thaddeus and I were too ill to read what he had written and prepare the necessary potions? Or, just this morning, what if, when we returned from the Terminus camp, Silvestrus's note had contained an urgent warning against danger? You wouldn't have been able to alert us because of your ignorance. I have persuaded Thaddeus this situation represents an unacceptable risk. Therefore, I have proposed a remedy."

"Oh, really? And what's that? You going to slit my throat?"

Anders paused as if considering this option. "Well, I don't know. Now that you mention it..." The young scholar laughed. "No, you urban urchin. I'm going to teach you to read."

"Read?" the astonishment on Rolland's face was almost palpable. "You're keeping me tied up against my will so you can teach me about chicken scratches? Why, you little—"

"Ah-ah-ah! That makes it take longer. Yes, read. That way, if we receive any important messages, we ignore them at our peril rather than have to always rely on you to get us killed. I think that sums it up."

Rolland struggled with his rage. "All right, Scholar. Can you at least tell me how long this is going to take?"

"Hmm. Do you see that little sign on the stick by your head?"

"Of course I do! I'm bound, not blind, ass wipe!"

"Ever the silver tongue. All right, what does it say?"

"How in the Hells should I know? I can't read, remember?"

"Well, I will release you when you can tell me what it says."

This response generated a series of invective, personal criticism, and complaint.

"We really don't have all that much time, Rolland, so if you feel a need to comment on every suggestion I make, we'll be here well into dark. Or, alternatively, I could always stuff one of our leftover trail rags in your mouth. Have you a preference? Good, silence is always best." Anders rotated the sign on the stick so Rolland could no longer see the writing. He unrolled one of the scrolls of parchment and took up a blackened stick. "Now, attend to me, sirrah, and learn. This is the letter *A*..."

* * *

As it turned out, after a rocky start, Rolland began to view the alphabet and written word as a coded puzzle to be deciphered. Anders smiled, as he had suspected from the beginning that this approach might have the best chance of success.

The Meadsville scholar was a patient and gifted, if relentless, teacher, while the Fountaindale thief proved a clever and astute, if captive, student. Following a short interruption for eventide, during which Anders spoon-fed his friend, teacher and student returned to work, lighting candles as darkness advanced.

* * *

Thaddeus had taken it upon himself to perform the necessary campsite chores, reasoning, correctly, he was better suited to that task than he was to what Anders had called "the Pedagoguery."

The moon, still full this second night, shone down with silver light when Anders finally nodded and addressed his student. "All right. Let's see, shall we?" With that, he turned the stick around and held a candle up to it. "Read it."

Rolland sounded out the words hesitantly. "It says, 'Ha!...Blue Nose!...How...do...you...like...it?

Morphia.' Why, that—" Catching Anders's expression, Rolland changed direction midsentence and regarded his friend for a long moment. He sighed. "I, um, want to thank you, Anders. This is something I couldn't—wouldn't—have done on my own. You've given me quite a gift. I, well, that is—thank you."

His short friend reached out and patted his shoulder. "My pleasure, Thief. I know you'd do the same for me. There's much, much more to it, of course, but this is a good start—even for someone with a sky-colored trunk. Now, let's see to those bonds."

Anders fumbled at his belt for his small trail knife, then methodically severed the confining ropes strand by strand.

Rolland moved slowly and painfully, first rubbing his wrists, then his legs and ankles, before shaking his limbs one at a time. With effort, he rolled onto his stomach and gradually worked himself up onto his knees, where he paused before shoving himself into a standing position. He wobbled at first but was soon moving under his own power. He made his way jerkily over to the hanging water skin and sloshed water liberally over his head and neck.

Thaddeus, who'd been watching the process with interest, came over and clapped him on the back—gently. "I've found some wild purberries and washed them. There's some honey, yet, in the crock Morphia left. What say you to a reward for your efforts before repose?"

Rolland said the berries were excellent, but the loose bowels that followed on toward dawn, he said, were not. The thief's condition, however, had run its course by midmorning.

He glared at Thaddeus. "You could have told me, you know, that eating so many would give me the runs," he said accusingly for the fourth time that morning.

And for the fourth time that morning, Thaddeus gave him the same response. "I did tell you to be careful about eating handful after handful, you know. It's not my fault you trusted your own urban sophistication over my humble backcountry lore."

"Yes, well if you'd only—"

Thaddeus raised his hand. "Wait. Someone's coming."

Within moments, Silvestrus and Asullus trundled around the bend in the trail with their canvas-covered cart overflowing with all manner of goods made fast with ropes. After waving and hallooing, the boys rushed to see what their master had brought them.

"...also, tents, blankets, cloaks, boots, gloves, and so on. Where we're headed, boys, it'll be cold enough to see your breath some mornings—even at this time of year."

After the excited recruits had superficially sifted through the new stock from the Moorstown Emporium, Anders assumed the role of quartermaster and began inventorying and dispensing the supplies. He seemed happiest when faced with tasks such as this. The boys prepared midday and gave Silvestrus a review of their night at Terminus and Rolland's new course of study.

"You know, it is an interesting coincidence, is it not, that I share the same name as the sorcerer who cursed those soldiers of the *Legio Leopardinus,* the Leopard Legion? I am somewhat familiar with curses of that nature, and it is entirely possible that the Centurion Major—Helveticus, was it?–had the right of it. No one in, no one out for as long as the curse lasts, though typically curses are not so open-ended. They usually have some defining point of extinction, though I am not sure what it would be in this case, perhaps some service to a higher good. It is hard to know, as their crime was significant—desertion in the line of duty. On the other hand, it could well have saved their lives, that is, if you want to consider it 'saving.' It was quick of you boys to discover how they experience time differently."

"Actually, Master, it was Anders who ciphered it out."

"Ah, clever Anders. Once more, you are able to use your noggin for something other than a cap hook. And Rolland, among the *Litterati* at last—good. Very good. If you like, I have some scrolls in my scrip which may be of interest to you. You are free to use them in your practice—only treat these scrolls with care, and return them whence you obtained them."

"Thank you, Master."

"Quite all right."

Of purple wings and clinging vines, there was no mention.

After excitedly looking through the equipment, the boys set up their new tents and prepared eventide.

Following the meal, Silvestrus rummaged through his personal pack and presented Anders and Rolland with three scrolls for reading practice. The two worked until late, with Thaddeus looking on and offering suggestions and recommendations from time to time until repose.

The following morning, true to Thaddeus's prediction, the party turned left and began the last leg of their journey up the Great North Road. Anders continued his role of *Praeceptor Legere,* and Rolland continued to impress his friends with his quickness and aptitude. Once he had mastered the rudiments, his thirst for knowledge proved insatiable, as if his ignorance were an intolerable itch he was at last free to scratch. He addressed it with a single-mindedness that daunted even his erstwhile tutor.

"But why does *e* go before *i* when it comes after *c*? That doesn't make any sense."

"I don't know why, Rolland," Anders spluttered. "It just the rule. That's all you need to know. So memorize it—it's important."

"Oh, very well. But I say it's stupid."

Such exchanges, however, were rare, though they amused the party. Thaddeus was glad for these lighter moments, as he had become aware, over the passing miles, that he was drawing nearer his Destiny, which was proving unnerving. What could he expect? What would be expected of him? Would he be able to do it correctly? Or would he be sent home in disgrace? What if...? That and many more questions played through his mind one after another.

At midday, Master Silvestrus approached the boys. "Lads, I have found some more scrolls for you to review for your practice. They represent a variety of topics. I hope they will prove useful." The old man handed a bundle of parchments to Anders. "I'm going to take a stroll around the area and have a pipe. I will be back in a bit."

Anders immediately sifted through the scrolls. "Here, Rolland, this looks like a good one to begin. Tell me what it says."

Following their meal, the boys packed their things and waited for their master to return. When at last he appeared, they set out on the Great North Road again. As the grade was easy and the likelihood of trouble low, Master Silvestrus made a place for himself amidst the bundles and was soon asleep in the warm afternoon sun.

Thaddeus walked at Asullus's shoulder, as was his custom, and was soon joined by the other two apprentices.

"Aye, Asullus," Rolland queried, "why didn't you tell us about that *Faerrae,* Morphia, who's been spying on us this whole time?"

"Well, 'tis a fair question. I said nothin' because I was bade so. The master an' the young *Spritae* met up soon after we left the College this *Mense Maio* past, an' she ha' been wi' us since that time. 'Tis a sweet lass, she is, e'en if she be a little flighty—an' she an' her sisters, who I can ne'er keep straight, ha' been shadowin' us e'er since. She do ha' a taste fer the honey, though, 'tis so. She was ecstatic when she learned we were to be headin' to Beewicke."

Asullus nodded in Thaddeus's direction. "In fact, now as I think on it, I'm wonderin' if the master ha' that in mind *ab initio,* as he says. In any means, she an' her tribe were willin' to work fer the nectar, an' the master seemed sure it was their type o' work he needed. I'm tellin' ye, lads, this trip—with ye three in it—was high on his mind from the beginnin'. I mean to say, ye lot are very, very important to him. But as to the why o' it, I'm bejabbered to think on any reason successfully."

"Maybe it has something to do with the Prophecy?" Thaddeus ventured.

"What?" Rolland asked.

"The Prophecy. He seems to put a lot of stock in that idea. Perhaps we're involved in it in some way."

Rolland snickered. "Thaddeus, tall friend, you've been out in the sun way too long. Think on what you're saying. How in the world could some junior librarian, a dung-footed hayseed, and a low-life pilcher have anything at all to do with something so grand as this Prophecy the master is always going on about?"

"Rolland, he isn't *always* going on about it. Where did you learn to always exaggerate using only absolutes all the bloody time? I think Thaddeus has a point, though," Anders considered. "Maybe the three of us—whatever our humble origins—fit into this Prophecy of his in some way. If he considers us that important, it would serve to explain a number of things."

"Ah, me short 'un, the keenness o' yer reasonin' could shear the smallest atomie. I think yer scholar's got the right o' it, lads, though I canno' fill in the details. All I know is this trip ha' been different in so many ways from any other we e'er took, I be runnin' out o' hooves to count 'em all."

Rolland snorted. "Well, if we're so special, the old master has a funny way of showing it. We should be treated like princes at the very least. I mean, if we're all that important."

Anders waved the comment away. "That makes no sense whatsoever. Look at how you're responding now. Do you think that's the kind of person a sorcerer should be—believing he's so great and everything? No, I think the master's been feeding us humble pie because humble pie is exactly what we need for now. What do you think, Thaddeus?"

"Anders has a point. We've been made to do things that help us to become more self-sufficient and, as a result, more confident, mayhap. It's possible he's doing it apurpose."

"All right, all right. But if I had my druthers, I'd druther be a prince—not that I could ever be one, or even have a chance at knowing one, come to think."

"And I'd rather have my Nannsi by me. And you, Thaddeus?"

"I'd just as soon know what's in store for us once we get to the College—but have Marsia be the one to tell me," he said with a grin.

As they headed north, Thaddeus realized it was getting cooler. His fingers were stiffening. He was more aware of chills, especially at night. And, he could now see his breath after even a small exertion. Master Silvestrus bade Anders break out the heavy cloaks, gloves, and boots. The young clerk thought each of them should sign a chit for their draws, but Rolland flatly refused and just walked off with his treasures.

Following eventide, Silvestrus smoothed his brows and cleared his throat. "Boys, if we keep on as we are, weather holding, we should reach *Arx Montium* sometime in the next five to six days. I plan for us to abide there overnight; then it's a relatively short piece to the College.

"Now, once we're there, things will be different for you. Here, you are young lads under my—if I might say—benevolent protection and valued highly in my eyes, believe it or not. There, however, you will stand alone on your own wits. You, the *Advenae*, will be beginners and Initiates to the Mysteries, along with others, and subject to the expectations of all those above you, including the *Indiginae*, the upper class. That is a very different position than what you have become used to. Know, for example, that the common word for the fresh *Tironis* is "scum."

Silvestrus cleared his throat and continued. "A fraternity exists there and a close one at that. However, in some ways, it is like a soap bubble. If you have ever had the experience of holding a soap bubble in your hand and poking a finger or stick into it, you will recall that there is a certain surface tension, until you finally push through to the inside of the bubble. It is the same in any new circumstance, the *Collegium*

Sorcerorum not excepted. Keep that in mind, and, perhaps, the experience will not be so daunting." The old man excused himself once more to take his pipe in solitude.

"Hmm. There's one thing he didn't mention," Anders said thoughtfully.

"What's that?"

"Usually when you push on a bubble to get inside, it ends up popping in your face."

Once cleanup was completed, Anders and Rolland fell to examining the scrolls again.

"Anders, doesn't *Reverte* mean to go back?"

"Why, yes. As in 'revert' or, perhaps, 'restore.' Why?"

Rolland pointed out the unfamiliar words, one by one. "Look at this line. Um, let's see—'to...use with... spell *Reverte*, as in to restore...to original.' Anders! I think this is a restoration spell."

"Here, give me that. 'Return to original...in conjunction with others, depending on strength. Use *Reverte*...intention important to apply when...' Rolland, I believe you're right. Good read. Now go on to the next."

"Wait a moment. Anders, what do reversal spells do?"

"I'm not sure, exactly. But the texts concerning the various spells we've been reading about so far all seem to imply they perform according to their title. So, in this case, a reversion, or restoration, spell should put things back the way they were previously. But what's so impor—Oh. I see. Let's look at this a bit more closely."

Thaddeus, who had been listening over his shoulder, joined his friends and reviewed the manuscript. "I think you're both right. I think this is a reversion or restoration spell. And I also think you were not given that scroll by accident. I think the master has just said, 'All right, boys, this is how you do it. Are you game?'" Thaddeus looked penetratingly at his urban friend. "Well, are you?"

"Yes."

"Well, why don't you get to it, then?"

"Yes!"

Anders and Thaddeus helped Rolland go over the text several times to make sure he understood what was required and how to go about it.

"Now, Rolland, think back to how you felt the first time you used sorcery, when we met that madman in the cabin with Bellis." A sharp pang shot through Thaddeus's heart as he spoke of his absent golden dog. "I've done sorcery twice now, and it's felt the same both times. Focus on what it is you want, embrace your Belief, then give the command. The timing's important, I think, but you have to Believe you can do it—just like the master says. You'll know when it's right."

The redhead nodded and took a deep breath, concentration furrowing his brow. "*Nasus Reverte.*" The blue nose stiffened and stood straight out from his face for a full minute before slowly wilting and falling back to lie limply on his chest. Rolland's expression reflected dashed hopes, and he hung his head. "It's no good."

Anders took his friend by the arm. "Maybe if we—"

"Forget about it, Anders. Thanks anyway, but it's just not to be. I have a strong feeling that no matter how many times I try it, nothing's going to change."

"Let me finish, dolt! What I was going to say was that maybe if you and I work it together, like the master and mistress did for our feast that time, it'll go better."

"Oh. Well, all right. You don't mind?"

Anders smiled. "No, Rolland, I don't mind. Now together—*Nasus Reverte.*"

With this effort, the nose again stiffened. Then its surface began to ripple, turning from deep blue to light blue to flesh and back again, all the while shortening, then lengthening. However, after several moments, the member again fell, sagging to his chest, blue as the bluest sky.

The thief kicked a stone, sending it flying. "*Stercus!* Just what does it take to do this?"

"Rolland, remember who it was put that spell on you. That wasn't just some journeyman conjurer."

Thaddeus joined the group. "What if all three of us try it together?"

"Maybe physical contact would help, too," Anders offered. "Here, grab my hand. Yes, I'm serious. Just do it."

The three boys stood with Rolland's hand out, covered by Anders's, then Thaddeus's.

"Good," Thaddeus said. "All together now. Wait for the tension to build. Wait...wait...wait...now!"

In unison, the three boys, eyes tightly shut in concentration, shouted out, "*Nasus Reverte!*"

The nasoid sprang outward as if stung, its surface rippling and wavering wildly as its colors changed from one second to the next.

Within a minute, the transformation was complete. The apprentices stood panting from their effort, perspiration running down their faces, but Rolland's face looked as it had when they first met, except now it was cleaner—and full of gratitude.

Rolland touched his nose in wonder, then smiled. "Thank you, thank you! That's two big favors I owe you both now."

"Ha!" Anders grinned. "You've taught me enough about commerce that you can be sure I'll collect on them."

"You're welcome, Brother," Thaddeus said, a serious expression on his face.

Rolland looked at his tall friend, eyes widening. "You...you mean that?"

"Yes," Thaddeus replied, extending his hand.

Rolland grasped it eagerly.

"I, as well," Anders said, capping the two others as he had in the madman's cabin. "Secundus gave me a scroll once. It had something to do with three men who fought with swords a lot for a king and had accents. But the thing I remember most was that they were really good friends and used to say they were all of them for each other and each other for all of them. Well, I think this is like that."

"Done!"

"Done!"

A moment later, Master Silvestrus returned from his walk. He stared thoughtfully at each boy in turn and nodded. "Good work, lads. Good work. Well, time for repose, I think. No bright lights tonight, eh, boys? Off you go. Oh, and you might want to try the extra blankets. I think it's going to be a little chilly."

The old sorcerer's prediction proved true, and by morning, the boys were glad for their heavier bedding. The smells of the new tents, clothes, and gear were a delight as well and an excitement in themselves. Rolland appeared most taken with their treasures, having said often enough that he'd never had anything new in his life unless he'd stolen it from someone else. Anders, raised in the lap of prosperous surfeit, always looked guilty at such times and said nothing. Thaddeus, no stranger to outdoor outfittery, pronounced the items of the highest quality and appreciated them as much as Rolland, though in a different way.

Thaddeus noted with interest that performing the same old chores with new tools made the tasks seem to go more quickly and with less effort. He was unsure, however, whether it was merely an artifact of perception or really true.

The boys' buoyant spirits lasted throughout the day of travel and on into the night. As they prepared again for bed, Silvestrus touched Thaddeus's arm. "Walk with me, lad, will you not?"

Thaddeus's friends went on with their preparations without comment as the first apprentice and his master toured the camp's periphery.

"Thaddeus, are you ready?"

"Ready for what, Master?"

"Ready for what you will find at the College, I would say."

Thaddeus avoided a groundchuck's hole as he considered his response. "I'm not sure, Master. I am worried a bit. About how I'll do. If I'll be worthy."

His old mentor laughed softly. "Oh, you are worthy, never fear. Thaddeus, on a different subject, I notice you picked up a new possession over Midsummer's Night. A stone, I believe. A special stone, perhaps. I wonder if I might see it?"

Thaddeus drew back slightly. "Why would you want to see it, Master? It's just an old stone."

Thaddeus became aware of a blue light surrounding them.

"Nevertheless, lad, I would like to take a look at it. It may hold some secrets worth knowing. What say you?"

"I, well, I suppose...I mean, uh, no, I don't believe so, Master. I mean no disrespect, but a special, that is, a friend gave it to me. I think...I think I should like to keep it."

The blue light faded and vanished. The sorcerer stopped pacing and faced his apprentice, his brows knitted together. Thaddeus braced for the storm that he was sure would come. Then the old man let out a long breath and shook his head.

"I see. Well, it is always best to respect a friend's gifts. Especially that of a special friend, I suppose. Very well, Thaddeus. But heed my advice. Hold that gift closely. Of course, if you are able to refuse me, I expect you will have little difficulty with others." The old man glanced up at the moon. "Oh, see the time it is getting to be. All right, Thaddeus, off to bed with you. It is certain there will be more adventures on the morrow. Good repose, lad."

"Good repose, Master." The boy turned and made his way back to his tent. Opening the flap, he saw two pairs of eyes reflected in the moonlight.

"Get in! What did he want?" came a hoarse whisper with Rolland's accent.

"Nothing, really. He seemed to want me to tell him how I felt about coming to the College. But then he asked to see my greenstone—the one Marsia gave me. At first I was going to, but then I felt I didn't want to. So, I said no. Then he said I should get some rest. That was all."

"Thaddeus," Anders hissed, "he was using his blue stone on you! We both saw the light. I think he might have been trying to influence you."

"Why would he do that?"

"I don't know, but if you think on it, consider. He has a stone that can get people to do things for him. What if you were he and had discovered one of your students had a similar stone? What would you do?"

"I'm not sure. Probably try to teach him how to use it."

"Ah," said Rolland, "that's what you'd do, but you aren't a thousand years old, or however many it is, and you're not concerned with trying to shepherd some earthshaking Prophecy into being."

Anders interjected. "Ssst! But that's not the half of it, Thaddeus."

"What do you mean?"

"We were lying here watching you through the slit in the tent flap. When he was using the blue stone, did you feel that you should really do what he wanted?"

"Well, yes, at first, but then I didn't. Why do you ask?"

"Because," the young scholar replied, "when the blue light flashed, it was but a moment before we saw a faint green light shining up from inside your tunic. It shone on your neck and chin. We could see it! It had to have been coming from that stone in the pouch inside your jerkin. Thaddeus, Marsia has given you your own Stone of Resonance!"

"Not only that," Rolland added in an awed tone, "but I'd bet my last half copper it was defending you from his stone—interfering with its effect, somehow."

Thaddeus's mind whirled with the implications of this discovery. A *Lapis Imperii,* or Stone of Power, and it was his! Much of the rest of the time before sleep was dedicated to theories concerning this topic. The last thing Thaddeus remembered before he dozed off, however, was a question Rolland posed just before sleep took him.

"But why would the master use such a stone on his own apprentice? What does that mean?"

"I don't know. I really don't know."

* * *

The slim, pale girl with jet-black hair hanging down in ringlets sat in a reclining chair in the sun of the villa's southern veranda, a partially unrolled scroll of epic poetry in her lap. She idly watched the workers tend the rows of vines in the vineyards spread out before her. Though wrapped in several blankets, she shivered still. It seemed these days she was never truly warm. A lidded wicker basket on the tiles next to her chair held several bloodied kerchiefs. Other kerchiefs, snowy white and neatly folded, were stacked in a small pile on her lap, beside the scroll. The one in her hand went often to her mouth, dabbing away crimson spittle following frequent spells of coughing. A half-empty crystal goblet of a rich amber vintage sat on the tiles on the opposite side of her chair.

Her thoughts turned to her benefactor. Poor Ormerod had been losing weight lately and already looked ill. He had only recently begun to produce that same dry cough she had, though he'd shown no blood. Not yet, anyway. Ethne was sure it would just be a matter of time, one or two months, if not weeks, at the most. She knew he had contracted the consuming sickness from her, and she felt badly for him. He had no heirs and no surviving family. He would die hard—the course of the illness always seemed to be more virulent in men—and when he did, his estate would likely be looted by the tenants, and the lands divided up among his greedy neighbors, who, she suspected, were already licking their lips in anticipation. All the more urgent reason for her to make her peace with Morella and her daughter, Lallie. She would soon need them. Everything depended on their willingness to help her. Everything.

She felt a small, but powerful, kick in her belly and smiled to herself. *My little Emperor,* she thought lovingly, *how eager he is to be about his business and how strong for one so new to this life. Life,* she mused, and a pang passed through her. It would be his life to save. But she would have to give up her own to ensure it. This was an old problem for her, however, and solved a long time ago. Still, the pangs did pass through from time to time.

It was happening just as the four old women, the faggot peddlers, had said it would—at least according to what her mother had endlessly recited to her until she had it by heart.

* * *

"But, Mama, why do I have to learn this?"

"Never you mind, child. Just learn it. It is the most important choice you'll ever have to make. My own daughter could be the mother of the new Emperor!" How proud she'd always looked when she said that. But then it only made her remember to test Ethne again about the Choice. This her mother did till the day she died.

After her mother's death, Ethne's older cousin, the mayor, anxious to be rid of his responsibility, had sent the girl packing off to that School for Young Ladies in Fountaindale. She still wondered, occasionally, if he'd known all the time it had been a brothel. Oh well, that was water under a very old bridge.

More to the point had been the tale of the four old women. According to the story, the four ancients had come knocking on her mother's door one midwinter, ostensibly selling firewood—but Ethne had always wondered about that. Old women tended not to go out in winter, nor did they tend to sell wood, and she'd never heard of any going around in a pack of four. But her mother had been adamant on that point.

"I was in my last three with you when I heard a knocking at the door. I wondered who could be calling in midwinter, and why. When I opened the door, there they were, four old women, yet their eyes were not old, but fierce. They only spoke briefly of their wood, then straightened and spoke in unison. They did not sound like old women.

> Myrtelee, we are come to tell you tidings of great moment! Listen and attend. The fruit of your womb will become the Lady of the Flowers of Sorrow, for if she would choose to live, all things you know will die. Yet should she choose to die, all things will live. They will live through her son—a boy who will be gotten by a boy. Thus, mighty the greatsire, mightier still the sire, and mightiest of all the son. That son an Emperor shall be. Tell your daughter, and tell her well, till she knows it front and back. It will be her choice—to stay safe in the City of the Pleasures or seek the Country of the Vintner, where she will be consumed in whole. But not before she has known the Keeper of Bees. It will be through him the fruit will come, and

for him, the Choice will be made, the Flower of the Nations. Tell her, and tell her well. She must choose: keep her life to herself and live in comfort for long years until the Darkness comes, or give up her life to her son, he who will beat back the Darkness and bring the Light—the White Rose, the Lion Rampant. Tell her she must choose.'

And saying that, they left. Long had Ethne pondered the meaning of those words. Now she believed she knew.

The mother of an Emperor—my wonderful son! I know your name already, oh, ancient hero, now to come among us once again. And, oh, my Thaddeus. You must know, yet you must let him be. But how to do this?

Ethne endured another spell of coughing, wiping away the scarlet foam.

I shall have to consider that, thought the black-haired *Domina Dolosa Florum. I will have to be very careful. Very soon.*

* * *

Caerulea fussed and fretted as she always did after laying her eggs, at least for a day or two. But this was not her usual clutch of eggs, but a solitaire, and, oh, what an egg—large, white, and gleaming! Not one of her realm could name, in living memory, a single egg so big and never one alone. It must be from the boy, Thaddeus. Silvestrus had implied as much during their visit the summer before. Wondrous things he had told her, though it was hard to know what to believe. He had spoken of directions, north, south. It had all been a bit confusing. But he had been definite on one point. It was centered on the boy. And the boy would beget on her, if she willed it, a daughter unlike any other—a daughter of fire, the light of the father.

So now, all she had to do was wait. First would come the larva, and what a larva that would be! A great worm with a human face—what loremaster had ever conceived such an image? And how it would eat! She'd had her entire court scouring the Queendom for weeks to gather only the most tender and succulent leaves. Next the chrysalis—not a cocoon. She was no moth! Then her beautiful daughter and her beautiful wings. What delight in imagining who and what she would resemble.

It was nice to have the pleasure of her inner thoughts. Certainly little was to be had in her home. My Lord Spadix seldom spoke to her these days. He seemed to take her egg as some sort of personal affront, as if she had done it apurpose to humiliate him. Well, not entirely. But it did serve him justice.

He and his trollops! Her own mood had been a bit dark of late as well, she had to admit. Perhaps she should not have been so quick to tear off Cecropia's wings when she had discovered her with My Lord in their own bower. But Caerulea was not Queen of the Butterflies for nothing, and she would not tolerate others laughing up their chitin at her. And Luna—well, Luna was a different story. But she had been very, very angry that day. Imagine the pale-green slut thinking to replace her on her throne just because she had been able to catch My Lord's eye on one occasion. Well, she had been well served that day. Caerulea smiled in wicked satisfaction recounting the surprise of the discovery, the shrieks, the denials, the mad flight. Moths always tended to forget their bearings once daylight had come. Yes, the mad flight, more like being herded. Herded by an angry pursuer—an angry Queen. Herded right into a spider's web! Ha! How she had screamed then. More than Caerulea herself ever had. Right up until the end, when she stopped screaming. Luna did look better then all dressed up in white spun silk. A great improvement. Ha!

Remembering the spider made her think again of Thaddeus, as she often did. My Lord Spadix believed the egg was the product of some dalliance of hers with one of her courtiers—as if any of that lot could produce an egg this size! Of course, his suspicious nature had, so far, opened several new positions in her court among that group, but then new faces were always ready to take the place of those who had gone beyond.

But yes, Thaddeus. She would have to get word to him after the metamorphosis. Perhaps she would send one of the new young courtiers. She was sure she could find a volunteer. Any of them would willingly die in the service of their Butterfly Queen, especially such a beautiful Monarch.

* * *

The *Regina Draconum Marinarum* lay languidly on the achingly white stretch of sand in front of her cave while the waves washed gently onto the beach in their timeless rhythm. She regarded the great crimson bulk of her companion with, certainly not affection, more a combination of boredom and fear. Always best to show him respect, though—the last time had almost cost her her life.

She addressed the bloodred beast. "The point, Attacondros, is that I cannot see how I can try to thwart the Stars. Some things are beyond even our powers."

"To the Hells with the Stars, I say! Besides, you cannot say for certain you have seen them rightly. Even I have been known to err on an interpretation. Let me plead again, Mari, relent! Couple with me, and I shall shower you with treasures of which even you are unaware. Then, when I leave, you may keep the egg and raise the whelp as you see fit. I will even send a portion of my servants to tend you if you like. After, I can visit you from time to time as my desires allow. You will be happy, after a fashion, and well-protected. None will dare disturb the mate of the *Draco Ruber!* None." He ran a clawed foot slowly down her front leg, perhaps as a sign of tenderness, but it made Mari shiver.

"Not that your supplication gives me no pause, Red King. However, there is a certain price to pay for all this...largesse, is there not? What am I to do with myself in those tedious years, perhaps decades, between your loving interludes? True, raising an eggon will distract for a time. But then? Also, and not insignificant for me, my formidable red suitor, is your temper. You will recall that the last time we had this conversation, you drove a spear straight through my breastbone."

"Yes, and I have said I was sorry for it, have I not? And I healed you, did I not? And stayed with you till your strength was as before?"

"That you did, and gramercy for it. But it would not have been necessary, Great Lord, if you had not thought to stick me in the first place, yes? Again, though, that is not the point. The point is that the Stars have shown me their truth. And their truth declares I must wait." She did not dare add that she had not only been told to wait, true enough, but to wait for another.

"The Stars have shown you their truth, but only as *interpreted* by that seaweed-headed, lyre-plucking, endlessly hair-combing, fortune-telling fish girl! I do not see how environmental indecision in one's body form makes for accurate soothsaying."

The *Draco Viridis* gazed at Attacondros, noting the trail of moisture seeping down from the small opening in his left temple. She knew he was seeping on the other side as well. Yes, he was truly under the grip of his "excitement," or should it be more properly described as "tension"? She would have to tread carefully here. He was half mad with lust already.

"I am able to read the Stars as well as any, as you should know. Pisca is merely a servitor in my court, one of many among the Mer. She has studied the Heavens only a little and thinks to know more than she really does. But she is of no moment in my decision. I cannot accede to your request, my Lord. The Stars say I must wait, and wait I shall."

The red dragon threw his head back and let out a terrible roar as gouts of orange fire swept the sky. "You make a great mistake when you deny me what I deem mine!" He appeared to struggle with himself for a moment. "Very well, *Draco Mari.* I will respect your choice, chiefly because to obtain what I desire most, I trow I would have to kill you first—then, what pleasure? I am no necrophile. My mates have always been eager and willing, till now, it seems. But hear me, my lost love. This decision will cost you dearly. It will cost you your court as well as your subjects and all who bow to you, and in the end, you will die horribly—and alone. Then all will know how the Red has triumphed over the Green!" The crimson Lord of Fire leaped into the air bellowing so loudly it seemed even the waves paused in their cadence. In moments, he was gone out of sight.

Mari sighed. She hoped this foretold Star child would be worth it. For him, she was risking everything.

* * *

On a small islet out of sight of the shore, Attacondros finished the unanticipated, but welcome, repast that had interrupted his flight. A lengthy journey lay ahead of him before he could rest again. Perhaps, however, he would come across that older Gray he'd heard tales of years before. It was said she summered in these climes. Better an experienced and grateful dame than a haughty and ignorant maiden in any case. Nodding his massive horned and crested head in self-approval, he launched himself into the air, heading west, his wide-spanned, leathery wings seeking the sea's uplifting air currents.

The waves continued their rhythmic lapping of the small islet, rising slowly higher and higher with the tide until eventually they washed away the blood, part of an arm, and a portion of a tail fin—but leaving behind a tortoiseshell comb.

* * *

The interior of the ancient oak was roomy, neat, and dry. A brazier provided warmth, and carefully tended candles provided light. As always, sources of heat were closely guarded in the interiors of such bower homes. Fires in the living room did no one good. The sparse furniture included a rug embroidered with mystic symbols, two chairs, a table, a desk, and a small altar off to one side. A thin column of the tree's central core ran from the middle of the floor to the middle of the ceiling, a tall, sturdy pillar. It was how the tree managed to support a Chief Druid's dwelling.

Luperca leaned forward, careful to keep her tawny braid to the side, out of harm's way. She set down the carved wooden cup on the small stump table in front of her chair. She liked tea, but the oak brew was always a touch too bitter for her taste. Her eyes returned to her host in his white, rope-belted robe. With graying hair and a long beard, he looked the part of the ideal Druid Sachem. The only difference she could detect was the sprig of black lysle placed in his Aureole—the sign of mourning.

"Thank you for seeing me, Madigan, and my thanks for the tea. Allow me again, however, to express my sorrow for your loss. Mattom was a great Chief Druid and was kindly to me always. I am sure, though, your own stewardship will bring no shame to your family name, but honor only."

The priest ducked his head in acknowledgment. "Thank you, Great Pack Leader. Your presence brightens this otherwise sad time of loss and reflection. To what do I owe this consideration, however? And what, if any, service may I render you?"

"I want for nothing, good friend. I am passing through, going from one place to another, and I thought to stop here and renew our bond. Also, to share information."

"Ah," the man said. "You have seen the boy, then?"

"Yes. Not only have I seen him, I have been his 'puppy'—yes, that's it—and, for a time, traveled with him. We have even played *Pila Ludere* together. I made the winning goal." She smiled with pleasure at the memory.

"Excuse me, Pack Leader. *Pila Ludere?*"

"Yes, football." Luperca regarded the man's questioning eyebrow. "It's, well, it's a game where you... Well, let it go at that. It is a modest recreation bringing simple gratification. In the course of it and other endeavors, I was able to form an opinion of the boy. He it is of whom we have spoken. I have no doubt."

The man let out a long breath. "Then it is happening at last, just as predicted in the Oaken Ring."

"Yes."

"Um, then you have...been together?"

"Ah, no, worse luck. A girl was present to whom he developed a singular endearment. She has given him a magical stone. This may be her means of attachment, or then again, perhaps not. In any case, it became clear his interest lies solely with her at this time. I shall have to abide and be ready. It is of no consequence, however. He is the one. So tall, so brave. He saved me from Corrigan, you know."

"No, I did not know. I am sorry. I thought my stepbrother sufficiently bound, but madness gives one divine strength at times, it seems. He hurt you?"

"Yes. Very much. But he will not do so again. He is now, and forever shall be—thanks to my Thaddeus—a cur, madness and all."

"I thought as much. Lately I have heard a lost soul howling in the wilderness at night. I imagined it was he."

"He is lucky at that. Were I to see him now, I would rip out his throat. I would not even bother transforming."

"His punishment is, perhaps, even worse than that, Great Leader, though it may seem hard to see it so, just now."

"I concede you may have a point, Madigan. It must be difficult to lose two family members in the space of such a short time. But you spoke of the Oaken Ring. Have you seen anything new?"

The Chief Druid smiled. "Come with me, Luperca, if you will."

The two rose, and the druid indicated a narrow passageway that led to another room almost completely taken up by a great wheel of wood lying flat, perhaps a hand's width thick. It was supported off the floor by four short, stout carved wooden legs. The two traveled clockwise around the circumference of the Oaken Ring until the man stopped and pointed.

"There. You see that variegation in the ring?"

"Yes—there."

"That is where the convergence begins. I had not seen it so clearly till just the other day. It is remarkable how something that is supposed to be fixed and unmutable suddenly changes as if it were the wind blowing across a pasture."

"Or, perhaps, that an elderly priest, beginning to show the infirmities of age, has just noticed something that was under his nose all the time," the tawny-haired woman said with a sly grin.

The Chief Druid grimaced ruefully. "Alas, that is ever more frequently a possibility. My thanks for your clever insight, however, and may I extend an invitation to you to stay the night. You may rest on the love chair for the evening, that is, unless you fear you will fall off while trying to scratch behind your ear with your sandaled foot." Madigan's grin was no less pointed.

"Ah, my dear Madigan, ever you are as you were when we played together around the Great Tree as pups." The Pack Leader reached out and patted his arm affectionately. "I would be honored to accept your invitation. But, to return to the variegation..."

"Yes. Of course. See here, here, and here. It is so clear now that I have studied it. You will be in great danger. The boy will come. He will sire upon you the High Priestess. She it is who will have her part to play to bind together all of *Gens Totus Canum et Luporum* when the Dogs of the East fall upon us."

A low, involuntary snarl escaped the young woman's lips at his mention. "I see it. But are you sure it speaks truly to you? This Ring is over two thousand years old, and this part, at least five hundred."

"Be assured of it, Luperca."

"Very well, then. I am for repose. It has been a long day, and I have farther to go on the morrow."

"As you wish, Great Leader." He indicated another passageway leading off to the left. "There you will find I have laid out those things I believe will be needful to you. Good repose, Luperca. And sleep well."

Chapter 11

AD COLLEGIUM

* * *

The troop resumed travel the next day, heading north. They had not gone a half *milla passa,* however, when clouds began scudding across the sky, gray and threatening, and the rain began to pour. Within a short time, the clay-based road had mired up, which slowed the party considerably, thus allowing more opportunity for the rain to soak them through to the skin. Sometime later, a chill wind descended on them from the North.

The boys spent their time slipping, sliding, and cursing. Thaddeus, stationed abreast of Asullus, hung on to the mule's bridle, as much to steady himself as his quadrupedal friend.

"Easy there, laddie. If ye falls, ye falls. But do no' be takin' me down wi' ye!"

Thaddeus turned at a snort from behind to find Rolland grinning broadly. "If you're finding something funny in this weather, then it has to be good, indeed. It's the first time I've heard you stop swearing all morning."

MOUNTAINGAARD
(ARX MONTIUM)

"I just had the thought that out there somewhere"—the redhead waved expansively with his free arm—"our little violet nixie and her multihued sisters are struggling mightily against the buffeting winds and sodden air. The image has given me a certain sense of warmth and strength to carry on."

"I hope she doesn't hear you, Roddie. It wasn't so long ago she had you strung up like a roast at the butcher's, you know."

"Ah, beef. Now there's another warming thought. My idea of paradise—a side of cow, a barrel of ale, my good knife, and leave me alone for an hour."

"My auntie Silvie says a constant diet of red meat is not good for you and can cause crook-shank," Anders warned in a condescending tone.

"Oh, well, we all know that's the closest your auntie Silvie ever came to red meat—from a cow..."

The heated sparring managed to distract them from their climatological misery, however, and it wasn't long before Silvestrus called a halt to make camp.

The rain continued a steady downpour for the remainder of that day, the day after, and the day after that. While the boys were miserable and complained frequently—some more than others—the old sorcerer and the mule adopted a philosophical stance.

"Aye, an' what's to be done concernin' it, anyway? Will ye throw away, p'rhaps, thirteen months o' yer sorcerous life to cast a rain-away spell just to see to yer local comfort, then? An' besides, ye could all use a washin' down as it is, I'm thinkin'."

The routine became depressingly regular. Each day the leaden skies wept openly, allowing not one warming ray to shine through. The party slipped and slid for twenty or so miserable *millae passae*, then set up camp and tents, groomed the mule as best they could, stretching a fly over his halter line. They tried to find some reasonably dry firewood to prepare their meals and attempted to be pleasant to one another until it was time to crawl into bed between sodden blankets.

Rolland's freely expressed misgivings regarding his choice to join the party assumed the form of a daily lament.

After the fifth drenching day from Moorstown, the ground started to rise, following which, the weather became colder.

Two days later, the boys awoke to a chill crispness in the air. Thaddeus stumbled out of his bedding and poked his head through the tent flap to behold a sun-bright morning. To the northeast, a majestic and imposing snow-covered mountain range stretched from horizon to horizon, standing in blindingly white contrast to the brilliant blue sky. The young apprentice's heart soared, all cares and troubles washed away in an instant. He turned back to the tent, shaking his fellow apprentices awake.

"Anders! Rolland! Up quick! You've got to see this!"

Anders sat up, rubbing sleep from his eyes, while Rolland quickly put back the dagger that had sprung to his hand at the shaking.

At the tall boy's prodding, his two friends came out to join him, gazing silently at the grandeur of the not-so-distant mountains.

"Behold *Arx Montium*—the Mountaingaard!" a deep voice declaimed behind them. "The great pinnacle and last stanchion of the defense of the West. Or so the story goes. It is beautiful, boys, is it not? No matter how many times I see the magnificence of these peaks, the feeling is always the same." Silvestrus stood regarding the towering tops.

Thaddeus thought his craggy profile and that of the mountains were rather similar.

"All right, lads, let us shake a foot. We are almost home now, and our journey nearly done. Mine, that is. Yours, however, is just beginning." He gave a short laugh and turned back to his tent.

The boys looked at each other, the spell broken, shrugged their shoulders, and began their preparations.

The road they followed wound back and forth up the skirts of the close-knit foothills, making its way toward the higher ranges. With each winding, they drew closer to the crest and soon became aware the trail was leading them to what was surely a gap in the mountains, a pass—a guarded pass.

As they, at last, trudged up to the opening, the path widened into a road that was paved with stone slabs similar to those at the City on the Plain.

Rising forty paces on either side of the pass, immense pillared walls carved from the living rock formed a columned fortress. Blocking the pass entirely were towering twin gates, rearing up massive and foreboding, with great iron bindings and bronze spikes projecting from the surfaces at intervals. Thaddeus didn't understand how even raw rock could support the weight of the gates, though his eyes told him it clearly did. Crenellations and arrow slits revealed the true nature of the architecture and its purpose—as did the armored men intently peering down at the party.

"I count thirty-five men-at-arms with crossbows aimed at us, with four men each manning a pair of *balustradae* on either side," Rolland whispered to the Beewickean.

"Then we should probably behave ourselves," Thaddeus said.

A tall man, uniformed in overlapping stiff leather sheathing with a chain-mail hood that spilled down his chest, emerged from a door built into the base of the great gate, followed by two others, similarly outfitted. All had belted long swords, currently sheathed, and carried themselves as well-practiced professionals. The leader strode toward the party with easy authority, his two arms men keeping pace behind. Blond curls escaped from beneath the man's hauberk, and a sprig from some plant was tied over his left chest as if it were a type of insignia.

"That's broom over his heart," Anders said in a low voice. "He's an officer—and from an important family."

"You learned that from some scroll?" Rolland whispered appreciatively.

As the officer drew nearer, his wariness eased. A handsome man, he smiled and waved a greeting, hailing the group.

"Master Silvestrus! Good morrow and well met! Welcome again to *Arx Montium.* I see your fishing expedition was successful."

"Greetings to you, Captain Geoffrey. And yes, it worked out rather well, all things considered. New ingredients for our soup of learning, I think." The sorcerer indicated the boys as the mule snorted.

"Aye, an' ha' ye no fine greetin' fer an old beast o' burden, is it? Well, who should be surprised at that, aye? None livin' there be as comes close to acknowledgin' the source o' all the labor an' toil as is necessary to bring these fruits to the table o' delight. But enjoy 'em they do, wi' ne'er a thought gi'en as to how—"

"Peace, faithful and steadfast Asullus!" the young officer said, laughing. "I greet you only now as I, by my custom, have saved the most important for the position of greatest honor." He grinned with a wink at the boys.

"Well, now, that be more to me likin' wi' yer grand silver tongue an' all, though I thinks me as to how the truth in all that flowery speech has little difference between it an' the droppings I ha' left behind me on the road from time to time, coursin' me way up to yer establishment."

Rolland burst out laughing, but quickly stifled his guffaws at a look from Thaddeus.

"How stand the courses at this time, Captain? Any news of import?"

"Nay. Nothing of any consequence, Master Silvestrus. The summer has been quiet here, though we did see quite a display of the North lights and a rain of falling stars a few weeks back. None of the men could recall ever having witnessed such a spectacle." The young officer's eyes held a questioning look.

"Ah, yes. I believe we witnessed the same phenomenon, if I remember correctly. Well, such displays are not common, that is true, but it does happen from time to time. I am sure there is a natural explanation for it. Now, tell me, have any of the apprentices begun to report to the *Collegium* as yet?"

"Only the *Advenae,* in groups of two and three, beginning last week—all looking scared." The officer grinned again.

"As well they should. None of the *Indigenae*—the upper class—then?"

"No. I believe the only ones here about are those who stayed the summer, the Prince being chief among them, I'd say."

"I see. Well, thank you, Captain. We are, as always, in your debt for the peace your constant vigilance provides."

"My thanks to you, Master Silvestrus. It is an honor to serve the Order. And I don't mind the scenery, either. The winters are a bit frosty, I must confess. Perhaps I will allow myself, one day, the leisure to take a turn to the Southlands. I understand the ladies there, especially among the high, are most comely, with an ear to musics, and well resourced."

"An excellent plan, Captain. Were I in your position, the same thought would occur to me. However, should you decide to follow your fortunes in that way, have a care to train up one of your loyal subalterns to assume your considerable responsibilities prior to your absence from us."

"That I will, Master Silvestrus, on my word. Now, what other service may we provide for you this day?"

"There is no need for you to trouble yourself, Captain. We are just passing through. If there is no objection, we will refresh ourselves in the barracks and see if we can wheedle Cook out of a late midday in the mess. Then we'll be off. I wish to make midforest by repose. Oh! That reminds me, have any of the *Aelvae* been seen in this area lately?"

"None that I've heard of, Master Silvestrus, but then, you know how it is with the *Aelvae.* As regards the commissary, today's selection features Raugauld's culinary masterpiece—hash. Not on the order of that excellent bear stew you bring us from time to time—"

Rolland screwed his face in a grimace.

"But filling, nonetheless. I must return to my duties, but I will see to it that all are alerted."

The old man nodded. "My thanks, and fare thee well, Captain."

Silvestrus signaled to the boys, who fell in once again behind the cart, and the party made its way through the lesser gate door. The guards saluted smartly as they passed.

Thaddeus was not sure what he had expected to see, but what he did see was not what he'd expected.

Gazing northeast, a vast forested plain stretched out far below them. At the extreme limit of his vision, he made out a stark white border, though he couldn't be sure if this represented mountains or some other feature.

Glancing around, he found that the mountain gate sheltered a small military garrison with barracks, stables, storage, and administrative buildings, all laid out in straight lines. A squared-off yard was being used by at least two squads of gate soldiers. One group was drilling with pikes in marching formation, while another shot crossbows from varying distances at three straw men on uprights.

"All right, lads, we'll take midday in the mess with a proper table and chairs for a change." The old man stepped down lightly, handing the reins to Thaddeus. "See to Asullus's needs and the cart, and then join me. I will be inside that low building on the right. Do not neglect *Latrina et Lavatio*—commode and ablutions—afterward. Then come to me."

Following a plain, though generous, repast, the group left the mountain outpost and turned again northeast.

The trail led rapidly down from *Arx Montium* into the green curtain that spread out before them. In the distance to the north, Thaddeus glimpsed what he took to be the sun glinting off a ringed structure of some sort.

Silvestrus resumed his perch on the cart. "Well, boys, this is the last leg of our journey. It's straight across this great forest to the *Collegium.* We will follow that path you see going down into the foothills and camp tonight in midforest, then press on come morning. If all goes well, we should reach the *Collegium,* perhaps, by tomorrow afternoon."

Rolland stood forward. "Master, the valley below is lush and green. Yet, as we approached Mountaingaard, it seemed as if winter had already come. I didn't—"

"*Arx Montium* is a wall of ice and rock that protects this valley. They have four seasons here, as in any other place, but the spring comes earlier, the summer lingers longer, the falls are brighter, the winter snow less frigid. This forest lies on the path to a College of Sorcery, after all. I am sure you understand. So, let us get started. Asullus, I believe you know the way."

"Aye, as well as yerself, Master, as I think ye know. Come on, lads. I be a mule leader, no' a sheepherder. Haw haw!" The old gray mule moved sure-footedly down and out of the mountain fastness onto the green-carpeted plain, cart and passengers jouncing behind him.

Of a sudden, Thaddeus looked back over his shoulder and beheld a little purple *Spritae* hovering at tree height off to one side. As soon as she realized she'd been seen, she waved and, in a trice, turned in midair and was gone.

The sight of her reminded him of his earlier conversation with the diminutive Fey.

* * *

"But why is it you send off sparks every time you come within a pace of Rolland? Has he done you harm?"

Small red spots blossomed on the *Spritae*'s cheeks. "No. But I will tell you, Lord in Beewicke, if you shall give me your word you will tell no other. Ever."

"All right, Morphia. I give you my word."

"Very well. It is…my temper, I suppose. At the Convent of the Silent Sisters, I was so irritated that he was almost able to slip beyond me on several occasions. It damaged my pride and was embarrassing for me to have to admit such to Master Silvestrus. Then, he threatened me with his knife. The Fey do not well tolerate such behaviors toward their persons from humans. Additionally, I suppose I chose to believe that it was Rolland's idea to bind me with cobwebs, and I was looking for an opportunity for fair return. But now that we've been together, I-I've come to feel differently about him—about all of you. And I am sorry for my *Vanitas*. There! That's as much honesty as I choose to give this night, and usually we Fey do not give any at all." As Morphia finished, her eyes were shining brightly.

"Thank you, small one. I shall hold this in my heart always."

* * *

"And thank you, again, Morphia," he said under his breath. "For all you've done for us. I hope you never want for honey."

"Thaddeus, who are you talking to?" Anders asked.

"I was just saying good-bye to a friend. Morphia was leaving us."

"Oh. I see. Well, I'm sure we'll see her again. So, Taddy, we're almost there. I have to say I'm pretty excited. Are you?"

"Yes. Quite a bit, actually."

"Rolland, how about you? Are you excited?"

"I suppose so. I just hope it's a place where everybody minds their own business. I don't fancy a lot of ignorant questions about this and that."

They walked easily along the forest path and did not stop for eventide until moonrise. The boys went through their well-practiced camp routines and, in a relatively short time, were sitting on logs around a cheery campfire contentedly picking their teeth.

"Master," the short apprentice began.

"Yes, Anders?"

"May I ask a question concerning *Arx Montium?*"

"Of course."

"As I understand it, Master, the line of mountains comprising the Great Wall stretches from the gate all the way to the Great Northern Fastness, and from the Southeast to the towering Golden Range. It is but a long line of snow-covered rocks sticking up out of the Earth at an angle, cutting in front of the more regular geography. And the only thing, it is said, of any consequence that lies beyond *Arx Montium* is the *Collegium* itself—a peculiar construction of Nature, it seems. It was Primus who told me once he considered the range an 'unnatural formation.' Is that true, Master?"

The sorcerer puffed his pipe for a moment. "Yes, that would be the right of it."

Silence returned to the group.

"Master, would you tell us, then, of the Mountaingaard?"

The old man looked thoughtful for a time, then sighed. "Very well, Anders. I suppose there is no great harm in it. So, *Arx Montium.* We have spoken several times of the Invasion of the East under the last Emperor. During the final battle—but several hundred leagues away from where the Imperial Army was being chopped to pieces—a group of sorcerers from the *Collegium* had made its way, in stealth, to Cinoton, the capital of the Cin. They hoped to there find some way to render impotent the power of the Eastern mages and save what remained of the Imperial Army. In that they were, unfortunately, altogether unsuccessful.

"It was discovered, however, that the, um, magical energy from which the mages seemed to be drawing their power, appeared to have its origin, *Omnino,* in an ancient, tall, and rather ugly tower, the Minaret of Power, that sat in the middle of the square of that selfsame city. It was not difficult to identify, as it was bathed in all manner of glowing colors with bursts of lightnings and flames shooting out from it at intervals. It was almost as if it held some manner of life force.

"The leader of the Imperial sorcerous raiding party, if you will, was a practitioner named Portoman, one of the truly Wise with great powers and skills. He it was who first broached the idea of making away with the Tower. He intuited that the artifact was the source of the Eastern mages' power—a power so much different than ours—even at its great distance from the battlefield. That being the case, he put forth the argument that removing the Tower from the land of the Cin would be akin to striking away the burning torch set to ignite the bonfire.

"Now this was a bold and dangerous design. What if he were wrong, and the Tower was in no way connected to the mages' powers? Then the sorcerers' quest would have failed, and they would expose themselves, limiting any further attempt to succor the Imperial Army and forestall disaster. What if the Tower could not be destroyed or moved? The same result. And what if the forces with which the Tower were imbued would call an alarm and signal others to come to its aid, or, itself resist the attempted abduction and strike out? These and many other questions were considered in hurried and urgent debate. They knew lives were being lost by the second, you see.

"In the end, Portoman had his way, and the group of sorcerers gambled that if it could not be destroyed in time, removing the Minaret from its lodgings and safeguarding it elsewhere was the best they could hope for. So the sorcerers joined together—much as you three did with Rolland's nose—and the Minaret was uprooted and made off with."

"Master," Rolland spoke, his eyes alight, "were the Westlands sorcerers detected? What happened to them?"

"Of a surety they were detected. How could they not be? A great hue and cry was raised. However, something very strange occurred. It was as if water had, of a sudden, been poured over that hypothetical bonfire I alluded to earlier. The mages' flames went out, so to speak. Their power seemed to falter. They pursued the sorcerers, certainly, but as mortal men only. No magicks, no spells were employed. It was as if they had been drained of all force and initiative.

"Well, the Westlands sorcerers were as astounded as the Eastern mages, I dare say. No one had any inkling the mages' powers were so intertwined and beholden to that ugly congregate of stone and mortar."

"So, they made off with their score? They got clean away?" Rolland pressed.

"Yes and no, boy. The surviving sorcerers were able to make their way back to the Westlands with their great prize, but it was too late to save the legions of the Imperial Army, which, by that time, already lay butchered in the baking sun."

"Did the Cin mages and army follow the Imperial sorcerers and try to get the Minaret back?" Thaddeus asked.

"No, lad. It was most peculiar. Once the Westlands' sorcerers got just beyond the border of the lands of the Cin, the pursuers suddenly and abruptly gave up their pursuit—they just stopped. No one knows why. It is one of the several thousand mysteries that surrounded that disastrous campaign."

"The 'surviving sorcerers,' Master?"

"Ah, quick Anders. Yes, not all the sorcerers survived, so to speak. Portoman himself, alone of the group, did not return home, at least not as you might count such things. He, at some point in the theft, was struck with madness and never recovered, in spite of our best efforts to heal him. Adjurford, his second, later postulated that in his role as leader of the attack on the Minaret, Portoman witnessed or experienced something that overwhelmed him. None who were there could ascertain what actually happened to him."

"And what of the fate of the Minaret, Master?"

"Ah, well, that brings us back to *Arx Montium.* The Minaret—the very one of which we've been speaking—stands now, as it has for a thousand years, on the grounds of the *Collegium Sorcerorum,* which has, for the past millennium, played host to it, calling it the Tower of the East."

Anders shifted position. "Master, if the Minaret has been with the *Collegium* all this time, what has been learned from the study of it?"

"Another good question, Anders. The answer, however, is, very little. The knowledge the Tower holds has remained inaccessible as to its true function. It has, all this time, remained an enigma woven into a mystery—or, perhaps, a riddle—floating in a mist. In recent years, however, one of the junior faculty claims to have teased out some knowledge of its secrets, though it is difficult to determine the exact verity there."

"Master," Thaddeus queried, "what of the fate of the Emperor, Tyrannus Superbus? Was he killed with his men?"

"No. It is my understanding he was captured—wounded but still fighting. Concerning his subsequent fate, the records are impenetrably silent. All that is known from the few surviving Westerns with knowledge of the event is that he was still living when taken away."

"Master, if the Cin have not pursued it in all this time, why is the mountain fortress still necessary to protect it?"

"Because, young thief, that they did not come immediately does not mean they will not come eventually. But they have not—to date at least. And for that we should all be extremely grateful."

"Master, Thaddeus made the same point these few days past."

"Really? Is this so, Thaddeus? Tell me of your thoughts regarding the matter. Be sure to omit nothing."

Feeling exposed and uncomfortable, Thaddeus hesitantly outlined his reasoning and conclusions. He even added Helviticus's warning.

"Well done, Thaddeus. You have hit on exactly the problem that has been gnawing at the back of my mind for—well, quite a long time, anyway. If anything further occurs to you, let me know immediately."

"Yes, Master."

"Oh, Master?" Anders, head down, looked very uncomfortable. Beads of sweat stood out on his brow in spite of the temperate evening.

"Yes, Anders."

"There is a thing I have been, myself, puzzling over for some time. And I have desired to ask you about it. I think I may have the right of it by now, but it may represent knowledge you would rather wish we did not share at this time, or, perhaps, ever, really. I am, therefore, hesitant to make mention of it, though you have always taken pains to assure us of the inviolate nature of any quest for knowledge."

A quirk appeared momentarily at the corner of the old sorcerer's mouth. "That is quite a preamble, my boy. You should probably get on with it."

"Um, yes, Master. I, that is, I believe that it may be possible...What I mean to say is...Well, to begin with—"

"We are, all of us, only on this world for a relatively short time, young Anders. But before my own time is gone, I should like to hear your postulation."

"Yes, of course, Master. It is actually quite to the point. Master—"

"Yes?"

"MasterIthinkyouweretherethen!" The words tumbled out a rush.

"What? What did he say, Thaddeus?" Rolland asked, leaning forward.

"He said he thought Master was there, then," Thaddeus replied.

"What? Where, when?" Rolland said, looking puzzled.

"On the Eastern Campaign with Tyrannus Superbus—with the Great Invasion of the Cin, I imagine. Is that right, Anders?" Thaddeus posited.

Anders nodded his head slowly, not daring to look up.

"What! Anders, have you gone and lost those legendary wits of yours? How in the world can you—"

Silvestrus was smiling openly. He held up a hand of restraint. "It is all right, Rolland. He is right, you know. How did you find me out, clever boy?"

"What!" the thief sputtered in disbelief.

"Rolland, you've taken to saying that a lot lately. Why not listen to what it is he has to say?" offered the tall apprentice.

Anders swallowed, then continued. "Well, Master, nothing that was major. Mainly putting together small bits here and there you've let out—"

"Perhaps you mean 'let slip'?" the old man offered.

Anders smiled shyly and continued.

"I first thought about it that night in Meadsville, when you told us about the Eastern Invasion. You were talking about the last battle, and you said"—the young scholar adopted a thoughtful look—"you said, 'They bled; they cried; and they died. We only wanted to—.' It was after I had rehearsed that phrase over in my mind, I thought it sounded to me very much like something someone who had been there might say. However, there was the problem of the thousand-year interval between now and then."

"A formidable problem, I would have thought," the old man said, still smiling.

"Yes, Master, but you, I believe, solved that one by telling us that sorcerers were long-lived, even up to several hundred years, you said. So, if several hundred years, I thought, why not a thousand years every now and then? Then, during our recent sojourn at Terminus, the Centurion Major, Helveticus, told us it was a sorcerer named Silvestus who had cursed them.

The last bit of thought I needed came just now when you described the events leading up to the establishment of *Arx Montium.* It, again, sounded very much the kind of detail only one who had been there would possess. Taken all together, well…" The distiller's son spread his hands and shrugged.

"And so, you asked me the question of information regarding *Arx Montium* apurpose? No doubt. And most of what I told you, you had, perhaps, already learned from your erudite and seemingly omniscient tutors. Yes?"

The short boy nodded quickly.

"Ha! Outdone by my own cleverness. Well done, Anders, well done."

The young scholar blushed but looked pleased. Silence again descended on the group.

"Um, Master…may I ask a question about…about that time?"

"Ah, Rolland. I know you would like to know more from someone who had been there, so to speak. Know, however, that these memories, while they concern things of greatness, are not, for me, happy ones. And I am not in the habit of sharing such thoughts with my apprentices, in any case. However, since a great deal has been shared, I will share a few things more. But it will be up to me to decide which. That said, what is your question?"

"Master, why didn't the Cin come west?"

"Very well. No one knows why the Cin have not come west. Certainly nothing has stood in their way these long centuries. Personally, I believe it has something to do with the Minaret of Power itself, but I have no idea as to specifics. Perhaps one of you lads will be able to tease it out one day. But in the meantime, there is *Arx Montium*—sturdy and staunch it stands, unmoving, unchanging, unassailable. It has also another useful, if minor, function. It serves as a marvelous deterrent to the idly curious. In older times, I understand, commoners would travel from all over the Westlands to the *Collegium* demanding this remedy or that bag of gold from the Brothers at the College for any minor frustration or grievance. Nowadays, those who come must have, by definition, demonstrably greater motivation and, therefore, purpose. We, as a result, treat their petitions with greater gravity.

"In any case, that wall possesses only one vulnerability that I've ever been able to think of. It is, of course, something concerning which I never speak."

The boys looked at him questioningly but felt constrained from speaking further.

With that, Silvestrus laughed to himself and abruptly stood. "All right, my fine young *Advenae,* you have kept me at it long enough and teased from me already too much in the way of things best kept secret. Now, off to your bedrolls with you. Good repose. Tomorrow, the *Collegium!*"

"Oh, um, Master," Rolland called.

Silvestrus turned from the opening of his tent, one hand on the flap.

"Yes, Rolland? It is a matter to which great importance is attached, I hope?"

"Master, are we then to hold secret all you have told us?" There was an air of challenge in the young redhead's voice.

Silvestrus merely barked a laugh. "Who is there that would believe it? Again—and finally—good repose!"

It was some time before Thaddeus heard the regular snoring of his two friends. Their discussions concerning this new information had carried on through half the night. Speculations, theories, and web spinning presented themselves in equal numbers. But later, when it became quiet, Thaddeus still could not sleep. Too many exciting images were parading through his mind concerning the events of a millennium ago. It was as if voices of the past were speaking to him. After a time, though, he thought voices actually were speaking. They were coming from outside the tent, but he could not decipher their meaning. Gently, and with great craft, he slowly lifted the edge of the tent a hand span nearest his ear and listened.

"...asleep, as I've said. There is no watch, only the three children. Let us be about it and be gone."

"If you are certain concerning this, we should proceed."

"I agree. Such things are best done quickly. Here, give me that. Now stand away. This will not take long."

Thaddeus was immediately filled with alarm—intruders in the camp! And from the sound of it, they were preparing to attack the master. Without thinking, Thaddeus grabbed his dagger, yanked up the tent wall, rolled out, and jumped to his feet in one smooth motion. Only afterward did he consider that he had left two potential allies-in-arms still sleeping. Ah, well, no time for regret now.

"Hold, villains!" the young beekeeper cried, brandishing his knife. "Attempt to harm my master, and you will have to deal with me!"

It was difficult, later, for Thaddeus to recall the exact sequence of events as they occurred. The moonlight shone down, sufficient for modest illumination. His first thought was that he had surprised three young boys—Anders's height or less—who stood gaping at him. One was holding a scroll, while the one on the left proffered a quill and ink bottle, and the third offered his back as a writing table. The three were attired in forest garb, which caused them to blend in with their surround. Each carried a dagger on one hip and a short sword on the other, with a bow and quiver slung over each back. They were slight of frame, but as Thaddeus stared, he revised his opinion upward as to their age. Their hair, a pale, silvery color, covered their ears, the points of which, however, protruded proudly therefrom. Their faces were beautiful with delicate, chiseled features.

All this was noted quickly, for in the next instant, he was on his back with three sharp points at his neck. He could see the intruders more clearly now that they were leaning over him, staring intently.

"Hold, Al-Donn! This boy is *Amicus Faerrarum!*" Though serious in tone, the silver-haired fellow's voice had a musical quality.

"You are certain, Ko-Thas? He does not appear the type."

"A simple matter to resolve," said the third. With a flick of his wrist, he laid back Thaddeus's jerkin to expose the apprentice's left breast. Sharp intakes of breath came from the three. Suddenly, Thaddeus was quickly hauled to his feet by six hands.

"Our pardon, friend. We were intent upon our mission, and our preoccupation with it fostered carelessness. I hope you have taken no hurt." The trio regarded him with concern .

Thaddeus wished to present himself as fully in control, as if it had been his intention all along to lure these strangers into gross overconfidence by allowing himself to appear to have been taken so easily. Well, so much for wishes.

"Um, no. I'm fine. Who are you, and what do you do here at this hour of the night?"

"As you yourself have given us no name, I will assume, for the moment, you are, perhaps, an apprentice who travels with Master Silvestrus on his way to the *Collegium*. Yes?"

Thaddeus nodded.

"Ah. Then, young one, allow me to introduce myself. I height Non-Dar of the Forest *Aelvae.* My companions, Al-Donn and Ko-Thas." The speaker fell silent and joined the other two in looking expectantly at the tall apprentice.

"Oh. I'm Thaddeus, son of Cedric...of Beewicke." He had, of late, become hesitant in adding this last, beginning to dread the response.

"Ah, Beewicke. Yes. Where the honey comes from."

A brief grimace stole across the apprentice's face.

"I thought I noted the fragrance on you. Well met, then, Thaddeus of Beewicke. You ask after our mission. Know that we were traveling close to you this night and thought to leave word with your master that the wood is quiet and the *Orbis Magnus* silent. Finding all asleep, we desired to disturb no one, so resolved to leave a message regarding the above. Now that we find you awake and alert, might you be so good as to deliver the message for us?"

"Yes, of course. My pleasure to serve."

"Ah, excellent. Our thanks. Fare thee well, then, Thaddeus of Beewicke, *Amicus Faerarrum.* Travel with ease in this forest." In a swirl of shadow, they were gone.

Thinking he could do nothing more, Thaddeus returned to his tent. His excitement of the moment, added to that felt earlier, convinced him he would surely be sleepless for the remainder of the night. In this, however, he was mistaken.

* * *

Thaddeus sprang from his blankets with the first birdsong and shook awake his grumpy fellow apprentices, regaling them with a recitation of his nighttime adventure. While Anders showed a modicum of sleepy interest, Rolland quickly launched into his store of profane epithets, leaving the frustrated beekeeper to slouch out of the tent and seek his master.

He found Silvestrus sitting on a log with his morning tea. The old man motioned Thaddeus to join him.

"I believe we may have had visitors late last night, eh, my boy?"

"Yes, Master, but how did you—?"

"The warding, lad. You pick it up as you go along. Why not tell me all about it, though?"

Glad to have an appreciative audience at last, Thaddeus related the entire incident concerning his confrontation with the *Aelvae.*

"Ah, well, that is good news at least. We will all travel with lighter hearts for it."

"Master, I have not met any of the *Aelvae* before. Do you see them often in this wood?"

"Generally speaking, Thaddeus, you do not see the *Aelvae* at all unless they wish it—and that only rarely. That you, a green novice in this forest, surprised them, in addition, is unheard of. They are, no doubt, right now considering how to work through their shame at this lapse of concentration and considering how much of it they will be obliged to reveal to their fellows." Silvestrus laughed. "I may decide not to be so charitable in regards to their sensibilities, however, in holding back that one of my apprentices so easily took them unaware. Ha! They have had the better of me on occasion, and crowed about it, that is certain enough."

Silvestrus's expression of delight lasted a goodly while before he again turned to Thaddeus. "There are, of course, different types of *Aelvae.* These here in the forest are organized into small bands of several families each, joined together in loose tribal confederations. None excel them in woods lore. In general, we at the *Collegium* always strive to maintain good relations with them. They have proven staunch allies over time, though they have their own purposes and preferences. It is usually best not to intrude nor presume upon them. But it would be better for us to turn our attention to other matters now. Were I to go on regarding the *Aelvae,* we would be days late in reaching the College—not a choice you would favor, I think."

Thaddeus agreed, then, gazing around the camp, became alarmed, recognizing something that had been troubling to him. "Master, something has changed. This is not the same forest we entered last evening. It's different."

"Yes. Well, good for your powers of observation. Know that in this wood, one never finds the same path twice. Perhaps it is a ploy to bewilder potential enemies. Never fear, though. The way may change, but the destination does not."

Thaddeus nodded in acceptance, if not understanding, and continued. "Master, just one last question. The *Aelvae* mentioned the *Orbis Magnus.* I would think they meant to say the Great Ring, but I have not heard of it before. What is it, Master?"

"It is a construction, Thaddeus, lying a bit north of here, resembling a temple. It is said to have been built by the First."

"The First, Master?"

"The First were a people so designated because they are thought to be the original inhabitants of this land. A short, slender race—human, not Fey—and light brown in color, it is said. Timid they were but with significant skills in stone working and cooperative engineering. Little else is known concerning them. It is believed that the *Orbis Magnus* represents the culmination of their racial energies, the apex of their achievement, though its true purpose remains unknown." Silvestrus paused to sip his tea and exhaled slowly.

The tent flap fluttered, and Anders stumbled out. After visiting a nearby bush, he moved to join the group.

"This temple has a purpose, Master?" Thaddeus asked.

"It is believed to have been built over a period of approximately fifteen hundred years in three distinct stages. Its physical structure is that of an giant outer ring of thirty-six huge upright stones. There is a horseshoe arrangement of even larger interior stones—twelve pair in number—with a capstone connecting each pair at the top. Each pair of stones with a top stone is separate from the other trios. At special places in the structure, one can, by sighting along certain grooves in specific stand-alone stones, predict the sun's position on the four Cardinal days—the Vernal and Autumnal *Aequinoctia,* and the Winter and Summer *Solsti.*"

"So, it is a calendar, Master?" Anders asked, glancing back over his shoulder as Rolland emerged from their tent.

"Hmm. Almost more of a chronologue, a timepiece. But each pair of the larger capped standing stones possesses certain marks—*insigniae,* or a key, if you like—all different. For example, one pair of marks represents two vertical lines, connected top to top by a horizontal line. Another an arrow. A third a pair of wavy lines. And so on. As far as can be told, the marks were placed there by the original builders."

"Do these marks have any significance, Master?" Rolland asked.

"Oh my, yes. These marks, unique to each threesome of stones, appear to designate different destinations, I believe."

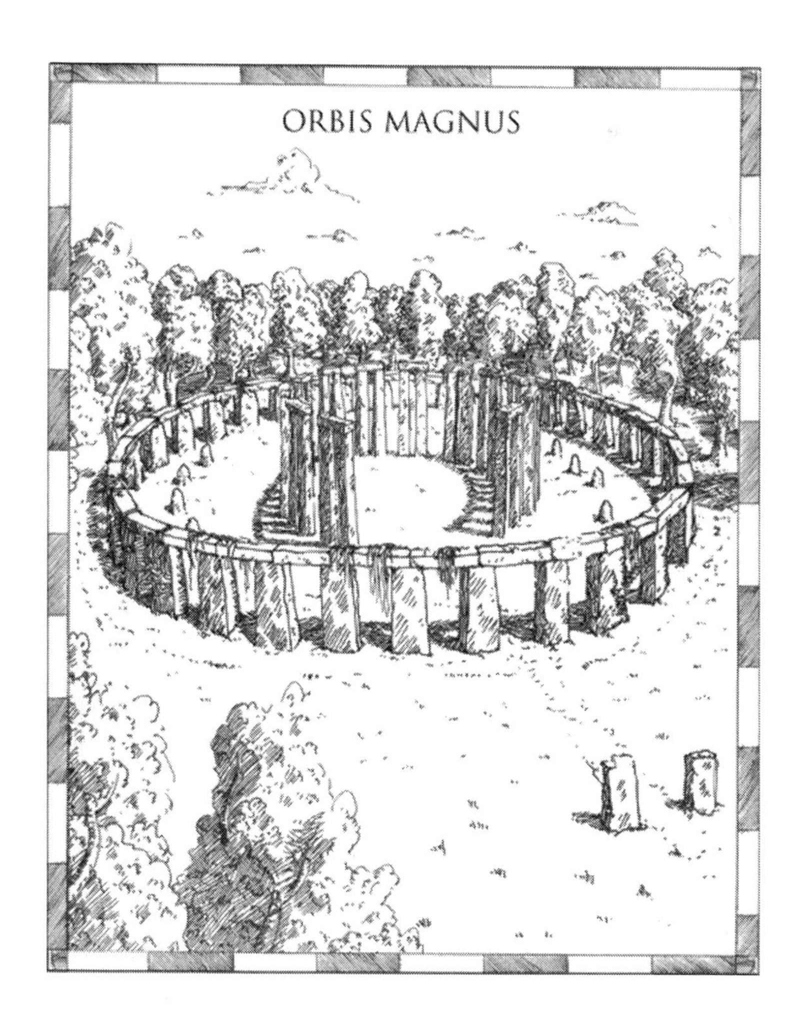
ORBIS MAGNUS

Thaddeus leaned forward. "Destinations, Master?"

"Yes, destinations, of a sort. Some individuals appear to be drawn to some of these stone pairs, while others to others. If such an individual should pass between one of these resonant pairs at a particular time, it is said they can venture to a place different from this. Little is known concerning such mysteries, as they seem to occur only rarely."

"What happens if an ordinary person passes between such a pair of stones, or one of the special people passes through the stones at a nonspecial time?"

"Nothing. They merely get to the other side of the stones. No one knows why."

"Have you ever had such an experience, Master?"

"No. I was told never to try. On those several occasions when I did try, a barrier always prevented me from doing anything other than passing through to the opposite side. Again, I do not know why. By the way, apprentices are forbidden to enter the circle of the stones."

"Why is that, Master?" Rolland asked with a little heat.

"Because, young thief, of the six hundred and sixty-some who are recorded as having made the attempt over the millennia, all have vanished. And none has ever returned."

"None?"

"None. One other thing of note concerning the Great Ring, it seems to be connected in some way with other similar stone groupings throughout the Earth, as near as can be determined. At certain times, for example, they have all been known to glow with blue light simultaneously."

"Are there other Great Rings like this?" Thaddeus asked.

"Not exactly like this. Bits and pieces, mainly. Of them all, however, this one is the most complete and intricate. You will recall, Thaddeus, that you have a Standing Stone in your own village. Some of the Wise suggest that this positioning of the Temple, lying astride the *Meridianus Primus* as it does, is significant. Well, now that you are all up, let us see to breakfast, then begin our trek. I will speak with Asullus."

During the morning preparations, Thaddeus was finally able to tell his friends of the visit of the *Aelvae* and the tendency of the forest to change. They discussed their views of the possible nature of the Great Ring. Thaddeus had difficulty assimilating so many new and startling experiences. He was having trouble digesting the myriad conceptions. It made his head spin. Anders's view was that, at the *Collegium,* they would surely find useful information on each of these phenomena, all carefully researched and reasoned out. Rolland, on the other hand, tended to believe little about all things new and strange, suspecting a ruse or errors in the recording or presentation of such events.

When the campsite was broken at last, the party set out with more trepidation *cum* excitement than usual—today they would achieve the *Collegium.* Silvestrus, on this day, did not take his usual nap in the cart but sat alert, reins in one hand, pipe in the other. The boys clustered around the mule, anxiety heightening each step that propelled them closer to their goal. They were relentless in peppering him with an unending stream of questions, which the faithful beast attempted to answer. Asullus's patience derived from a combination of the elements of his basic nature added to the experience of repetition of this same interrogation borne over many years of ferrying such promising youths to their destinies.

"Asullus, what does the *Collegium* look like?"

"'Tis as a big, hollow stone square set in a large meadow."

"What will our lives be like there?"

"Like what it's like in any new experience—hard at first, easier as ye learn it up an' go along."

"What are the masters like?"

"Mostly the same, though each be different."

"How many masters are there?"

"They tends, always, to have thirty-three, each wi' a different color an' callin'."

"Why?"

"Because."

"What about the other apprentices?"

"Much as yourselves."

"How many are there?"

"Varies from year to year, it does. Ne'er seen less than four in a class. Ne'er seen more than twenty-four—altogether, around fifty."

"What will we do there?"

"A big servin' o' hard work. Chores at the crack o' dawn, breakfast, chores, classes, midday, chores, classes, eventide, chores, study, repose, an' then it begins all over again the next day."

"It's like that every day?"

"Nay. Ye get some smidge o' time to yerselves on Saturn's Day an' Sun's Day. More, as ye advance."

"Will we all be together in our classes?"

"More so at the beginnin'. 'Tis no' unusual o'er the years, though, fer each o' ye to be seekin' out this master or that fer further study in some special area as ha' captured yer fancy or fer some topic as to which ye ha' shown a special knack."

"How long will we be there?"

"Varies, though wi' most 'tis four years. Some stay, some go, sometimes."

"What are the older apprentices like?"

"All different, one from the other, as ye might imagine. Some'll treat ye kindly. Some'll gi' ye a hard way to go. Most'll ignore ye 'less ye do somethin' as to trouble 'em, whether apurpose or by mischance. Then they'll make ye wish ye had no'."

"How about the masters? How will they treat us?"

"More or less the same. Ye'll wish to be on yer best behavior wi' them, however. Their way o' dealin' wi' those as irritate them can run to the harsh, don' ye know. An' yer knowin' Master Silvestrus here'll be no protection fer ye. Should ye transgress badly, ye'll be sent back to yer home wi' ne'er another chance to try again." The mule grew silent for a moment, then cleared his throat before continuing. "There be one o' the faculty, a younger fellow, ye'd best be 'specially wary o', however. Him 'tis worth avoidin', as ye can. An' ne'er gi' him an excuse to be at ye."

"Who is it, Asullus? Tell us."

"Nay, I canno'. 'Tis forbidden, I am, to mention a master by name in that way. But ye'll find out fer yerselves soon enough."

"Well, is it like that all year?"

"Nay, 'tis different o'er the warm months. Then, ye may ha' more time to yerselves or to visit yer home, if ye're allowed, or to be sent on a quest."

"A quest? What's that?"

"This here *Collegium* was built to educate the young as has certain talents. These talents are supposed to be used in the service o' the public weal. So, from time to time, folks here an' aboot as have trouble wi' one thing an' another will write, or e'en come in person to the *Collegium*, to petition the masters to help them wi' this or that problem. If 'tis a serious matter, a master'll go. If 'tis no' so bad, a likely lad'll often be sent to see what he can do. 'Tis a bit o' an honor to be selected fer such a task. I meself ha' ne'er heard o' them sendin' a *Tironis* on such a mission, though I suppose 'tis possible."

"How do they fare?"

"Mostly fair enou'. On occasion, one'll no' come back."

Here, a silence fell as the boys looked at each other in wide-eyed apprehension. But soon the torrent began again.

"What will they teach us?"

"All manner o' useful things. How to develop an' use yer powers fer the best. How to think. Mostly how to be a credit to yerselves while helpin' others as is less fortunate."

"There's another piece of it for us, though, isn't there, Asullus?" Thaddeus asked pointedly.

"How mean ye, laddie?"

"Our part in the Prophecy."

Asullus turned to toss his head while actually stealing a glance back at Silvestrus. The old man, however, was gazing placidly off to the left as a faun, perched on a tumbled-down log and playing a tune on his pipes, lazily nodded to him.

"Aye, lads, take a care wi' yer questions concernin' certain topics now, as we be approachin' the *Collegium.* I canno' help ye in matters such as these."

"Will we be able to use our sorcery right away?"

"Nay, 'tis strictly prohibited fer the *Tirones,* except fer yer classes where ye're closely supervised. Unallowed sorcery is dealt wi' mostly in a variety o' ways ye'll no' be wantin' to discover. An' do no' be thinkin' ye can test out yer talents down the hall or round the corner wi' no one the wiser. They always know when ye do it, an' they always responds to it right at the instant. Now ye be boys like any boys, an' from time to time, ye'll be sorely wantin' to see what yer limits be or to show off yer skills or ha' the impulse o' the moment to send a pie out o' thin air into yer friend's face an' such—but don' ye do it! There be no levity as will be worth what'll be sure to follow fer ye. An' ye mark me well on that, Young Master Rolland, in particular.

Sportin' a blue nose fer a time is as nothin' to what can happen should ye be bendin' the constraints. I ha' been at this fer some time, lads, an' I know o' what I speak." The mule ended his speech looking directly into the redhead's eyes.

"Do the girls have the same training?"

"I canno' answer fer certain, havin' ne'er been swaggled into their servitude as I ha' been here these many years. 'Tis me understandin', however, that 'tis much the same, though allowin' fer the differences as come from bein' o' an entirely different species altogether, don' ye know. Haw haw!"

"Their school is called the *Ludia*?"

"Aye. 'Tis in Northfast, I trow, far to the west o' here on the coast."

"I wonder if they're nervous about starting their first day?"

"Mayhap ye mean as nervous as yerselves? Well, 'tis no doubt there, I should say. But perhaps ye'll have an opportunity to ask 'em yerselves."

"How's that, Asullus?"

"Well, 'tis the tradition fer the young'uns o' each school to get together every year or every other year, depending on certain happenings, o'er the summers, usually, fer a holiday. Principally, I think, as the ones in charge wish ye to get all matched up."

"What? Why?"

"So there'll be more little sorcerers an' sorceresses o'er time, o' course. Would ha' thought that'd be obvious."

An extended and embarrassed silence fell over the boys—part outrage at being manipulated so and part in anticipation at the prospect of such a venture.

Anders nodded. "Well, if Nannsi would wish to consider spending some of her future with me, I wouldn't mind, I think."

"Now, there's a noble sentiment if e'er I did hear one," the mule said earnestly.

Thaddeus said nothing, but his thoughts were again filled—as they often were these days—with visions of a tall girl with long honey-blonde hair, green eyes, and a wonderful quiet way, who, at special times, might tenderly touch the side of his face as if she really liked him.

Further woolgathering was put aside when the master called the break for midday. Nothing new was learned, but what they had already seen and heard was hashed and rehashed. Master Silvestrus proved resistant to going into more detail, only saying, as he most always did, that Belief was the key to sorcery, and that anything else worth knowing would be revealed to them in the course of their studies at the *Collegium*.

Once their journey resumed, the boys again clustered around the mule, badgering him with more questions concerning what to expect—most of which, however, tended to be repetitious, signaling an increase in their anxiety as they approached their goal. After a time, Asullus declared he was tired of the pestering and offered no further responses. That left the boys to fall back on their earlier strategy of speculation without basis among themselves, which was most unsatisfactory, yet the best they could accomplish under the circumstances.

Near eventide, the party suddenly emerged from the forest onto a bright green meadow bedecked with uncountable ground flowers and an equally uncountable number of butterflies flitting amongst them. In the near distance stood a great stone building like nothing any of them had ever seen before.

"Behold, lads, the *Collegium Sorcerorum!* You are now come home."

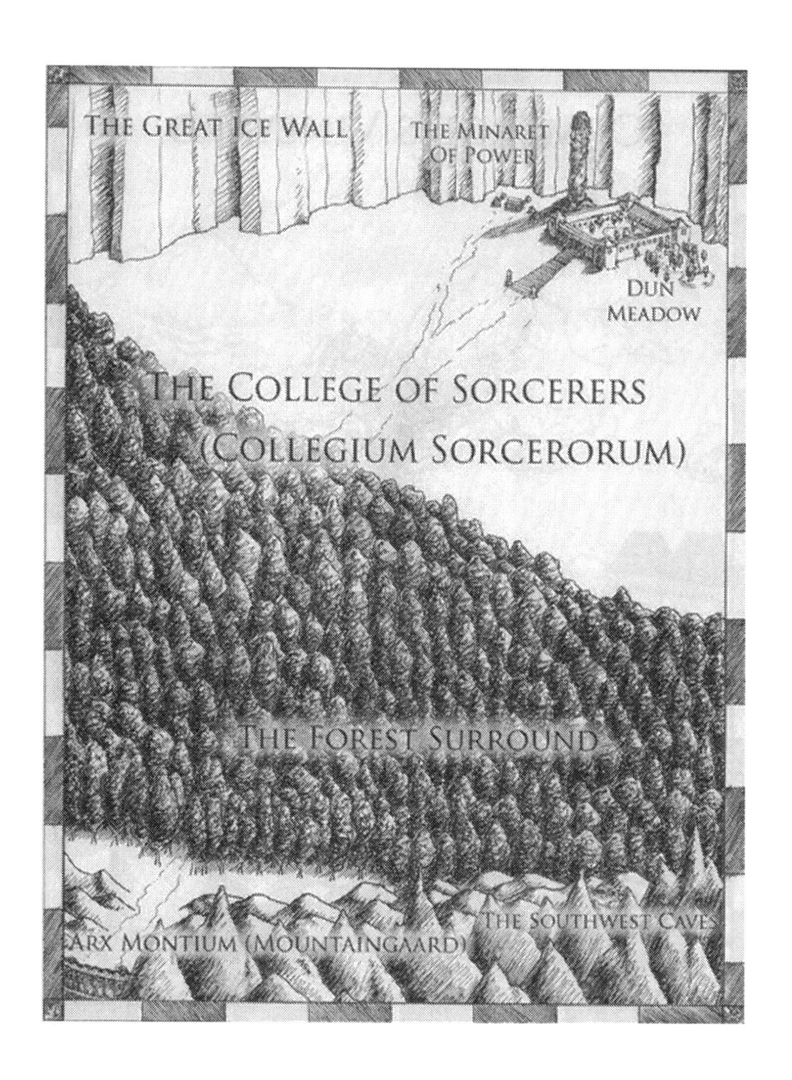
The Great Ice Wall
The Minaret Of Power
Dun Meadow
The College of Sorcerers
(Collegium Sorcerorum)
The Forest Surround
The Southwest Caves
Arx Montium (Mountaingaard)

EPILOGUE

[from the Prologue to *The Chronicles of Aberjanius, Book 1, The Restoration of the Empire*]

And so it came to pass in the last years of the Westlands' Inter-Imperium, Thaddeus, called the Faithless, working at the behest of the *Collegium Sorcerorum,* traveled east, retracing the steps of his youth, sent there in order to spy upon the land. For rumors of preparation for war had reached the ears of those senior in the College, and he was prevailed upon by his old mentor, Silvestrus of Somerset, to make the journey, seeking for what information he could glean. His choice for this task was twofold, his master had informed him—the first being that he had traveled in these lands as a youth and was familiar, therefore, with the peoples, their languages, and customs. And second, because it was suspected by some that there was a connection between the current activities of the Cin and that which Thaddeus himself had caused to have been restored to them in the relatively recent past. The Council, itself, however, was undecided as to whether it was Thaddeus's bold act that had set this process in motion, or whether this was an inevitable consequence of forces already long at work. Feelings ran strong in the course of the Council's deliberations, and it was by no chance that the young sorcerer was chosen for this mission, his mentor judging that his apprentice's absence from the College at this time would be prudent in any case. For his part, Thaddeus departed the Westlands only with great reluctance, as in recent years his heart had turned to a desire, at last, to make a home far away from the politics and annoyances of life in the community of the narcissistic and demanding old sorcerers found at the *Collegium.* It was his hope that such a home as he wished to build would be shared by the woman whom he had long loved—a sorceress herself—to whom he had given his heart many years ago, and with whom he wished to have a family. He was aware this was an unusual inclination for those of his calling. But it was not the first time he had assayed the unusual. Other sources, however, claim that...

...providing further elucidation. Thaddeus, called the Faithless, had seen but thirty-six summers when he set out upon his mission. He did not know at the time that he would travel the weary miles from the Westlands to the East and back again many times during the next five

> years. Nor did he know that while his dream of home and family would be granted, he would, on his travels, meet others of his seed—of whom he had no inkling—others who would come to play a pivotal part in the turning of the momentous events in the history of the world of that Age, a history that would include the birth of the *Imperium Restitutum*, the Great Invasion of the Cin, and the Death of the Fey. In fact, Wineskins, in *De Rerebus Cerebrus*, (qv), maintains that...

* * *

Thaddeus took a swig from the clay cup, then set it down on the table. It was hard to decide which was worse, the warm drink that passed for "ale" in this place, or the used water in the washbasin upstairs in his room. Then there was the ubiquitous sand and dust. Thankfully, the heat did not penetrate fully down here. He gave a moment's silent praise to the inn's architect, who had contrived to sink the tavern below ground level. Upstairs, however, was another matter entirely.

Thaddeus returned his attention to the grubby little man sitting across from him who was wiping his face with the back of his hand after gulping down some of the local swill. The unshaven one leaned forward and lowered his voice. Thaddeus winced—it was behavior certain to alert any real listeners out and about on the tavern circuit this afternoon.

"It is as I have said, Great One, the gates are barred. Two *Contubernia* of ten men each stand at every egress, and a half century is posted at both the Wailing Gate and the Emperor's Gate. This young commander is no fool. No one can get in, or out, without the closest scrutiny."

"I see. Well, that is...inconvenient. What can you tell me of their leader?"

"He is, as I have said, young—I doubt more than twenty-two summers. His rise has been meteoric, to say the least. Conflicting reports abound as to his origin, but most agree he is originally from the Westlands, beyond Grecolia. I have heard that his mother perished giving him birth. His father is unknown. The story goes that after his mother died, two servants took him to the local capital, a certain Fountaindale, but there either lost him or sold him. I do not know which. In any case, he became a ward of the state, but at age thirteen, he was noted to have astounding physical prowess and was sent to the local Proconsul, Marcus Quintessentialus. The boy evidently found favor with the man and was admitted to the Imperial Military Academy in Fornia at his insistence.

"It is said he graduated from that institution with honors and is as brilliant a strategist and tactician as he is an accomplished warrior. And his horsemanship shows no flaw. He held his first command at sixteen and was raised to the rank of full general just last year after the successful conclusion of his Aconian Campaign. The older members of the General Staff are said to be divided in their views concerning him—some encourage him, thinking to use him in their schemes because of his youth, while others fear him and his successes and would just as soon see him dragged down in disgrace. The younger members of the staff are reportedly rabid supporters, quite taken with him and doggedly loyal."

"Ah, Speculatoris, that tells me facts about the man but does not tell me of the man. Say on."

"Of course, Lord. Only permit me, please, to point out that obtaining such information as you request is not only time-consuming but inherently dangerous, especially given the current situation. Not only that, but I am a humble man of modest means, and the costs of accumulating what you desire increase disproportionately with—" The small man's protestations ceased immediately as a leather purse of some weight appeared in Thaddeus's hand from inside his robes and was discreetly pushed across the table.

The information vendor's eyes grew large, and his prosperous nose twitched as a crook-legged smile appeared underneath it, revealing an uneven row of gummy yellowed teeth, missing some companions.

"Many thanks, Great One! The blessings of my mother's mother's—"

"Yes. Of course. Thank you. Now, tell me more about our general."

"As you wish. Although granted great luck as well as talent, he is said to have led a riotous life in his youth, outside of his studies—dancing on tables, frequenting low places with unsavory company. However, once given command, it was as if a sorcery occurred." Here, the man shifted a furtive gaze back and forth, returning to rest on his deeply hooded employer. "From that point on, the young man gave up all drink, riotous living, and questionable associates, strictly dedicating himself to matters of military conquest. He already has two provinces under his control, and Oasia here will soon be his as well, I believe."

Thaddeus's eyes narrowed slightly.

"My beliefs are well-founded, Great One! All my sources agree, and I use only the best."

Thaddeus relaxed, reached for the clay cup, then thought better of it.

"Ah, to continue. He has no women for distraction—nor men, either, as it comes to that—and works without stop from dawn to midnight. He is extremely well educated—knows all the one hundred and sixty-nine classics by rote—and is fluent in five languages. All in all, a remarkable individual."

"Has he any passions? Interests? Goals? Ideals?"

"Ha! You mean aside from conquering the known world and resurrecting the long-dead Empire? No, none that are spoken of. Well, one, perhaps. But that is not—"

"Tell me."

"Well, it is said that he does have a passion, as you put it. In every city he conquers, he searches for his father. His agents are everywhere scouring for information. They say he will reward anyone with proof of this man's identity ten thousand gold Imperials. Of course, many have tried to claim that reward. But now, only with caution. Those he deems to be liars, or charlatans—all of them to date—end up with their wrists and ankles nailed to a wooden crosspiece dangling three paces off the ground. A slow and painful way to depart this life, in my view. Few there are who come forward these days."

"I see. Very well, Speculatoris. You have done well, and I am not displeased—thus you have been well paid. Should you discover further information concerning this man or his intentions here, come to me, and you shall see additional reward. Now, it's best if you leave, unless you know of some secret way out of this walled fortress that I do not."

"Thank you, Lord. Alas, no," he said, spreading his hands. "But if I hear..." With a slight bow, the small brown man made to depart but was stopped by Thaddeus's upraised arm.

"A moment, Speculatoris. What is his name, this young general of ours?"

"A-ki-re-u, Great One. General Akireu." With that and another small bow, the informant was gone, lost in the dimness of the smoke and wall hangings of the underground chamber.

Thaddeus swirled the contents of his cup—perhaps motion would improve quality—and sat lost in thought. The name sounded familiar, but he could not place it. Well, it would come to him in time. It always did. More to the current point, however, he had to leave this city and get back to the *Collegium.* Silvestrus would be wanting to know what Thaddeus had seen and discovered, not to mention news of the young conqueror. What if this invincible warlord were to turn his eyes to the Westlands? What then?

Uncertain of his next move, he rose from the table, deposited a few coins for the "Genuine Old Meadsville Ale, yes, sir!", and headed for the egress. He would take a casual stroll around the square and scout the situation for himself.

As he left through the glass-beaded exit, the snoring centurion at the next table suddenly sat up, alert, and grabbed his helmet, never taking his eyes from the cloaked figure just now leaving. The uniformed man stood quickly and strode toward the exit. At the top of the stairs, the square-jawed, iron-gray-haired soldier pushed through the curtained doorway, out into the sunlight, and hurried off down the Via Frontaga.

Thaddeus, making his way around the South Wall, was discouraged. Speculatoris had, unfortunately, been accurate. No other way out of the barricaded city existed. Of a sudden, a troop of soldiers in polished helmets, shields, breastplates, and spears, led by a young officer in a red cloak and red-crested horsehair helmet, turned immediately in front of him and halted.

"Your pardon, sir, but General Akireu requests a moment of your time."

Thaddeus heard another contingent of troops come to a halt directly behind him. He was caught as neatly as a bluegill in a net.

"Of course, um, Captain. Please lead the way." This was neither the time nor the place for thunderworks and molten sulfur. Best go along quietly—for now.

"Right. This way, sir, if you please. Troops! Forward!"

Within moments, Thaddeus was ushered into the Commanding Officer's suite at the compound. Having shown him in, the captain and six grizzled veterans remained standing in place, alert and at attention. Behind the only desk in the room sat a blond youth with curly cropped hair in a workaday leather tunic and breeches—standard military issue. A nearby bronze stand held a breastplate burnished to the point it hurt the eyes to view it. Above it hung an equally bright command helmet with a white ostrich-plume crest. A mirrored shield leaned against the stand. The figure of a tawny lion, rampant to the dexter, was emblazoned on its face. It seemed oddly familiar, though Thaddeus could not quite place it. An exquisitely blown crystal vase on the desk held a single white rose.

The young man finished writing, put down his stylus, rolled up the parchment, sealed it with hot wax, applying his signet ring, and stood, his green-gray eyes assessing Thaddeus from head to toe.

"Thank you, Captain Quintus. You may leave us now." The captain hesitated the barest second. "Really, Captain, it's quite all right. This man is no assassin." The captain and his coterie filed out, leaving the older man alone with the younger.

The general was tall, almost as tall as Thaddeus himself, though broader of shoulder and more solid—a trained physique, firmed by the hardships of military discipline and lengthy campaigning.

Thaddeus cleared his throat. "Forgive me for speaking, General, but do you fear assassins then?"

"No. I do not. However my staff, which seems to bear me some affection, does. But please, this is no formal inquiry. Seat yourself, and be at peace." The general indicated the nearest chair, rose, and turned toward a cupboard behind the desk. He spoke over his shoulder. "Wine?"

"No, thank you, General. I have already had my portion of spirits today."

"Yes. Genuine Old Meadsville Ale. Or so it is advertised." The young man smiled, turned back to his desk, and resumed his seat. His cup remained empty.

Thaddeus studied the blond conqueror before him. On the right side of his neck was a tattoo, a lion rampant, the same sigil as his shield. He was handsome, open, and friendly, but also intelligent, even shrewd. Thaddeus would trust this man's judgment regarding anyone.

"Perhaps you are curious as to why I have had you brought here?"

"Perhaps you seek information?"

"Yes, I do. You know, not many people living in this region of the world would know, or care, about ale—let alone one called 'Old Meadsville.' You, perhaps, have lived in the Westlands? I understand that is where it is brewed."

"Yes, General. You have the right of it. I have lived there."

"I thought I heard it on your tongue. And, are you, by chance, familiar with one of the larger towns in that area, a city called Fountaindale?"

"I am."

"Then let me introduce myself. I am General Akireu, though you know that already. But would you please tell me your name, sir?"

"Peregrinus. Peregrinus of Fountaindale, General," Thaddeus replied without hesitation.

A look of disappointment briefly crossed the young general's features. "Ah. Well. I want to thank you for answering my questions, Master Peregrinus. You've been quite accommodating, given the circumstances, in doing me this service. Is there any service I may do for you in return, sir?"

"Well, yes, now that you mention it, General. I understand the town is under military quarantine for a time. I have, however, urgent business in those very Westlands to which you were referring. I wonder, therefore, if I might be granted a pass and safe conduct out of the city so I may continue my journey?"

"Of course—it is a reasonable request. I will see to the necessary papers. Captain Quintus!" The man appeared as if by magic. The general explained his wishes, and the captain left to see to the details. The young man nodded to Thaddeus. "Thank you for your time, and a safe journey to you." He resumed his seat and returned to his writing.

As Thaddeus was ushered out, he pulled his right hand farther back into his sleeve so the fading green glow from the ring stone on his finger was hidden. Following a contingent of the guard, the sorcerer went first to the inn, collected his belongings, and settled his account. The general's escort showed him safely through the town, out the Lion Gate, and past the Army's perimeter, two *mille stadiae* down the road.

Thaddeus was now due for two weeks' worth of sand, heat, and more sand—depressing. He was tired to the bone of this solitary life of constant dust, travel, and cheap inns. He would settle himself and build a tower—and not just any tower, one on the seacoast, by all the Gods! The young general's face came to him. In spite of the situation, he liked the man, and knew, under other circumstances, they would be friends. And something about the name...It would come to him. It always did.

* * *

Back in the general's headquarters, a small, scruffy man in a dirty robe stood before the Captain of the Guard. "And so you are clear, then, what it is you're to do?"

"Yes, Captain," Speculatoris replied. "I am to follow the hooded man without being detected and send periodic reports back to you for the general."

"I did not say these reports were for the general, Spy!" the captain snapped.

"Of course not, Captain. You are correct. I was in error. Now, um, as to the matter of the fee..."

* * *

The day was sunny but with winds starting up along this section of the coastline. Random gusts blew up the cliff side, trying to remove Thaddeus's cloak and robes—or at least twist them around so he couldn't see where he was going. No doubt sea nyads amusing themselves at his expense. In any case, he slowed his dapple gray stallion, Viator, to a walk and continued his survey, heading north, with the sea on his left.

He was looking for a place, a place he had once seen in a dream, or vision, or in any case, it was a long time ago. It was a place with a Tower, or that might someday have a Tower. It was, he fancied, his Tower—a Tower on a coastline. *Turris Septentrionum*, a place of contemplation, peace, and safety—he would see to that—where he could raise a family. A place free from outside influences, or at least mostly free. He would know it when he saw it because he had already seen it. Now it was just a question of finding it.

He looked down at the simple map the local Quaestor had caused to be made for him last week when he'd passed through Pontesport. This looked like the area, all right. In fact…

Thaddeus looked up again to see a young maiden some distance away standing on the edge of the cliff. Everything froze in time for him. A young girl in a short tunic with a long blonde braid down her back and a pack carried on her shoulders faced toward the sea. The figure raised both arms as if in supplication, then dove straight off into space.

"No!" Thaddeus shouted, kicking Viator hard in the ribs. "Damn!" was followed by "Go!"

In a second, the huge horse was eating the distance between them and the cliff's edge. Thaddeus leaned close to the horse as he had been taught. He was there in a matter of heartbeats and off his mount before it had a chance to slow down.

"Fool girl!" he swore. Probably trouble with some pimply-faced, worthless pig-farmer's drunkard son with whom she was taken at the moment—or, perhaps, pregnant by.

Thaddeus ran the short intervening distance and skidded to a halt to peer over the edge. *Ascende* should work. There she was, knifing down to the rocks below in a graceful swan's dive. Now...

But just then, her "pack" opened, billowing out into a pair of great white gossamer wings. The girl pulled smoothly out of her dive at the last possible moment and began swerving and swooping in a series of intricate maneuvers—truly a dance of aerial grace.

After his heart slowed from its previous pounding, Thaddeus sat down on the cliff's edge to watch. The girl's elegance captivated him. After some time, the winged one's progress brought her back up the cliff face, where she saw Thaddeus watching her. She hesitated a moment, then added a swirl or two to complete her design, finally alighting several paces away from him.

Now that the girl was still, Thaddeus could appreciate her finely chiseled features and form. Her bright-blue, heavily lashed eyes were a perfect match for her equally bright-blue fingernails and toenails and the paler bluish tint of her skin. She was only chest high, though, if that—a miniature woman, with extraordinary wings.

She was wary, but unafraid. "What do you here, sirrah?" she demanded in a voice particularly haughty for one so young.

"I was looking for a Tower. But I saw you dive off, and I thought…"

"That I would be dashed to pieces on the rocks below? And you came to rescue me? That is quite charming, though, of course, unnecessary. I was merely testing what My Lord Spadix calls 'the thermals.' It is very exhilarating, though, I suppose, technically I'm a bit young and therefore forbidden. But, so be it. My name is Avolare. What is yours?"

"I am called Thaddeus."

The girl stiffened and peered at him with more interest. Her wings began to beat back and forth, shimmering in the sun, as she took a step nearer. "And what village or town do you hail from, Master Thaddeus?"

"Well, it's a tiny place, a bit inland from here. I doubt you've heard of it."

Taking another step, the girl stared at him intently. "Nevertheless, sir, humor me. What is the name of your town?"

"Beewicke," Thaddeus replied, "although I've not been back there for some time—and now I have other names that I go by, so…"

Avolare had gasped at the name of the town and cautiously approached even closer, her great wings fanning more rapidly. "And what, Thaddeus of Beewicke, is the chief product of this tiny village of yours?"

Thaddeus had the feeling something important hinged on the answer to this question, but he had no idea what. He was curious as to the girl's ignorance of Beewicke, but she was clearly Fey, and perhaps her education had been different.

"Why, honey, of course."

The girl uttered a shrill cry and leaped into the air, rushing toward him at blinding speed. Before he could begin to defend himself, she collided with him, knocking him to the ground. Phosphenes appeared in his vision as he strove mightily to suck air back into his lungs while trying, unsuccessfully, at the same time to ward off a torrent of kisses raining all over his exposed face. His brain, whirling with the events of the past several moments, was attempting to remember her cry as she'd launched herself at him. What was it now?

Ah, oh yes—"Papa!"

The sorcerer sat on the ground with his legs crossed and hands behind him, supporting him, facing the butterfly girl, whose legs were drawn up with her chin resting on them and her arms wrapped around as her wings fluttered lazily back and forth. The wind, puny in comparison, held no candle to the great breezes stirred by the inundation provided by the blonde girl's speech.

"And then, of course, Mama had to decide whether I should be raised in the human world or with the *Faerrae,* but there really was no choice, naturally, given my beautiful wings and all and they are beautiful, don't you think because everyone says so, even if they are larger than all the others', but then I'm larger than all of the others, too, but Mama says that's because of you, because you're human though I've often wondered if a sorcerer—and Mama says you're a very powerful sorcerer, but I tell her, of course, my papa would be, wouldn't he, I say to everyone—means it's easier to have children with the *Faerrae*, but it's probably different for everyone, depending, of course, on the circumstances though sometimes I've seen Mama cry for you, and she always speaks well of you, and I've heard her, a thousand times, talk about the night you rescued her from that terrible spider—like you were going to rescue me just now, I mean before you found out who I am and what I am. My Lord Spadix is not always so pleased with me, but Mama won't let him send me away, though sometimes I think he'd like to, because he resents me, as I'm proof that he's not so great and all knowing as he pretends to be..."

As the Fey chattered on, Thaddeus found himself lost in this tidal wave of words, but once he had sorted out their import, he realized he didn't mind at all, really, not at all. In fact, it reminded him of...

Suddenly, a shadow fell over them, and Thaddeus looked up to see another great winged shape approaching.

Avolare, cut off in midsentence, gasped, "My Lord Spadix!"

The intruder landed a short distance away. Large and muscular, he was kingly in bearing with great brown wings and coloring. But as he drew nearer, it was clear that he lacked, perhaps, a thumb's height on Avolare.

"What do you here, girl, and who is this stranger?" he barked at her.

"He is only a traveler passing through, My Lord Spadix. He saw me flying over the meadow and stopped to watch. I did not see him until just now. I alighted to tell him to forget this scene as if his life depended on it, or it would go ill with him."

"Saucy girl. You are always showing off your wings—just like your mother. Do not think for a moment I will not be telling her of this adventure of yours." The *Rex Blottarum* glanced briefly at the cliff's edge. "You did not, I presume…"

"Oh, no, My Lord Spadix. You have forbidden it, and I would not disobey you."

"It is just as well you do not. As for you, stranger, it will be best for you to forget all that you see here." The King of the Moths casually raised his arm, and a handful of fine dust flew out of it and was borne on the wind to Thaddeus. "I doubt anyone would believe you in any case. Now, Avolare, you are to come with me. Your mother, the Queen, is worried about you, though I am not sure why she should be. Be that as it may, she sent me to find you. We must leave now if we are to be back before dusk. I have, um, important business this night with my subjects. It is the Fall Carnivale, and I must be there by First Star. Come!"

With a quick glance back and a blown kiss Thaddeus was certain My Lord Spadix did not detect, Avolare leaped into the air, obediently following her stepfather. Thaddeus gazed after them until they were lost from view. After a bemused moment, he contemptuously brushed the moth dust from his cloak. Someday, My Lord Spadix might be in for a bit of a surprise. Though whether he, Thaddeus, would be the agent to deliver it, or his daughter, was a throw of the dice.

Laughing to himself, he looked around and knew without doubt that if he were going to build a Tower, he was going to build it on this very spot.

* * *

The tall figure landed lightly on the ground near the recently completed gray stone tower. Transformation was not so much painful, as he'd heard others claim, as it was just plain hard work. The northern wind and cold rain pounded his cloak, quickly soaking it through and through, and produced in him a strong desire to return to his sunny southern shores. This was important, though. He had just come through a long and deadly battle, and he was compelled to stop here. His mother would have wished it.

* * *

Thaddeus sat at his letters desk, quill in hand, absently rubbing his eyes and considering what to write next. The single fat candle waxed to the skull of Morag the Unlucky guttered and spat from time to time as the wind from the storm pounding the coast buffeted his tower. The stars and moon hid behind a curtain of sheeted rain—a thoroughly miserable night. But the gloom of the night was softened by the prospect of the morrow. His bride was coming. She would be here tomorrow, or the next day at the latest, to start their life together. Assuredly, she was not alone. Her family, his family, their friends, Anders and Nannsi, Rolland and Sonnia, Zoarr and his Molly o' the Willows—all welcome, of course, but his eyes would be for one, only. The crackling and popping of the fire in the pit at the end of the room seemed muted, expectant.

With no warning, a measured pounding rattled his study door. Odd. Who else knew to find him here? And in this foul weather? And at this time of night?

He replaced his quill in the heavy pewter inkwell—a prized possession for several years now—and made his way to the door. A moment only to prepare, and, at his pull, the thick oak yielded and pivoted on its massive brass hinges for several hand widths before slowing to a stop.

A cowled stranger in a sodden wool cloak stood before him, rivulets of water running down, forming puddles on the floor. Thaddeus glanced past the visitor at the torches set in sconces at intervals down the hall. The stranger's path was clearly marked by receding pools reflecting the flickering lights. There were not many who could come this far unannounced and unaided.

The man—if man he was—was taller than Thaddeus. Gracile, rather than robust. A long object protruding from behind his cloak on his right hip was certainly a sword. Sturdy workaday leather gloves covered both hands, and heavy boots shod his feet. His tunic and trousers were of a thick, unfamiliar material.

A cockleshell pendant hung from his neck by a heavy gold chain. There was the smell of the sea about him.

"Thaddeus? Called the Faithless?" The voice was deep and resonant.

"I am he." A moment passed. "Your name, sir?" It was not a command, but it brooked no disregard.

"I am called Ultoris. I have sought you for some time. May I come in?"

Thaddeus was unafraid. He had little to fear these days, and he was curious. "Yes. Of course." He stood back and motioned for his visitor to enter.

Thaddeus indicated the chair across from his desk, turned to the nearby cabinet, and took down two goblets, which he filled from a crystal decanter. He placed one on the edge of his desk nearest Ultoris and resumed his seat. Sipping the Frantillian vintage slowly, he regarded the stranger with interest. He was unable to discern his visitor's features—this Ultoris had, so far, shown no inclination to throw back his hood. His guest sat without moving for some moments, his head inclined toward the proffered glass. Quickly, he took it and tossed down the contents, then replaced the glass carefully on the desk. The sudden movement struck Thaddeus as serpent-like.

The sorcerer started to rise, but the stranger spoke again. "No more, thank you. It is an excellent choice, but what you've given me already has been enough for the task, though I do not refer to the wine."

Thaddeus resumed his seat, aware he was being regarded in turn, even weighed. He waited. The stranger leaned forward.

"I am here on behalf of my mother, the Queen. And for myself as well. I never knew her, of course, but I've no doubt she'd have wanted me to give you this message: The Red is fallen. The Green, avenged."

A moment passed. "That, then, is the extent of your message?"

"It is. Now I must depart. Forgive my abruptness, but my kind is not, by nature, social. Still, family bonds are the strongest. I would have you know it pleases me greatly to see you at last. You are as I imagined you would be. My thanks for the wine. Farewell." With that, the stranger rose and strode to the portal, where he stopped and turned. "Perhaps we may meet again…" And he was gone.

At his desk, Thaddeus stared at the fire a long time, lost in thought, considering the night's events. He knew what he had seen as his visitor crossed the room—the shadowed face briefly illuminated by flames from the burning logs. Not a human face, rather, humanoid. Leathery, almost scaly—and verdant. A long scar, perhaps the mark of a burn, trailed diagonally across that countenance. And the eyes—so very green. Sea green.

He took another sip of wine. Recollection came, coupled with understanding.

Ah, how long ago it seemed. And how difficult it must have been for his young guest.

* * *

Ultoris left the Tower satisfied. It had gone very well, and his mother would have been pleased. Now, south, and farewell to this cursed cold wind and stormy rain. Moments later, he was eyeing the countryside from a different perspective. He was reminded that it had been some time since he had last eaten. Perhaps he should have accepted the sorcerer's implied invitation and stayed for a late repast. No doubt he would have been offered delicacies and fine pastries. Looking down and spying movement, he mused that while delicacies and fine pastries were all very well, they did not always compare favorably to, for example, a fresh whole sheep. His great leathery wings banked, and he went into a practiced steep dive, talons flashing in the lightning.

* * *

Thaddeus rode at a steady pace through the rain. He would need to seek shelter soon, as it was getting late, and the light was perceptibly fading. He'd want an early start tomorrow, of course. It would likely take him another day or so to make the coast, next south for another part of a day, then home. By that time he'd be racing the White Eaglet—bringer of babies, according to Saphie, his youngest so far—as to who would make it to the Tower first, him or the new arrival. He'd been on the road longer than expected, but at least most of the Westlands' defenses were now in place, according to Silvestrus. That was enough for now. He'd done his part. So, to home.

He had passed this way before and recollected a clutch of caves up in this area. He slowed Viator to a walk and turned off the Northern Road into the forest.

An hour further on, a roaring and snarling brought him to a halt. Normally he would avoid investigating anything that sounded like conflict—he'd gotten soft, as Rolland of Fountaindale had said more than once. But peace meant a great deal to him these days. Still, if he was to bed down around here, it would behoove him to know what it was that transpired. He dismounted and tied Viator to a nearby tree limb and followed the sound of the disturbance.

Coming to a clearing, he espied a grotto abutting several cave openings. In front of one was the source of the disruption. *Spelaeus!* Standing tall and roaring fiercely was the largest cave bear Thaddeus had ever seen. It was a towering mass of fury fully five paces high. Bellowing and slavering, huge paws with terrible claws capable of ripping apart anything that opposed it, it stood astride the entrance to one of the caves. Between its massive legs, two little cubs huddled together—a sow protecting her babies.

The focus of the great bear's attention was a large brown wolf pacing an arc back and forth, snarling between feinting forays to the cave's entrance. It was clearly wounded, a great bleeding gash down its left shoulder and chest. Hobbling, it alternately eyed the grotto, seeking a way to leave without being torn in half, and the cave entrance—a dilemma.

Thaddeus wasn't sure what could be accomplished here, but he'd never find a place to rest with this ruckus, not to mention being able to trust that his horse would not become an entrée for these carnivores. While he thought Viator would probably give a good account of himself, nothing could stand against that bear. And wolves tended to travel with friends.

"Ursus!" he called in the Language of Those Who Hunt. *"What do you here?"*

The bear swung its massive head around to face him, though its eyes flicked back frequently to the cringing wolf. The wolf likewise gazed at Thaddeus, eyes widening momentarily, but quickly turned its attention back to its much larger adversary.

"Ha! Sorcerer! I smelled you coming, but first I must deal with this dog!"

"Tell me, Great Bear. What has this little one done to offend you?"

"It came into my home. I was resting, but my pups were curious. I awoke immediately. All should know it is death to come near my family."

"Did it seek to harm you or your babies?"

"No. It lives still, does it not? If it had…"

"Yes, of course. I understand. I see it is gravely wounded. Perhaps it would leave you in peace if given the opportunity?"

"I had thought that as well after I had given it that scratch, but it will not leave, though I have given it several chances. Now, however, my patience is at an end, and it will die."

"Great Bear! None are there who could fault your reasoning, yet preserving life may yield benefit. With your leave, I would speak with this intruder and understand better why it is behaving in this odd fashion. What say you to postponing its death this little while?"

Several moments passed as the great beast mulled over the request.

"Very well. You may have a small time to do this thing. Know that I do this only because I know you of old, though you may not recall a young cub who found a beehive kept by humans and what happened then. But none of your tricks, Sorcerer. Discover what you need to and end it quickly!"

"As you say, Great Bear." Cub? Beehive? Oh yes...

The wolf had slowed its pacing and now stood shaking in one place, head lowered and panting heavily.

"Lupus, what do you here in this place?"

"I was traveling west...seeking someone...It was important to me...was in my other fur...got caught in the rain... went into the cave...smelled of bear, but I thought it was gone...My smelling is poor in my other fur...put my pack and staff down...cubs came to me...They were so cute...knew I should have left sooner...Then herself appeared...more than I bargained for...wanted to run, but I must have my staff and pack...They're still in there...can't leave without...I'm so cold...feel dizzy..."

The wolf collapsed to the ground, head rolled back, tongue lolling.

Pack? Staff? Then it came to Thaddeus. A demi-wolf! He moved cautiously to the limp form and examined it briefly.

"Great Bear, this one is gravely injured and near death. She lingered only for some rags and a stick she left in your home by error—for which she is truly penitent. They are important to her, however. If you have no need of them, I ask to be allowed to remove them so they disturb you no further. Also, I ask to be allowed to remove this dog from your presence as well. I am willing to see to her remains."

"You ask too much, Sorcerer! The bitch will die! I will rend her corpse as a reminder to all who it is that rules here! As for the trash she has left in my home, I will shred it till none is left!"

"I understand your anger, Great Bear. And, truly, it is justified. However...I wonder if you would be willing to consider an exchange?"

"Exchange, Sorcerer? How mean you?"

"Perhaps I have something you would find of value. I ask to be allowed to present it to you. Then, if you deem it of worth, we would exchange, and I would be allowed the dog, rags, and stick I have spoken of."

The huge cave bear snorted. *"You have nothing I would find of value—unless you mean that horse I smell on you. I do not mind horse. I have not had any for two seasons. They are skittish and prone to run when I approach. All right, then. Bring me your horse. If it pleases me, you may take the cur and her garbage and depart immediately. I grow tired of this charade, and when I am tired, I am likely to become irritable."*

"Ah, Great Bear, of course you would like my horse, but I find, unfortunately, I have some further need of it just presently. In its place, however, let me offer this..." Thaddeus gestured and spoke. *"Fiat Mel!"* There was the familiar roaring and rushing sound.

The cave bear's eyes widened, and it began to drool. *"Well done, Sorcerer! Take what you need and leave us. Now!"*

"Of course, Great Bear! As you wish."

The mother bear lumbered back into the cave. Thaddeus ducked as the demi-wolf's backpack and staff sailed out of the cave in a high arc and landed near him and the wolf with two thumps and a bounce. Thaddeus slid his cloak off his shoulders, gently laid the wolf upon it, tossed in the slivered staff and ripped pack, and dragged the lot carefully backward out of the grotto to where Viator waited, never letting his eyes leave the form of the stupendous beast and her cubs until he and the injured wolf were safely away.

* * *

After assuring herself the meddlesome human and wolfish intruder had truly left, the mother bear grunted, signaling her pups to join her. They came quickly and were soon sitting on the ground, one on either side of their mother, who had already dipped one of her great paws into the sorcerer's wondrous gift. As she licked up the sticky, wax-flecked golden treasure, she reflected that while mercy was said to be its own reward, compensation, on occasion, was tolerable as well.

* * *

Viator presented not at all pleased with the addition to their party but seemed less concerned once he appeared to understand the wolf's condition posed no threat. After a brief search of the area, Thaddeus discovered a suitable cave a safe distance away from the bear's grotto. Besides its proximity to a rushing stream, it had other advantages—chief among these that it was uninhabited. After they settled in, he turned his attention to his new charge.

With care, he dressed the semiconscious wolf's wounds. She seemed to bear the ministrations with patience, still on his cloak, far back in the cave, away from the elements. He considered giving the animal a sleeping draught, but as he was about to offer it to the wolf, the creature opened its eyes and spoke.

"It is all right. I do not require your drug. I will sleep well this night, and I am grateful. Thank you, Father." And with that, she drifted off to sleep.

Dawn brought continued rain and a remarkable improvement in the demi-wolf's condition. And information.

The young woman in a torn tunic and long brown braid falling to the cave floor sat carefully with her back against the etched rock wall, away from the small fire. Her left shoulder was swathed in simple bandages. In her lap was a wooden bowl half filled with broth. Between measured dips and sips from her spoon, she related her story as Thaddeus squatted nearby, his arms resting on his legs and hands clasped loosely in front of him.

"Mother named me Sacerdotia, knowing I would become a priestess. Concerning you, she told me she knew you from the beginning—right after she returned to where she and her pack had killed the ogre. She kept track of you and decided to see you in person. The local townsfolk, of course, knew her from her other, dog, form, but the village demi-wolves all knew who she really was, of course—their Golden Pack Leader. Then came the incident with that mad religious fanatic, and there you were. She was immediately attached, and the rest you know, I am sure. And, so, here I am, the result—a Druidic priestess half-wolf shape-shifter gone looking for her father. I had heard about your Tower and thought I'd pay a visit there."

The girl took some more sips, then shifted her position slightly with a wince. "I had been making fairly good time walking. I had my oaken Staff of Relevance and my magic paraphernalia in my pack. But then it started pouring...That was a near thing yesterday, Father. Your arrival was timely. I knew you right away, of course, family scent and all. I was relieved, but so surprised to see you there, of all places, coming in as you did. I was thinking this morning that there must be more to this than appears on the surface, but I have not yet recovered sufficient strength to parse it all out so far. I do acknowledge, though, that it has saved me a longer journey. I've always wanted to meet you, and..." Her voice trailed off.

"What is it, Sacerdotia?" Thaddeus asked.

"Father, you must be away home soon. Your family needs you."

Thaddeus, alarmed, stood casting about, but the comely hazel-eyed brunette reached up and placed a gentle restraining hand on his arm. "It is all right, Father. I did not mean to disquiet you. You are needed because it is near Nature's time for your tall woman. Rest assured, all will be well. Not only for this one, but for the next—and the next, and the...Oh my. Twelve altogether. Oh my." The girl's eyes widened, and then she giggled. After a moment, and with some obvious effort, she got slowly to her feet. "Father, you go on. I will rest here a bit and tend to the camp. With my staff and pack, none will disturb me. I am truly well now, and you are needed elsewhere. I have achieved my purpose." She stood on tiptoes and kissed his brow. "I shall tell Mother that I found you and that you are well, and all the rest. She will be amazed, and pleased." She frowned briefly. "And I will probably get another lecture about woodcraft and animal-animal interrelations. Oh well. She's a parent, and that is what they do, is it not? Good-bye, Father. This has been very special for me."

Thaddeus kissed his newfound daughter's brow in return, retrieved his belongings from the cave, and strode out to where Viator was waiting. He untied the tether, mounted quickly, and with a wave of farewell rode down from the forest. Without difficulty, he found the Northern Road again and resumed his journey westward. The rain had stopped by now, and the sun shone bright with promise.

As he rode, Thaddeus considered what his daughter had said. Twelve? And now he had met the fourth of his four Fey children. He wondered briefly concerning the others of his kind. Was this true of them as well? This thought led him to think of Silvestrus. His mentor had never mentioned in detail this aspect of a Sorcerer's Ethos, only to say they rarely married and settled down with just one person. And he did have an age on him—centuries, it seemed. Was spreading the seed of sorcery widely a part of his plan? Did it have something to do with other sorcerers who had followed? Did it have something to do with himself? He must give this some thought. He would mention it to his 'tall woman,' as Sacerdotia had called her. It may be she could offer some perspective. But perhaps not right away. First things first. And that was going to include a lot of changing cloths. He grinned and nudged Viator into a canter.

* * *

To the east, a young woman wearing a sling crumbled herbs into a small pot of boiling water, with other ingredients, then gazed into the ferment. Long she looked, her expressions changing from one to the next. First pleasure, then turmoil accompanied by great danger—then anger and retribution. At the last, she saw great joy, then peace. But peace for whom? That was the problem with visions—they could be vary nonspecific. She would have to parse that out, too. When she felt better. For now, weighty events and earthshaking cataclysms would have to give precedence to a nice long nap.

* * *

> ...which has been the question raised not only by Geoffrey of Mothmount, but others of similar stature—to wit, how much of what transpired in those days was Silvestrus of Somerset knowledgeable of, or, possibly, a party to? In the end, it is, perhaps, after all, only a matter of speculation.

Yet, how far can one stretch the concept of coincidence? In the following, the author presents his theory, supplemented by texts written at the time and, most importantly, with excerpts from the personal journals of Thaddeus, called the Faithless, himself—but recently come to light following decades of intense search. Though weathered with time and, apparently, sea air, they are nevertheless able to shed much light on this nagging question. The reader should know, incidentally, that these writings were obtained only at great personal cost to the writer, in contrast to what my 'esteemed' colleague from South Noblebarns dismissively seems inclined to refer to as 'dragon's lair, indeed, pishposh...truth from brandy—ha!' and other similar attributions. However, let me assure the reader, I now know they do exist. However, moving on, it should be noted that Freebooter of Westwallia, herself a correspondent to the *Ludia* for some years, has proposed that...

[excerpt from the "Address to the Committee on Documentary Integrity Concerning Verifiable Source Material from the Ante-Deluvian Age," Master Dunlop of Crudus presiding, Professor Derrick One-Arm presenting]

DRAMATIS PERSONAE

A First and greatest Demon. Creator, by will alone, of all. It is the character of the Demon, unavoidably suffusing its creation with its own essence, that accounts for the imperfections observed everywhere in the Universe and in Man himself.

Adjurford Sorcerer of the *Collegium Sorcerorum.* Second-in-command to **Portoman** during sorcerous raid on the capital of the Cin in the time of the Eastern Invasion occasioned by the greed of the last Emperor of the Westlands, **Tyrannus Superbus**. Their original mission was to destroy the Minaret of Power. However, following **Portoman**'s descent into madness, **Adjurford** assumed leadership of the small band of sorcererous brothers and succeeded in making away with the Tower, instead. He was able to return to the *Collegium Sorcerorum* with all his men and the severely compromised **Portoman**. Speculation later arose that a young **Silvestrus** of Somerset may have been a member of that party.

Adrocles Superstitious house servant to **Sophia** and **Astonius** of Brightfield Manor.

Akireu Eldest of four feral children of Thaddeus of Beewicke, whose mother, **Ethne** of the Flowers of Sorrow, was the Beewickean's first love. Brought by servants of the vintner **Ormerod** to Fountaindale, he was sold to **Chiron**, Centaur and Horse Master of the *Collegium Sorcerorum.* He was taken by **Chiron** to Fornia, where he was raised and trained by the Centaur, until word of the boy's prowess reached the ears of **Marcus Quintessentialus**, regional Proconsul, whose favorable influence assured **Akireu** a place at the Academy of War.

Aldo Male servant employed by **Oliffe**, innkeeper of the Sword in the Scone, a Fountaindale establishment.

Al-Donn *Aelvae.* Lieutenant to **Non-Dar**, Lord of the Greensward *Aelvae.* Favors acorn soup.

Alistair Profane member of a pair of black marble gargoyle statues charged with guarding the main entrance to the *Collegium Sorcerorum.* Claimed by some to be, on occasion, both sentient and mobile.

Anders of Brightfield Manor. Only child of **Astonius** and **Sophia**, successful distillers near Meadsville. Intelligent and clever, well tutored by his teachers and apprenticed to **Silvestrus** of the *Collegium Sorcerorum.* First of the three brothers to **Thaddeus** of Beewicke. Later affianced to **Nannsi** of Zorbas in Grecolia. He is Cardinal Point *Occidus* (West) of the *Octipes Circuitus Magnus,* the Great Compass.

Annis Male servant to **Ormerod**, master vintner of Figberry.

Antigonis Monitor lizard. Familiar of **Silvestrus** of Somerset, he abides at the *Collegium Sorcerorum* in his master's study. He has a special dietary predilection for soft-feathered, nocturnal avian predators, to the distress of some of the other Masters at the College.

Apiarius Magister Chief Beekeeper of the Hives in Beewicke, having inherited the position from his father.

Arbuta Sister to tavern keeper **Dawber** of Bannock. She lives alone in a small manor on the Frantilline coast.

Arch-Iten *Aelvae* Bow Master at the *Collegium Sorcerorum* and cousin to **Non-Dar**, local Lord of the Greensward *Aelvae,* who are, by tradition, allied to the College.

Ardens Sister. Septuagenarian member of women's religious Order of Nurses, residing at the Convent of the Silent Sisters. Impulsively sought to disavow Holy Orders after the advent of **Rolland** of Fountaindale at the convent.

Argentus Silverfoot. One of silver-haired and pointy-eared half-*Aelvae* twin cousins. He is in his first year of study at the *Collegium Sorcerorum.* Along with his twin, **Platinus**, he befriended **Thaddeus** of Beewicke and his three human brothers.

Argus Loyal hound, eager companion, and early protector of **Thaddeus** of Beewicke.

Argutia Intellect. One of the four daughters—the *Intelligentiae*—of **Mater Naturae**, who together are tasked with preventing the demons at the Earth's core from breaking through to the surface via the Minaret of Power to ravage the planet.

Arnius Apprentice and *Tironis* classmate of **Thaddeus**. Largest and slowest in his class but loyal to a fault.

Astonius Master distiller and astute businessman at Brightfield Manor, he is husband to **Sophia** and father of **Anders**.

Asullus Sentient mule, born in Cobbly Knob in the year of the Great Comet, and chattel of the witch woman **Lillith**. Achieved capacity of speech and other gifts through his mistress's magicks and has not been silent since. Father to **Asummus**.

Asummus Coal-black mule with striped tail. Son of **Asullus** and, like his sire, sentient, verbal, and productive. He is later tasked with taking his father's place.

Atreus Albino griffin, traditionally employed by seniors at the *Collegium Sorcerorum* as access coordinator and personal assistant to his masters. He but recently worked for **Wil Rathboneson**, and later for **Thaddeus** of Beewicke.

Attacondros King of Red Dragons. Passionate suitor for the favors of **Mari** the Green, Queen of Sea Dragons. Frustrated by the failure of his suit, he pronounces a terrible curse upon the Green Queen.

Avolare Second of four feral children of Thaddeus, mothered by **Caerulea**, *Regina Papilionum*, Queen of Butterflies. Tall for a butterfly, she is blonde haired and blue eyed with a bluish tint to her skin. Abhors silences in conversations.

Barcus of Poosia. Recruited by **Apiarius Magister** of Beewicke as replacement for the abruptly absent **Thaddeus**. Over time, he gains the respect and confidence of **Hycynthya** and **Cedric**.

Barnabas Cleric and Brother of the Order. One of only a small number of members of the Holy Orders allowed by the Council to study and teach at the *Collegium Sorcerorum.* He has a passion for the study of Law and serves as an Administrator of the College.

Bartsome Innkeeper of the Friend in Mead, Bostle's premier, and only, inn. He keeps a good and generous table known as "**Bartsome**'s Best."

Beatus Master sorcerer and current *Princeps Accademiae, Collegium Sorcerorum.* Benign shepherd to his flock. Many believe that upon his retirement, he is likely to be succeeded in that position by **Silvestrus** of Somerset.

Bede Venerable Master Sorcerer and early *Princeps Academiae, Collegium Sorcerorum,* to whom **Silvestrus** of Somerset was apprenticed.

Bellis Golden hunting dog rescued from a beating by three apprentices. She decides to travel with the boys on their journey and is thought to be associated with a tawny-braided woman, a young girl and the blonde alpha female of a wide- ranging wolf pack.

Bernardus Soldier of the cursed and ghostly 1001st Leopard Legion—the Deserter's Legion—encamped on the City on the Plain, Terminus, a city visible only on nights of the full moon.

Binarius (fka **Digitus**) Professor of Mathematics. Undeterred by loss of facility with decimal system, has borrowed idea from alternate source (**Thaddeus**) to devise system of numbers based on two digits only.

Blumena Kindly laundress and nursery matron at the Fountaindale thieves' guild. She took especial interest in the career of **Molly o' the Willows**.

Caecus Nearsighted Master Sorcerer with strong ties to the current *Supremi* class of *Indiginae* at the *Collegium Sorcerorum.*

Caerulea *Regina Papilionium,* blue Queen of Butterflies. Life mate to My Lord **Spadix**, *Rex Blattarum,* King of Moths, who is widely known to be both unfaithful to, yet jealous of, his Queen. Mother of **Avolare** by **Thaddeus**.

Callidus of Agilitium. Albeit left-handed, he was the most accomplished apprentice in sword work of the *Imperium* but perished during the Invasion of the Cin. Some believe his weapons—a sword and shield marked with a —were eventually destined for **Thaddeus**, called the Faithless.

Carlus (aka **Charles**) Minor Brown Demon of the Lower Vale, whose existence was spared long ago by **Silvestrus** of Somerset following the loss of a mortal wager. Per agreement, **Silvestrus** can summon **Charles** to perform tasks—typically involving combat—with the proviso that the spoils of such contests are afterward the Demon's to do with as he pleases.

Carolle Former Governess to **Anders** of Brightfield at Brightfield Manor, whose niece, **Nyree**, took a fancy to her young charge.

Carthago of Cannae. He is a roustabout, seaman, rascal, and swag. He is also the cousin of a cousin of **Pontius**, Magistrate of Vexare. His loyalties are to family, crew, and the Goddess of Profit. He is said to be good with a knife but confesses that his ultimate goal is to marry, settle down in the town of Zama, give up his seafaring ways, and raise a large family in peace—as soon as he can find the means.

Cartographus Cleric and Brother of the Order. One of only a small number of members of Holy Orders allowed by the Council to study and teach at the *Collegium Sorcerorum,* he has a passion for geography, maps, travel, and travelers' tales and serves in the library of the College.

Catria Personal maid to **Sophia** of Brightfield Manor.

Cedric Assistant to **Apiarius Magister**, Keeper of the Hives at Beewicke. Married to **Hycynthya**, the old miller's daughter, and father of **Thaddeus**.

Celsius Skilled Master of the Healing Arts at the *Collegium Sorcerorum.* Enjoys drama and attention, typically arriving in a cloud of green smoke. He is eternally anxious concerning compensation for his services.

Charles (aka **Carlus**) Minor Brown Demon of the Lower Vale, whose existence was spared long ago by **Silvestrus** of Somerset following the loss of a mortal wager. Per agreement, **Silvestrus** can summon Charles to perform tasks—typically involving combat—with the proviso that the spoils of such contests are afterward the Demon's to do with as he pleases.

Chiron Centaur and Horse Master at the *Collegium Sorcererorum.* He is given the task of training apprentices in the use of non-edged weapons and mounted combat. Later, he leaves the College to seek the infant **Akireu**.

Coqua Last living female of the Fathers of Man, wife to **Specus**. She later became adoptive mother of **Faran** of Fountaindale at the encouragement of **Silvestrus** of Somerset but died in an attack on her home by local townsfolk.

Corrigan the Mad. He is the alcoholic stepson of **Mattom**, Arch Druid of River's Wood community. From childhood, he was a darkly moody youth who jealously harbored suspicions regarding his playmate **Luperca**, with whom he shared his stepbrother, **Madigan**.

Dawber Tavern keeper of Bannock. He longs to retire to the South, especially after recent events in his inn.

Digitus (aka **Binarius**) Professor of Mathematics. He is responsible for the conception and development of the decimal system but should have spent more time on social skills development.

Ephemerus First new apprentice recruited for the *Collegium Sorcerorum* following the disastrous Invasion of the Cin by **Tyrannus Superbus**, one thousand years in the past. He had a penchant for uttering obscure prophecy after consuming strong drink.

Eques Sir. Knight Master and leader of the Battle Masters of the *Collegium Sorcerorum.* He is the most knowledgeable and skilled of the Combat Masters in the use of edged weapons and armor.

Equus Demi-God of those as be four-footed, don' ye know, and frequent mount in service to **Mater Naturae**.

Eryops Ancient and evil giant Amphibian living in swampy land near the Southwest Caves of the forest surrounding the *Collegium Sorcerorum* who, for his own reasons, reports the comings and goings of various folk in the forest to Master **Perditus** of the College.

Ethne of Tarandon, Lady of the Flowers of Sorrow. Mistress of vintner **Ormerod** of Figberry and, later, mother of **Akireu** by **Thaddeus**.

Fabia One of twin girls born to the union of **Silvestrus** of Somerset and **Merriwhiddle** of Martanius, who was sacrificed by her mother to the evil sentient tree, **Garrungroot**, in return for power, immortality, and invulnerability.

Fabrica One of twin girls born to the union of **Silvestrus** of Somerset and **Merriwhiddle** of Martanius, who was sacrificed by her mother to the evil sentient tree, **Garrungroot**, in return for power, immortality, and invulnerability.

Falswar Comptroller of the thieves' guild in Fountaindale.

Farouj *Nom de voyage* of Prince **Zoarr**, in Bannock, given him by **Rolland** of Fountaindale.

Faran of Fountaindale. Redheaded adopted son of **Specus**, last of the Fathers of Man and Master Cook to the *Collegium Sorcerorum,* and his wife, **Coqua**. Unrecognized relationship to **Rolland** of Fountaindale and former leader of **Faran**'s Falcons, the young thieves' guild. Later, he became Guild Master of the entire thieves' guild of Fountaindale.

Fastus the Fowler. Reputed lover of **Lallie**, servant to **Ormerod** the vintner of Figberry. Also, he is reputed father of **Somada** by **Lallie**.

Floria of Copperville. Jilted fiancée of a thieves' guild member, who exacted a dramatic revenge on her espoused.

Fondula Mate of **Iam**, the First, Keeper of the *Orbis Magnus.*

Fracilia *Pixae* and Queen of the Ice *Faerrae,* indebted to **Non-Dar**, Lord of the Greensward *Aelvae.*

Franciscus Soldier of the cursed and ghostly 1001st Leopard Legion—the Deserter's Legion—encamped on the City on the Plain, Terminus.

Garrungroot Evil, sentient tree Spirit with whom failed sorceress **Merriwhiddle** of Martanius strikes a deadly bargain. He has knowledge of all that trees know and observe and is able to become mobile with sufficient incentive.

Gethin Male servant to **Ormerod**, vintner of Figberry.

Geanninia of Glascoton. Imposing sorceress and Professor at the *Ludia.* She has been romantically linked with **Silvestrus** of Somerset in excess of a lifetime.

Geoffrey of the Broom. Lord, skilled warrior, and commanding officer of the Iron Company of the *Arx Montium,* Mountaingaard, Defenders of the

Collegium Sorcerorum. He has a long-held desire to retire to the South, marry well, and start a dynasty.

Georgus Along with **Loffi**, is stablehand to **Ormerod**, the vintner of Figberry. He is one of the few servants remaining at the estate following the illness and death of his employer.

Gertie Female servant employed by **Oliffe**, innkeeper of The Sword in the Scone, a Fountaindale inn.

Gladitoris Unpleasant youth and member of **Faran**'s Falcons, of the young thieves' guild of Fountaindale. Considered a bully, he worked under the direction of **Sagar**, **Rolland** of Fountaindale's former colleague and chief competitor in that organization.

Grada Faithful servant to **Ormerod,** the vintner of Figberry. She was the last of those remaining at the manor and buried her master next to his mistress, **Ethne** of Tarandon.

Groton Arms Master to the thieves' guild of Fountaindale. Came to Fountaindale after losing niece placed in his care to violent son of Chief of Grecolian family. Sometimes linked to later mysterious disappearance of this same Grecolian son. In Fountaindale, developed strong ties with **Molly o' the Williows** and took singular interest in teaching her the arts of self-defense. Died in barroom brawl said to have been random occurrence.

Grunius Master sergeant and second-in-command of the Iron Company. Stationed at *Arx Montium,* Mountaingaard, he is charged with limiting access to, and defending those in residence at, the *Collegium Sorcerorum.*

Hadrout Irascible centaur. Formerly partnered with **Silvestrus** of Somerset in the recruitment of likely lads for the *Collegium Sorcerorum,* he resigned from that post following a dispute concerning the centaur's lack of willingness to carry either the recruits or the Master Sorcerer on his back.

Hap-Sung Mother of Prince **Zoarr**, and wife to **Zauda**, House of Abdomoolano, King of Mauretesia. Former acrobat and contortionist, she was originally employed at the Temple of the Seven Pleasures in the capital city, Mellisol.

Hectorus Seaman and lover of **Melephan** of Fountaindale, a prostitute working for the thieves' guild. He was the biological father of **Rolland** of Fountaindale. Dark haired, with a sinewy frame, several golden teeth, and tattoos. Good with a knife and horses.

Helveticus *Centurio Prior,* Centurian Major, of the encampment of the City on the Plain, Terminus. He was the leading spirit of the cursed camp of the ten thousand, whose souls had been recruited for the ill-fated Eastern Campaign against the Cin. Husband to **Marta** and father of four sons.

Horatius Soldier and scholar of the cursed and ghostly 1001st Leopard Legion—the deserter's legion—encamped on the City on the Plain, Terminus.

Hycynthya Mother of **Thaddeus** by **Cedric**. She is the daughter of Beewicke's old miller and only survivor of a curse placed on her family when she was a child.

Iacus Fallen former apprentice to **Silvestrus** of the *Collegium Sorcerorum.* Later, he becomes a leader of the Black Sorcerers, and serves as consultant to the thieves' guild, and others, for exorbitant fees.

Iam Last of the First, the initial tribe of modern human sentients spreading up from the Land of the Sun to occupy the northern continent. The First were builders of the *Orbis Magnus (Lapidum Pendentium),* a structure of standing stones lying in the northwest corner of the forest surrounding the *Collegium Sorcerorum.* It is a construction, marked with twelve symbols, whose precise purpose is undetermined, but may be related to time and place management. Though the current building is now a ruin, this was not always the case. Legend speaks of a connection between the *Orbis Magnus* and the land's other standing stones.

Iam tends over the structure as he has for millennia since the mysterious disappearance—all in one night—of all his people, save his wife, **Fondula**, who remained with him until her death some time past. He is tattooed and wears an orange blanket, special beads, and two Great Golden-Crested Eagle feathers. His greatest virtue is patience. He has had a passing acquaintance with **Specus** and **Coqua**, and has developed a benevolent interest in the career of **Thaddeus** of Beewicke.

Ingenia Wisdom. One of the four daughters—the *Intelligentiae*—of **Mater Naturae**, who together are tasked with preventing the Demons at the Earth's core from breaking through to the surface to ravage their Mother's planet.

Jadell Youngest daughter of **Zauda**, King of Mauretesia, and his wife, Queen **Hap- Sung**. She is very close with her older brother, **Zoarr**, and loves to tease him. She lives under a cloud, however, having been declared, at the time of her birth, to carry a Mark of Doom according to a short-lived Court Soothsayer.

Kenneth of Walworth County. He was the childhood sweetheart of **Melior**, the *Mater Amplior* of the *Sorores Silentii*—the Convent of the Silent Sisters.

He was left at the alter following a last-minute, gut-wrenching decision by the Mother Superior.

Ko-Thas *Aelvae* Lieutenant to Lord **Non-Dar**, whose tribe abides in the forest surrounding the *Collegium Sorcerorum.* He enjoys willow bark and beans.

Labienus Titus Lieutenant sent by his old commander, General **Iulius**, to assume command of *Arx Montium,* Mountaingaard, relieving Lord **Geoffrey** of the Broom, Captain of the Iron Company. He quickly falls into conflict with Sergeant **Grunius**, the fort's second-in-command.

Lallie Daughter to **Morella** and, with her, house servant to **Ormerod**, the vintner of Figberry. Recently delivered of **Somada**, her daughter by the estate's fowler, **Fastus**, but then abruptly abandoned by the same after he was confronted by her mother, **Morella**, regarding his intentions. She nursed **Ethne**'s son, **Akireu**, by **Thaddeus** of Beewicke, along with her own daughter.

Lilith Witch woman of Cobbly Knob, and third cousin to **Silvestrus** of Somerset. She is an animal trainer, and owner of the mule **Asullus**. At the request of her cousin, she imbued **Asullus** with the ability to speak, an act generative of a peculiar and unintended consequence. Rival with girlfriend **Eve** for the affections of her Man.

Lillia of Falling Stone. Formerly a nanny for a lord's large household some fifteen hundred years in the past, she demonstrated unique capacities in early adolescence, thus capturing the attention of a local priest, through whose support she was eventually able to achieve admission to the College of Sorcerers. Later, she became engaged to **Longius** of Adventitia but disappeared one night under mysterious circumstances.

Lilyput Ancient green Goblin, House Mistress of the *Collegium Sorcerorum.* She is uncommonly skilled with sorcerous enchantments and unaccountably knowledgeable concerning sorcerous prophecy and politics. She is rumored to have the special ability to appear simultaneously in divers settings and to have a long-standing, albeit obscure, relationship with the College's spectre, **Brother Longbone**.

Loffi Along with **Georgus**, a stablehand to **Ormerod**, the vintner of Figberry. One of the few remaining servants left at the estate following his master's illness and death.

Longbone Brother Doomed, as a result of a curse, to roam the Spaces Behind at the *Collegium Sorcerorum*, living forever, never eating, never drinking, and never having direct contact with others. Thought to have some obscure relationship with **Lilyput** and, at her behest, rumored to perform late-night punitive visits to the chambers of young boys who have promulgated behavioral infractions of the College's Articles of Conduct and Comportment.

Longius of Adventitia. Apprentice at the *Collegium Sorcerorum* over fifteen hundred years in the past. Clever artificer and one of only a handful at the College who was ever able to discover the secret of the Spaces Behind. Affianced to **Lillia** of Falling Stone. However, he is said to have disappeared one night under mysterious circumstances.

Luctarus of the Empty Hand. Short, slight, and usually dressed only in a partially wound sheet, he is, nevertheless, one of five Battle Masters at the *Collegium Sorcerorum.* His specialty is unarmed combat, and he carries a Medallion of Power inscribed with the ancient Symbol of Duality.

Luperca Ancient minor Goddess, usually found in the company of wolves. She is said to be able to take the form of a tawny-braided woman, but is also apparently associated with a small girl and a hunting dog. The mother of the fourth of four feral children, **Sacerdotia**, fathered by **Thaddeus** of Beewicke.

Macro Enforcer, loyal to **Faran** of the thieves' guild of Fountaindale.

Madigan Arch Druid and Sachem, son of **Mattom**, Arch Druid before him, and step-brother to **Corrigan** the Mad. He officiates from the Holy Grove in River's Wood. He is a childhood friend of the current avatar of **Luperca** of the wolves. He is the custodian of the predictive power of the Ancient Oak, the Great Wheel.

Malia Gifted and talented woman of the Classic Age, who achieved amazing success as a singer of verse until her performance career was abruptly cut short by a bout of swamp fever. Following her uncommon remission, she gave up all singing for the study of Medicine under **Relso** the Wise. Following the birth of her child by an unknown paramour, she spent the few remaining years of her life at the Convent of the Silent Sisters, whose faculty she herself had, at one time, trained. Unfortunately, the swamp fever, against which she had so valiantly striven over the years, claimed her at the last. In her honor, the illness henceforward came to be known as **Malia**'s Aria.

Marcellus Leader of patrol of legionnaires of the 1001st Leopard Legion—the Deserter's Legion—marking the perimeter of the cursed encampment of the City on the Plain, Terminus.

Mari the Green. *Regina Draconum Marinarum,* Queen of Sea Dragons. As a young adult, she was once caught off the coast of Frantillia by a sudden, violent summer storm. Badly battered, she awoke to find herself on the beach of a small coral island off the coast of a quaint fishing village, where she was attended by a young man toward whom she developed a deep affection but who later left her. To seek news of local matters and obtain needed supplies, she assumed the form of an old woman, living apart from the town of Vexare. There she was always welcomed and well treated, later coming to act as the village's midwife and wise woman. She eventually met her destiny at the hands of a spurned suitor. Mother, by **Thaddeus** of Beewicke, of **Ultoris**, who was, from conception, imprinted with the task of achieving vengeance against his mother's slayer.

Marsia of Dorset Downs, Northfast. She is the fourth of four daughters of a local college professor. A tall girl, with hip-length honey-gold hair, she carries a pair of greenstones, split from a single source and said to have special properties. She was recruited to the *Ludia* by Mistress **Geanninia** and traveled with her, joining with **Nannsi**, **Sonnia**, and **Molly o' the Willows**, in turn. She has special knowledge of a future with **Thaddeus** of Beewicke and has determined not to shirk from it.

Marta Wife to **Helveticus**, *Centurio Prior*, currently stationed with the 1001st Leopard Legion, City on the Plain at Terminus.

Mater Naturae Mother Nature. Important figure of prehistoric times enraged at the violation of her Earth avatar by Demons from **Bellona**. In response, she has charged her four daughters, the *Intellegentiae*, with the task of thwarting any attempt by those same Demons to win their freedom from the Earth's core—into which they were cast and entrapped—by escaping to the planet's surface.

Mattom Former Chief, or Arch Druid and Sachem, at River's Wood. Father to **Madigan**, current Arch Druid at River's Wood and stepfather to **Corrigan** the Mad. He was able to persuade **Luperca**, an ancient Goddess, to bring to fruition her part of the Ring's Plan, by assuming her alternate forms for various periods of time so she and **Madigan** could be raised as childhood friends. Before his death, **Mattom** was able to pass on this knowledge to his son, the subsequent Chief Druid, **Madigan**.

Melaphen Fiery, redheaded prostitute and mother, by **Hectorus** the sailor, of **Rolland** of Fountaindale. Following the loss of her seaman before the birth of their child, she strove to devote her remaining time and energy to raising the baby boy. She was later slain by a drunken customer during the boy's infancy, and the responsibility for his care passed to **Faran** of Fountaindale. Cautious rumors hinted at some manner of special relationship between

Melaphen and **Faran**. Some few even considered her demeanor, at times, otherworldly.

Melior *Mater Amplior.* Abbess of the convent of the *Sorores Silentii.* Early on, she was betrothed to **Kenneth** of Walworth County, but following a soul-searching weekend retreat, gave up the prospect of a husband and family to enter a religious Nursing Order. Though an excellent and highly skilled healer, she always found issues of human relationships versus the greater good a struggle.

Merriwhiddle of Martanius. Failed student of sorcery, and competitor with **Geanninia** of Glascoton for the love of **Silvestrus** of Somerset. Convinced by that sorcerer to allow him to accompany her to her homeland, she left the *Ludia* in her fourth year, unfulfilled. **Silvestrus** then abandoned her after she became pregnant with twin girls, **Fabia** and **Fabrica**. In a rage, she formed a compact with the evil Tree Spirit **Garrungroot**, who promised her power, knowledge, invulnerability, and immortality in return for lifelong servitude and the lives of two others.

Modus Porter of the *Collegium Sorcerorum.* He frequently traveled outside the *Collegium* to obtain supplies and deliver messages. He was recruited, over time, to perform various tasks by one of the young Masters there.

Molly o' the Willows Orphan sold to **Faran** of Fountaindale of the thieves' guild. She had an especial talent with the young and tended the children of the guild's night ladies with great affection. She was mentored by **Blumena** of housekeeping and was instructed in defensive arts by **Groton** of the House Guard. She developed a sentimental attachment to the stands of willows lining the banks of the River Fountaindale. She often expressed ambivalence concerning relationships with those of differing social class.

Morad Demon son of **Morag**. Ambitious, say some, to a fault.

Morod Arch Demon and father of **Morag**. Slain by **Silvestrus** of Somerset. The son
has vowed vengeance.

Morag Arch Demon who long cultivated a connection with the Minaret of Power, after being placed by his kind in the land of the peoples who would come to be known as the Cin. However, he abruptly lost power when a ragtag band of Western sorcerers, in a surprise maneuver at the height of battle, purloined the Minaret, transporting it to, and securing it on, the grounds of the *Collegium Sorcerorum.*

Morella Mother of **Lallie** and servant to **Ormerod**, the vintner of Figberry. She held a low opinion of **Ethne** of Tarandon, **Omerod**'s mistress, yet took

Ethne's only child to Fountaindale, after his mother's death, and kept him safe to await the advent of the Horseman.

Mores Iusti Lived some fifteen hundred years in the past. Youngest *Princeps Academiae* of the *Collegium Sorcerorum,* achieving the post with surprising ease. Once ensconced, he discovered the Spaces Behind and began to indulge voyeuristic impulses concerning **Lillia** of Falling Stone, among others. In his fourth year of administration, he mysteriously vanished, coincident with the disappearance of **Lillia** herself and her fellow student and love interest, **Longius** of Adventitia. Despite significant efforts, these absences were never fully explained, nor were their bodies ever recovered.

Morphia Purple-winged and often somnific representative of *Spritae* family of the *Faerrae.* Such Fey are often sought after to accomplish tasks and fetch items. Some are said to be exquisitely sensitive to the addictive powers of *Pixae* honey, especially the strain found in Beewicke.

Myrtelee of Tarandon. Mother to **Ethne** of Tarandon. Peasant woman to whom, at the height of a harsh winter, four women appeared, initially identifying themselves as faggot peddlers. This pretext was rather quickly abandoned, however, and the four visited upon the unsuspecting woman an annunciation that her daughter, at a certain time, would be given the choice of everlasting fame or long life. She was instructed to ensure that her daughter learned this pronouncement by heart.

Nannsi of Zorbas, Grecolia. Her father is a successful merchant. She is the only short and dark member of her sib line, resembling none of her brothers and sisters. Attentive to details, she objects to much that is “frivolous” in life. She searches for a soul mate and puzzles over how to convince that person of his inevitability while simultaneously seeking the means to meet the requirements for sorceress practice.

Non-Dar Lord of the Greensward *Aelvae* dwelling in the forest surrounding the *Collegium Sorcerorum.* He is traditionally the ally of the sorcerers and a blood enemy of all Goblin-kind. He is often experienced as a bit stuffy and full of himself but is considered steadfast and handy to have around in any altercation.

Nyree Niece to **Carolle**, former Governess to **Anders** of Brightfield Manor. She was a frequent visitor at Brightfield over the summer months, during which times she struck up a troubling relationship with the boy.

Nytus Former Grand Master of the thieves’ guild of Fountaindale. Found slumped in his chair one morning with a red, corded silken scarf of highest quality lying in his lap. By the following week’s end, **Faran**, but recently returned from the East, had assumed the very same chair.

Oliffe Innkeeper of well-appointed Fountaindale inn, The Sword in the Scone, standing between a smithy and a bakery. He suffers regularly from predations periodically visited upon him by **Faran**'s Falcons of the young thieves' guild.

Orbis Sister. Chief librarian at the Convent of the Silent Sisters, who, through her research, was able to delve the existence and purpose of the Rings of Resonance.

Ormerod Well-regarded vintner of Figberry, whose purberry wine vintages are famous in the region. Longtime acquaintance of **Silvestrus** of Somerset. Takes a mistress, **Ethne** of Fountaindale, a former lady of the evening. He eventually succumbs to a type of pulmonary consumption not uncommon to that city at that time.

Osiric Great Golden-Crested Eagle. Formerly lord of his kind but blinded in a forest fire while trying to save his mate, **Qinda**, and their fledglings. He subsequently developed enhanced and compensating senses of smell and hearing, which contributed to a renewed interest in life.

Pegotta Resident of Beewicke, assistant to local baker. Later she became enamored of **Barcus** of Poosia, replacement apprentice to **Thaddeus** of Beewicke.

Perditus of Skara Brae. The youngest Master to sit on the Governing Council of the *Collegium Sorcerorum.* Unpopular, antisocial, yet brilliant and ambitious, he is a dedicated student of Eastern magicks, especially their rumored links to Otherworldly powers. He has made a life study of the Minaret of Power, the only known artifact extant in the Westlands to date from before the time of the great Invasion of the East. Some consider that his confidence in his ability to control events may be overdetermined.

Peregrinus *Nom de voyage* of **Thaddeus** called the Faithless used during his travels to the East.

Pertangus of Mauretesia. Life Arms Master to the House of Abdomoolano. He traditionally considers the end product to have precedence over the means by which it is accomplished.

Phoebe Friendly dapple mare recruited by **Silvestrus** of Somerset to distract **Asullus** from his preoccupation with the imminent drudgery of towing a sorcerer-laden barge up the Greater Flatstone River to River's Wood.

Pisca Mermaid and seer to the court of **Mari** the Green, *Regina Dranconum Marinarum.* She brought the Sea Dragon Queen's attention to patterns in the stars foretelling the advent of a young human male by whom the Queen would bear a child of great importance who would grow to avenge the mother of a great wrong. She met her doom at the claws of **Attacondros** the Red, frustrated suitor of her mistress. It is believed that she was first ravished, then devoured by this personage.

Piscelius Old man of the sea and captain of his own fishing boat. He has a distant relation to **Pontius**, Magistrate of Vexare, who engages him to provide both shelter and transportation back to Vexare for the Magistrate and his young charge, **Thaddeus** of Beewicke, at the conclusion of the adventure of the Green Dragon's treasure.

Platinus Silverfoot. One of the silver-haired and pointy-eared half-*Aelvae* twin cousins, he and his close kin, **Argentus**, befriend **Thaddeus** of Beewicke and his three human brothers in their first year at the College before, by chance, running afoul of one of the Masters of the College.

Polyphemus Cyclops. Having been bested by **Noman**—and through a number of peculiar circumstances—he ends up having his vision restored but his head subsequently nailed to the door leading to the Hallway of the *Indiginae,* or Seniors, at the *Collegium*

Sorcerorum. He is charged with seeing that those in their last year of study are not unduly disturbed.

Pontius Magistrate of Vexare, Frantillia. In his youth he was a skilled guide to boats and ships both entering and leaving the local harbor. He has written to the *Collegium Sorcerorum* for assistance in combatting a recent infestation of Red Tide, suspected of being of arcane origin. He is made aware of a Green Dragon's treasure by **Thaddeus** of Beewicke and must devise a course of action that brings the greatest benefit to the greatest number of his constituency.

Portoman Master sorcerer, *Collegium Sorcerorum.* One of a company of sorcerers volunteering to serve the Empire during the invasion of the lands of the Cin. It was **Portoman** who intuited that the Cin's unanticipated success in first repelling, then slaughtering the Imperial legions was related to a magical concentration of dark energy stemming from the Minaret of Power, lodged in the enemy's capital city. He and his companions, therefore, contrived to steal away the Minaret, but at great cost to **Portoman**'s sanity. He was eventually brought safely back to the College along with the mysterious Tower. His broken mind, however, never healed, despite best efforts, and he did not long survive his return.

Prestis He is a tanner who frequently has dealings with the thieves' guild of Fountaindale.

Primus First of three tutors engaged by **Sophia** and **Astonius** of Brightfield Manor to educate their only child, **Anders**. He is bilious in nature.

Protervus Imp. He has been impressed as guardian of the pantry at the *Collegium Sorcerorum* due to the natural predilection of young boys for caloric surfeit regardless of time of day or night.

Providentia Foresight. One of the four daughters—the *Intelligentiae*—of **Mater Naturae**, who together are tasked with preventing the Demons at the Earth's core from breaking through to the surface to ravage the planet.

Psittica Four-hundred-year-old parrot pledged to House Abdomoolano of the Kingdom of Mauretesia. At this time she is assigned to Prince **Zoarr**, sole surviving heir to the Leopard Throne, currently in study at the *Collegium Sorcerorum.* The parrot can authentically assume the color and shape of similarly sized objects and is also an exceptional verbal mimic.

Publius Only son of **Tyrannus Superbus**, accompanying him on Westlands' campaign to the lands of the Cin. Legend suggests he was taken alive, with his father, at the conclusion of the last battle and was yet living when taken away.

Pumilis of Upcrag. Dwarf, Master of Small Arms, and one of five Battle Masters of the *Collegium Sorcerorum.* He is the only dwarf on record who is known to speak with a lisp.

Qinda Great Golden-Crested Eagle and life mate to **Osiric**, lord of his kind. She perished in a forest fire protecting her fledglings, while her spouse vainly tried to beat back the engulfing flames.

Quintessentialus, Marcus, Proconsul. He was an early sponsor of **Akireu**, local student of Chiron the Horseman. His endorsement secured his young protégé a place at the Academy of War in Fornia, thus initiating the boy's formal military career.

Quintus Captain, skilled warrior, and aide-de-camp to his military academy classmate, General **Akireu**. From the beginning of his career, he faithfully served his General and was eventually rewarded with the position of Chief of General Staff of the Armies of the Imperium. He steadfastly demonstrated a fierce loyalty to his General, taking pains to carefully investigate all who came near **Akireu**. He never married.

Rastius Master sorcerer and Sergeant-of-Arms at the *Collegium Sorcerorum.* He is of large stature, second in volume only to Master Cook Specus.

Rathboneson, Wil *Indiginae* in senior year at the *Collegium Sorcerorum.* He formerly studied under Master Sorcerer **Perditus** of Skara-Brae but was dismissed at the end of only one year. It was speculated that the Master may have mistaken him for another. He is a lover of horses and captain of the senior-class *Pila Ludere* team.

Raugauld Cook to the Iron Company, *Arx Montium*, at Mountaingaard. Makes passable stew.

Relso Master of Medicine in the Classic Age and attentive mentor to the opera singer **Malia**, later turned medical student. There is speculation he may have fathered her only child.

Rolland of Fountaindale. Only surviving child of **Hectorus**, seaman, and **Melaphen**, redheaded prostitute. He is a street thief, Excelsior class, youth thieves' guild, **Faran**'s Falcons. He is rumored to have some special relationship with the very same **Faran**. Later, he is apprenticed to **Silvestrus** of the *Collegium Sorcerorum.* He is the second of the three brothers to **Thaddeus** of Beewicke. He engages in a personal rivalry with **Zoarr** of Mauretesia. **Rolland** is Cardinal point *Orientem* (East) of the Great Compass.

Sacerdotia Female cleric and fourth of four feral children of **Thaddeus** of Beewicke, by **Luperca**, great golden pack leader. She is an Arch Druidic priestess in her own right, and a demi-wolf.

Sagar Lieutenant to **Faran**, leader of **Faran**'s Falcons of the young thieves' guild of Fountaindale. He is an early, close colleague of **Rolland** the Red, later charged with his friend's capture following that boy's oath breaking.

Sanadar Loyal House Captain to the court of **Zauda**, King of Mauretesia. He is an exceptionally large fellow with massive earrings, ample wit, and a deep and hearty laugh. He favors peach brandy.

Sapientia Wit. One of the four daughters—the *Intelligentiae*—of **Mater Naturae**, who together are tasked with preventing the Demons at the Earth's core from breaking through to the surface to ravage the planet.

Secundus Second of three tutors engaged by **Sophia** and **Astonius** of Brightfield Manor for the instruction of their son, **Anders**. He is phlegmatic in character.

Sennead Great Golden-Crested Eagle, son of **Osiric**. He assumed the lordship of his tribe after his father's loss of vision in a forest fire. Subsequently, he implemented a policy of benign neglect toward the efforts of his sisters, who sought to comfort their father following his injury.

Sennacis House manager to **Sophia** and **Astonius** of Brightfield Manor estate. He is choleric in nature.

Shire Reeve Chief officer of law enforcement in Fountaindale and surrounding communities.

Silvestrus of Somerset. Instructor at *Collegium Sorcerorum*, mentored by Master **Bede**, whom he considered venerable. Early in his youth, he is known to have studied serpent habitats along the coast of southern Frantillia. At the time of the Invasion of the Cin, circa 8500, he was elected to the Sorcerers War Council, in spite of his young age, and thus accompanied the Imperial Army of the Invasion to the East. Following this disaster, **Silvestrus** became a tireless proponent of the Doctrine of Sorcerous Pan-Semination. Over time, he was recruited as a Disciple by the Mother, serving her will through the four *Intelligentiae.* He was the father of twin girls by failed Sorceress Apprenticiatrix, **Merriwhiddle** of Martanius. He is currently affianced to **Geanninia** of Glascoton, Headmistress of the *Ludia.*

Sin-Dol *Aelvae.* He is a member of the tribe led by Lord **Non-Dar**, who dwell in the forest surrounding the *Collegium Sorcerorum.* He has studied the procurement of the rare and elusive substance ambrosia.

Somada Infant daughter of **Lallie** by the fowler **Fastus**, born one month before **Akireu**, son of **Ethne** by

Thaddeus. **Lallie**, already nursing **Somada**, went on to nurse **Akireu**, as well.

Sonnia of Frantillia. She is the second child and only daughter of a successful merchant who has spoiled her outrageously. Sea life was her major interest until she was recruited to become a sorceress at the *Ludia.* She is of average height and typically wears her waist-length brown hair in a braid, but her brilliant smile is judged her best feature. If she has any faults, it may be her ambition and attention to classist positions.

Sophia Mistress of Brightfield Manor, wife to **Astonius**, and mother of **Anders**, her only child. She is known for her superb business acumen.

Spadix *Rex Blattarum,* King of Moths, life mate of **Caerulea**, *Regina Papilionum,* Queen of Butterflies. A great brown moth, he is always referred to as "My Lord **Spadix**." He is particularly jealous of his wife's interest in others and so tends to resent **Avolare**—daughter of **Caerulea** by Thaddeus of Beewicke—whom he believes, but cannot prove, is not his child. His moth dust is said to have certain special properties.

Speculatoris Information monger. He is employed by **Thaddeus** the Faithless while visiting Aconia to learn of the history and intention of the young general **Akireu**. He is subsequently hired by an officer of General **Akireu**'s staff, without the General's knowledge, to learn of the history and intention of the sandy-haired traveler who identifies himself as **Pertangus** of Fountaindale.

Specus The last surviving member of the Fathers of Man. Husband to **Coqua**, the last surviving female of the Fathers of Man. Unable to have children, he adopted eight-year-old Faran in an arrangement orchestrated by **Silvestrus** of Somerset for the sorcerer's own purposes. He possesses uncommon culinary skills. Following his wife's death, **Silvestrus** convinced him to travel to the *Collegium Sorcerorum* and assume the duties of Master Cook for the school. The Master Cook's physical features are striking and unlike those of any other living human being.

Stooks Acneform adolescent member **Faran**'s Falcons of the young thieves' guild of Fountaindale, under the leadership of **Faran**'s lieutenant, **Sagar**. He is killed by the mule **Asullus** during an attempt to capture **Rolland** the Oath Breaker.

Suttonus, William of. House burglar and ne'er-do-well uncle to **Anders** of Brightfield Manor. Originator of well-known, folksy sayings, one of which speaks to his credo that if one seeks resources, it makes sense to frequent only those places as have the resources one seeks.

Tertius Third of three tutors engaged by **Sophia** and **Astonius** of Brightfield Manor to educate their only child, **Anders**. Later dismissed following a reputed difficulty with the cook. He is sanguine in nature.

Thaddeus of Beewicke. Only child of **Cedric** and **Hycynthya**. He is apprenticed to **Silvestrus** of the *Collegium Sorcerorum,* and is lover to **Ethne** of Tarandon, **Caerulea**, *Regina Papilionum,* **Mari**, *Regina Draconum Marinarum,* and **Luperca**, Great Pack Leader, with resultant issue of **Akireu**, **Avolare**, **Ultoris**, and **Sacerdotia**, respectively. He later proposes to **Marsia** of Dorset Downs, sorceress. After losing Belief, he is identified as **Thaddeus** the Faithless. He is the Cardinal point *Septentrio* (North) of the Great Compass.

Thra-gora Beatific member of a pair of black marble gargoyle statues charged with guarding the main entrance to the *Collegium Sorcerorum.* She is claimed by some to be, on occasion, both sentient and mobile.

Threkor He was one of the last of the Fathers of Man and greatfather to **Specus**. Killed by hunting party of Others, using dogs, in a slaying that was, on later reflection, almost certainly racially motivated.

Tigellinus Enforcer loyal to **Faran** of the thieves' guild of Fountaindale.

Tyrannus Superbus *Imperator Ultimus*, the last Emperor of the Westlands, reigning from the Imperial capital at Fornia, who led—one thousand years in the past—a million-man army consisting of a thousand Imperial legions at full strength in the Invasion of the Cin of the East. The campaign, however, proved a disaster, ending in the total annihilation of the invading force by the Cin's employment of their Ancient Ones—skilled users of magicks—thought to have been aided and abetted by Demon-kind. Two of the very few survivors of the entire campaign later vouchsafed on oath that at the conclusion of the final battle, they witnessed the Emperor and his son, **Publius**, who had accompanied him on the campaign, being led off by the enemy.

Ulina Older female servant to **Pontius**, Magistrate of Vexare.

Ultoris Third feral child of Thaddeus. He is the son of **Mari** the Green, *Regina Draconum Marinarum*, Queen of Sea Dragons. He inherited, as dragons do, all the knowledge of his mother during the period of his incubation. By the time of his hatching, his mother had perished due to poisoning from the Red Tide, leaving her son with the Burning of Vengeance toward his mother's slayer, the mighty **Attacondros** the Red.

Wineskins Diligent, erudite historian and late-century author, whose *De Rerebus Cerebrus* is considered the definitive work chronicling the life and campaigns of the first Emperor of the Restoration.

Zauda King of Mauretesia, of the House of Abdomoolano, married to **Hap-Sung**, seventh and only surviving wife, formerly acrobat and contortionist at the Temple of the Seven Pleasures, dedicated to Goddess **Dyanya**. He is father to **Zoarr**, Prince and sole surviving heir apparent, and **Jadell**, Princess of that House.

Zoarr of Mauretesia, seventh, and only surviving, son of **Zauda**, House of Abdomoolano, King of Mauretesia, and **Hap-Sung**, former acrobat and contortionist. He is an apprentice to **Silvestrus** of the *Collegium Sorcerorum,* recruited one year earlier than the typical age as a result of regional political considerations. He is the third of the three brothers to **Thaddeus** of Beewicke. He is a skilled student of the martial arts as well as a musician. He later seeks to court **Molly o' the Willows**. He is the Cardinal point *Meridies* (South) of the Great Compass.

Glossary
Lingua Imperatoria

Ab – from
Abitus – departure, of a departure
Acini – of a grape
Ad – coming to, arriving at
Administer – manager
Adrogantia – hubris, nerve, chutzpah
Advenae – newcomers, those just beginning study
Advenarum – of, or pertaining to, those just beginning
Adversa – bad, unfortunate, adverse
Aequinoctia – the two annual occasions of equal night and day
Aequinoctium – equinox
Aelvae – largest of the *Faerrae;* bold warriors, archers without peer, excellent in sports
Aetate – Summer, in Summer
Alvis – from the bowels
Amazones – women warriors
Amici – friends
Amicus – male friend
Amores – affairs of the heart
Amplior – superior, larger
Anima – breath
Anni – of the year
Anno – in the year of
Antiqua – old

Anus – old woman
Apiarius – beekeeper
Aprilis – fourth month of the year
Aquila – eagle
Aquilo – North wind
Arbiter – referee, judge
Arbor – tree
Arborea – pertaining to a tree
Arcanum – secret
Argutiae – wit
Arx – arc, range
Ascende – ascend, rise!
Astacus – lobster
Atrium – hall
Auferre – take away
Auster – South wind
Autumnale – autumnal, pertaining to the fall
Ave – hello, good-bye, hail
Bellona – Sister to Mars, the God of War; also, one of a pair of Mars-sized bodies striking Earth early in its history, leading to the formation of the Moon (*Luna*)
Blattarum – of the moths
Brevis – short
Bruma – Winter solstice

Caeca – blind
Caelum – heaven
Caeruleus – blue
Calcitra – kick!
Caninum – pertaining to dogs

Canis – dog
Canum – of dogs
Cantare – singing
Caput – head
Cardines – Cardinal, or major, points of the compass (N, E, S, and W)
Cardinis – Cardinal, or major, point of the compass (N, E, S, or W)
Castra – encampment
Castratus – castrated one
Caupona – inn
Cerealis – eighth month of the year
Cibus – food
Cincinni – curls
Circuitus – circular instrument, as a compass
Circulus – of a circle, circular
Cogitatio – one's cognition, thinking process
Collegii – of a college
Collegio – college
Collegium – institution of higher learning for boys
Cometae – comet, of the comet
Commuta – transform!
Concidit – give up, surrender, deny, cease!
Condicio – proposal
Conloqui – talking, speaking
Conloquium – negotiation
Contrahe – shrink in size!
Contubernia – Imperial military unit composed of ten members
Conventus – convent
Convivium – feast

Coquere – cooking
Coronifer – slave holding a wreath over the head of the Triumphant, while speaking a formulaic warning in his/her ear
Cortina – cauldron
Creationis – of creation
Cultri – knives, cutlery
Cum – with
Custos – gatekeeper, guard

Daemon – demon
Daemonis – of a demon
Debellatum – war, contest, conflict
Decem – ten, tens
Defundat – may it pour forth
Destrue – destroy!
Dicit – speaks
Diem – day
Dies – day
Discere – learning to
Dissimulator – camouflage artist
Dolorosa – of sorrow
Dolorosus – pain
Domina – lady, housemistress
Dominus – head man, boss
Domo – going away from, or leaving, home
Dormi – sleep!
Draco – dragon
Dracones – dragons
Draconis – of the dragon, dragon's

Duodecem – dozen
Duri – hard

Epulae – foods
Erroris – of error
Est – *is, is completed*
Et – and
Eurus – East wind
Ex – from
Extende – expand in size!
Exitus – consequence

Facere – making
Facite – make, restore
Factum – making, rendering
Faerrae – one of the major orders of the Fey, who are divided into *Pixae, Spritae,* and *Aelvae* primarily by increasing size
Faerrarum – of the *Faerrae*
Fatuus – fool
Faunus – nonhuman sentient animal
Februarius – second month of the year
Ferias – holidays
Festivus – festival
Fiat – let it become, make it so, let there be
Fides – a Belief, faith
Florum – of flowers
Forfices – scissors
Fortuna – luck, fortune
Fur – thief
Furiae – the Furies

Furis – of the thief
Furum – of thieves

Gens – nation, kind, grouping
Globi – balls
Globulus – globe, sphere

Heus – hark, listen!
Hominum – of men

Ianuam – doorway
Ianuario – of January
Ianuarius – first month of the year
Ignave – coward
Ignesce – ignite!
Ignis – fire
Illos – them
Imitatrix – mimic
Impeditus – thwarted, the thwarted one
Imperator – Emperor
Imperatoria – Imperial
Imperii – of power, of the Empire
Imperium – Empire
Impetus – attack
In – in, at
Incendat – let it catch fire!
Incipe – start!, begin!
Incipere – starting
Indigenae – those already present at their study; those of the second, third, and fourth years at a school
Inferni – inhabitants of the infernal regions

Inflationis – flatus
Inflatus – inflated
Ingenia – cleverness
Ingenium – spirit of
Inquisitio – quest
Insanus – insane, mad
Insignia – insignia
Insigniae – more than one insignia
Intelligentiae – mindful ones
Intellegis – do you understand?
Inter-Imperium – period between empires, interregnum
Inverte – turn inside out!
Invicti – victorious
Invictus – invincible
Iovius – seventh month of the year
Iter – journey
Iudex – judge
Iudicare – to judge the status of
Iudicium – judgement
Iunii – of the sixth month
Iunius – sixth month of the year
Iusti – high, just

Lapidum – of the stones
Lapis – stone
Latrina – toilet
Lavatio – washing
Leavus – left-handed
Legatum – bequest, legacy
Legere – read
Leges – law

Legio – legion
Leopardinus – of the leopard
Lex – law
Liberate – be free of bonds, restraints!
Liberi – books, scrolls
Librum – book
Ligate – bind!
Limine – threshold
Lingua – language
Litterae – letters
Litterati – literate ones
Locus – place, place of
Luctator – fighter using no weapons other than hands, feet
Ludere – play!
Ludi – game
Ludia – institution of higher learning for girls
Ludos – classes
Luna – the moon
Lunares – Men of the Moon
Lunaris – Man of the Moon
Luperca – she-wolf, archaic goddess
Luporum – of wolves

Magister – master, expert, chief person
Magna – great
Magni – great
Magnus – great
Maio – of May
Maius – fifth month of the year
Manes – ghost, undead

Maritima – of the sea, marine
Martius – third month of the year
Mater – mother
Mathematicarum – of mathematics, mathematical
Matris – of the mother
Maximi – greatest ones
Mea – my
Media – mid
Medice – physician
Medici – of the physician
Mel – honey
Mellum – honey
Membrum – member
Memento – remember
Mense – in the month
Meridianus – meridian
Meridies – South
Mille – thousand
Millibus – distant by thousands of paces
Minimi – least ones
Minor – minor
Mitra – religious head wear
Monumentum – monument
Montium – of mountains
Mores – morals
Mori – to die, to be mortal
Mortui – dead
Mundana – world

Nasus – nose
Naturae – of Nature

Neglegere – breaking
Neptunius – tenth month of the year
Nivei – snow
Nihil – nothing
Nova – new
Nox – night, night's eve
Numeri – of number, numbers
Nuptiae – of marriage

Occasus – downfall
Occidus – the West
Octipes – eight-footed, eight-pointed
Omnino – wholly, entirely
Oratio – speech
Orbis – ring
Ordines – Ordinal, or minor, points of the compass (NE, NW, SE, and SW)
Ordinis – Ordinal, or minor, point of the compass (NE, NW, SE, or SW)
Oriens – East
Orientalium – of Easterners
Orientalis – Eastern
Orientem – of, or pertaining to, the East

Papiliones – butterflies
Papilionum – of the butterflies
Papyrus – paper
Parare – to prepare, preparing
Parthorum – of the Parthians
Passus – of paces
Patefacta – yielded up, given up, surrendered

Pax – peace
Pendentium – of those hanging
Per – through
Perditi – lost, perished
Peregrinus – foreign, strange, stranger
Philologe – scholar
Physica – female scientist, biologist
Pila – ball
Pilae – balls
Piscatorum – of the fish
Pistoris – of a baker
Pixae – smallest of the *Faerrae;* frequent pollinators, fond of gyre and gambol
Plutonius – eleventh month of the year
Potestatem – power
Prave – depraved one
Prima – main, primary
Primus – primary
Procax – bully
Prodi – go, get going, giddyup!
Prolatus – offer
Populusque – and the people
Protervus – imp
Providentia – foresight
Prudens – rational
Puella – girl
Puellae – girls, dolls
Pueri – boys
Pueros – children
Pugil – boxer
Pugna – fighting

Pugnare – fighting
Pulchella – pretty, beautiful
Pulicium – of fleas
Pumilus – dwarf
Purgata – cleansing
Pustula – pimple

Qua – which, that
Quaesitor – inquisitor
Quaestor – official
Quartus – fourth one
Quercus – oak

Recludite – open!
Regina – Queen
Regulos – rules
Rerum – of matters
Respica – look behind
Restitutum – restoration, restored
Reverte – return to previous state!
Rex – King
Ruber – red
Rumpite – swell to bursting!

Saccularii – of the pickpockets
Sacra – holy
Sacrum – holy
Sana – sane
Sanguis – blood
Sanum – healthy
Sapientia – wisdom

Sapo – soap
Saturnalia – annual "farewell old year, welcome new year" festival
Saturnius – twelfth month of the year
Saxum – rock
Secundi – those in the second year of study
Semper – always
Senatus – the Senate
Senex – old
Septentrio – North
Septentrionum – of, or pertaining to, North
Sepulchri – tombstone
Sepultura – burial
Sidera – planets
Silentii – of silence
Sine – without
Sint – let there be
Sis – may you be
Sit – let it be
Solares – Men of the Sun
Solaris – Man of the Sun
Solitarius – hermit
Solsti – the two annual occasions comprised of the longest and shortest days
Solstitum – Summer solstice
Somnia – dreams
Sorcerorum – of, or pertaining to, sorcerers
Sordida – outdoor, trail, rough, common
Sorores – sisters
Spadix – brown
Speculi – of the mirror

Speculum – mirror
Specus – cave
Sphaerae – balls, spheres
Spiritus – spirit
Spritae – mid-sized *Faerrae;* often sought to accomplish tasks and fetch items
Spuma – foam at the mouth as with soap!
Statim – immediately!
Statuis – statues
Stercus – feces
Stola – woman's gown
Sub – under, preceding
Subtercollem – under-hill
Supremi – those in the fourth, final year of study, the most advanced of a group
Supremorum – of those in the last year of study
Supremus – those in the fourth, final year of study

Tace – silence, be silent!
Tauri – of the bull
Te – you
Terra – land
Tertii – those in the third year of study
Tertius – third one
Tirones – recruits, those of the first year of study
Tironis – recruit, one of the first year of study
Totus – all, entire
Tres – three
Turre – tower
Turris – tower

Ultimus – last
Uranius – ninth month of the year

Vernum – spring
Veni – one, come!
Venite – more than one, come!
Venereus – of Venus, love
Vermes – worms
Vesanus – madman
Vesica – bladder
Vespertiliolis – little bat
Vestimenta – clothes
Via – road
Vicerunt – they have won
Virgines – virgins
Vinarii – of the vintner
Vincite – entangle!
Vires – power
Viridis – green
Vites – vines
Volans – flying one

Zephyrus – West wind

Made in the USA
Charleston, SC
21 August 2013